Next Time

Ron Ward Jr

For Stormy

Next Time

Prologue

Hurry. Hurry, goddamn it.

Jim Radcliffe pressed the gas pedal to the floor of the black Ford Focus, speeding along the dark stretch of a two-lane back road at two in the morning. Train tracks ran parallel to the road on his right. To the left, an occasional house or side street. The engine hummed loudly as he pushed it to its limit. This wasn't a race car, but tonight, speed was its only purpose. In the past, he'd regularly used this route to travel home from work, but the increasing deer population in the area, along with no streetlights, had persuaded him to take the main highway. The alternative route added a few minutes to his after-work, early-morning homeward commute, but it was preferable to totaling out a paid-for car on the hefty leaping body of a confused deer.

Tonight, though, he wasn't headed home. There was another destination along this path. One he needed to get to in less time than allotted, and this riskier way was quickest.

Sweat beaded on his forehead. His brown and usually unkempt hair matted to his scalp. Windows down and wind beating against his face. The "fasten seat belt" tone sounded persistently but was ignored. As he sped along, his hands shaking on the steering wheel, and his heart pounding as if it were a machine about to overwork itself and explode, he turned on his brights. He couldn't slow down. He couldn't lose a fraction of a second, but he wouldn't reach his destination at all if an animal of any kind ran out in front of him and he didn't avoid crashing into it.

Ahead, a car approached in the opposite lane. The driver of that car, annoyed by Jim's bright lights, flashed headlights at him as it neared, either trying to signal Jim to dim his lights, or simply to send Morse-coded cursing in the form of blinking illumination. Jim didn't give a damn. The car passed, heading the other way, blaring its horn at him. Jim continued on. There was no time to worry about pissed-off drivers. He had to hurry.

Even at ninety miles per hour, this stretch of road seemed so much longer than it had in the past. He could see the curve to the left ahead, but it felt as if he crawled toward it. After that bend, he would cross the railroad tracks and turn in to the neighborhood where his destination was.

A shadow to the right startled him, a deer just off the side of the road, and he swerved into the left lane. It was more a flinch than an intentional action. He kept control of the car and brought it smoothly back to the right. His breathing accelerated. His hands were so wet with sweat, he worried he might lose his grip on the steering wheel. So he clenched harder, as if he were trying to crush it. He had no idea if the deer had run out into the road, but it didn't matter now. It was in the rearview, and he wasn't concerned with anything behind him.

Unless he was noticed by a police officer, possibly hidden by the darkness of night, running radar on this long stretch of a nearly desolate back road, nothing or anyone else mattered. Jim traveled at speeds that would earn him more than just a warning or a fine. If pulled over going this fast, he would likely be arrested for reckless driving. He didn't care, though. If the law were to suddenly fall into pursuit, lights flashing and siren wailing, Jim wouldn't stop. A potential night or two in jail couldn't deter him. He only had so much time. The consequences of evading the police were far less than the ones awaiting him if he slowed down or stopped.

Slowing down was something he suddenly had no choice of, though. A sharp curve to the left had finally arrived, and just after the bend, a train track crossing and a four-way stop. The three other streets at the intersection were in clear sight, and no other headlights approached from any of them. Nothing obstructed his view, so he slowed enough to take the curve, glanced in all directions, flew across the tracks and straight ahead.

Another long reach of nearly lightless roadway. He picked his speed back up, pressing the gas pedal until it moved no further. Now he was on the primary artery through a neighborhood. There were houses on both sides of the two-lane road, and the posted speed limit was thirty-five. He was already up to seventy and his speed increased: 73. 75. 78. 80. If something came out in front of him now, the car would be totaled, and he would likely end up at his own funeral. It was wise to slow down. Better to get there a little late than not arrive at all would be the sensible thought. Not this time, though. It was all or nothing. If he relaxed his haste, he would lose precious moments. He still wasn't sure what to do when he finally arrived at his destination, but he prayed something would come to him, either during the transit or once he arrived on the scene. He knew what was happening but wasn't sure how to handle it just yet.

Some houses had porch lights on. Some didn't. The ones with the lights seemed to blur past as if he were in a spaceship traveling at warp speed. The homes melded into one another; their driveways became one. Trees in front and side yards became green smears in reality. Driveways were merely stripes on what seemed like a twirling amusement park ride.

Hurry. Hurry. Come on, damnit.

Sweat trickled into his right eye and caused a burning sensation. Jim blinked several times. His vision distorted for an instant and already fuming panic became more intense. He needed *something* to go right. If this had been a leisurely drive through the scenic route on his way home from work, there would have been no distracting shadows, no slippery grip on the steering wheel, no sweat in his eye. But now, when he needed things to go smoothly for just a few minutes, the universe threw obstacles at him.

"This wasn't part of the deal!" he yelled after wiping his eye with his left shirtsleeve.

With both hands on the wheel again, he could see another four-way stop ahead. That was his turn. He slowed the car but only so much, as if he planned to gun straight through. He had to proceed through this intersection with a little more caution, though, because a tree in a home's front yard, and bushes on its border, obstructed the view of the street to the left. As Jim quickly neared the stop sign, he still couldn't see that left road, which meant any driver about to speed up through the intersection probably didn't see him. If Jim crashed into an innocent commuter and killed him or her, he would not only suffer the rest of his days knowing he'd taken a precious life, but he would also not reach his destination.

But every second mattered. The deal wasn't fair. The entire composition of the agreement was a wicked prelude to someone else's entertainment. *Who the hell got off on something like this? Who found it entertaining to put lives at risk? What kind of soul or entity thought it satisfying to cause such anxiety and potential chaos?* The most wicked of minds. The most evil of living, thinking things.

Jim slowed the car enough to take the right-hand turn, but he intentionally didn't look to his left. There wasn't enough time. He just hoped someone wasn't coming from that direction. He held his breath, braked, and took the right-hand turn so quickly it was a task to hold on to the steering wheel. He turned onto the street, tires squealing so loudly he probably woke up half the neighborhood. His car went onto the left side of the road, the driver's side wheels into someone's yard for just a brief moment; he pulled the Ford back onto the street, barely missed a mailbox, and sped forward again.

He released his breath as he zoomed through the neighborhood. One more turn would put him on the street of his destination. He looked ahead and to the right, and already saw the glow of the fire in the distance. His legs suddenly felt weak as dread filled his soul. So feeble, it became a struggle to keep the gas pedal to the floor. Anxiety gripped him and complete terror threatened to render him useless.

God, hurry. He had to hurry. *Don't lose it now.* Composure was vital. If he allowed himself to panic, his decision-making would be fatally compromised. He needed a clear head. But Jim was no hero. He was a warehouse worker. A father of one. A husband. A tax-paying citizen. His favorite food was pizza. He was just a guy. Just a man. A regular person. Yet, on this night, extraordinary circumstances required him to have extraordinary resolve. This wasn't a rush to the post office to get a package off on time. It wasn't running a few minutes late for work. This was life-and-death. If not that, then maybe it was a chance to fix things. A chance to undo something that caused so much grief and anguish. A chance. The deal wasn't supposed to be just an opportunity. That wasn't the signed agreement. Yet, now, there was no time to challenge the rules or file grievances with the powers that be.

Jim swung a hard right onto another neighborhood street. Now he was in the unfinished part of the neighborhood. Wooden skeletons of homes on both sides of the road. Dirt yards and unpaved driveways. There was only one house finished, purchased, and lived in on this street. The first of many that were slowly rising around it. That house was the one on fire straight ahead and to the right. Jim's eyes widened with horror. He could see the fire.

The home's roof was completely engulfed in flames. An eerie glow emitted from it and illuminated its surroundings. Orange and yellow flickering light with a backdrop of nighttime. He could even smell the burning of the home's manufactured ingredients. It was something Jim had never seen in his life. Or maybe he had, but the personal involvement in this situation made it seem like a unique experience.

Terror gripped him. Panic shook him. He wanted to cry, but now was not the time. He was scared. Not just of what he knew was happening inside that house right now, but that he might not properly rise to the occasion. He pressed the gas pedal as hard as he could to the floor panel of the Ford. The car raced toward the house. The fire warned of destruction and death.

Fifty yards. Thirty yards. Twenty. Ten.

Part One

Fire

Chapter One

A beautiful summer day. Mother Nature had shown some mercy and given the region a break from the usual scorching July weather. Eighty degrees and clear blue skies. A placid breeze from the west was instant physical therapy to Jim Radcliffe as he flipped the burgers on the grill. With each turn, fire shot up through the grates and immediately settled down again. Hamburgers flipped; hot dogs turned. He pivoted away from the sizzling food and faced the backyard, looking at his family through dark sunglasses. Several feet away and under a canopy sat his only son, Todd, his pregnant daughter-in-law, Beth, and his wife of twenty-three years, Alice. They had married when they found out Alice was pregnant with Todd, and it had been a mostly blissful life.

Todd, in his white collar shirt and blue jean shorts, his brown hair parted down the middle, saw his father looking his way and stood up from the table. Alice and Beth continued to chat with each other, smiling and laughing, breaking into serious talk, giggling and joking, then more conversation. Alice's shoulder-length, curly brown hair and Beth's long blonde hair both waved gently in the light summer breeze. Todd made his way to his father, who seemed to watch more than his family, but also stared off past them, toward the privacy fence at the yard's border. Along that fence, several maple trees offered shade for two lawn chairs.

"You okay, old man?" Todd playfully asked his father.

"Yeah. Those trees. I like how they run along the fence line. They offer extra privacy."

"One of the reasons I bought this place," Todd said. "Me and Beth sit under them all the time. It's our favorite spot."

"Well, for now. You have no neighbors yet."

"Oh, but they're building. Houses are popping up around here. We're lucky to be the first to buy and move in, but that won't last."

"It amazes me. The prices on these homes. How quickly they're selling. People making that kind of money are common?"

"I guess so. Though I doubt many of them got as lucky as I did." Todd winked at his father.

"Lucky?" Jim asked. "You earned that promotion."

Todd emitted an entertained scoff. "Oh, come on, Dad. I'd been on that job for three years. When I submitted a résumé for that position, it was nearly a joke. I didn't expect to get it. I didn't even expect them to read it. As young as I am, the résumé was nearly blank."

"It's that charming charisma." Jim grinned.

"Are you saying I don't have charisma?" Todd asked lightheartedly.

"Oh, you've always had that. Since you were a newborn. Always been a charmer."

"Definitely smiled and bullshitted my way into distribution manager. Do you know how many people with far more experience are probably pissed off? They all hate me now."

"Someone saw something in you." Jim took off his shades, laid them on the grill's side table, and regarded his son with seriousness. "They're not wrong. You've always been the best at everything you did. Just like your father."

"Only I'm willing to take on more responsibility."

Jim grunted. "What a terrible word. No, thank you."

Todd let out a quick laugh. "What word? Responsibility?"

"Yeah." Jim grimaced with fake disgust. "That word. I'm happy where I'm at. Just a foot soldier. Under the radar. Do my job and go home. Nobody calling and waking me up early in the morning with problems."

"That part only somewhat sucks. I kind of like it, though. It's like I'm captain of my own starship. There's a thrill to solving problems and having those solutions praised. I can pat myself on the back over my ingenuity."

Jim nodded toward the two wives sitting under a canopy in the yard. "That's plenty of responsibility right there. You'll see, in due time."

"I'm sure I will. But a kid can't be that hard. After all, raising me was easy."

Smiling and seeming to look back in time, Jim said, "You weren't that easy, but you weren't difficult. Maybe raising children isn't what I'm talking about, son." Jim winked.

Todd let out a quick chuckle. "You mean Mom? You couldn't have done it without her."

Jim nodded in agreement. "That's a truer statement than either of us will ever know. She's always been amazing. From the day I met her, to right this second. The most amazing thing I've ever known." And he looked directly at his wife with love.

She noticed his expression and smiled back at him. "What are you two talking about over there?" Alice called out.

"Divorce," Jim teased with a straight face.

Alice playfully scrutinized her husband for a few seconds and then returned to chitchat with her pregnant daughter-in-law.

The sizzling from the grill grew, and both son and father looked down at the cooking meat.

"You going to just burn supper, Dad?" Todd joked.

"Shit." Jim moved to flip the burgers and turn the hot dogs. Fire shot through the grates once more and then calmed down. The aroma of cooking meat filled the backyard and added to the pleasant feeling of a perfect summer day. Family, sunshine, and privacy: this was all Jim ever needed in his forty-three years of life. It was all he ever wanted, and he'd always been fortunate enough to keep it.

Raising his son had been a smooth experience. And marriage to Alice was always wonderful. He felt as if he loved her more every day. They were made for each other. He knew so way back then, and it was confirmed every moment of their existence together. The perfect team. The most astounding love story. Happily ever after had started in high school and still continued on now. Every single moment was special. Every day was cherished.

"It'll be the perfect night for a fire," Todd said as Jim turned the meat.

"Not for us. Gotta work. Double-time Sunday. There's money to make."

"You can take *one* Sunday off."

"Not this one. We could always try next Saturday. Or any Saturday during the summer. Mom and I don't hit the Gulf Shores till late August."

"Maybe we could tag along," Todd suggested.

"You could," Jim agreed.

"Depends on what's going on at work. Sometimes I can handle issues remotely, but every so often I have to make surprise visits. You know, to keep all my peasants on their toes."

Jim chuckled. "Peasants, eh?"

"Subordinates. Whatever word fits."

Jim said, "You know, I drive by here almost every day on the way into work. Out there on the main road. On the way in, the highway is too busy, so through this neighborhood is the back way for me. No traffic. Scenic. I like it."

"Probably not much to see at night, though."

"I take the highway home at night. It's actually quicker when there's no traffic. But during the day, from the main road out there, I can see the back side of this house. I remember when it popped up after they bulldozed this area into lots and put them up for sale. I wondered what the homes would cost in such a nice and quiet area."

"A lot," Todd said. "Too damn much. But she fell in love instantly, so I had no say-so in the matter."

"You'll get used to that. If she's not happy, you're not happy," Jim advised.

"Seems to be the case. But I love it, and I love her. She's a vibrant person. She glows with happiness and kindness."

"Just like your mother," Jim said.

"They say we marry people like our parents," Todd said.

"Then they will get along great."

"They already have. It's been a few years. Beth loves Mom."

"And vice versa," Jim agreed.

And it was at that moment Jim was startled by what he saw in the corner of his vision.

As soon as he turned, Todd followed his father's sudden change of demeanor and sight.

Coming through the open backyard gate was a figure. As both of them faced it, they realized it was a man. A filthy man. A dude in his early forties with skin so soiled it looked as if he'd rolled around in mud a month ago and hadn't showered since. He wore only a pair of blue jean shorts, which looked as if they hadn't been washed since the day he first put them on, and a worn-out pair of sneakers. He was a white man, but his skin was so tanned it appeared as if he'd been under the sun during every second of daylight since summer began. His hair was brown, wild, and oily. His eye sockets highlighted dark bags underneath them, and his face was so sunken in, his cheekbones protruded. The man's eyes were bloodshot, and he looked as if he were in the middle of a drug-abusing bender.

He staggered slightly as he entered the backyard, stopped and glanced at the women, who were now watching him with profound alarm. The man had a pistol in his right hand, and it was pointed outward, as if he were looking for a random target to quickly take a shot at.

Immediately on guard, Todd's face became serious, his smile turning into a frown of concern, and he started as if he were going to charge the mysterious character.

Jim's attention quickly turned to Todd, and he raised his hand in a stop gesture toward his son, shot him a glare of authority, and slowly shook his head in more an order than discouragement.

At the table, the two women, who had been engaged in pleasant conversation only moments ago, now watched both their husbands and the suspicious intruder. Alice's smartphone laid faceup on the table, and she instantly reached out for it. She didn't pick it up, but she touched the screen and swiped her security pattern to unlock the phone. She then hit the dialer app, quickly typed in 911, and hit Send.

The intruder only glanced at the women for a second and then focused on the two men at the grill. Smoke rose and the food sizzled. The entire demeanor of the backyard barbecue changed from ease and relaxation to fear and tension in an instant. It seemed even the summer breeze stopped to watch in suspense.

The man spoke, and his voice cracked as he did so. "You," he said accusingly as he looked at Todd. "You."

Jim watched the situation unfolding with the need to do something, but he wasn't sure what that something was. The unidentified man held a gun, and he was too far away to charge at or make a move toward. The gun was up and the muzzle pointed toward Jim and Todd, but Jim wasn't sure which of the two the intruder meant to aim for. He wanted to say something but wasn't even sure what words to mutter. If the man was as messed up on some kind of substance as he looked, the wrong word could send him into a shooting spree. There were five innocent lives in this backyard, including the unborn granddaughter within Beth's womb.

At the table under the canopy where the two women sat wide-eyed and frozen in fear, Alice listened to the ringing of the 911 call coming through her phone. It wasn't set to speakerphone, but she could still hear the faint sound of the ring through the earpiece. There was a click, and she heard a female voice answer on the other end.

"911, what is your emergency?"

"You," the intruder said again.

He made eye contact with Todd, who was now thumbing through his memory, trying to recognize the man whose tone suggested familiarity.

"Why should *you* get another chance?" the man asked.

He was angry. His voice was one of hatred and envy. But envy of what? Todd couldn't recognize him.

Jim looked at Todd in search of a sign of recognition on his face but saw only confusion. He looked back at the man, whose gun hand trembled lightly. It wasn't fear that kept him from steady hands, but so much rage. The look in his sunken eyes, his expression, indicated a hatred as pure as the eternal battle between good and evil. His demeanor was as if he wanted to pull that trigger but held back. He seemed to fight the urge to kill because it was wrong, but it also appeared as if he might lose that struggle. He wanted to shoot, and he didn't want to. But he wanted to more.

Todd stood speechless in a pool of fear.

Jim finally said, "I'm sorry, sir. Do we know you?"

The intruder turned his attention toward Jim and peered at him. "You don't have to know me. I'm nobody to you. I'm nobody to anybody. But I know things. I see things. I know you two are going to cheat. I want to know why you think you have the right." The man's voice shook when he spoke. It was ragged, as if he'd been smoking cigarettes since he was five years old.

"Cheat what?" Todd asked, an intentional steadiness in his voice. He eased the words out, issuing them as softly and politely as possible. Walking on eggshells. Skating on thin ice.

The man seemed to stare right through Todd, as if he were shooting laser beams from his own eyes into Todd's brain. The anger and hatred were so intense, Todd could feel it.

The intruder said, "Death. Why do you get to cheat death? Why is it fair for you to do it?"

Todd looked at Jim in confusion, who returned the glance. Both their attentions went back to the man with the gun.

At the table, Alice watched the scenario unfold, but also spoke softly to her phone. She was giving the 911 operator her address, hoping the man wouldn't notice.

Beth stared at Alice in fear, worrying that if the intruder heard, he would open fire.

Alice started with, "There's a man in the backyard with us." So softly, but not a whisper: "He's got a gun on us. Come now."

The 911 operator said something that neither of the women heard. Alice said toward the phone, "Man in backyard with gun. Come—"

"You!" the intruder yelled toward the women. He pointed the gun toward them. "Throw that phone. Throw it now. Throw it out there!" He used the pistol to gesture toward the tree line at the back of the property. "Throw it now! Throw the fucking phone!"

Instantly, but without hanging up, Alice tossed the phone. "There," she said. "There. It's gone."

The intruder turned his attention back to the father and son.

Jim almost made a move toward him but didn't act in time. They were now targeted again and still too far away to attempt a takedown of the gunman. Jim trembled not just with fear, but with frustration, too. He was supposed to do something. He was supposed to protect his family, but he was no hand-to-hand combat expert. He hadn't been in a physical fight since his middle school days. He wanted to take action, but his mind couldn't imagine the proper method of approach.

So, for now, they were just all held hostage to some junkie who obviously randomly chose this gathering of people to terrorize. The situation was delicate and could explode into tragedy at any moment. Jim looked at his son, who was succeeding early in life. Without moving his head, he looked over toward his wife and daughter-in-law, who watched with terror frozen on their faces.

"Nobody else gets second chances," the man said to Todd. "Why should you? Why are you above everyone else? Why do you think you have the right to interfere in God's plan?"

In a low and cautious tone, Todd said, "I don't know what you mean. I've never cheated death. I've never even faced it. I think you have the wrong—"

"No! I have the right person. The right people. You too." The intruder changed his glare from Todd to Jim. "Why do you get to save your son? When so many others have faced their grief, why do you get to cheat yours?" The man took one step toward Jim and Todd's position. He pointed the gun directly at Jim. "If I kill you right now, I stop you from cheating. Everyone dies as they should, and I stop the paradox."

"You don't have to shoot anybody," Todd said carefully. "You don't have to hurt anyone."

"But I want to, so bad," the man said to Todd. "I'm not a bad person. But I want to, so bad."

Jim said, "Why do you want to hurt us? You don't know us. Why—"

"Because you're a cheater!" the man yelled, his voice near an escalation there might be no return from until violence finally broke out. "You're the one who will do it. It's you. You are the one who's going to fuck everything up."

"Going to?" Todd asked.

"I saw it. I see a lot of things," the man said. "I see things that happen. I don't know why I was chosen. But I see things. I see your death. I see your dad changing it."

Jim said, "Do you want us to get you some help? Is there someone we can call? Family?"

"I don't need any help!" the man yelled, nearly hysterical. "I don't want help!"

Jim said, "You keep waving that gun around, you're going to hurt someone. Can you at least point that thing at the ground and maybe we can all talk about this?"

"What's to talk about?" The man jabbed the gun in Jim's direction. "You're going to do a terrible thing. I can stop it right now. I can prevent you from fucking everything up."

"From fucking *what* up?" Todd asked.

Watching from several feet away, and still sitting at the table, both women were afraid to move or add to the strange conversation now taking place between their husbands and some intruder, who was obviously delusional and off his rocker. Alice hoped the police were on the way. She prayed to herself the 911 operator had understood the urgency of the call and heard clearly the address given to her. The police needed to be en route. They needed to be pulling into that driveway any second now. The situation was escalating. The crazed intruder seemed to edge closer to pulling that trigger. He was irrational and unreachable. Alice and Beth could both see in their husbands' eyes the want to take action, but they were obviously being cautious. Waiting for the right moment to spring like a cat on its prey.

The man threw Todd a look of disgust. "Time. From fucking up time. Changing the past has its consequences. Everyone will pay for one man's selfishness. Everybody alive now. Everybody not yet born. All of history. You don't have the right to do that. *He* doesn't have the right." The man nodded toward Jim.

Jim said, "Change time? We don't know what that means. What do you mean by changing time?"

"I mean by going back and stopping something from happening. Interfering with what's already occurred." The man's voice quivered. It was as if he spooked himself when he spoke. His words slowed. His demeanor became one of fear or dread. He kept his focus on Jim. "When they die and you go back to save him," he gestured the gun at Jim, "instead of letting it be. Instead of going on with your grief and recovery. Instead of just fucking dealing with it like everyone else does with lost ones. You're going to change it. When you change it, you alter every life from that point forward. Time is not meant to be redesigned once it has occurred. You don't have that goddamned right."

Jim and his son looked at each other in bewilderment, realizing together that this man with the gun, this intruder in Todd's backyard, was not only on drugs, but was likely quite the delusional character even when sober. Whatever drugs he was on that made him sweat and shake like that, that made him bold enough to burst into a family gathering, waving a gun around and pointing it recklessly at innocent bystanders, only intensified a mental illness that was already present.

Several feet away, Beth stood up suddenly, as if she meant to take some action. Her pregnant belly out in front of her, she stared at the man with profound scrutiny.

He noticed her movement and pivoted toward her, then checked Jim and Todd, and looked back at Beth again.

His stance was threatening toward her, and Todd wanted so badly to charge him, but once again, Jim threw his son a solid, commanding stare.

"You stay right there," the man said to Beth. "You really have no part in this. You and your unborn daughter won't be saved." He nodded toward Jim, while still focused on Beth, and continued. "He will only save his son. You won't be brought back."

Alice stood up and said with a stern voice, "Who are you? Who do you think you are? Do you hear yourself? Are you on drugs?"

"I'm someone who sees things. And I see your husband altering an event that should be left alone." The man's voice was still shaky.

Something about his nervousness seemed to escalate. His hostages all detected this situation nearing a dreadful climax.

"I'm going to stop your husband."

"By shooting and killing him?" Todd asked. The man faced him, and Todd continued. "Are you not altering the future by taking his life? Are you not disrupting the flow of time by killing someone, causing them to die outside of natural reasons?"

"I'm stopping a catastrophe. This is the present. I'm not changing anything that's already happened."

"But if you shoot and kill him, you *are* altering a timeline. Without you being here, without you pulling that trigger, he lives a normal life. *You* are about to change that."

"The future isn't written. The past is. You're just trying to save yourself. You don't really give a fuck about anything else."

"No," Todd disagreed as he shook his head, adamant. "I don't believe a word you're saying. I think you're delusional. What if you are? What if you kill him for no valid reason at all? What if you're about to become just a murderer and not some kind of temporal hero? Is that what you are? Is that what you're willing to be?"

"I'm saving the timeline," the intruder replied bluntly and raised the gun toward Jim.

Just as it seemed he was about to take aim and shoot, from beyond the doorway of the surrounding privacy fence came a sudden cocktail of sounds. Cars pulling up. Doors opening and closing. A multitude of voices: one emitting orders and others replying with confirmation. Then, through the front gate, came a Black police officer with his gun raised. Immediately, the intruder lowered his weapon as he spun around to face the officer, who was already issuing a stand-down command. And the officer knew the intruder by name.

"Billy, put that goddamned gun down now," the policeman ordered.

Behind the approaching officer, two more police officers, a female and a male, came in through the gateway with their guns drawn, but pointing downward. All three stopped just a few feet from Billy. The first officer not only looked focused on the current mission, but he also looked angry, as if he were sick and tired of dealing with Billy's bullshit.

Billy lowered the gun but didn't drop it. He looked not only surprised, but somewhat ashamed of himself. As if the speaking police officer was an elder mentor who he had just disappointed. Billy looked at the ground and then at the speaking officer. "Tony, what are you doing here?"

"Don't you Tony me. What the hell are you doing, man?" Tony spoke with firm authority, as if he wasn't worried in the least that Billy might raise his gun and shoot at him. "A gun, man? You're pulling a gun on these folks?"

These folks—all four—watched with more curiosity than fear now. Somehow, Tony's approach toward Billy set them at ease, as if they now saw Billy as a harmless child instead of a deadly potential perpetrator of extreme violence. Yet they all four remained frozen where they stood because Billy still had a gun and he seemed no more sane than he was just moments before the police appeared on the scene.

"You don't understand," Billy said to Tony. "They're gonna cause bad things. This guy," he nodded toward Jim and Todd, "is going to change the timeline. I dreamt it."

"Now, Billy, that makes little sense," Tony said. "You high again?"

Billy snapped, obviously offended by the accusation, but didn't deny it. "That's got nothing to do with it. I dreamt it. Just like those other things that happened. I dreamt it. They're going to cheat death. I can stop them. I can save the timeline."

"You don't need to stop anything with that gun." Tony gestured toward the firearm in Billy's hand. "You really want to be in this much trouble? You've always been small-time, Billy. This is a whole other level. You're already looking at a felony. Put the gun down. Just bend down and lay it on the ground. Stop before you bury yourself."

Jim was relieved that the two knew each other by first name. It meant that this officer, Tony, had dealt with the crazy man, Billy, on numerous occasions and probably knew exactly how to handle him. But the one thing that kept Jim at unease was the fact that, evidently, Billy here had done nothing this bad before. So now the standoff was in a territory unfamiliar to everyone here on the scene. Not just Jim's family, but the perpetrator and the police officers in relation to him. Billy's voice continued to tremble as he spoke, which indicated to Jim that he hadn't necessarily calmed down just yet. He wasn't ready to give up the gun, as he still clasped it. But he was pointing it at the ground, so there was hope he might relinquish it still.

"You have no idea what's at stake here," Billy pleaded. "You know I've been right before. So many times. You know it. You've seen proof of my dreams. You...know I'm right."

"I don't know anything other than you're holding a gun on innocent folks. You need to put it down. Billy, I want you to walk away from this. Just put the gun down and let's go through the routine. Put it down, Billy. Nice and easy. Put it down." Tony spoke with caution in his voice. He was authoritative, but with careful treading.

Billy glanced toward Jim and Todd and back to the officers. He was thinking and thinking hard. His face showed he was weighing his limited options. Obviously, he was leaving here in handcuffs. Only the charges remained to be determined at this point. He looked at the gun in his right hand, still pointing toward the ground, then back at the police officers.

"You have no idea what's going to happen if I don't stop it," he mumbled, almost like a pouting child.

"And you know what's going to happen if you raise that gun again. Look behind me, Billy." Tony was talking about the officers behind him with their weapons drawn. He then used his head to gesture toward the women standing under the canopy. "We can't let you harm these people. Billy, listen to me. Put. The gun. Down."

Tony looked toward Jim and Todd who were, from his perspective, standing right behind Billy. They were in a dangerous spot if Billy forced the officers to open fire on him.

Making eye contact with Jim, Tony gestured with his head toward the backyard.

Jim immediately understood and tapped Todd on the shoulder. When Todd looked at him, Jim whispered, "Come on, son." Jim then led Todd out into the yard, but not near the women, who were yet still frozen in fear and awe under the canopy. Well aware the threat wasn't over yet, and if crazy Billy did decide to shoot, Jim didn't want the ladies getting hit in any kind of crossfire.

Billy had been facing the officers until he saw Jim and Todd moving in his peripheral.

He turned halfway toward them and stopped cold when Tony yelled with full authority in his voice, "No, Billy! Don't fucking move, man! You face me! Do it. Face me, Billy!"

Billy turned once more toward the officers, gun still pointing at the ground. He looked defeated, but it was only in appearance. He wasn't ready to give up yet. To Tony, Billy pleaded with frustration in his voice, "You don't know what you're doing. You have no idea. You're going to be on the wrong side of whatever history the entire world will eventually face if you don't just turn and leave." His voice rose as he spoke. His tone deepened with agitation. "You can't fuck with the timeline, man. *You can't fuck with the timeline!*"

"Put it down," Tony demanded yet again. "This is about to get really ugly. Just please, Billy, put the goddamn gun down. You don't trust me by now? As much as we've been through, you don't trust me?"

"I can say the same thing to you," Billy snapped.

"Billy, when you sober up, you're going to regret this day. Don't make it any worse. I'm going to come to you. I'm going to walk over to you, nice and easy. When I do, Billy, don't you dare raise that gun. Do you understand me?"

Billy looked at his gun and back at Tony but didn't answer.

"Do you understand me?"

Still no reply. Just a stare filled with irritation.

Tony took one careful step toward Billy, still holding the gun on him. Billy didn't move. Another step. As Tony took the second step, he pulled one hand from his gun, reached to his side, and slowly withdrew a set of handcuffs from his utility belt. The chain jingled loudly in the tension-filled atmosphere.

Billy let out a long sigh, and when he did so, his entire body moved with it.

Tony froze, pointing his weapon right at Billy's chest. Gun in one hand and cuffs in the other, Tony said softly, "Nice and easy, Billy. I'm going to come to you and put these cuffs on. For everyone's safety, I'm going to put these cuffs on. Billy, do not make a move. Don't move. Don't move that gun. Nice and easy."

Tony took another step closer, his eyes focused on Billy's. Another step, gun in hand. Another slow, cautious step. Billy watched. Tony edged closer.

Jim and Todd scrutinized, wide-eyed. The women trembled in their stances. The officers behind Tony had their aim on Billy's chest.

Another step. Tony was almost within reach. Billy stood still, yet his demeanor wasn't exactly one of surrender. He looked as if he waited for the right moment to make his move. As if his personal space were a trap—he was the bait, and Tony was the prey.

Tony was now within arm's reach of Billy and fell still. Still meeting Billy's glare, Tony said, "Now I'm going to take that gun, Billy."

Uneasiness tinged Tony's voice. "I'm going to reach out and take that gun. Don't you move it. You understand me? I'm just going to gently pull it out of your hand. Don't you move an inch, Billy."

Tony slowly lowered his weapon and placed it in its holster at his side. Handcuffs in one hand, he reached downward toward Billy's gun. As he edged toward it, he mumbled, more to himself than Billy, "Nice and easy, man. Nice and easy." He gently wrapped his fingers around the barrel. "Nice and easy," he whispered.

Tony cautiously tugged on the gun and pulled it from Billy's hands. Once it was secure in his grip, Tony held the gun behind him. The female officer put her gun away, rushed to him, and took Billy's firearm from Tony. Quickly, Tony secured one handcuff around Billy's wrist, then grabbed him, spun him around, and engaged the other handcuff around the other wrist. Tony offered no resistance but mumbled something hateful under his breath.

Everybody in the backyard seemed to exhale in unison. Tony now had a good grip on Billy's left arm and the two were face-to-face. Billy, in frustration, jerked forcefully as if he were trying to escape, but Officer Tony was stronger.

"You don't know what you've done," Billy said with ire. "You don't fucking know."

Tony looked back at the other officers. "Get his ass in the car. I'll be out there in a few minutes." He then faced the women. "Folks, you okay?" He looked at Jim and Todd. "You guys all right?"

A cardinal landed on the edge of the house's roof, on the gutter, and looked down at everyone. It squeaked a few times and then flew off again. A warm, comfortable breeze blew through as if Mother Nature herself let out a sigh of relief. Beth plopped down into her seat. Alice went to Jim and Todd. As she approached, she said, "Jesus, Jim. Jesus."

Chapter Two

A warm July evening. The full moon was high above, its powerful, illuminating glow keeping absolute darkness at bay. The insects of nightfall guaranteed a summer night of chorus and mating calls. Somewhere off in the woods on the outskirts of the new neighborhood, an owl called out its familiar question to the world. On a lot where construction of a new house had begun just a few weeks ago, a black cat scurried across a stack of plywood. It stopped dead center and sat down, looking out intently over the construction site, in search of mice or bugs to play with and then ultimately kill. On the second floor of the only house that was complete, light outlined a bedroom window from within. In that bedroom, Todd lay in bed in his boxers, reading a Dean Koontz novel titled *Lightning*. From the bedroom's bathroom, the sound of a running shower suddenly went silent.

Todd looked up from the book toward the bathroom door, then placed it on his nightstand under a bright lamp. He couldn't remember a word he'd read in the last twenty minutes. His mind was still obsessed with the events from earlier that day. The crazy gunman and his ridiculous babbling about death and changing the past. The raving lunatic's accusations that Todd's father, Jim, would somehow do something that might screw up a timeline for the entire world.

An electric hair dryer came on in the bathroom.

Todd couldn't get it out of his head how close he might have actually come to losing his wife and his unborn daughter today. How such a perfect afternoon could become a life-and-death situation, during which he became more afraid than he'd ever been in his life, picked at his brain from the moment it started until the instant that baffling junkie was in handcuffs. And he also obsessed over the fact that if there could have been that close of a call today, then every day was a risk. Perfect moments with family. A warm, breezy July day. Food cooking on the grill. A moment of complete happiness and contentment could turn dangerous at any random time. Beth and unborn Stormy Dawn would never be safe in this world.

It was Todd's job to keep them sheltered, defended, unharmed, and yet somehow today he had failed to do so. He should have charged at that man, and had wanted to in the moment, but the perp was too far away. Todd reminded himself at least a hundred times in the past several hours that if he'd started toward the raging idiot with a gun, he would have put his loved ones at possible fatal risk. Yet, still, he inwardly accused himself of cowardice, of not doing enough, of becoming a complete chicken-shit in his family's moment of need for his bravery. There was no bravery today. No courage. Nothing at all. He'd just stood there, scared, frozen, and unable to act when needed.

Now the whacko guy was behind bars. At least Todd hoped so. There was no telling for sure with how today's criminal justice system worked. Innocent people were on death row while guilty people accused of violent crimes were out on five-hundred-dollar bonds. If today's perpetrator was actually out of jail, free and roaming, there was a chance he'd come back, looking to harm Todd's family again. After all, the man seemed focused on them specifically. He didn't just wander into any backyard waving a gun around. He had come for them, accusing them of something they were going to do in the future.

If the psycho was out and free, then the next time he got high or strung out, he'd come this way again.

There were no guns in this household. The only weapons of defense were cheap steak knives and locked doors and windows. What if next time, Billy, the crazy man, hid in the shadows and struck without warning? The direct approach had not worked for him, so another attempt might be more planned and calculated. Todd realized he was just as afraid now as he was in the moment of direct threat earlier today. Even the arrest of the man offered no relief.

The hair dryer in the bathroom shut off, the door opened, and Todd's beautiful wife appeared in the doorway. Her baby-full belly led her out into the bedroom, covered only by a long, purple nightgown. Her blonde hair, usually long and well to the middle of her back, was up in a nightcap. Blue eyes and a tiny nose. A small mouth and smooth cheeks. She was the woman of his dreams. As long as he'd known her, he had been in love with her. Having met her his junior year in high school, that hadn't been long at all. They were still young and not settled into who they were going to be, but he felt as if he'd loved her for ten lifetimes. When he looked at her, every good feeling flowed through him. She made his heart warm. She aroused his sexuality with just a glance. His blood flowed and his heart beat because of her. And soon, another female would steal his love: their daughter and first child. Stormy Dawn Radcliffe. In about two months' time, they would become a family of three.

As Beth seemed to struggle to get into bed, her extra cargo making it an awkward task, Todd reached toward his nightstand light and turned it off. Beth grunted in effort, finally snuggled under the blankets, stretching her legs out. Her belly looked like a hill in the middle of a field of flat plains. She reached to her left and turned her light off.

The bedroom went dark, but not completely, as the outside moonlight seemed to offer backup illumination.

"I'm not sure I can make it another two months," Beth said as she stared at the ceiling.

"Maybe it won't be a full two months. You know they can't usually call it right on the money," Todd replied as he also stared upward.

"It feels like she's about to burst right out of me, whether or not it's time."

"Looks like it too," Todd teased.

Beth glanced over at him with a phony, stern look.

He pretended to avoid her glare and smiled.

"You carry a growing, living human being inside you for nine months and see how you feel."

Still looking at the ceiling, but now with a grin, he replied, "Nope. Don't have to. I'm a man."

"God's cruelest imposition on women. Why couldn't we both have to give birth?"

"Considering where it comes out, it would likely kill males."

"It would be an honorable death, though," Beth said. "Dying while giving birth to your child."

"How about we keep it like it is and nobody dies?"

"How about men can just squeeze the baby out through their but-tholes?"

"Ouch." Todd playfully flinched. "How about not?"

Looking at the ceiling again, Beth suddenly changed the topic, and a blanket of solemnity covered the bedroom. "Honey, I was really afraid today. I thought that was it for us. For one of us. For all of us. If he'd started shooting, maybe he wouldn't have been able to stop himself. Maybe he'd gone into some kind of violent frenzy that wouldn't have ended until—"

"Stop it," Todd interrupted, turning to his wife with a serious glare. "That didn't happen. We're safe." Even though he felt the same way, his job as protector was to at least make his wife *feel* safe. He agreed with every word she said, but if he verbalized that, he was failing her. Todd had already let her down enough for one day. "He's just some random junkie. He's behind bars now. Even if he was out, he was too high to know where he was. He couldn't find this house again if his life depended on it."

"I sure hope our lives don't depend on him *not* finding it," Beth said ominously.

"It doesn't. He was just a nutjob."

"What do you think he was talking about? All that stuff about changing the timeline? About cheating death?"

"He was a junkie strung out on something. *He* didn't even know what he was talking about."

"You say that but...sometimes it's the crazy people who know things. Their minds aren't restrained by the rules. Because of that...they can...see and feel things normal people can't. What if he's onto something?"

Todd looked at his perfect wife, his beautiful sidekick in life, and marveled at her. He assured her, "Not druggies. Maybe old people on their deathbeds, within their final moments of life, have some kind of eerie clairvoyance. But not junkies, Beth. The man was high and babbling. He doesn't know anything about the future. He was probably on a combination of drugs and hallucinating."

"Maybe you should stay home from work tomorrow," she said. "It wouldn't hurt to miss a day just to make sure. Just stay home with us and be safe." She put her hands on her belly under the blankets. "Just stay home with me and Stormy. We can have a big breakfast and sit around, watching soap operas all day. It wouldn't hurt for you to miss just one day."

"You're getting yourself worked up over nothing."

"Nothing? A sweaty, dirty, drugged-out hippie in our backyard wanting to blow us away, over a future he claims to have seen, is nothing? I'm glad you're so okay with it all."

"I'm not okay with it. But it *is* over. The police officer told us that weirdo would be in jail for a long time. Said he's been in and out of jail for the last several years but never did anything really bad. With his long rap sheet, he'll be headed off to prison for a few years now. By the time he gets out, he will have forgotten all about us and his fucked-up dreams."

"Just one day," she repeated in a stubborn tone.

Todd sighed. "I can't stay home on a Monday."

"What's the difference between Monday and any other day?"

Todd replied, "The first day of the week? I have to be in there. It's not a good look. I may be a big boss, but I have even bigger bosses."

"One day."

Another sigh. Then Todd said, "Say this psycho was right about his nonsense. He didn't give a specific day, date, or time. What if whatever is going to happen occurs on a Tuesday or a Wednesday, or a Saturday? I can't stay home every day."

"It's just one day. You can't give that just to humor me?"

"Beth..."

"One day and I'll shut up. I won't mention it again."

Todd sighed, still staring at her.

Beth flinched. Her face lit up with glowing excitement and she reached out, grabbed Todd's hand, and pulled it under the blanket to the top of her belly. She whispered, "Our daughter agrees."

Todd smiled as he felt the movement of their daughter, Beth's hands on top of his, in his wife's belly. A nudge. Rolling motion. Another poke. More fluid movement. Then stillness.

Beth turned her head to face her husband and met his fascinated expression. She smiled warmly. "Don't tell me you can resist her. She wants you to stay home. No better time than now to start spoiling our baby girl. Don't you think?"

He hesitated, still grinning at Beth.

"One day," she said.

"One day," he agreed.

A sudden childlike excitement came over Beth's manner, along with a sigh of relief. She reached toward Todd for a kiss, and he met her halfway with reciprocation. One kiss. Two kisses. So soft and gentle. So full of love everlasting. He pulled his hand out from under the blanket and touched her cheek. She smiled. He grinned.

"I love you so much." She put her hand on his and kissed him again.

"I love you, Beth. I love you more than anything."

Chapter Three

J im swiped his work badge at the outside turnstile, waited for the confirmation beep, and went through it into his job's parking lot. The warehouse and tonight's shift finally behind him, he stopped just as he stepped onto the pavement and looked up at the clear summer night sky. It had been an eventful day before he'd left for work, which made the past eight hours on the job drag by like a snail making its way through mud.

The parking lot's abundant lighting made it nearly impossible to see any stars as he stared upward, but the moon was at its fullest, and no city lights or artificial illumination could out-blare its powerful glow. Behind him, the gate beeped repeatedly as his coworkers made their way through it and walked past him toward their vehicles. Jim looked away from the sky and watched his fellow associates in their after-work motions.

Some were conversing, joking, laughing. Others hurried toward their vehicles, not as if they were leaving a job for the night, but like they were making a hasty escape. And a few others moved as if they realized hurry was pointless because life was a routine and tomorrow they had to do the same thing over again. He stood there, watching them in his dirty T-shirt, messy hair, baggy blue jeans, and worn-out steel-toe shoes.

Jim was exhausted. He wondered if he could lie down right now and right here in this parking lot and fall asleep immediately. From the moment the irrational man had invaded his family's little Sunday afternoon get-together to the second he clocked out, his mind hadn't stopped. Flashes of what could have happened today at the hands of the intruder weren't the only things on his mind, though.

It was the things the man had said. The foretelling of something tragic happening to Jim's only son, and then the even more spectacular predictions of Jim saving Todd's life and somehow altering a universal timeline, had weighed heavily on his thoughts for at least the past ten hours. What bothered him the most was that he entertained the idea that the weirdo might actually know something. Every time Jim told himself the guy was just bat-shit crazy, on drugs, and babbling in a doped-up stupor, something inside him stopped short of completely dismissing everything the man had said. What if the stranger had been right? What if something was about to happen, and Todd was in danger? What if Todd, Beth, and unborn Stormy were teetering on the edge of their own doom and there was nothing anybody could do to stop it?

Sometimes the craziest of circumstances occurred out of nowhere. Life moved along nicely and smoothly, and then, at the snap of a finger, tragedy struck. Death and grief dropped in like a sudden summer downpour on a bright and mostly cloud-free day. Just one dark cloud, just one burst of wind, and suddenly what seemed so perfect was completely darkened.

These thoughts ran through his mind like a music player playing one four-minute song on a loop. Persistently, Jim fought off the visions of gloom and doom without success. Now he realized he was exhausted from it all, especially after working an entire shift during which he just wanted to go home and be with Alice.

As more coworkers walked by, Jim snapped himself back to here and now, and made his way to his car. He pulled his car keys from his pocket, aimed them ahead, pushed the unlock button on the remote, and got in. As soon as he was inside the car, he pulled his smartphone from a pant pocket and placed it in the passenger seat. Jim engaged his seat belt, put the keys in the ignition, and started the car. The radio immediately blared with sports news. He muted it by pushing in the volume knob. The front windows rolled down when he pressed a button on the inside of the door. He turned the air-conditioning, which was pushing cold air into the car immediately and at full force, off. The time on the digital dash clock read 2:13 a.m. Both hands on the steering wheel, he leaned back in the driver's seat, rested his head on the headrest, and closed his eyes while releasing a long sigh of surrender. Jim's body and mind were exhausted, and he dozed off right there in the parking lot.

"Jim, wake up!" came the sudden, sharp, and loud male voice right into Jim's ears. Startled, he opened his eyes, and his entire body jerked away from the driver's window. Eyes wide open, he looked to his left and saw Adam Crane, a coworker, standing beside his car, looking in at him.

Adam chuckled. "Are you okay, man?"

"Long day," Jim said. "Thanks for jolting me back to the world of the living."

"You should go have a beer with us, man. Long days end well with a few drinks. You definitely look like you need it."

Adam was in his early thirties. A tall, skinny, bearded man, he always seemed to be in the best of moods. He'd been a coworker of Jim's for ten years now, and there had been many times Jim had gone to the bar after work to have a couple beers with Adam and other coworkers. It was always a pleasant experience, but it had been awhile since Jim was social with his colleagues. It wasn't that he'd grown tired of them, or disliked them, but he preferred to just go straight home after work. There were a few times during those social events Jim had a few too many to drink but still drove home. At some point, he figured he'd pushed his luck with potential DUI charges a bit too far, and realized if he wanted to drink after work, he could do it at home. He *did* miss fraternizing occasionally, but once going directly home became a comfortable routine, he hadn't swayed from it.

"Man, I appreciate the offer, but I'm too tired for even that. I just want to go home and crash."

Adam made a pouty face. "Ah, come on, Jimmy! It's just a handful of us. We're not looking to party all night. Just have two or three beers, shoot the shit, and head home."

"Can't do it." Jim shook his head. "Maybe next time. You guys don't get yourselves into any trouble tonight."

"Oh, sure thing. You know me. I'm Mister Responsibility." Adam grinned and winked at Jim.

Jim forced a quick laugh. "Right. Mister Responsibility." And he chuckled again.

"Well, see you tomorrow night, man."

"See you tomorrow night."

Adam walked away and left Jim to himself, sitting in his running car, exhaustion heavy within him. He sat there for a few minutes more as the rest of the shift's departing employees came through the turnstile one by one, watching them but not paying attention to them. His mind was elsewhere. Even in its worn-out state, it was profoundly active with the day's events. As often as he tried to dismiss the crazy man from Todd's backyard and the lunatic's ravings, Jim couldn't help but feel like there was some accuracy to them.

As his brain replayed the scene—the man waving a gun around wildly, taking aim, and then waving it again, the things he said, the predictions of future turmoil and disaster—Jim realized he believed every word of what he had heard. He could see, in his memory, the man had been sweating profusely. Something in his eyes showed he was not just mildly high on drugs, but completely blasted and out of this world. He hadn't seemed sane at all. Not even close. A poor fellow who had gone off the edge, likely because of a life-changing and ruining event, shouting warnings and a foretelling of events yet to come.

"I have to go home," Jim whispered to himself. He adjusted his posture from laid-back and relaxing to driving mode, put the car in reverse, and checked the rearview mirror. All clear. It was time to get home and get some sleep. It was time to move on from this nightmare day.

***

Jim almost took the back roads home. He could have turned left out of the parking lot, taken the scenic route, and driven by Todd's house just to make sure everything was okay. After all, he passed it on the way in to work every afternoon. And, ever since his son had purchased that house, Jim had ridden slowly past the road it was built on. It was just two turns off the main road, and he could actually see the back of Todd's house through the row of homes that lined the main street.

With potential disaster on his mind, Jim considered just riding by, glancing toward the rear of his son's house, and then continuing on home. That might not be enough to satisfy him, though. In order to settle his nerves, he would have to turn in to the neighborhood and drive slowly past the residence, glancing at the front yard, the side yard, the driveway—watching for any shadows that might show a stranger on the property.

But if he did that tonight, wouldn't he need to do it every night? And what if Todd looked out a window, even though it was two in the morning, and saw his overly concerned father stalking his house? Not only might it rouse Todd's nerves, but if he relayed any sighting to Beth, she might stress, too. She was seven months pregnant and unnecessary anxiety was the last thing she needed. Besides that, Jim assured himself that Todd was a grown man, and could handle any life disruptions that might occur. Surely he didn't want his father treating him like he was a child. Especially when he was about to father his own daughter.

So Jim turned right out of the parking lot and drove toward the main highway. At this time of night, it was the quickest way home and there was less of a chance a deer would come running out of nowhere into his path. That back way was littered with them, especially during the summer, because of its proximity to a large area of woods, and nearly void of any artificial lighting.

It was when Jim was turning right onto the main highway, running a red light completely, without stopping to look first, that he really began to understand how tired he was. And then, when he ran straight through another traffic light on the highway, he grasped the fact he was thoroughly exhausted. He knew he was lucky nobody was traveling through that intersection from adjacent streets, and even luckier no cops had witnessed his reckless moving violations. He wasn't sure how much a ticket was for that kind of infraction, but knew whatever the cost, he didn't want to pay it.

Exhaustion wasn't the only thing distracting him. That gun-pointing, accusing psychopath from earlier today was living rent-free in

Jim's head. He couldn't erase the images. He couldn't turn deaf ears to the man's words. All night at work, in the parking lot after, and now during what should be a short drive home, he heard the words repeated.

I see your death. I see your dad changing it.

Nobody else gets second chances. Why should you?

Changing the past has its consequences.

The crazy man looking at Beth.

You and your unborn daughter won't be saved.

Jim shuddered, as if hit by a blast of cold air, while he struggled to focus on the road. Streetlights passed in a blur. Closed businesses. Empty parking lots. Wide open roads at two a.m., hours before the chaos of morning rush-hour commutes. Traffic lights glowed green. Power lines ran parallel to the highway.

I see your death.

You and your unborn daughter won't be saved.

Jim felt a rush of emotion. He felt as if he was choking up, about to cry, like something tragic had already happened. He envisioned a funeral for his son, his daughter-in-law, and his granddaughter, and tears formed in his eyes. As if the foolish man's predictions had already come true, a wave of grief and sorrow came over Jim. He felt loss and mourning. He felt regret, as if he could have prevented their deaths, but didn't. A tear crawled down his cheek.

As he sped under a green traffic light, Jim shook his head and got hold of himself. Nothing had happened. Nothing was *going to* happen. Right now and in this moment, Todd and Beth were peacefully asleep next to each other, safe and sound in their own home. Stormy was snug and protected in her mother's womb. The night was a peaceful one, not one of disaster and tragedy.

This was what the man who invaded their family gathering had wanted. He'd hoped to instill fear into the minds and hearts of people who were enjoying life, family, and the perfect day. Something he could no longer do without drugs and crazy thoughts, for whatever reasons or circumstances had taken his sanity and hope from him. Because that man was without enthusiasm for the future, or lacked any reason to find happiness in his current life, his thrills came from trying to take away goodness from the innocent.

Jim's grip on the steering wheel tightened. He now had another emotion overwhelming him: anger. This feeling was so much better than the ones that had come before it. There was no despair in being pissed off. There was only a focus of ire and fury on a deserving target. Billy whatever his last name was. He was the target. And Jim swore to himself, in that moment as he turned off the highway onto a main road leading to his neighborhood, that if he ever saw that man again, he'd physically make it clear to the psycho to stay away from his family, and any other innocent folks he might come across.

As Jim pulled into his driveway and saw the upstairs bedroom light on, as it usually was when he arrived home from work, he breathed a sigh of relief. Alice was likely lying in bed, reading a book, waiting for her husband. She waited up for him every night, without fail. It didn't matter whether his shift was twelve hours or eight hours. She refused to turn that light off and drift away into the land of dreams without Jim being in bed right beside her. In sickness or in health, in joy or anger, in contentness or melancholy, she always waited for him. Even if she was exhausted and fighting off the sandman with everything she had in her, she waited.

He sat in the car just outside an open garage door for a few minutes, watching the bedroom light and smiling. Suddenly, all was well again. He was home. His wife waited for him. And he believed his son and his family were home safe and sleeping soundly, too. The crazy guy had been just that: crazy. The world was fine.

Chapter Four

S unlight blazing through the window directly in his face woke Jim. He stirred, rolled over away from the brightness, and then opened his eyes. Under the blankets in his sleeping shorts, with the air-conditioning running on high, he was comfortable and not ready to be up for the day. He looked at the nightstand, saw his smartphone faceup, and reached out for it with reluctance.

He didn't really want to see the time, but usually once his eyes were open, he felt it was time to get up. And his routine had him waking on his own every day around nine a.m. If it was any earlier, he would put on an eye mask and go back to sleep. But if it was nine a.m. or later, he'd crawl out of bed and get his day started. Working the night shift, he hated sleeping the day away, wasting moments of life in slumber. Even if he worked later than usual the night before, and if dragging ass was required all the way until bedtime once again arrived, he still forced himself up.

He unlocked the phone screen with a swipe and the digital clock numbers informed him it was 8:47 a.m. Too early to get up, but too late to go back to sleep. He put the phone back on the nightstand and rolled over to face Alice, who was not in bed. Her side was empty, with her half of the blanket piled into the middle of the mattress. She rarely woke up before Jim. The normal routine was him getting up around nine, making himself a cup of coffee, and watching the morning news for about an hour before making Alice coffee and waking her up. Jim listened intently and could hear the television on in the living room. The house they had raised Todd in was the same one they'd lived in since their marriage: a small, modest three-bedroom, attached garage accessible through the kitchen, one-level house in a middle-class neighborhood. Sound carried quickly from one end to the other. The master bedroom, which wasn't *much* of a master bedroom, was at one end on the back half of the house, and only about fifteen feet from the living room and the kitchen. Along the hallway, two smaller bedrooms on the front side of the house, and a small laundry room on the back half.

Jim sat up, turned and planted his feet on the carpet, and stretched. He heard sounds in the kitchen. Coffee cups clanging. Water running, then stopping. Alice must have awakened just before he did. Perhaps it wasn't the sun that pulled him out of sleep, but feeling her movement as she threw off the blankets and climbed out of bed. He picked his short-sleeved T-shirt off the floor and pulled it on over his head. Jim stretched again, stood up, and walked out of the bedroom.

When he stepped into the kitchen, Alice was stirring her coffee cup with a silver spoon. She set the spoon down just as he said, "Good morning, beautiful wife."

She turned and smiled at him, but her face showed something was disturbing her. "Good morning, handsome husband."

He went to her, standing eight inches taller, and put his arms around her. She held her full coffee cup outward, so not to spill its contents, and hummed with pleasure. Jim kissed Alice on the top of her head several times and then looked her in the eyes. Something was definitely on her mind. "I love you," he said.

"I love you," she replied, sounding as if she were trying to force pleasantness into her voice.

"What's wrong?" Jim asked with obvious concern.

Alice looked away and then back at him, and lied when she spoke. "Nothing. A little tired. I don't think I slept well."

"Looks like something is bothering you more than just a little lack of sleep."

She sighed and sipped her coffee. Alice acted as if she wanted to say what was on her mind but felt embarrassed about it.

"Let me make my coffee and we'll talk about it."

"It's really nothing," she insisted. "I didn't sleep well. That's it."

He scrutinized her for a moment and then surrendered. "Okay. If you say so, I guess."

"Really, Jim. Just lack of sleep. I'm so tired."

"Then maybe go back to bed and get a nap?"

Another sip. A defeated expression appeared on her face. She said, "I'll give the coffee a chance to kick in. If it doesn't, then I'll nap."

"Sounds like a plan to me," Jim said.

"I'm going to go sit down." Alice then puckered her lips and tiptoed up toward Jim's face.

He met her with a soft kiss. "I'll see you in there."

Alice turned and left the kitchen.

Jim opened a cabinet to find a coffee cup. But as soon as he reached toward the one he wanted, he heard a crashing sound in the living room. Something had fallen and broken into several pieces. It sounded like glass shattering. Jim instantly bolted out of the kitchen and saw Alice standing there, staring out the living room window, which had its curtains tied to each side. A clear view of the front yard and the driveway. She looked as if she'd just seen a ghost.

Jim followed her gaze, and saw a police car in the driveway and an officer climbing out of it. Another marked cop car pulled in behind the first. Jim stared for just a second, and then saw Alice pick her smartphone off the coffee table, completely ignoring the broken pieces of porcelain and the spilled coffee on the hardwood floor.

"No," she whispered with dread as she held the phone in one hand and touched the screen. She swiped, typed, and then pushed. "No, no, no." Her voice was filled with building terror. She held the phone to her ear.

Jim watched curiously as a police officer exited the second car, and both cops met up in the driveway and started to converse. One looked toward the house and then back to the other. They continued to talk.

"Honey, calm down. They're just here to follow up with what happened yesterday."

The police officers were still chatting with each other. One looked at the house, then to the right of it. The other looked around as he talked, wiped his forehead as if clearing away nervous sweat.

"Todd's not answering the phone, Jim," Alice said shakily as she looked at her husband and then back at her phone. She pushed on it again and once more held it to her ear for just a second. "Goddammit, Jim. It's going straight to voicemail!" She was panicking.

"Honey, let's just see what they have to say."

Alice dialed the number again.

The two police officers talked between themselves. It was as if they were stalling. Jim watched, looking anxiously from his wife, to the window, at his wife, at the window. His legs were weakening. He felt like something was wrong here. Something was off. Maybe his wife's nervousness was influencing his own dread, or maybe something really was wrong.

"Straight to voicemail!" Alice said frantically. "Fuck! Answer the phone, Todd!"

She dialed the number again. And again. And again.

The police officers finally walked toward the house, one in front of the other. They were plodding.

Jim was suddenly so afraid, he felt like he might go into cardiac arrest. He tried to calm himself and started toward the door. As he took his first step, Alice threw her smartphone down the hall.

It crashed against the corner wall and hit the hardwood floor, slid for a few inches, and then stilled. "Goddammit!" she yelled desperately.

"Calm down," Jim said as he unlocked the inner front door. "This is about yesterday." He was trying to reassure her, but his voice gave him away. It was obvious he wasn't so sure himself. Jim pulled the inner door open, then opened the screen door just before the police officers had a chance to knock or ring the doorbell.

***

With his sobbing and nearly hysterical wife in the passenger seat, Jim smashed the gas pedal and turned right onto the highway, running the traffic light, which had just changed from yellow to red. The tires protested in high-pitched screaming against the pavement, and drivers in the vehicles going straight, whose light was now green, angrily hit their horns. With absolute concentration on his face, Jim sped away from them.

Speed limits didn't matter. Traffic laws ceased to exist to him. He had to get to the hospital. He and Alice had dressed and left the house within two minutes of the police officers' departure. They had delivered the most dreaded of all messages. A house fire. Todd was in the hospital, hanging on to life by a thin, hopeful thread. Beth and the baby had perished in the fire. A gas explosion wasn't the cause of the disaster, but the final, explosive conclusion to it. Emergency personnel had pulled Todd from the house, but his body was covered with severe burns, and he was suffering from smoke inhalation. When the explosion happened, firefighters were rushing back in to pull Beth from the home, and two of them lost their lives too. An early-morning disaster had taken four souls and was about to claim a fifth.

Jim's hands shook as he gripped the steering wheel. It felt as if they would weaken to where he'd have no control of the car. Apprehension flowed through his body in the place of blood. He wanted to scream and cry, but he had to be strong, at least until they got to the hospital. Alice was mumbling and sobbing in the passenger seat. She was a mess already, and if what Jim was dreading actually became reality, he wasn't sure how he could hold himself and his wife together. Made-up visions of the disaster—the fire, his son burning alive, his daughter-in-law, the unborn baby—forced their way into Jim's imagination. The suffering. The helplessness. The police officer had said the fire must have already been at full force when Todd and Beth finally awoke to it. They tried to escape but didn't make it past a few moments after waking up.

Jim could see it in his mind. The smoke. The fire. Todd and Beth's lungs were unable to handle anymore, waking to coughing uncontrollably. Robust flames all around them. The heat. Melting their skin already. One might have awakened first and then shook the other frantically. Both running into the hallway, already struggling to breathe. Beth collapsing. Todd trying to help her. Both being overcome. Falling. Unconsciousness prevailing. A cruel plague of fire surrounding them. Emergency responders arriving and rushing into the house. Finding the fallen couple together in the hallway. Pulling them down the stairs. Emerging through a fire-engulfed front entrance with Todd first. An explosion. Beth, the baby, and two firefighters still inside. The blast throwing the ones who were carrying Todd well into the front yard. A night lit up with disaster and tragedy.

"No," Jim mumbled as he shook the vision from his head. Tears flowed down his face. His mouth trembled. It felt nearly impossible to breathe.

A traffic light ahead had changed from green to yellow. Jim was too far away to beat it. He willed the Ford to move faster. The light turned red as they were about one hundred feet away from it. Jim glanced at both side roads. Cars were moving forward, signaled by a green light to do so. Jim didn't slow down and raced through the intersection. More horns blared. They didn't know his circumstances, and he didn't give a damn if they were mad.

"We're not going to make it," Alice said in between sobs. "Hurry, Jim. Hurry, goddammit!"

He *was* hurrying. Jim was breaking every traffic law in existence to get them there quicker. He didn't reply but tried like hell to focus on driving and speed.

"Jim, please hurry," Alice said again, her words barely comprehendible through her crying. "He's going to go. He's going to go before we get there. Our son is dying!"

Jim snapped at her, "If I crash the fucking car, we won't get there at all." And he immediately felt remorse for his tone.

"I know, but hurry!" Alice yelled and then continued to cry.

A right turn through a major intersection ahead. The traffic light, once again, was already red, and cars from the opposing lane were turning left. Jim slowed just enough to make the turn and cut in front of them, smashing the gas pedal again after committing to the turn. Cars slammed on their brakes. Irate horns resounding was becoming a regular occurrence during this emergency run. He gunned the Ford ahead.

Alice was now crying uncontrollably. Jim wanted to console her. He wanted to tell her it would all be okay. Todd wasn't dead yet. According to the police officers, he was fighting for his life in the hospital. He would make it through. He would survive, recover, and, in time, live a normal life.

But it wasn't just Todd they were mourning. Beth and the baby were deceased. They didn't get the opportunity to fight for survival because they had perished on the scene. So young, so full of life...Beth was a good daughter-in-law. The unborn baby girl never saw the first light of birth and life.

Jim held back his own crying. He was choking back the tears as he drove, flying through traffic, hearing his suffering wife beside him. Sobs made their way to the surface, and he fought them off. He had to focus on getting to the hospital. If he broke down and lost concentration, they would crash. If he wrecked the car, and if Todd was destined to not survive, they wouldn't even be able to say goodbye to their only child.

Another right turn. This time, the light was green. Jim took the turn at nearly full speed. The car almost slid left into the oncoming lane, but he pulled it back and sped forward. The hospital was about three more miles and two turns away. Jim wasn't religious, but inside his mind, he begged God to at least let a devastated mother and father say goodbye to their son if death was inevitable. There was light traffic on the road, as if the man above himself had laid out a clear path for them. The thought of that made Jim dread what might be ineludible even more.

"Our son," Alice sobbed. "Our only son. Please, God. Please."

"He's going to make it. We're going to make it." Jim faked confidence and tried to pass it on to his already destroyed wife.

"Why? Why him? Why them?" Alice asked, as if she expected a solid answer. "They're good people. They work hard. The perfect family. Todd never hurt anyone. Oh, dear God, why!?"

"He's going to make it, baby. He's going to make it, I promise."

She put her face in her hands and cried. Alice wanted to cry out words that made sense, but there were none. She couldn't speak anymore. Words refused to form. Prayers were impossible. Hope was a once beautiful day, soiled by gray clouds and emotional storms.

The final turn onto the hospital's road. Jim cut the car hard right and pushed the gas pedal with all his strength. The car wanted to swing left, but Jim held it steady. Just ahead and on the left, their son was in a building, in a hospital bed, fighting for his life. Within moments, his parents would be by his side, battling with him and cheering him on with everything they had in them.

Chapter Five

Jim and Alice came through the emergency room sliding doors like an invading army with a noble cause. He was in sweatpants, sneakers without socks, and a baggy brown T-shirt with a breast pocket; she wore blue jeans, a wrinkled green blouse, and flip-flops. The matching expressions on their faces were ones of terror and dread.

The main waiting room, which they hurried through on the way to the counter, was nearly empty. An older lady and man sat side by side, watching a soap opera with the volume down, trying to be distracted from whatever reason they were there. The lady behind the counter was a short, dark-haired woman in her thirties. She made no attempt to greet the Radcliffes with a smile, as their expression and tone suggested there was no need for pleasantries.

Alice, with tears running down her face and biting her fingernails, remained silent as Jim did the talking. "Todd Radcliffe. He's in here. Fire burns. From earlier this morning. We were just notified. Todd. Radcliffe."

"Okay, hold on." The woman behind the counter typed on a keyboard and watched a small monitor in front of her. Her fingers moved quickly, and her demeanor was one of absolute seriousness. Within just a few seconds, she said, "Yes, follow me."

She stepped out from behind the desk, and pulled a plastic card from her breast pocket, waved it in front of a metal plate, and double doors opened. "This way." Her voice sounded as if she were in just as much a hurry as Jim and Alice.

That didn't sit well with Jim at all. The urgency in the greeter's voice indicated she read Todd's condition as critical. The police had already informed them of that back at the house, but Jim had hoped that during their speedy transit, things would change for the better. He had begged for it internally, pleading with a God he was sure didn't exist.

They followed her through the doors and down a corridor. Twenty feet and to the right, the three of them stepped into an open room with a nurse's station occupied by two female nurses and a male. The male had a more authoritative look about him, a middle-aged Black man with a dusting of gray in his six-o'clock shadow and the hair on his head, a stethoscope around his neck, and a nametag that appeared more official than the nurses'. Jim and Alice realized immediately he was a doctor.

The greeter went to the station and said something to the doctor, who then looked at both Jim and Alice with profound concern.

At that moment, Jim realized the prognosis of the circumstances was dire. Before the doctor came around the counter and approached them to speak, suddenly Jim felt like he couldn't breathe, and nearly forgot Alice was standing beside him, and that she'd been mumbling soft prayers since they stepped through the double doors with the greeter.

"Todd Radcliffe's parents?" the doctor asked, mainly speaking to Jim.

"Yes, that's us." Jim's voice cracked with fear.

The doctor sighed, and his look of worry grew in definition. Both Jim and Alice immediately understood. Alice grabbed Jim's arm and clenched it, drawing herself as close to her husband as possible without shoving him aside.

The doctor said, "He's burned over his entire body. The paramedics had to bring him back twice. Once on the scene, and once in the ambulance on the way here." He paused, searching for words that were soft instead of brutal. "Your son is in really bad shape. He suffered severe smoke inhalation along with the burns."

Another pause.

Alice's grip on Jim's arm tightened. Jim's chest clenched as if preparing for a devastating blow.

"When you walk into that room, you're not going to like what you see. We had to treat and wrap his entire body."

"Is he going to live?" Alice bluntly asked, her tone demanding.

The doctor looked down at her. He was a tall man, hovering over both parents. The look on his face was one of sorrow and condolences. "He's got a chance, but it's very slim. Go in there and be with your son. Go stand beside him. Talk to him. Tell him how much you love him. Let him know you're here." He gestured toward a room just across from the nurse's station. "Go to your son."

Alice let out an anguished sob and immediately fought to keep herself together.

Jim looked at his wife, tears dammed in his eyes. He then looked back at the doctor. "Thank you." And he led his wife across the hall into the hospital room, where he assumed he would say goodbye to his son forever.

***

When Jim and Alice came through the open door, Alice gasped at the sight of her son. Todd was lying in the hospital bed with no sheet or blanket over him. His entire body, from head to toes, was covered in white surgical dressing. His legs. His feet. Only his toes were exposed. His torso, his arms, and most of his hands with his fingertips protruding—his neck, his head, and even a fraction of his face were wrapped. His nose was uncovered, as well as his mouth and eyes. A heart monitor beeped loudly, and occasionally there were additional tones and beeps from the machines next to his bed. An intravenous line went through a small opening in the dressing on his left arm. He was looking straight up, as he was restrained by the bandages to move his neck in any direction. When they arrived bedside, the two distraught parents could see that even Todd's eyelids were blackened, as if they'd been overcooked.

"Oh, God," Alice said under her breath as she started to turn away.

Jim stopped her and held her firm. "No," he told her. "He needs us."

Tears ran down her cheeks. Her gaze was one of mourning. She whispered to him nearly frantically, "Jim, I can't see this. Our son. Oh, God, I can't do this."

"This is about him now. Not us. Come on." He gently tugged her toward the bed, and she surrendered, allowing him to lead her.

Todd's eyes opened, and he stared at the ceiling. With effort and only eye movement, he looked as far to the left as he could, and saw his mother and father standing beside him. He made a sound, as if he tried to speak but couldn't—an effortful and quick grunt.

"Son," Jim said, holding it together the best he could.

"We're here, Todd," Alice said, fighting off sobs.

Todd's lips moved again, but no sound emerged from them.

"It's okay, son. You don't have to say anything. We're here and we love you," Alice said.

The heart monitor continued to beep in a steady rhythm. To Jim, the room smelled too clean. The obvious smell of a hospital. It was odd to him how such sterility could be associated with something as terrifying as death. A place that was bright and should resemble life and healing, but indicated the complete opposite. How could something so pristine represent something so despairing?

"Dad," Todd whispered, his voice raspy and cracking.

"I'm here, son." Jim reached out with his free hand and touched Todd's fingertips. "I'm right here."

"The...the crazy guy." Todd struggled to speak, but was determined. "He was right."

"No, he wasn't. You're not dead. You're going to survive," Jim assured with fake confidence.

"Beth...the baby...my daughter."

Jim looked at Alice, who was already staring at him with dread. He lied and said, "They're fine. They are in another room under observation. They made it out okay."

Alice let out a quick, sudden snivel, and then covered her mouth with one hand to silence herself.

"They're not hurt bad?" Todd asked.

"No," Jim said. "Just under observation. The doctor said they're going to be just fine. It looks like you caught the brunt of the accident. They are fine. Beth is sedated and sleeping. Not a mark on her."

Todd smiled and then grunted, as if the smile itself had caused him pain. Then he said, "I'll be okay."

"Yes, you will," Alice agreed, though her voice indicated otherwise.

Todd's eyes met Jim's directly, and he spoke with a continuing struggle. "It's okay... It's okay because you're going to bring me back."

"I'm not bringing you back from anything. You're not going anywhere, son. You're going to fight and you're going to make it."

"The man...he said you'll bring me back."

"The man was crazy," Alice said firmly. "You're not going anywhere."

Todd winced suddenly, closing his eyes tightly for several moments. He then slowly reopened them. "God, it hurts. It hurts...everywhere."

Both Jim and Alice wanted so desperately to offer words of encouragement, but knew their son was well aware of his situation, even if he was barely hanging on to a state of consciousness.

Still only capable of eye movement, Todd looked at his mother, who stood there with one hand tightly holding her husband's arm, and the other against her own face. Her look of concern was so deep, there was no hiding she was bracing for impending tragedy. He said to her, "My house?"

"You can build a new one," Alice replied gently. "It's just a house."

Jim added, "You can stay with us until you get better."

Todd's eyes, suddenly filled with alarm, glanced at his father. "Just me? You mean...you mean *we* can stay with you. Beth...Stormy...we."

Realizing his error in choice of words, Jim quickly agreed with his ailing son. "Yes. All of you. We have that extra bedroom. We'll figure it out."

"None of that is to worry, son," Alice said, her voice shaky. Her effort to hold back tears was too obvious to hide. "You only need to focus on getting better. Getting out of here."

Todd coughed, winced, coughed again. His face tightened. His eyes fluttered. His lips moved slowly, as if he fought off a foul taste of something. He looked at both his parents. "I love you."

Just as they started to reply, an alarm went off on the machine beside the hospital bed. A loud, frantically beeping alert. Todd's eyes were still open, but he was suddenly staring off into some place other than this world. His mouth fell agape, and he exhaled a breath slowly, as if in relief. The heart monitor, the rhythmic beeping, suddenly became one extended tone.

There was a rush behind them from the doorway. Several hospital staff poured into the room in a hurry, all with expressions of embarking on an important mission on their faces. The doctor was leading them.

Just as Alice said, "Oh, God no," Jim pulled her by the arm away from the bed so the hospital staff could do their thing.

The alarm still sounded. The heart monitor tone blared. Their son was dying.

The medical staff surrounded the bed. The doctor in charge pulled a defibrillator from one machine near the bed. He gave orders. One nurse, a female in her thirties, replied. To Jim and Alice, none of the words were clear. They heard the nurses and the doctor conversing, sending orders and confirmation back and forth, but it all sounded like a foreign language. Todd was no longer in sight due to being surrounded by the staff, all with white hospital overclothes on.

"No, no, no," Alice muttered and then put both her hands to her face as if she were trying to hold her head in place.

Jim, trying to remain strong, grabbed his wife and pulled her to him.

Someone yelled, "Clear!"

A loud sound, like something heavy crashing against flimsy wall paneling. Todd's body flopped in the hospital bed. Silence and waiting from the nurses and doctor. The heart monitor stuttered, then continued in its melancholy tone.

Someone yelled, "Clear!" again. Once more, the sound of the defibrillator's power. Todd's body fluttered. The heart monitor's tone continued without interruption again.

Alice buried her face in Jim's chest, her hands over her ears. She was crying, her sobbing muffled by the sounds of the current rescue efforts and Jim's body. She pressed harder, harder, as if she wanted to crawl into his chest and hide from reality.

Jim looked down at her, pulled her tighter, kissed the top of her head through her frizzy morning hair. Tears flowed down his cheeks and fell onto his wife.

Her weeping increased, louder, beyond possible sound suppression. Her body moved in motion with each wail.

The heart monitor. Beeeeeeeeeeeeeeeeeeeeeeeeeeeeeeeeeeeeeep.

The taunting sound of the defibrillator.

Nurses and the doctor put all their lifesaving skills in motion. Voices echoed around the room. Alice cried harder than she ever had in her life, refusing to back away from the safety of her husband's protecting body. Jim sniffed and didn't look up.

The heart monitor—that monotonous, tragic sound. Something they would remember for the rest of their lives.

Todd Radcliffe, their son, their only child, was gone forever.

Chapter Six

The funeral included about sixty people—family, coworkers, friends—on one of the prettiest days of the summer. Clear blue skies, a soft breeze flowing through, and lower than normal humidity. A day that appeared as if it were meant for family and friend gatherings of a more cheerful and jubilant nature. To the people attending the burial of an entire family—father, wife, and daughter—somehow the sunshine was unseen, the breeze unfelt, the air thick with grief.

As Jim stood beside his wife, him wearing the only suit he owned and her wearing a funeral-appropriate dress, he wondered why destiny had chosen his family, his loved ones, and couldn't help but think if there was a God, then He couldn't possibly love His children as much as everyone believed. That there must be a sinister side to Him, to allow for such tragic deaths. Why did good, genuine people have to die so soon, and under such random circumstances?

The authorities involved had determined the fire started from faulty wiring in the kitchen of Todd's home. A brand-new house that, within its confines, three innocent victims had met their ultimate fate so early. There would be an investigation into the inspection process, and then the construction of the house. Someone would be blamed and likely lose his or her or their jobs. But that wouldn't bring back this beautiful young family to the world of the living. Whoever's error it was, it was one that gave permanent consequences. There was no undoing this.

Prevention was well past the stage of possibility. Three lives were lost. Three lives snuffed out for the remainder of this universe's lifespan, and any further existences that may come and go in the far distant future. Their one chance at the beauty of life had been taken from them forever.

The funeral home reverend spoke. He quoted Bible verses, which, to Jim, only offered more doubt about the good of God, if he existed at all. There were moments when he wanted to interrupt the man in his funeral garments, reading from a Bible, believing every word he spoke, though none of those words had any proof of solidarity. Just as Jim felt like he might not be capable of holding back, when he thought he might just interrupt the whole sermon, he heard his wife beside him crying. He heard people in the surrounding crowd sniffling. He saw Beth's parents and family, tears in their eyes, hope lost from their gaze upon the two side-by-side caskets hovering over a double burial plot in the ground. For Beth and the unborn daughter, it had been a closed casket service. The expectant mother was only identifiable through DNA and dental records. Of course, the baby had never been born, never offered a single breath of beautiful weather such as today's. All three so unfairly cheated of life.

Alice hung tight to Jim's arm as she cried. Some moments she was loud and others she tried to restrain her sobbing. He had not yet given himself a moment to weep uncontrollably. During the past several days, he knew his mission was to be one of strength and support. When around his wife, who hadn't stopped crying since her son passed away in the hospital days ago, he had to be her solid ground. And in moments of solitude, he held strong even then, because he couldn't allow himself to break character. He had to keep it going on one long train, and after everything was over, he would permit himself to lose it completely. He would find a few moments alone during which he could cry, scream, curse God and any other force of nature that might be involved in this tragedy, throw things, swear, stomp the ground and raise his fist to the sky in anger.

Jim also thought of the crazy guy, who seemed to predict these deaths with an eerie accuracy. Though one thing was wrong: Jim had saved no one. He didn't arrive on the scene and bring his son back to life. Somewhere during the memory of some dude named Billy waving a gun and insane prophecies around in Todd's backyard, Jim wondered whether somehow the lunatic was responsible for the fire.

Had he been released from jail? Had he somehow snuck into the house and set a fire, covering his tracks and making it look like a random accident with the skill of a professional killer? The fire had been ruled an accident by those who were practiced in the investigation of such occurrences, but what if they got it wrong? What if Billy had been so desperate to see his delusions transform into reality, he had seen to it himself?

Jim was suspicious that there was more to this than was obvious. The coincidence was too damn visible, and he wondered whether he was the only one who saw it.

"Let us pray," the reverend said. The gathering of mourners followed those instructions by lowering their heads in unison. As he began a prayer which asked God to welcome the fallen into heaven, to accept them into His open arms, to embrace them and show them the glory of an afterlife in heaven, Alice's sobbing escalated into bawling.

She tried to control herself but was unsuccessful. Jim could feel her body shaking with every wail, and he put his arm around her, pulled her closer, offering a comfort she wouldn't be capable of accepting or utilizing.

From speakers nearby, a flute rendition of "Amazing Grace" played softly and grew louder as the prayer continued. When the words finally stopped, crying from several people in the crowd seemed like a melancholy addition to the melody. Jim wanted to cry as loudly as those around him. He wanted to let go of his strength and grieve, to release his anguish the same as everyone else. But Alice needed him. She needed him more than she ever had or ever would. He held her and realized he was also holding her up. Without his help, she might fall to her knees.

The music settled at its final volume and filled the area with the feeling of loss and hope. The two emotions danced and intertwined with the breeze, the smell of a summer day with leaves whispering and birds chirping. A passenger plane flew over so many thousand feet in the sky, its roar just under the volume of the music. Cars drove by on the surrounding roads, people on their daily commute or running errands, all alive and likely not thinking of the dreaded circumstances of death.

Chapter Seven

Night. The freshly blacktopped road is two lanes. Yellow broken lines in the middle. To each side, a heavy fog blanketing everything nearby. Ahead, more fog. Visibility no more than thirty feet. Looking back, the fog is so close it is as if he's emerging from it. Ahead again. So dark. He hears his own breathing. The silence of this night is as if nothing exists in the universe, other than himself, that can make a sound.

The darkness is not absolute, however. Above, there is dim illumination barely penetrating the vast and thick blanket of mist. Possibly from the moon. He walks forward cautiously, realizes he is barefoot as his feet touch the smooth road. It's almost too smooth, too perfect—a flawless street paved with a technology that must be of supernatural nature. It felt like a hardwood floor as he moves forward. Not even the slightest chip, imperfection, or even a crack. He is surprised he can even walk without sliding and falling, as the smoothness of the road should result in a slick experience. His footing holds, though, and he continues on.

He is not sure why he's walking forward. The only reason must be that all other directions were too invisible. To the right and to the left, only a few feet each way to the edge of the road, and then the fog—a substance of warm air and mist which seemed to be alive, with a conscience, and following him. He walks in the middle on the yellow lines. As he looks forward, it is the lines he follows and not just the road. The lines guide him.

He is terrified. His heart thumps wildly, yet he can't hear it. Still, only his breathing is audible. The silence alone is as frightening as the unknown on all sides of him. Especially the unknown behind him, which, as he turns back for a quick look, is still nearly at his heels, though maintaining a constant and precise distance. If he stops, will the fog from behind swallow him? If it *does* take him in, what next?

The fog couldn't have a mind of its own, so perhaps there was someone, or something, inside it, controlling it, steering it as a human does a motor vehicle. What if that something or someone is an evil entity? What if when it finally catches him, it kills him, inhales his soul like he does cigarette smoke? What would happen to Billy Wagner's soul once it was inside the evil being keeping pace with him, using Mother Nature's innocent creation for cover? Was it a path to hell?

He doesn't think he deserves to be side-by-side with the most wicked of all life-forms in a place known for eternal suffering. Even though he doesn't live an honest life, he has hurt no one. He isn't deserving of agony without end. He may not be a candidate for the other place, but he at least belongs somewhere in the middle.

He continues forward at a steady pace, while nervously glancing from side to side, front to back to front. There is no reason to hide his fear, though he knows he can't, even if a reason arises. He's horrified. Something is coming. Something sinister and merciless.

This was the most perplexing of situations. If he stops, the fog from behind catches him. If he continues forward, he eventually disappears voluntarily into the mist. There is no escape in either choice, and he wonders if he should just stop and surrender now. His legs are growing tired. His heart may burst right out of his chest. Fatigue settles into his mind, too. He wants to sleep. He wants to close his eyes, make this all disappear, and sleep a visionless slumber.

Forward. Step after step. Racing heartbeat after racing heartbeat. His breath grows louder. Forward. Step. Step. Step. Step. Then, the fog ahead stirs, as if something huge is moving within it. Nothing emerges into the open. The mist swirls about. Behind the scenes, a sudden hum. A vehicle's hum. The sound is approaching, yet its maker is not coming into the open. The fog finally settles to stillness again. After a quick winding down, the hum stops. Silence once more.

Billy is still afraid to stop walking. He moves forward reluctantly. A quick glance back, and he sees the murk has not fallen behind or moved closer. It is staying with him. It waits for him to stand still so it can take him. Yet, whatever is ahead, if he continues, he will suffer the fate of what is planned for him from that direction. There is no choice but to keep moving because he fears what is behind him is worse than what's ahead. At least in the forward direction there has been sound. Behind him, no clue of what awaits.

Forward. Step. Step. Step. Step.

Another sound. Something quick. A car door shutting. Not slamming closed. Not gently shut in an attempt to hide. Just shut. Coming home from work, shut. Arriving at a family function. Nothing sinister about it. Nothing to be afraid of, yet, somehow, Billy's terror intensifies. Panic is rising above anything he's felt in a long time.

Patient footfalls from inside the haze ahead. Someone walking toward him. He looks back, hoping there is a distance between himself and the cloud in that direction, but it still keeps pace. And now he wonders if it is only there to urge him forward into whatever disastrous encounter lies ahead.

Billy moves forward still. Step. Step. Step. Step.

Whoever is coming toward him, he realizes, is matching his pace. Step. Step. Step. Step.

His eyes are wide. His jaw is dropping further as he walks. He feels himself trembling as if he is standing in the middle of the Arctic Circle. Uncontrollable shivering. He bites down gently on his tongue to keep his teeth from chattering. He clenches his hands into fists. Billy wants to stop. The footfalls are getting louder, yet no figure emerges. Louder. Louder. Approaching. He continues forward, but he wants to stop. He needs to stop.

Suddenly, whatever is behind him is preferable to what is ahead. Something bad is ahead. Something beyond evil. His neck hairs vibrate, warning him of danger. He wants to stop. He wants to turn and run into the mist behind him. Perhaps it will offer cover and is actually there to save him. Maybe either direction is doom. A monster behind him, and a deadly character ahead.

He wants to yell or scream, but he has no voice. He can only breathe so loudly. His heart can only race so furiously until it explodes, rendering him lifeless. He doesn't want to die. Not yet. It's too soon. He feels like he has a reason to live. There is a cause for him in this world. Since the dreams started, he's always felt they revealed his purpose in cryptic form. He just needs to figure out what he's supposed to do. He's tried to do so much good, yet he's always in trouble. People see him as bad, but *he's not bad!*

The footfalls still approach. He's going toward them. He should turn and run. At least stop. Stop going toward whatever evil nears from ahead. Cease and freeze. Stop and wait. Just stop going toward it!

Step. Step. Step. Step.

Now, suddenly, a figure appears in the fog. It is a human. Only a shadow because the mist conceals any vivid details. It looks like a man.

It walks like a man, moving toward Billy. Long sleeves. Billy can make out cuffs around the wrist. Long pants. The tapping of the man's steps implies dress shoes. Click, clack; click, clack. He is still at least twenty feet from clearing the fog. Coming right at Billy, and Billy is moving right toward him. They will meet in the middle in only a matter of a minute or so. Billy realizes he doesn't want to see this man's face. He doesn't want a clear image of who or what he is. Billy understands there is something sinister about the approaching figure.

Step. Step. Step. Step.

Click, clack; click, clack.

The terror is rising. Billy thought he had already reached a peak in his fear, but it's growing to a level he knows his mind can't tolerate. Perhaps it's a rising madness. What is worse: being dead or being alive and truly insane? There is no positive outcome from coming face-to-face with the stranger. He is something worse than incarnated maliciousness. Billy can feel it emitting from him like heat from a radiator.

Billy stops. Assuming the fog behind him will swallow him up, he braces himself. He closes his eyes and holds his breath. Every muscle in his body tenses for whatever impact is coming. Nothing, though. He feels nothing. Slowly, he opens his eyes. The fog hasn't overtaken him. Ahead, the diabolical figure's walking slows and then stops.

Click, clack; click, clack... Click...clack... Click—

Billy waits. He can't see the figure's face, but it is obvious the unholy stranger is staring at him. Perhaps he is disappointed that Billy has stopped. What if the fog detains the man, and he can only attack Billy's soul if Billy voluntarily comes to him? Billy wonders if he misinterpreted the fog. Perhaps the eerie mist is a protector. A guardian sent by benevolent forces to give Billy a fighting chance.

Something stirs, but not just from one direction. All around. Above and below. Left and right. Before and behind. A slow breeze runs its fingers through Billy's wild hair, causing a frigid chill to pass through his body. The breeze is consistent. It doesn't speed up or slow down. It brushes against Billy's face and the back of his neck. The sides of his arms. Through his fingers in both directions, it seems. Through the space between his legs as he stands there, he now realizes, in boxers and no shirt at all. This is the same attire he sleeps in. He looks down at his own chest and sees the hairs moving in the nonstop current of air.

The sound of the wind is changing even though its speed isn't. It's becoming a growing whisper. A person taking a breath before speaking. All around him. All directions. A whisper. So soft at first. Louder. Stronger. Bolder. Finally, it forms words.

I want to make a deal.

Billy wants to run but remains frozen. What deal? He wants to flee with everything in him. The fog will protect. He can turn and disappear into it. No. The man is *in the fog.* The mist may protect Billy from the man only because the man is trapped within it. That's where the protection comes from. If Billy enters the fog on any side of him, he will be willfully sacrificing himself to the demon inside it.

He remains frozen, but turns his head from left to right, behind and before again. Looking for a clearing to run through. There is none, though. He will stand here, forever, waiting out the thing inside. Eventually, he'll lose his sanity and his will to live. There is no escape. Not now. Not today. Not tonight. Not twenty days and nights from now. The evil force inside will have him, regardless of what he does.

Let's make a deal, Jim.

Jim? Billy thought. *Jim? Jim, Jim, Jim...shit.*

"No deal," Billy finally answers softly, but with courage in his voice. Then louder, "No deal. Fuck off. You hear me? Fuck off! Fuck off! *FUCK OFF!*"

Billy sat up, gasping for breath, kicking his blankets off, screaming the same words repeatedly until he realized he'd just wakened from another dream. Sweat-drenched from his hair to his toes, as if he'd just run for his life for the course of a marathon. He looked to his left and saw the other inmate he was roomed with, sitting up in his bed, watching him as if he'd just finished crawling on the ceiling. Billy calmed his breathing moment by moment, put his hand on his chest. His heart raced.

"Whoa," he whispered to himself. "Whoa there. All over. It's just a dream. Just a dream, man. Just a dream."

The man in the other cot, a younger man with muscles and a strange tattoo on his face, said with a deep voice, "Another one?"

"Just a dream," Billy replied quickly as he glanced at the bars of their cell. "All's good, man. Sorry if I woke you."

"You always waking a motherfucker. Can't you get some meds for that shit?"

With raised eyebrows, Billy glanced slowly at his jail-mate, then back to the bars. He was almost happy to be here. Nothing could get to him in this place. He was safe. Even though they were only dreams, he never felt safe from them out in the world—out in the open, in his homeless camps or his spots in the woods where he sometimes slept. It was as if being out in nature not only exposed him to the weather, but to other, more sinister forces, too. Those forces worked in obscurity. That's why they invaded his mind, instead of attacking him full front from the outside. Nobody else could see them in his head. Only him.

The visions were often not good. Some were, but more than not, they were of terrible things that would eventually happen. In the county jail, he was safe from them. He couldn't go mad in a jail cell. Not like he'd felt outside of it. The law thought he was a petty criminal, but they didn't realize he committed those minor infractions because he wanted to be arrested. The visions could get in his head in here, but he still felt as if they were only empty threats. In here, nothing would come for him. Out there, something would eventually have him.

He looked over again and saw his cellmate laying down, his back to Billy, and already snoring.

Billy was safe in here. Well, maybe not so safe if he kept waking up Big Bubba over there. If that continued, bad dreams out in the woods might seem like nothing.

Chapter Eight

F ive weeks had passed, and Jim knew life, as he'd always lived it, was long over. He'd taken a few private moments to grieve in ways he knew how to do so. There had been no bawling, but mostly staring up at the night summer sky, before walking into the house, after returning home from work. He would step outside the garage, and as the automatic door engine hummed, he would look back upon his life as a father and a husband.

He looked at the stars, the moon, peering into outer space, but his eyes saw none of that. Instead, he saw the birth of his only son, Alice pushing, the nurses encouraging, him standing there scared to death that something would happen to either of them or both. And when Todd was lifted to his mother, freshly cleaned of afterbirth and umbilical cord cut, Jim felt more than relief. He felt an excitement for the future. How he and Alice would raise this child, their son, together. How they would instill upon him their beliefs, their ethics, their hopes and dreams for him.

He would smile at these memories, but then his mind's rendition of what happened on that tragic night would break in like a bad commercial during a feature film. Sometimes Jim could skip through it to the next pleasant memory, and sometimes he was forced to watch.

When he finally went inside, he would find Alice asleep with tear streaks on her face. Photo albums lay open on the bed, showcasing family moments they had captured in their forever still form. Birth-days. Cookouts. Trips to amusement parks. Water fun in the backyard with various methods, including a blowup pool when Todd was just a toddler. Alice didn't wait up for Jim anymore. Instead, she focused on a past, which was now the only place she could find her son. She cried herself to sleep every night.

Jim felt as if he was letting her down. After four weeks of vacation to stay home with her, to be her leaning post, to hold her up in a life she seemed to no longer want to live, he had no choice but to return to work. The bills had to be paid. He wasn't deflecting the tragedy that happened and he definitely couldn't ignore it, but life had to go on. Todd wouldn't want them to lose everything, to fall to rock bottom, because of his sudden exit from this world. Falling over in life wouldn't bring their son back. Life *had* to go on. Todd would want them to find happiness again. He would want them to move on and forward.

It wasn't just a cliché, but it was the truth. Their son had loved them deeply, and if he could see his mother right now, if he could witness her struggle, somehow from the other side, then he would not only be sad for his own early departure, for the ending of his family, his wife, his unborn child, but he would mourn his parents' ongoing despondency. It did nobody any good to continue on a path of depression and self-destruction. Jim knew this, and he fought to stay on a road that, he assumed, would lead away from the gloom and doom.

Yet, Alice wasn't so strong. She was falling further every day into a void she might eventually have no hope of emerging from. Even though it broke Jim's heart, he remained strong for her. At least, that was the front he portrayed. Inside, though, he struggled to keep it together. Always reminding himself what Todd would want, what Beth would want, what Stormy Dawn would want had she been born.

It was just past three p.m. on Monday. Jim was in the kitchen, standing at the counter, packing two bologna sandwiches into plastic sandwich bags for his work lunch. Sunlight shined through the kitchen window, illuminating the room in a bask and glow that seemed like a scam for hope. He used to be more creative with his sandwich making. After all, lunch was supposed to be a pleasurable break in the middle of an otherwise dragging work shift. Nowadays, it seemed pointless to care about taste and pleasure. He packed the sandwiches plainly and quickly. A slice of bologna in between two slices of bread. That was enough to put something in his stomach for energy to make it to the end of the night.

Alice was outside in her tomato garden, where she spent most of her days now. They no longer had their morning routine of drinking coffee together in the living room. She was up before Jim, and when he did awake and make his way to the kitchen, he could peer through the window and see her sitting in a lawn chair on the edge of her garden, staring at the plants as if they might offer her an answer to all the questions she now had. Most importantly was "why." Why did this happen to them? Why did it happen to their child? Why did it happen to Todd and his family? Why did it have to happen the *way* it happened? Why now? Why them? Why? Why? Why?

Sometimes, Alice looked as if she was frozen in her stare by some supernatural power. She would look in the same direction for hours, with tears streaming down her face, her lip quivering. Sometimes she cried, bawled, as if the tragedy had occurred moments ago. And other times she held it together while the tears flowed, her hands firmly on the armrest of the lawn chair, staring out at the plants, hopelessly lost in emotional anguish.

Often, Jim went out, pulled up a chair, and just sat beside her. He would stare at the sky, at the garden, fidget his fingers, tap his toes, look at his wife whose beauty was still there but hidden on the other side of ceaseless mourning. He would try to talk to her, bringing up the nice weather, the progress of the tomato garden, the taste of the coffee, the appearance of the lawn. Whatever he could pull out of the metaphorical hat to get her to respond. Most of the time, though, she answered with nods, quick, zombie-like replies, and sometimes just plain depressed silence.

Just as he was putting the two sandwiches wrapped in plastic into the sports bag he used for work, there was a sudden commotion from outside. A shriek of frustration, something hit something. An impact. He immediately dropped what he was doing and rushed out the back door. He saw the toppled-over lawn chair first, then he eyed his wife in her garden. She stood in the middle of the several rows of tomato plants, sobbing loudly, grabbing the plants, yanking them from the ground, and tossing them to the side. With each pull, she grunted angrily. With each throw, she sobbed uncontrollably.

Jim hurried to her, reached her just as she was pulling at another plant that refused to come out of the ground. Frustration on her face, anger in her moans. She pulled, pulled, pulled. The tomato plant finally gave in and came up as if it had pressure behind it. With a shriek of misery, she threw it with all her strength. It flew about twenty feet before crashing into the toppled lawn chair. Jim grabbed her arms as gently as he could and pulled her to him.

She resisted, yanked herself back, stumbled and almost fell, recovered her balance, and grabbed another plant.

"No!" Jim shouted as he took her by the wrist. She struggled to break free from him. He held her against his chest. "No, baby. You'll regret this."

She tried again to pull away, but he asserted his superior strength and held her tight. The side of her face against his chest, she wailed uncontrollably now.

"Baby, don't do this," he mumbled to her. "Your garden is your solace. You love this garden. If you do this, you'll regret it later. Please, sugar. Let me hold you. I love you. I love you so much, Alice."

She stopped crying just long enough to get a few words out. "What's the point?"

He continued to keep her close. He clung to her. Not in restraint, but in deep and profound love. Eternal love, pure and genuine. He kissed the top of her head several times. He said, "The point is, this is something you adore," soft and careful with his words.

"We can't eat all these tomatoes." She sobbed. "This garden was for everybody. They're gone now, Jim." She pulled away just enough to look up at him.

Her demeanor broke his heart a million times in just a few seconds. Tears in her eyes and rolling down her cheeks. A look of emotional torture in her glare. A woman defeated, who had lost all hope. His heartbroken and devastated wife. And there was nothing he could do to mend her wounds except hold her and remind her that he loved her dearly.

"They're gone," she whispered, buried her face in his chest, and then cried uncontrollably. She wrapped her arms around him and pulled as if she was trying to climb inside her husband. As if the only safety from her mourning was within the frame of his very existence. She sniffed and whimpered, and he could feel her slipping downward as her legs weakened from grief.

He strengthened his hold on her delicate frame, kept her from falling to the ground, as her one and only guardian.

"Don't go," she said without pulling away from him. "Please don't go. Don't leave me. Please, Jim, don't leave me."

He kissed the top of her head again and whispered, "Okay. I'm right here. I'll stay home tonight."

Tears in his eyes threatened to explode outward as he held his devastated wife. Jim looked out at the garden, at the small path of destruction she'd made only moments ago in a fit of grieving rage. He looked beyond the garden toward the backyard of their neighbor. He glanced even beyond that, toward the southern horizon. And then upward into a blue sky.

"I'm not going anywhere," he reassured her again, holding back the urge to fall apart himself.

Part Two

Mr. Brimstone

Chapter Nine

Jim walked into the district police station with just one thing on his mind: some whacked-out man named Billy, who had accurately warned an impending death of an entire family. A husband and a son, a wife and a daughter, and unborn child all perished and it was that Billy guy's words that echoed mercilessly inside Jim's head for weeks. To him, that was too powerful a coincidence to let disappear into trivialness. Jim had decided there was only one person to wring answers out of and that was Officer Tony Mitchell, the man who had arrived on the scene and ultimately arrested the delusional stranger the day before the very night the tragic fire would occur.

He stepped into the police station, walking so purposefully into the lobby and approaching the front desk. A female officer, blonde, about thirty-five, was behind it. He instantly caught her concerned attention. She regarded him with caution as he stood on the other side of the counter and spoke in a tone that implied anger.

"I need to speak with Officer Mitchell," Jim said, nearly demanding.

Even though his approach had tried to prepare her for unpleasantness, she was still surprised by his tone. The look of concern on her face grew as she replied. "Is he expecting you? Your name?"

"Jim Radcliffe. And no, he's not expecting me. That doesn't matter. I need to see him."

After a brief, cautious pause, she asked, "Can I tell him why some-one named Jim Radcliffe is here to see him?"

"The fire that killed my family," Jim replied, staring straight into the officer's eyes.

"I'm sorry, Mr. Radcliffe. I...I'll go get him," she said nervously and left the counter, disappearing through glass double doors directly behind it.

As soon as she left the room, a phone on the counter rang. It sound-ed an incoming call for five rings before stopping, and Jim assumed an automatic answering service had picked up. He glanced around the room. On the walls, framed pictures of the surrounding community. A park with kids playing. A public swimming pool with adults and children enjoying a refreshing dip on a hot summer day. There were pictures of several individual officers with years of service printed on gold plates. As he viewed the surroundings of the station, a male police officer, who didn't look a day older than twenty-one, walked in, nodded at Jim, and then disappeared off to the left around a corner.

The phone rang again. It was on its third ring when the female officer came back through the doors and told Jim to come around the counter and follow her. As they both went through the double doors, with her in the lead, the phone stopped ringing and then started again.

"You don't have someone to answer the phones?" Jim asked. "What if that's an emergency? That's the third—"

"Mr. Radcliffe, it goes straight to a central calling center if we don't answer. No need to worry."

"Ah," he replied.

"In that office straight ahead, sir."

"Thank you, ma'am," Jim replied as he moved past her with near worrisome haste.

She remained somewhat on alert and watched him all the way down the hallway. She waited a few moments after he'd stepped into the office before returning to front-desk duty.

As Jim crossed the threshold into the office, Officer Mitchell, in full uniform, stood up behind his desk with purpose. He looked at Jim with pitying eyes. "Mr. Radcliffe. Let me start by saying I offer my sincere condolences to your family. I can't even begin to know what—"

With unwavering confidence, Jim interrupted with, "He had something to do with it. You can't tell me he didn't. He was there. He made the threats. Goddamn it, he actually foretold it. That's too—"

With his hands up as if in a defensive posture, Tony said, "Whoa, whoa, sir. Who made the threats?"

"You know who. That crazy Billy guy. He said it himself—"

"Billy Wagner," Mitchell confirmed. "Sir, that fire was investigated by arson specialists. The fire was an accident."

Jim waved Tony away. "Yeah, I know. Faulty wiring or whatever. Explain to me how the hell he stood in my yard, claiming people were going to die, and then hours later they're gone." His voice rose some, but he was trying to keep a reasonable lid on his vocalized anger. "How the fuck did he know?"

"Mr. Radcliffe, he was in jail the whole time. He's still in jail. He's been in jail since we pulled him out of your son's backyard in handcuffs." Officer Mitchell made intentional eye contact and continued, "*He couldn't have done it.*"

"Then he's paid someone to do it. Some thug from the streets. Maybe it was all planned out. He gets himself arrested. Then he has an alibi while his co-conspirator is out there actually committing the crime. He's behind it. Somehow, he is responsible. He killed my fucking son." Jim choked back emotion as he spoke. His anger mixed with grief, tears of both welling in his eyes.

Officer Mitchell saw Jim's face and pitied him. This man had just experienced something no parent should ever have to endure. Not just the loss of a son, but of an entire family unit. Tony's expression was one of empathy as he gently replied, "Sir, I know what you're going through is hard. It's got to be so damn hard. I wouldn't want to be in your shoes. There's no way I would hold it together. But Billy doesn't have any resources to pay for a hitman. He barely survives on the streets. The man is homeless. He shows up at the soup kitchens and meal donation facilities, starving most of the time. When he gets some money, however—he gets it through begging or petty theft—he catches a buzz. Usually he drinks. Sometimes he smokes weed. Every so often, he gets hold of something stronger, like pills or meth.

"What he did in your son's backyard was the worst thing we've ever arrested him for. It's his first felony charge and those of us who know him are profoundly baffled by his behavior that day. I know you want to point a finger. That's how people work. When something awful happens, we need to blame someone or something. But I'm telling you, you're looking in the wrong direction. Find an attorney. Sue the pants off the construction company, or the people responsible for the electrical inspections. Someone in those entities fucked up. If anything or anyone is responsible for that accident, it's them. It's not Billy."

Jim looked past Tony, toward the wall behind him. A plaque, with Tony's picture, listing his years of service, his promotions, and even a few awards. He looked back at the understanding police officer, who was staring back at Jim with patience. Jim wanted to be mad at him, wanted to accuse him of not doing enough, but even in a heightened emotional state, he couldn't do it. This was a man just doing his job, and according to the wall hanging behind him, was damn good at it. This was a true police officer standing before him. A loyal public servant. Jim realized he had nothing more to say, but still stood there in silence.

Tony Mitchell, a man full of understanding, spoke again. "Let me tell you about Billy. He's thirty-five years old. He's had a very rough time of it, thanks to his own mind. At one time, he had a wife, a good job, a modest house in a decent neighborhood. Just like you and every other normal, law-abiding citizen, he went to work, got paid, came home to his spouse, paid bills. He cut his grass every week. Took out the trash on Mondays. Told his wife daily that he loved her. The American dream." He paused, sighed, and his eyes showed a shift from focus to sadness.

"When he was around twenty-eight, he started having weird dreams. One night, he dreams about their cat running out into the road and getting run over. Two days later, it happens. Then, he has a dream about a car crash just outside his neighborhood. Two kids were killed in that wreck. It happens a few days later. These dreams he's having seem to be visions of the future. Now, they weren't always bad things. Sometimes they were of pleasant occurrences that eventually happened. He dreamed of his promotion at his job and got it. He dreamed of his wife getting her dream job and it happened. But even the good dreams fucked with his head. The fact that he could foresee things scrambled his brain and his sanity.

"Eventually, he became afraid of those dreams. He didn't want to see them. He wanted them to go away. He realized that when he went to sleep drunk, he slept straight through. If he saturated his brain with something that knocked it out, there were no dreams at all. No visions. No prophecies. And his drinking got out of control. Eventually, the drinking didn't work anymore. His body adapted to it. So he started small with marijuana. When that didn't work, he mixed weed with alcohol. Again, he slept soundly for a while. But eventually, that didn't work either. So he started switching it up. Pain pills, meth sometimes, alcohol, the weed. Sometimes he switched from one to the other, and other times he combined them all. The man just wanted to sleep."

Another sigh, as if bracing for the impact of something terrible. "His wife divorced him. Besides all the substance abuse, he was becoming unhinged. She became afraid of him. He never hurt her and, as far as she's said, he never threatened to. But she didn't know if or when abuse toward her would begin. His rantings and his substance abuse, to her, could only be a precursor of worse things to come. She left him, divorced him, and moved away from him and this town. That didn't help things at all for Billy. He sunk further. Spiraled out of control. Missed work a lot and eventually got fired. He didn't have much in savings because he'd been spending foolishly on booze and drugs, so it wasn't long after he got fired that he lost everything else.

"Car got repo'd. House foreclosed. He couldn't find a job because he showed up for interviews fucked up. Within a few years' time, he went from living the average dream life to being a homeless, burned-out alcoholic and drug addict. Yet one thing from all of that remained: the dreams." He paused, breathed, and continued. "One time, while we were booking him for shoplifting, he talked about a dream he'd had. Said he saw the winning horse for the Kentucky Derby, which was only a few days away. Just for the hell of it, a few of us put a few bucks on that horse. Now I wish I'd have bet the whole farm because that underdog horse won. The payout was forty-seven dollars for every two dollars bet. I won ninety-four bucks. It was the only dream like that he'd told us of, but we all knew if he ever told us of another one, we'd listen."

"Why didn't you tell me? Why didn't you warn us that day?" Jim asked with a pleading voice. "We could have saved them."

As if he were a parent speaking to a misunderstanding teenager, Officer Mitchell replied, "You think you would have believed me? You didn't believe him, did you? He told you. Besides that, not all of Billy's dreams come true. A very few select of them do. It is just when they do actually happen in real life, they happen in precise detail of his dreams. He was so high and drunk that day. It took him two days to even completely sober up. All the way to jail, he babbled about changing the past and its consequences. Of all the things he ever told us, whatever he was going on about was extraordinary. Completely out of the realm of possibility. He wasn't talking about a wreck or a natural disaster or lottery numbers. He was yelling about time travel and universal paradoxes. As much experience as we've had with Billy, it's never been a bunch of crazy shit like that. Even I thought he was just high and carrying on."

Jim seemed to ponder Officer Mitchell's words for a few seconds and then asked, "What's his last name again?"

Tony scrutinized the question for a moment and replied, "Wagner. Billy Wagner."

"And he's in the county jail right now?"

"He is, and he'll likely be there until his trial. After which, he's probably going down the river for a few years."

Jim nodded slowly in acknowledgment. "Thank you, Officer Mitchell. I hope you have a great day." And with that, Jim turned to leave the office.

"Sir." Tony stopped Jim, who paused at the office threshold and looked back. "Let it go. Look, sue whoever you have to sue. Let your attorney handle it. I don't want to sound insensitive. I'm *not* insensitive to your circumstances. What you and your wife have lost, what the other parents have lost, is tragic. People we love are irreplaceable. But go on with your life. You're not young anymore. You're not old, but you're not young either. Grieve. Cry it out. Be sad for a while." His voice sounded pleading.

"But push through it with the goal of getting past it. Your son, your daughter-in-law...they would want you to be happy. They would want you to move on and enjoy this beautiful world we live in for as long as you can. Don't go looking for revenge where there is none. You'll miss out. Suddenly, you'll be an old man with a walker, looking back on the past twenty-five or thirty years wishing you hadn't wasted it. They're gone. Grieve. Memorialize them. Then, move on. You get one tour through this life. Just one." He held up his index finger in a one gesture. "Don't waste it."

Jim released a slow sigh. "Do you have a family? Kids?"

"A wife of thirty years and two grown daughters."

Jim nodded several times and sighed again. "Have a nice day, sir."

He turned and left the office. He came through the double glass doors into the lobby, passed the female officer at the counter, who was now on the same phone that had rung repeatedly earlier. When he stepped outside the station, he felt like he was hit by a wave of something besides the summer heat. Today was a hot one. Temperatures in the high 90s and a heat index well over 100.

He stood in front of the building for a moment, glancing at the police cars in the closer parking spots. Jim looked out farther, saw his car; looked past it toward the highway. He watched the rush of midday traffic. People coming and going in their daily routine. How many of them carried heavy grief, yet continued on with their lives as if nothing happened? Was it that easy? When tragedy took things so dear to them away, he wondered how they drew strength.

In his car, engine running, air-conditioning blasting, the radio on silent, windows up and putting a barrier between the sounds of the world and his own personal space, he stared at the steering wheel. Jim wanted to cry right now. He wanted to lose it. Break things. Scream. He wanted to hurt someone. Whoever was to blame, he wanted to wring their necks. He wanted to throw them in a fire and ask them how it felt. Now, he couldn't do that. He had to keep it together not just for him and his life, but for Alice and *their* life.

There was no room for him to go off the deep end. Alice needed additional strength, because her own was insufficient. There was only one set of shoulders that task could weigh on: Jim's. He tapped his fingers on the steering wheel. He clenched it with both hands. He squeezed as if he were trying to strangle it. So tightly, lines formed in his face, his forehead. He was trying to crush his grief out through the inanimate object.

Finally, he loosened his grip. Strength—emotional, mental, and even physical...he had to be strong. There was no other option for the time being.

Chapter Ten

Upon returning home from his visit to the police station, Jim smelled an unfamiliar aroma as he came through the front door and kicked his shoes off in the foyer. He immediately saw Alice on the sofa, asleep in her nightclothes, one leg hanging off, and snoring so loud he was surprised he didn't hear it before entering the house. When he saw the half-empty bottle of cheap bourbon on the floor, laying in a puddle of its own contents, he realized what the scent was. Strong alcohol. On the side table to the right of the sofa, a shot glass.

He crossed the living room and stopped just in front of the couch and his slumbering, suffering wife. Looking down at her, he wanted to cry. The shot glass and the alcohol that was kept in the house was purchased by Jim. Every so often, when he had a full weekend off from work, he liked to sit in the garage, listen to '80s music, and sip on either bourbon on the rocks, or the occasional, simple cocktail of vodka and orange juice, also known as a screwdriver.

Alice was not a drinker. In their younger years, she drank with him occasionally, but that was a long time ago. She didn't like the taste of any form of booze and especially wasn't too happy about how it made her feel the next day or two. Now, she lay there on a sofa, passed out from having drank what looked like half a bottle.

He'd only been gone two hours and when he left, she'd been sitting outside, staring at her dying garden. She must've hit the bottle as soon as he departed. He figured Alice probably didn't want to drink in front of him because it was yet another sign of how deep into depression she was slipping. She had already passed the border into a territory where she definitely needed the professional help she was already receiving, because Jim couldn't be enough for her.

He picked the bottle up off the floor and set it on the table beside the shot glass. Jim then went to the kitchen, pulled off several paper towel sheets from the hanging roller over the sink, came back to the living room, and soaked up the bourbon mess on the hardwood floor. He set the saturated disposable cloth on the table and looked at Alice once more.

As usual, her cheeks had tear streaks. There were new wrinkles on her face, on her forehead. Her hair was greasy and matted, as if she hadn't showered in days. The cloud of melancholy that had settled in this home was one that had not cleared at all in the past weeks. In fact, it seemed to thicken.

Jim wanted his life back. He wanted his son to be alive again. He wanted his granddaughter to be born so he could hold her, so Alice could hold her. Jim needed to see his daughter-in-law and her perky demeanor, always smiling, always joking, always the shiniest of presences. An entire family had perished, and those left behind were fading in slow, torturous waves.

Jim lowered beside Alice, knelt on the floor, and looked at her closed eyes. They were fluttering, and he wondered what she was dreaming about. Her facial expression was one of anguish, and he hoped she wasn't dreaming about the fire. He wished at least in sleep she could find places or visions of pleasantry. That didn't seem the case, though. It appeared there was nowhere she could turn to find even a trickle of peace.

He picked her up off the couch, her legs over one arm and her head resting on the other, and carried her across the living room, down the hallway, and into the bedroom. As he laid her gently on the bed, she stirred. She babbled something incoherent and then fell silent again. He pulled the comforter over her to her neck and stepped back to watch her.

Her eyes opened. They were bloodshot so bad it appeared as if she'd been on a multiple-day alcohol bender. She looked up at him and stared for a moment before mumbling, "Where have you been?"

"I went for a drive," he lied. He didn't want her to know the truth. Because the truth meant that he wasn't as strong as he was portraying for her. It meant that he'd started a journey of investigation and revenge. If she saw such weakness in him, then how could he be a safety net for her misery?

Alice sighed and looked straight up. Her line of vision was toward the ceiling, but it was obvious she saw something else beyond that. Something from another time and another emotion. She stared, unblinking.

"Are you okay?" Jim asked in a whisper.

Her eyes moved toward him, and she waited a moment. Then she replied softly, "No."

"Tell me what I can do. Just tell me, baby. What can I do to make you better again?"

She looked back toward the ceiling, past it into that far-off place again, and didn't answer.

"Alice, I love you. Let me help you. Please."

"Bring them back," she said, still looking upward. "Bring back my family."

"They're not coming back," he replied so gently. "We've got to accept that. We can't undo death."

"So apathetic," she said with a sigh and a trace of contempt.

"Apathetic?" Jim asked. "I care. I just can't work magic."

"You should have gone by there that night." She turned her head toward him, a hint of anger in her voice. "You told me that day when we were at the hospital. After he died. You said you'd thought about taking that way home but didn't. Why didn't you, Jim?"

He realized she was still drunk. She was stretching her words and slurring them.

She continued, "Why didn't you check on our family?"

"I never take that way home. The long back road. No streetlights. There are so many deer through that way. How was I to know?" Defensiveness in his voice.

"You knew what the man said. If it had been me, I would have ridden by their house every night. I would have never taken the highway again. On the way to work and on the way home, Jim. I would have checked on my family every day."

"Honey, we can't base our lives on the words of some drugged-out crazy guy."

"But we should have. You could have saved them. The fire was just as you were leaving work. The arson investigators gave a time. It was the same time you left. You could have saved them."

She sat up, paused, and looked as if she might fall back down into the pillows, but steadied herself and glared at him through drunken anger. "You didn't care. You cared more about getting home than you did your own kid's life."

"Oh, Alice, don't say things like that," he begged. "You're drunk. Don't say shit like that."

She swung her legs around, lowered her feet off the bed, and balanced herself again. Her eyes...they were so red. She looked like a female Satan, drunk and angry, hatred and accusation in her glare.

"Why not say it? It's the truth." Her voice was so nonchalant and careless. As if she wanted to hurt him.

"No," Jim said. "It was coincidence. The man was insane."

"Was he?" she asked sharply as she stood up, and then fell back onto the bed. She grunted with frustration and pushed herself slowly to a standing position, only a foot from Jim, looking defiantly into his eyes. "Our son died. Our grandbaby. His wife. They don't get to stand here and call that man crazy. You could have saved them. You didn't care, Jim." She waved one finger in the air like a mother gesturing a no-no to a child. "You didn't care about our son."

"Alice—"

Her voice deepened with building ire. "Don't Alice me. Don't act like you gave a shit or even do now. Look at you, out riding around like nothing happened. Already over it. Going to work every night and coming home as if everything is the same. You moved on easy, didn't you, Jim? Do you know our son is dead?" Her voice was still rising and near a hollering volume. "Dead!" She staggered past him and out of the bedroom.

He turned and followed.

In the hallway, Jim kept his distance as Alice waddled toward the living room. She bounced off one wall and leaned on another, scoffed in disgust, and then stopped with one hand against the wall for balance. Then she leaned forward and retched. As pure liquid ejected through her mouth and to the hardwood floor, making a disgusting wet impact sound, she mumbled incoherently. Alice wiped her mouth with the filthy arm of a blouse she'd worn for days, leaned forward, and threw up again.

Jim approached her, saying, "Alice," softly. He reached toward her from behind.

She spun around, fury in her glare, and frantically waved her arms at him in an attempt to ward off any assistance. "Stay away from me!" she demanded, swaying as she tried to maintain a stance. "Stay the fuck away. Why care now? Why care now when you didn't care about our son?"

"You're drunk," he said, strengthening his voice for show. "You're going to be sorry for everything you're saying when you sober up. When you sober up, Alice, I hope you remember everything."

"Haven't you ever heard the saying? Hmm? Drunk words are the ones we're afraid to say when we're sober. Booze gives us the courage to say what we were already thinking."

"What you're accusing me of is so horrible. Can't you fucking hear yourself?"

"Oh, I hear myself loud and clear," she said with a rebellious smirk. "Is it to you, Jim? Father of the fucking year. Father of the fucking century. Am I loud and clear?"

"Why are you doing this?" he pleaded. "Why would you feel like that toward me? I've always been good to you. I've always loved you. Why would you let what's happened drive you to hating *me*? I'm here for you. Who's here for me, Alice?" He stepped forward. "Who is here for me? You think I'm not hurting? My son, Alice. My son is gone. *Our* son. Did you forget that? He's *our son,* Alice!"

"Did *you* forget it? Did *you* forget it that night you should have checked up on him? That night you let him, his wife, and their child burn to death?" She stepped toward him and took up a stance of defiance. They were nearly chest-to-chest now. She looked up, fire in her eyes. "Did you forget who he was, Jim?! You let them die! You fucking let them die!"

"No," he shot back.

"Yes!" Her face nearly looked demonic, there was so much spite in it. "Yes, Jim! You! You let them die, and I hate you for it!"

Jim inhaled deeply, paused, and spoke with forced gentleness. "Do you think this is what they would want? Do you think Todd would want this? What's happening right here? What you are doing right now...do you think your son, his wife, our grandchild would want it? If they're watching right now, do you think—"

"Watching right now? Ha! They can't watch, *Jim!* They can't watch because you let them die. You think they're watching from some heavenly platform? Is that what you believe, you dumb sonofabitch?"

She turned and stumbled into the living room. Jim followed but stopped at the hallway threshold. Alice was in the middle of the room, sunlight shining through the unobstructed bay windows. She put her hands in the air, as if she were making a gesture to someone or something that existed upward. As if she were raising her hands to heaven itself. "Are you watching, son?" She looked straight up. "Beth, are you watching? Stormy, did they let you birth into heaven? Are you there? Any of you? Son! Are you watching?"

She turned in slow motion, her hands not lowering even an inch, and still looking toward the ceiling. "Todd! Tell your dad he let you die. Look at your father." She looked at Jim and pointed one finger at him. "Look at him! Going on with his normal life. No signs of grief. Look at him! He didn't care then, and he doesn't care now! Look at your pathetic...worthless...piece of shit father."

She lowered her hands and gave Jim a matter-of-fact grin. "You hear that, Super Dad?"

Silence.

She held a hand to her ear, gesturing focused listening. "You don't hear anything? I don't hear anything." She turned a full circle, hand still to her ear. "I don't hear them. They're not answering. How are they watching and can't answer, Jim?"

She started toward him, stumbled over her own feet, miraculously managed to not fall, and stood firm only a couple feet from Jim, who was so dazed he couldn't even speak.

He was frozen, watching his wife with pity. His heart hurt. His soul was in agony, but he couldn't allow that to be seen. Even with her words spearing right through his illusory tough skin, he had to be strong for her. This was not who she was, and these words were not how she felt. He willed himself to believe that.

"They're gone," she continued. "They can't hear a fucking word. You understand how death works, right? The brain doesn't work anymore, Jim. They're buried in the ground. Beth was such a sloppy mess from having been melted to almost nothing more than bones, her parents couldn't even officially say goodbye to her. Closed casket, Jim! That baby. That poor little baby whose first life experience was to be burned to a crisp, Jim! You could have saved them all!"

With that, she turned and started forward. She wasn't watching her steps and her leg caught on the coffee table. She fell over it, knocking off three framed pictures. One of Todd's high school graduation, with him in his cap and gown. Another one of Todd and Beth, both with a hand on Beth's belly. And another one of the unborn daughter's first ultrasound. The pictures fell to the floor.

Alice fell over the table, rolled off it, and landed on her front side, crushing the pictures. She lowered her head and laughed. A chuckle of deep frustration mixed with grief. She laughed louder. And then she raised her head and shrieked. She screamed so loud the entire neighborhood might have heard it and assumed she was in agonizing pain or immediate, life-threatening danger. Her howling was cut off by a cough, and then another one, and then a full fit of hacking and inhaling. She puked again. More liquid poured from her mouth and splattered on the floor just under her face. She cried. She wept not only from her body, but from her soul.

Alice rolled over onto her back and continued to sob. She raised a fist and screamed, the back of her head and hair now soaked in her own vomit. Screaming, crying, screaming some more.

Jim watched in horror. He wanted to cry with her, but again, not yet. *Strength. Be her strength.* She had none of her own right now and wouldn't for a long time.

After several minutes, which seemed like hours to her terrified husband, her emotional breakdown concluded. She eventually fell silent, rolled away from the pool of bile, and fell asleep.

He sat on the sofa and watched her for a time he couldn't calculate, because suddenly time didn't seem to have any existence. It was no longer relevant because hopelessness had blacked it out. Alice wouldn't get better today, tomorrow, next week, next year. And Jim wondered how much longer life would matter to her, him...them together. She was fading from the life they had known. Now, it seemed all they would ever understand again was grief and misery. Despondency and despair forever.

She snored. And instead of moving her again, Jim laid down on the sofa and stared at the ceiling until he fell asleep too. In his slumber, he dreamt of the past. A happy past. One worth remembering if, for anything, to simply survive the present. Birthday parties. Beach vacations. Todd and Beth's wedding. Alice giggling in joy like a little girl after finding out she was to be a grandmother. So many good times that were only memories and dreams now.

Chapter Eleven

Jim awoke to the consistent rumbling of a lawnmower from a neighbor's yard. He was stretched out on the sofa, laying on top of his shirt, which he had apparently pulled off during the night. When he heard the lawnmower engine growling, opened his eyes, and was nearly blinded by sunlight coming through the living room windows, he realized he'd slept all the way through the remainder of yesterday afternoon and on through the night. His sight and mind foggy from a fresh awakening, he glanced toward the wall clock near the foyer. The short arm pointed at a fancy seven, and the long arm pointed at a likewise three. It was early morning. He'd been so exhausted, he'd crashed and slumbered for over sixteen hours. He had also completely missed his work shift without calling in.

Alice was no longer lying on the floor, and her mess of vomit had been cleaned up. Jim felt it ironic that he'd slept longer on a sober mind than she had on an intoxicated one. He laid back down and listened for any audible signs she was currently active inside the house. All he could hear was the lawnmower outside growing louder and then quieter in an obvious pattern as his neighbor pushed it from one side of his yard to the other and back again.

Jim needed coffee. He slowly emerged from the comfort of the couch, moving like an old man who had just endured physical activity he hadn't dared to engage in for years. His arms and legs felt tired.

His thoughts were murky. The stress was taking a toll on him, not only emotionally, but physically as well. He hadn't wanted to get up. He just wanted to lie there, go back to sleep, and stay in comfortable darkness until the current trials of grief and despair ended. Maybe he could just exist in a dream world, where everything was good, until Alice was finally better again. However, he also wondered whether she would ever recover. For now, her behavior only indicated a deepening plunge into a depression that was pulling her in like a black hole would. And if light itself couldn't escape such gravity, how could a grieving human?

He dragged himself into the kitchen and made a cup of coffee while glancing out the back window. She was out there again, finally in fresh clothes, sitting in her chair just on the edge of her garden. The plants didn't look good. At one time, they had been thriving thanks to her constant care and maintenance. Now, with rows of slumping crops, withering leaves, and even empty spots where she'd pulled them out of the ground in a fit of rage and sorrow, the garden looked like a sloppily shaven face.

He sipped his coffee and continued to look out the window at his wife. The only way to save her, he feared, was through the route of an impossible act: bringing her son back to life. Bringing her grandbaby back. Rescuing the trio of this family who had been sent to the afterlife for a forever stay. It saddened him even further than he already was when those thoughts introduced themselves in his mind. The only way to make things right was to pull off a stunt that couldn't be performed. He couldn't bring them back any more realistically than a Hollywood stunt double could jump a ramp in New York City and safely land across the country in San Francisco.

She'd already been to see a psychiatrist, who simply listened to her cry for an hour and then prescribed her medication to help her fits of extreme depression. That's likely why she acted the way she did yesterday: meds and alcohol weren't a good mix. As a matter of fact, there was probably a label on the prescription bottle that warned against drinking while taking the medication.

Jim wondered whether she remembered her cruel words from yesterday. He wondered whether she was sorry, or whether she was too lost in despondency to care about anything but the losses they had suffered. He felt like he should go outside and be with her, but he really didn't want to. There were two potential outcomes: she would still have the attitude and thought process of yesterday, or she would simply ignore him. Either way was rejection, and even though he knew he should go to her regardless of how she might act, he simply didn't want to deal with her foulness again today.

He almost couldn't wait to go to work. At least there he was busy. At least on the job he was not at home, fighting a battle it seemed he was destined to lose. He realized his current line of thinking wasn't husband-like. He was being selfish, but when the hell was it his turn to grieve? Weeks of holding his wife up, not only being a mental wall for her to lean on, but now also a verbal and emotional punching bag. He also felt guilty for experiencing this new frustration toward her. But again, when was it going to be his turn? What about him and his grief, his regret, his anger?

He turned from the window but still stood in place. His thoughts switched from his wife to the man he now knew as Billy Wagner. The lunatic who predicted the demise of three innocent human beings and was now safe and sound himself in the county jail. Immune from prosecution because the police believed he couldn't possibly have anything to do with the house fire. Billy was a new focus of Jim's anger. And hatred.

Even though Jim didn't actually know Billy Wagner, he hated him. He despised him even if he had no role in the event that turned Jim's life upside down. Were those rational feelings? Maybe not, but the harsh perception of Billy made Jim feel a tad better. Just a tiny tad, but something was better than nothing.

Jim sipped his coffee. It was time to pay Billy Wagner a visit. Jim needed answers. He had to talk to the person he suspected of so much evil, face-to-face. Suddenly, Jim knew exactly what he was doing today before work.

Billy Wagner.

Chapter Twelve

Inside the county jailhouse, the lighting was appropriately dim. It felt like what Jim would expect from a dungeon setting. The concrete walls were barren of anything decorative, the overall mood that of a dark melancholy. It was a hot summer day outside, and when he stepped into the building, there was a rush of cool air. But, as he went through the process of signing up to visit an inmate and then was moved to the waiting room, the comfortable air was replaced with that of dry warmth. It was as if even visitors needed no mercy from the elements the same as those being held here against their will for committing crimes.

Jim waited a good half an hour in that transitional area, sitting in a hard, uncomfortable plastic chair. His smartphone did him no good to pass the time because the building's walls were so thick of concrete, no cellular signal made its way inside. All he could do was sit there and wait, staring at blank walls and preparing for what he might say when face-to-face with Billy Wagner once more.

Only this time, there were no guns involved. The perpetrator he was here to see had held an advantage over him during their first meeting. Now, they would be in the same place, only a few feet apart, on even grounds. Though there could be no physical confrontation between the two of them, Jim wouldn't have to tread carefully through his own words. This time, he could say what was on his mind without the worry of himself or a loved one catching a bullet.

He shared the waiting room with one other person: an older woman who sat quietly with her hands folded in her lap, and her oversized purse on a chair beside her. Her lips moved occasionally, and Jim could hear a mumble coming from her. At first, he thought she was incoherently babbling to herself. But as he focused on her whispering voice, he eventually realized she was praying. He wondered who she was here to visit. He assumed she was too old to have a younger child, someone just entering adulthood who had ventured into the wrong side of the law. If she was here for a son or a daughter, her child couldn't possibly be any younger than his or her mid or late thirties. If that was the case and she was here to see an older child, then Jim figured she'd probably been dealing with this kind of situation for a long time. He wondered whether years of stress, that an adult problem child could cause, had made her look older than she was, which was in her early sixties at least. She was alone and not with a husband. Could that be who was on the other side of the wall, waiting to speak with, possibly, the one person in the world who still loved and supported him?

A heavy steel door, across from the less secure entrance they'd come through to enter the waiting room, rattled and opened. A bulky, young, uniformed and armed male security guard stood in the doorway and said, "Jim Radcliffe to see William Wagner."

"That's me." Jim stood up.

"This way, sir."

Jim followed the guard through a long hallway of concrete walls, ceiling, and floor. At the end of the dismal corridor was a metal detector with a conveyor running through it and a table at both ends. Standing on each side of the metal detector, two more guards. They watched Jim as he approached. When he stopped at the first table, the guard standing beside it said, "Empty everything you have on you," and he nudged a small plastic rectangular basket toward him. Jim put his smartphone and keys in the basket. He then pulled his wallet out of his back pocket and placed it in the container.

"Is that everything?" the guard asked.

"That's everything," Jim replied politely.

"We're going to pat you down," the guard said. "Legs apart, hands up."

Jim obeyed and the guard, who had walked him in, ran hands along the insides of his legs, the outside of them, along his sides and his underarms. He then patted Jim's backside, then his front side, avoiding one specific area for obvious reasons.

"You're good," the guard said.

As he was being patted down, his belongings in the basket were on the conveyor, passing through an x-ray machine to the other side.

"Step through please," the guard at the table instructed.

Jim walked through the metal detector, and once on the other side, that guard pushed the plastic container toward him.

"Get your things," the second guard commanded.

"This way," the guard who had guided him through the hallway said as he stepped in front of Jim and into a large, open room. On the other side of the room was a plexiglass wall. In front of that wall, a line of partitioned booths, each with phone handsets in place on one side. People sat in several of the booths, with the phones to their heads, talking to prisoners, all dressed in orange jumpsuits, on the other side of the plexiglass. Each booth was numbered. There were fifteen of them.

"You got number twelve." The guard gestured toward the corresponding booth. "From the time he sits down, you'll have ten minutes.

When you're told that ten minutes is up, hang up and stand up. There's no extra time given. You have more to say, then come back tomorrow."

"Got it." Jim stepped into the booth, sat down in another uncomfortable plastic chair, and waited.

On the other side of the plexiglass, another heavy steel door opened. Through it came Billy Wagner, matching the other inmates' attire, handcuffed in the front. He was clean this time. His hair wasn't slick and stuck to his head as if he'd just emerged from a grease shower. His face wasn't filthy, as if he hadn't bathed in weeks, like it had been during their first meeting. He didn't appear to be hyped up on hard drugs. He looked calm, cool, and even somewhat content. There were two guards in the room with him, one male and one female. The female went to him, uncuffed him, and gestured toward the booth where, on the other side, sat Jim.

At the sight of Billy, Jim's pulse raced. So many emotions stirred within him, but the leading one was hatred. Even though he knew very little of the man in the orange jail jumpsuit, Jim despised him with everything he had. He wanted to break through the transparent barrier between them, grab Billy by the neck, and slowly squeeze the life out of him. He wanted to fling him about like a rag doll and ultimately smash his face, repeatedly, into one of those concrete walls.

But Jim reminded himself to remain cordial in his tone and words. If he threatened Billy or showed spite toward him, this endeavor might be cut short. Jim wanted Billy to talk. He wasn't sure what he wanted him to say, but he wanted him to speak.

As Billy turned toward the booth where there was a phone on the inside of the partition on his side, his face showed he recognized Jim. His demeanor had been one of detachment when he came through the steel door, but now it changed instantly to interest and curiosity.

He went into the booth and sat down, but did not immediately pick up his handset.

Jim sat still also, as the two stared at each other, both with their own cautious questionings of this meeting.

Finally, Billy picked up the handset and held it to his ear. He waited for Jim to follow suit, but Jim only stared. Finally, Billy pointed to his own headset and sent a look of encouragement to his adversary. After a few more moments of hesitation, Jim picked up his headset and put it against his ear. Neither of them spoke immediately.

Finally, Billy said, "If you have nothing to say, why are you here?"

A few more moments passed without Jim speaking.

Billy said, "I can go back to my cell. It's actually cooler in there. Feels like they turned off the AC in here."

"My family is dead," Jim finally said bluntly.

No look of surprise came from Billy, but he seemed sympathetic. "I'm sorry to hear that, Mr. Radcliffe. I really am. I offer my condolences."

"My son, my daughter-in-law, my grandchild. All burned to death."

"I'm sorry."

"The same night you came into our backyard. It happened the same damn night."

Billy was silent but held eye contact with Jim.

Jim continued, "How could you know?"

"Dreams," Billy answered plainly.

"What did you have to do with it? Coincidences don't exist. What did you have to do with that fire?"

"I agree with you about the coincidences part, but I had nothing to do with it. I only saw it before it happened."

"No." Jim shook his head. "You planned it. You paid someone to do it while you were sitting in jail with an alibi. You were behind it."

Billy sighed, but not in frustration that he was being accused of such a sinister act. It was pity.

"Why?" Jim asked. "Why would you do such a horrible thing to any human? Do you understand they burned to death? They fucking burned to death. They suffered."

"I had nothing to do with it," Billy replied, scoffed, and continued. "I wouldn't do that to anyone. I should have shot you, but that wouldn't have been just for the thrill of the kill. I've never hurt anyone in my life. I should have pulled the trigger, and I didn't. Now the world will suffer the consequences."

"What consequences? Why? What the hell are you talking about? Are you sober right now? You're in jail. You have to be sober. Do they allow drugs in here?"

"I was high on that day, but I didn't need to be to know what should be done. I was only fucked up because I needed the courage to do it. Even then, even knowing what was coming and knowing I could stop it, I still couldn't pull the trigger. Hurting people isn't my thing, Mr. Radcliffe. Not even when the fate of the world depends on it."

Jim pulled his headset away, held it as if he wanted to crash it against the plexiglass, and then returned it to his ear. "You keep babbling about this shit. You did it while you were high on who-knows-what, and you're doing it supposedly sober now. What are you talking about? Explain it to me. I'm all ears, man. Explain it to me. Right here and right now. Tell me what the fuck you're talking about."

Billy's expression became one of heavy thought as he took a deep breath and released a long sigh. "You're going to do something you shouldn't do. You're going to save your son. And when you do that, you're going to cause a string of events that lead to something...horrible. Terrible. Death. So much death. All for one person."

"That doesn't tell me anything. What's going to happen? How can I save my son? How the hell can I save someone who's buried and dead? I watched the coffins lower into the double grave. All three of them are gone. His wife was burned and melted so bad it was a closed coffin service for her. The baby...there was nothing left of her. Gone."

"If I tell you too much, I risk fucking the timeline up even more. I don't even know the complete details of what's going to happen. I just know it's something horrible, and a lot of people are going to die. You're not going to listen anyhow. If any of it was to be stopped, I had to pull the trigger. I didn't. So I let the world down by letting you live."

"Why can't you tell me? Even if I could believe you, why can't you tell me?"

"Because I've told you too much already."

"Your brain is warped. You know that? Your mind is shot. Fucked up from too much drinking, too much drug use. You're fucked up. You don't make any sense."

"You think I don't know that? This messed-up mind is something I try to saturate. I try to block out the dreams. I can't, though. I've tried and I can't."

Jim stared straight through Billy Wagner. He wanted to come through the only thing separating them and beat the man until he elaborated on his words of ridiculous prophecy.

Billy asked, "Is the weather nice outside?"

"What does that matter? You're not going anywhere for a long time," Jim taunted. "You're where people like you belong. Away from society. People like you hurt others just for a sick thrill. I know you had something to do with it. I know you had my family killed."

"Is it hot outside? Muggy and humid? It must be. That's why it's so hot in here."

"You're a psycho."

"I've known for quite some time that I'll die on a pretty day. A beautiful day. Sunny, seventy-five, clear skies, and a comfortable, soft breeze. The kind of day we're supposed to enjoy in the outdoors. Nap in a hammock under a shade tree. Wear comfortable clothes and it's not too hot or too cool. A perfect day."

Jim only stared.

Billy continued. His eyes seemed to watch something far from where he was, in another dimension of existence, a time and place nowhere near the county jail or Jim. "You see, my dreams tell me things. They show me glimpses of what's coming. The future. Just bits and pieces, but I can usually put the puzzle together. I can usually decipher the cryptic prophecies of my own mind."

"I don't care about any of this," Jim said blatantly.

"Shhhh. Let me tell my story."

"I don't give a damn about your story."

"Oh, but you do. That's why you're here, Mr. Radcliffe." Billy almost smiled but didn't complete its formation. "It was in one of my dreams. I'll die on a beautiful day. So when it's cold outside, snowing, freezing, hard winter grounds and brisk winds, I know I'm okay. When it's hot outside, scolding and humid summer days, I don't worry. Thunderstorms, tornado warnings, flash floods, destructive winds and thunder and lightning—those are good days for me. While you cook out in your shorts and sneakers and no shirt with your family and friends on near-perfect days, I'm wondering if this is it. The dreams don't tell me how...they just tell me I'm going to die. So all day, every perfect spring, summer, or fall day, I'm cowering away somewhere, wondering which breath is my last."

"I don't care when you're dying. You can die right now. I wish you would. I wish I could do it with my own hands." Jim tried to shift the subject back to its original content and said, "You keep saying I'm going to save my son. I'll play along. Tell me how."

After he said that, Jim realized he wasn't just playing along. He knew that deep within him, a hope was rising. Like a hot-air balloon filling and patiently lifting off from ground to air, a belief that maybe Billy *could* see the future, and in that future, he foresaw Jim somehow turning back time and saving Todd. Jim's desperation to save his family was making him irrational, and even though he recognized that, he still wanted Billy to talk. Of all things, surely going back to that night, and rescuing his son, was impossible.

But the more Billy insisted that very action was going to happen, the more Jim wanted to believe him, and the more Jim *did* believe him.

Billy stared at Jim for a few seconds, then said, "Do you love your son?"

"This is ridiculous," Jim snapped. "What am I even doing here? What am I doing?"

"*Do* you love your son?"

"That's a stupid question."

"Do you love your son?"

"Of course I do. Of course I love my kid. What kind of question is that?"

"And you'd bring him back if you could?"

Jim scoffed. "What the fuck is your point? Can you get to it?"

Billy smiled as if entertained and replied, "You're not very good at answering questions, are you?"

"I'm not very good at entertaining some psychopath jailbird. Some loser who chose a life of crime over a life of legitimacy."

"But you came to me."

"Because I thought after what you've done, you might want to return to some kind of human decency. I thought just maybe, just *maybe,* you'd want to rectify some of the bad you've done. But no. You don't. You just want to sit here, getting some kind of pleasure from watching me suffer, asking stupid questions."

Silence fell upon both of them. Billy watched Jim as if observing a rat's behavior in a science lab maze. Jim looked back at Billy, trying to figure out what the man was reaching for with this line of questioning.

Finally, Jim answered, "Yes. I would save my son if I could. I would pull him from that fire if I could. If I could go back further and get him out before the fire starts, I would. If I could give my own life so that he'd live, I fucking would. Does that answer your question?"

"And you'd do so at the risk of millions of lives. Maybe even billions. Because *you* want *your* son to live. Because you want it for yourself, not for him. In your selfishness and narcissism, you don't care about anything but what you want. You'd sacrifice the world for your one beloved son. Why? Because you can't handle the grief? Because it hurts so bad?"

Billy slammed both his hands against the plexiglass, and Jim flinched. The guard on Billy's side of the barrier took notice, but only watched with caution.

"Is it your son you love or yourself?" Billy asked as he pulled away from the glass and leaned back in his chair again. "Do you want to bring him back for him, or for *you,* Mr. Radcliffe?"

Jim leaned forward and slammed *his* hands against the glass, and this time, Billy flinched. Holding his hands in place, Jim said, "You worthless piece of shit. I can slam fists for dramatic effect, too. You're just a cracked-out showboat. That's all you are. Your dreams aren't real. Your history is phony. You didn't turn to drugs and alcohol because of terrifying visions. You did it because that's just the kind of person you are. Weak. Pathetic. Worthless. You let yourself down and, in the process, you let your wife down. You let everyone who's ever loved you down. Where you are now..."

Jim paused, looked Billy up and down, and continued. "That's where you belong. Behind this glass. In that orange suit. Nothing more than an eyesore on humanity. Nobody even misses you, do they? I'm the only visitor you've had. Poor little drug-addicted, drunk Billy. Nobody loves him, so he has to fuck with people who *do* have love in their lives." Jim pulled away from the plexiglass and sat back in his chair. "Nobody even fucking knows you're in here, except for people who *despise you.*"

Billy sighed in disappointment and said with finality, "Mr. Radcliffe, when the time comes, don't do it. You will only create suffering well beyond your own. And your misery will only escalate. You'll not be fixing anything; you'll be breaking everything. Endure your grief, your family's grief, and move on with your life."

Jim leaned forward. "How? How am I going to save him?"

"*Don't* save him. Leave the universe as it is supposed to be."

"How, goddammit? How am I going to do it?"

Billy stood up and signaled the guard. "I'm ready to go back now."

Jim shot up out of his chair, almost near panicked, and repeated, "*How?*"

The guard came to Billy and urged him toward the steel door. Billy cooperated, not looking back toward Jim, who stood at the glass, his hands on it, yelling, "How am I going to save him?! Don't you walk away now!"

The guard handcuffed him in the front, opened the steel door, and waited for Billy to walk through it.

"Tell me, goddammit! Tell me how!"

Billy looked back at Jim and regarded him with a sympathetic glance.

"Tell me, you asshole! How do I save him?!"

Billy turned around and stepped through the doorway.

"Goddammit, you come back here! You tell me how to save my son! My son! Tell me how!"

The guard and Billy disappeared through the doorway, and the door shut behind them. In profound frustration, Jim pounded the plexiglass repeatedly.

"You piece of shit! You fucking piece of shit! I'll kill you! I'll kill you myself! I know you hear me!"

He beat on the plexiglass. He was trying to hold back tears while still screaming at someone who was, by now, out of audible reach. "I know you hear me! I'm coming for you! *I'm fucking coming for you!*"

Chapter Thirteen

Alice stood outside in the day's heat in her ragged nightgown, just on the border of her struggling garden. She sipped from a glass of whiskey on the rocks, sweating profusely but not caring. For years she had taken joy in keeping the plants alive, nourishing them, caring for them as if they were living pets. She spoke to them often and enjoyed how they listened without offering judgment in return. Sometimes, when a soft breeze came through, it was almost as if the plants had a consciousness, waving back and forth to her voice, assuring Alice they could hear her words and feel their meaning.

Now, they were shriveling, leaning over, falling down. Her neglect of them had taken its toll, and it seemed their very souls had abandoned them. They no longer listened, or paid attention to her, in reciprocation to her treatment of them. A once flourishing relationship now only a thing of the past. She had always believed in the rule that the other side of life was death, but also the other side of death was life. She knew this in her heart and deep within her soul. Yet, somehow, she'd never really faced the death side of things in this extreme. Sure, her parents had passed away some time ago, but they were supposed to go first. But, her own son, his wife, and their daughter? Destiny had ultimately decided that three loved humans would perish well ahead of having lived a full life. And in doing so, not only were three beautiful people gone forever, but those left behind would never live another peaceful day.

For Alice, now death was everywhere. The death of her son and his family, the death of this garden, and the death of her will to advance forward in life for even another second. She could fall to the ground right now, well aware she was taking her last breath, and would likely welcome a forever darkness.

She realized she was letting her husband down. Alice knew that, in a drunk rage, she'd said words she didn't mean. Those accusations she'd thrown at him had come from an inebriated mind, not a sincere heart. But she didn't have the energy or the willpower to make it right. She felt remorse for her actions. Deep remorse. Yet, somehow, she couldn't fix it. And she was sorry for *that,* too. Sorry that a man who loved her so unconditionally had to stand aside and watch her willingly leap into her own demise. She loved Jim. She loved him so damn much.

But he was a part of an entire unit she loved. With most of that unit now perished, she simply didn't have the energy to hold what was left of it together. Jim was a vigorous man. If he stood by her or ultimately left her, he would eventually return to a happy life. He'd often preached the words "you only get one chance at life." She knew he truly believed that. Alice also knew Jim to be the kind of man who listened to his own advice.

She wasn't giving up on her marriage. She was giving up on life. It wasn't a matter of throwing in the towel because things got tough. No. It was simply not having what it takes to move past something. Now, even waving a white flag would be too much. She could barely make herself shower once a week. Even pouring this drink, which was now empty, required more energy than she cared to expend. She was spent emotionally, mentally, and physically. Her husband couldn't help. A professional psychiatrist could only prescribe her medicine for her anxiety and depression. There were no words to guide her from this maze of tortured turmoil. She merely existed now and wished she had the courage to end it all.

Alice looked at the empty wineglass in her hand, which she had used for a whiskey on the rocks. There was barely a drop left in the glass's bottom, which she tilted from side to side for a few moments and then threw down with a shriek of agony. The glass broke into several pieces with a loud crack as it crashed against the garden's ground. The power of the action had thrown her off-balance. She staggered. The sun was beating down as she looked up. She stared directly into its center in defiance. Finally, she could hold her gaze no longer and looked back at the garden, black spots in her vision, which took a few moments to clear.

She screamed again and didn't stop until she was out of breath.

***

Inside, Alice staggered into the kitchen and poured herself another drink, using a new wineglass. When she pulled the ice tray out of the freezer and cracked it, all the ice popped out and fell to the floor. She tossed the tray across the room, bent down, picked up two pieces of ice, and dropped them in her glass. They clanged and spun around the bottom. She then poured her bourbon, lost her focus, and overfilled the glass.

As the bourbon rose over the rim and flooded onto the counter, she didn't tilt the bottle back up, but continued to pour. The alcoholic beverage puddled on the counter, spread to the edge, and leaked onto the floor. When the bottle was finally empty, she ignored the mess she'd just made, threw the bottle against a far wall, and hypnotized, watched it shatter, and then looked down at her drink. The glass was too full to pick up, so she leaned down and sipped from it as it sat on the counter.

Alice licked her lips, enjoying the strong taste of the bourbon. This was the only pleasure in life she had anymore. The alcohol did more for her than just pleasing her taste buds. It numbed her. The meds she was on seemed to have nearly no effect on her daily misery. Sometimes, when mixed with several shots of whiskey, they helped to tire her. But even when she passed out from drug- and alcohol-induced sedation, she only stayed under long enough to sleep the buzz off.

If only she could just sleep life away to a future point in which the pain and suffering had come and gone.

To her right, a prescription bottle filled with the pills she was supposed to take as needed. As needed, to her, was every waking moment. She looked at the bottle while stirring her drink with an index finger. She raised the finger to her mouth and licked it. Inhaling deeply, she continued to scrutinize the prescription bottle. She had read the label on it repeatedly since first filling the prescription weeks ago. One of the warnings cautioned against driving a vehicle after taking the medication. Another instructed what to do in case of accidental overdose, which was only to call 911.

If there was a route in which one could accidentally overdose, and it was implied such an action was dangerous to life, then wouldn't intentional overdose end this miserable existence? Her head swam in the rough waters of an alcoholic inebriation. She swayed, grabbed the counter. *Right now, could she not end it all?* It would be easy, especially as drunk as she was. She could swallow every pill in that bottle, finish her drink, lay down, fall asleep, and never wake up again. Her pain would not only be eased, but erased. An eternal slumber instead of the brief ones she enjoyed here in life. And the forever sleep would be a dreamless one.

The visions she encountered now, while unconscious, were ones of torture. Even the dreams stemming from pleasant memories were hard on her because, when she awoke, she returned to a reality she despised. And the nightmares of burning houses and screaming, suffering victims she recognized as her son, his wife, and their unborn daughter only shook her awake to a world away from fire, but back to the absence of those she had loved so dearly. Alice had never prepared for their deaths. Not even a single thought had occurred to her, during their living years, that she would someday have to exist when they no longer did.

Alice reached out and slid the medicine bottle across the counter, and through the spilled bourbon, closer to her. When it was directly before her, she stared at it again for several moments. *Would it hurt at all if she swallowed all those pills and waited for death? Would the pain even matter?* Because there was no possibility of it matching the agony she trudged through in this life. If she overdosed, perhaps she would physically suffer for moments or minutes before the darkness, but it wouldn't be like the forever misery she lived in now.

She turned the bottle around without lifting it from the puddle of bourbon. She turned it and turned it. Slowly. Seeing the label's words but not reading them. She turned the bottle. Turned it. Sighed. Looked upon it and then beyond it. Somewhere in the distance, a far distance, another existence. One of peace and tranquility. One where she either would be nothing or she would be with her son. Both options were better than this state of being. This melancholy presence in a world where she no longer wanted to be.

Alice picked up the overfilled wineglass and turned away from the counter, leaving the bottle full of its pills, and dragged herself into the living room. As she crossed the threshold, she heard a child laugh. The sound came from the 65-inch smart television mounted on the wall. She stopped in front of the TV and looked at it. On the screen, ten-year-old Todd playing in a swimming pool with his father. They were splashing, swimming, laughing. Jim lowered his hands, joined together, to create a step beneath the water's surface. Todd stepped into his father's hand, and Jim launched him several feet into the air. Todd then splashed into the water, went under for a second, and came up laughing and cheering.

"That was a high one!" Todd exclaimed.

"Again?" Jim offered. "I think we can beat that one."

Out of the scene because she was the one recording the pool play-time, Alice heard her own voice say, "I don't know. That one was pretty good."

The smart television was connected to the internet, and played several family videos on a loop from a website where Todd and Alice had saved them over the years. Alice had turned it on and set them all to play before she'd taken her first sip of bourbon for the day. Once she fell into an alcoholic daze, she'd wandered off to her garden and forgotten about the videos. Now, drunk and disoriented, she'd found her way back to them.

On the screen, Jim lifted Todd into the air once again. Another splash. Todd laughing. Jim laughing. Alice laughing.

"That was better!" Todd yelled victoriously.

"Seemed the same to me," Jim said. "How about you do me?"

"Now *that* I'd like to see," came Alice's out-of-scene voice.

Alice stood in front of the screen, watching it and cracking a smile. These memories were amazing pieces of the past the fire didn't take from her. These moments did happen and there was profound happiness. They were real.

Another splash. More unified laughing. Alice continued to smile and sipped her drink.

But there would be no more of these memories created. Alice tried to imagine a young Stormy Dawn, Todd throwing her into the pool, Alice still recording. She tried to force the vision of what the future might have been into her mind, and her thoughts became jumbled. It was not possible for her to do it. She couldn't fake the visions because not only had they never existed, but she *knew* they would never come to be. Her imagination refused to cooperate with the creation of an impossible fantasy.

The video ended, and the screen went blank. Then, a swirling circle appeared, showing the playback was buffering, and finally a new video played. This one was of eight-year-old Todd on a bicycle, Jim running behind him with a hand on the back of the bike seat, Todd stiff and wide-eyed in concentration.

"You can do this!" Alice cheered, once again the one doing the filming.

Todd's legs moved furiously to pedal the bike forward. Jim kept up the best he could, but the bike was slowly speeding away. Finally, Todd willed the bicycle away from his father, who lost touch of the back seat but still ran behind his determined son. Todd's face relaxed, and a smile appeared as he realized he was doing it. He was riding and balancing the bike on his own. More distance between son and father. Todd pedaled away, determined. Victory. He was on his own. Jim finally came to a stop to catch his breath, Todd riding away from him in glee.

"You're doing it!" Alice shouted from behind the camera.

"There you go!" Jim yelled in the video. "You got this. Go, go, go, go! You're doing it!"

Standing in the living room, watching the video with a nostalgic grin, Alice whispered, "You're doing it."

On the TV, Todd continued to race forward. His excitement was almost impossible to contain for the sake of concentration. Forward. Forward. Pedaling. Faster. Faster.

Jim applauded.

In the living room, Alice cheered. She dropped her glass. It shattered; she didn't care. She didn't even notice she'd made another mess of broken glass and spilled booze. She raised a fist and yelled, "You're doing it! Go, son! Go, go, go!" Louder: "You're doing it!" Louder still: "You're fucking doing it." She choked on incoming sobs. "You're doing it, son." Now, a sadness mixed with the cheer. "Go, son!" Her voice softened as she tried not to cry, but the tears came full force now, trailing down her face as if the floodgates of grief had once more opened. Her voice, trembling and low: "Go, Todd. Fucking go! You did it." Crying now, nearly uncontrollably. Sniffling. Tear after tear. A steady stream. "You're doing it," she wailed.

She couldn't make the happiness return. Instead, she came back to reality. Todd was dead, and this was a video from the past. A past in which he lived and thrived and laughed and splashed in pools and rode a bicycle without training wheels. A time long gone. The only place in which Todd could laugh or learn new things was in the past. There would be no more. No more videos, no more fresh memories. Her son was dead.

Alice stood, whimpering in front of the TV. Crying. Agony. Anguish. Turmoil.

Chapter Fourteen

J im sat at the bar, looking up at the several small television screens mounted above it. Every TV played the same sports news station, and now the focus was on the baseball games from earlier in the night. The Braves had beaten the Mets thanks to a walk-off three-run homer in the bottom of the ninth inning. The volumes weren't muted, but they were barely loud enough to hear, much less to make out what the sports news anchor was saying. From the speakers placed strategically around the inside of the establishment, classic rock from the '70s and '80s played. Right now, a track from Poison was blasting. A song in which the singer claimed to work too hard for little pay and needed a break, wanting nothing but a good time.

Jim had clocked out at work only twenty minutes ago. Although his coworkers hadn't invited him to come along to the bar with them this time, he decided he needed a post-shift beverage. Nothing too strong because he didn't want to drive home drunk. But he needed some kind of buzz, something to lessen the tension and loosen his mind. His phone sat on the bar in front of him, and he touched it to unlock the screen. The time was 2:13 a.m. He sighed, wondering why the hell it seemed to always be that exact time when he looked at his phone.

It had been 2:13 a.m. the night he left work, thinking to ride by his son's house, but drove straight home instead. That was the time he'd made the wrong choice, which led to his son's death. Had he not been lazy, or too tired, or, hell, had been even a little more concerned, he would have driven by that house. He would have seen it was on fire and he could have saved them all. Would Jim now be subconsciously nudged to look at the time at 2:13 a.m. for the rest of his life? He wanted to slide the smartphone down the bar and watch it fly off the edge. He wanted to never look at the time again, at least after midnight.

The bartender, a younger woman in her early to mid-twenties, placed a frosted mug full of draft beer in front of him. There was a thin layer of foam at the top. "Four-fifty. Would you like to start a tab?"

Jim's wallet sat on the bar right next to the beer. He opened it and handed her a credit card. "Yes, please. Thank you."

"We hold the card until you leave," she informed him.

"That's fine. Keep the beer coming, please."

She took his card and turned around to face a monitor with a keyboard below it. She typed in some information, likely his card numbers, and then placed the card in a drawer just below the keyboard. Then she was off to the other end of the bar to talk to a younger man, a friend or patron she had been conversing with when Jim sat down.

He sipped his beer and continued to look at the TV screens and their sports broadcasting. There was more baseball, and more baseball, and more baseball. This time of year, it was really the only sport drawing coverage. Within a few minutes, he had downed the full beer, and the bartender was sliding another to him. The television monitors, though he watched them, were far from his chain of thought. Eventually, he was staring at baseball, but saw other things instead.

He saw his son on the screens. Todd was running around in the backyard as a child, laughing and happy. He saw Alice chasing Todd in play, both with smiles on their faces—Alice saying something, Todd running and laughing. Jim saw them all sitting at the outside table with the huge, wide-open umbrella attached to it, providing shade as they ate the hamburgers Jim had just finished grilling.

After so many minutes of daydreaming about the good stuff, Jim suddenly saw Todd's house as if he stood in the street just in front of it. The house was completely engulfed in flames. Then, coming out of the front door with her son's lifeless body in her arms, Alice, tears streaming down her face, her expression toward Jim one of accusation and spite.

You could have saved him, the vision of Alice said. *You let our son die.*

No. I didn't know. How was I to know?

You knew. You were warned. You ignored it. You might as well have lit the fire yourself.

No, Alice. No. I loved our son. I loved his wife. I loved the baby.

Then why didn't you save them?

I didn't know.

You knew. You fucking knew and you did nothing.

No.

YOU KNEW! YOU LET THEM DIE!

NO!

Jim, his hand tight around the half-empty beer mug on the bar, closed his eyes to make the visions on the screens go away. He held his lids shut tight, as if bracing for a physical blow—as if someone in front of him was drawing back with a baseball bat, about to swing it at his head in full force. He saw darkness behind the closed eyelids. The darkness was protective. It held at bay all the memories coming at him, as if to chastise him for his errors, instead of simply showing him a time of his life in which his family lived happily and blissfully.

When he opened his eyes again, the monitors above his head were all playing the same commercial, plugging a certain brand of motor oil, showing racecars on an oval track traveling at high speeds.

Then something pulled his attention away from the televisions. He looked down and to the right, and that was when he saw the man. The man was sharp dressed, in a black suit and red tie, dark-brown hair well-kept and cut, a smooth, clean-looking face, aged somewhere in his mid to late thirties. The man stared at Jim, and was also drinking a draft beer from a frosted mug.

When the man lifted his glass toward Jim in a friendly gesture of acknowledgment, Jim's heart felt like it skipped a beat. The expression on the man's face was one of empathy, and Jim found that odd. It was like the man knew everything Jim was going through because he had been through it too. Jim raised his glass toward the man to return the gesture, then finished his beer in several long gulps. Still staring at the man, Jim set his empty mug on the bar. The man grinned, and Jim forced a return smile.

Something about the cordial individual had Jim suddenly on edge. He made himself look away from the stranger. He'd had enough shitty experiences with people he didn't know this year. Though there had only been one other, one was a count too high, considering the circumstances.

Jim stared at his empty glass, but felt the man was still watching him.

The bartender came with a fresh beer-filled frosted mug with a smile, saying, "Here ya go," and took the empty one away with her.

Intentionally ignoring the stranger, Jim took a swig from the mug. His mind was already buzzing from the previous two brews. He forced himself to look up at the televisions and saw the sports news was playing on a short loop. He'd been here less than a half hour, and already they were showing highlights from the Braves/Mets game again.

It's not your fault, a voice inside his head told him. A male voice, but not *Jim's* voice.

It is my fault, Jim disagreed with the voice. *I could have stopped it. I could have saved them.*

You didn't know.

I was warned.

You can fix it.

It's too late.

You can save him still.

Jim finished the beer off in one long drink. When he set the mug down, he did so with a little too much force. The heavy mug made a loud pop, but didn't break. He yanked his hand away from it and stared through the empty, sweaty glass. He looked at it as if it might offer solutions, or at least consultation. But it was just an empty mug, and Jim suddenly realized he was drunk. The room spun a little. He focused on the mug and brought the room back to stabilization.

The televisions: Todd and Alice running around in the backyard again. Once more laughing and being joyous.

The waitress brought him another beer, took the empty one.

The motor oil commercial again.

The house on fire.

Alice holding Todd in her arms. *You fucking knew and did nothing.*

The other voice, the unfamiliar male one, said, *You can still save him.*

Jim whispered, "I didn't know."

Alice, holding their burned and dead son: *You fucking knew.*

The strange male voice in his head: *You didn't know.*

"I knew," Jim mumbled as he stared at yet another empty glass.

Jim snapped out of his trance and looked across the room again. The man was gone. Jim realized he hadn't seen the man walk past him toward the exit. It was as if he had only imagined the stranger. He blinked his eyes several times, and the table where the man had sat was still vacant. There was no empty glass on the table. There was a salt and pepper shaker, a full napkin holder, and three chairs pulled to the table. *Had there been a man?* The table looked clean and untouched. *But how much of a mess does one make while having just a beer?* The table could look that clean if someone had or had not briefly sat at it.

Jim wiped his mouth with his hand; then he blinked several times and looked again. The table was still empty. Nobody sat there now, and it was likely nobody had been there when Jim thought he saw a friendly stranger toasting him from afar.

Jim touched his smartphone, bringing to life the screen and the digital clock on it: 3:27 a.m. The server came to him and saw his mug was empty. "Last call. You gonna want another one?"

Jim watched her as she spoke but didn't answer immediately. He realized he might give the impression that he was drunk, and finally said, "No, I... I'm done."

"I'll get your card and your bill." She then turned around to the same keyboard and monitor as before.

While she was calculating his bill and running his card, Jim glanced around the bar in search of the strange man with the suit and tie. There were four younger men playing pool in a back corner, and he recognized all of them as coworkers. On the other side of the bar, an older guy with gray hair sat with a shot glass, his eyes obviously blood-shot even from a distance, looking up at the TV monitors. Across the opposite side of the room from where the stranger had sat, a man and a woman, both middle-aged, sat at a table facing each other, both with a beer bottle in front of them, conversing heavily as if the rest of the world didn't exist.

Jim looked behind himself, and saw only the exit door, and the darkness of night beyond it. The stranger was either gone or hadn't even existed to begin with. Yet, Jim had seen that man as a solid form, not a distorted piece of reality. If Jim was hallucinating, wouldn't other things seem off or blurry too? And why the hell would he imagine a character he'd never seen, or at least remembered seeing, in his life? Why *that* character? Why that suit and that tie? Why the neat dark-brown hair and the smooth face? If it was an illusion concocted by Jim's mind, why was it such a well-groomed vision? Could it be the alcohol? Beer didn't cause hallucinations. Sure, it made things sway and spin sometimes, but creating characters and placing them in real life wasn't something booze was known for.

He wondered for a moment whether he was dreaming, and mentally backtracked through his day. Waking up to have coffee and seeing Alice in her garden. The jailhouse and his confrontation with Billy Wagner. The work shift. Driving to the bar.

Jim watched the waitress turn toward him and lay a receipt, an ink pen, and his credit card on the bar.

"Just need your signature."

Without looking at the receipt total, Jim signed it. He then pulled his wallet out and laid a five-dollar bill over the receipt.

"Thanks," he said, obvious confusion in his tone as he packed his card in his wallet, and then his wallet in his pants pocket. He then pulled his keys out of another pocket but glanced across the room once more in search of the strange man.

"You good to drive?" the waitress asked.

The man was still vanished, though Jim had expected him to be there, holding a full beer mug toward Jim in that same friendly gesture. Jim answered the waitress without looking away from that far-off empty table. "Yes. I'm good. Just a lot on my mind." He then looked at her, forced a smile, and turned to leave.

Chapter Fifteen

The moment he climbed into his car and started it, Jim realized he might actually be too inebriated to drive. He had almost lost his balance and leaned slightly into the other seat, but caught himself before doing so. He was sloppy putting the key into the ignition. And when the car fired up, he hesitated for several long moments. The radio was muted, as it had been for weeks.

Nowadays, he preferred to drive in silence. Especially at night. Night driving, the breeze coming through the window and massaging his face, the silence of a sleeping city, had been therapeutic in short bursts as he drove home after work. Sometimes he wished it was always summer and always nighttime. It provided the solace he needed to ponder, but the warm weather was still there, even without sunlight. It was the most comfortable outside conditions of the year.

And it was even better when the sky was clear and the moon was on the other side of the planet, its light not outshining the view of space and its millions of stars. Though even that intriguing sight had lost its effect as of late. Now when Jim looked up during the night, instead of wondering how many of those stars might have orbiting planets with abundant or intelligent life, he thought of his son and his family, no longer bound to the earth with physical bodies, but maybe, instead, exploring all of existence in a form not restricted by gravity or other laws of physics.

Jim had never believed in any such things, but now he hoped he was wrong. He hoped that death was a route to transcendence and enlightenment, and that this life was only the beginning of something that was more eternal and freeing.

Finally, he felt steady enough to drive. Jim put the car in reverse, backed out of the parking spot, and pulled out of the lot onto the street.

***

Because of the location of the bar, Jim decided to take the back roads home. There was likely to be less of a chance of getting pulled over by law enforcement if he made any driving errors on that route. It was one long road with train tracks to the right and an occasional house or side road to the left. Then a series of turns, another slightly long road off which was the neighborhood where the burned-down house was.

Jim hadn't visited that spot since the fire, but Alice had done so at least once a week. Jim assumed Alice thought she was doing good for herself, releasing the grief in small increments by returning to the scene of the tragedy. But he'd tried to convince her to stop going there for now. That it was only worsening her sorrow, and she was actively engaging in self-torture. However, she was too far gone to listen to anyone's advice, and with each day, her heart and soul mourned even more than the previous one.

A fog had fallen on the area, and Jim drove into it on that long back road. He found it somewhat odd that from the parking lot of the bar, it had been a perfectly clear night. But the moment he turned onto the main street, a thick mist seemed to suddenly be present. Almost as if the fog itself stayed on the road intentionally, following its own path to a specific destination. Though strange, Jim dismissed his notice of the phenomena and focused more on the road, the yellow broken lines in the middle, and the white line to his right. Now that he was in motion, he realized he shouldn't be driving; he had consumed too much alcohol.

He was thankful it was only a seven-mile trip from the bar to home, because a much longer route might put him at risk of catching a DUI charge or worse, crashing into something. His head felt off-balance even while sitting in the driver's seat. With both hands on the steering wheel, he fought for focus and the ability to maintain a straight line while he drove. He wasn't sure how many draft beers he had consumed, but he was well aware it was at least one or two too many. He should have gone straight home after work, but damn it, he needed that buzz. Even for just an hour or two, he wanted to loosen up and feel better.

This was not comfortable, though, driving carefully through heavy fog, trying to maintain control of the car while obviously intoxicated. If a deer ran out in front of him, his reflexes would be slow. If he crashed, even into a deer, he would likely be in deep shit. A cop would come along, stop to check whether Jim was okay, and notice Jim's slurring speech. So now, just on that dreadful thought, he slowed the car even more. If he'd stayed sober, he could have flown through this distorted obstruction without care. He would have been safe at home quicker.

"Never again," he whispered to himself, and realized he had difficulty even just saying two words without them sounding like inebriated babbling.

There was a loud pop. It sounded as though someone had shot a gun at him. At the same time, he temporarily lost control of the steering wheel. In the middle of the digital speedometer, a flashing warning advised him he had low air pressure in one of his tires. A thumping sound, something pounding at the road's pavement. The car wanted to go left, and Jim fought to steady it.

"Fuck," he mumbled.

A tire had blown. From the feel of the car, it was the back left one. *Thump thump thump thump thump.* The pounding of the deflated tire on the road was so loud, Jim was almost certain occupants of any nearby homes would hear it even in their sleep, wake up, and come outside to investigate all the noise.

Twenty feet ahead, just on the threshold of visibility and the murkiness of the heavy fog, there was a narrow shoulder. Jim guided the car to it, pulled over, and threw it in park. He slammed one hand against the steering wheel while muttering, "Shit. Damn it. Shit."

The sudden situation seemed to have sobered him up somewhat, because his mind cleared. He knew he had to get out and get a spare tire on in a hurry. If a pedestrian or a police officer came along, even if Jim kept his cool, they might smell the alcohol on him. Alcohol had a stronger fragrance to those who had not been drinking while they were around someone who had been. He didn't need to add to the current stress with a drinking and driving charge.

He turned the car off, but left the key in the ignition and turned on the emergency flashers. After doing so, he thought for a moment. Those flashers might bring unwanted attention. But leaving them off with the car parked on this narrow of a shoulder, and in a thick fog, could prove more dangerous. He elected to leave them on, flashing and ticking in a near annoying rhythm. Next, he reached forward and pushed a button to pop the trunk open. He heard the trunk click, sighed, and got out of the car.

It was the left rear wheel. As he walked beside the car, he stopped and looked down. The tire had blown so powerfully that some of it was shredded. It was completely deflated, with no hope of repair. The power from the blowout had taken the tire from the rim and forced it backward into its wheel bay. There was a strong, unpleasant smell of burned rubber in the air and Jim wondered whether he'd run something over or the tire was just bad. He did little driving besides commuting back and forth to work, and he'd just replaced all four tires only a year ago. Jim stood there, staring at the rearranged tire for a few moments before heading to the back of the car.

He pulled the trunk up, then the inside floor panel, revealing the spare. Attached to it was the jack that came with the car. He picked up the jack and set it on the ground. Next, he pulled the spare tire out and placed it behind the car. There was something missing: the lug wrench. Feeling sudden anxiety, he realized if he didn't have the one tool needed to change a tire, he would have to call a damn tow truck.

He lowered the floor panel and glanced around the empty trunk. The tool was not in there. He lifted the floor panel again. Nothing. He slammed the panel down with frustration and looked at the jack on the street shoulder's pavement, thinking maybe the tire iron was attached to it. It wasn't. He looked at the spare tire leaning against the back of the car: just the tire. No tool attached or screwed to it.

"Jesus."

Trunk wide open, jack and wheel on the ground, he stood there, staring at the back of the car for a few moments. If he had any luck at all, it was bad luck. Of all the nights he chose to have a few drinks before driving home, it had to be the one he would end up helpless on the side of the road. This could have happened at any other time and it would only be a minor inconvenience. Now, though, he was buzzed. He wasn't completely drunk, but he was intoxicated enough to draw suspicion from a police officer or even a tow truck driver. If he called for a tow, the responding person might not give a damn that Jim smelled like alcohol and had been driving. But, if he ended up dealing with some do-gooder, self-appointed outstanding citizen, this already awful night would get worse. He had no choice but to call Alice, who was likely deep into an alcohol-induced slumber, and have her come get him. He could only hope she hadn't been drinking too. Otherwise, he might have a long walk ahead of him. He was at least five or six miles from home. Although that wasn't a ridiculously long distance in a car, on foot, it would take at least a couple of hours.

He went to the driver's side of the car, leaned in the open door, and retrieved his smartphone from the passenger seat. He unlocked the screen, but it only dimly lit up. The screen remained faint as he tapped it, thinking it hadn't unlocked properly. The top right corner of the screen showed the phone battery only had one percent charge remaining. In a near panic, he frantically tapped on the contacts icon. It opened, and at the top in the search bar, he typed Alice's name. As soon as he hit the Call button, the screen went black. A message popped up, telling him to connect his phone to a charger, and then it powered off.

This was it. This was the moment he completely went over the edge. After everything that had happened in the past several weeks, this moment finally snapped him. Rage flowed through him, cocktailed with frustration and despair. He faced the direction from which he'd driven to this point and launched the phone with all his strength into the fog. Jim didn't wait to hear its impact against the pavement, likely exploding into several pieces.

He turned to the car again and pounded his fists numerous times against the hood, so hard that two small dents appeared, while screaming at the top of his lungs. When he ran out of breath, he paused, then screamed again while once more crashing his fists against the car. An adult temper-tantrum. There was no more patience left in him. The powerful man he tried to portray had given up. It was his turn to lose it. His time to snap. He had no more emotional resolve remaining. This was his tipping point.

After punching his car as if it caused every problem he'd ever endured in life, he folded his arms on top of it, rested his face in them, and cried. He cried hard, sobbing and wailing, inhaling and exhaling in bursts of hopeless emotion. The tears dropped from his eyes as if a dam had finally burst behind the pressure of life's trials. Everything Jim Radcliffe had bottled up for so long was now released into this cruel world of helpless circumstances and unjust consequences.

There was no fairness and there was no hope for ultimate happiness. Everything good always ended and was followed by everything bad. Trying was futile and proudly walking through every obstacle only resulted in a beating that even the strong couldn't help but succumb to eventually. His son. His daughter-in-law. His granddaughter. His wife. And now, himself. He wasn't strong at all and had only been faking it. He raised his head from his arms and looked around, tears falling.

The fog was a perfect representation of his life. He'd do anything to go back to that night. *Anything*. To save the ones he loved so dearly, he would do any damn thing. *Billy Wagner*... Had he been right? If he was, then what did Jim have to do to be allowed to go back and pull them from that fire? *Anything*.

"I'll do anything," Jim said in between sobs, staring back toward the fog. His emergency flashers reflected against the wall of mist, a consistent reminder that his life was in complete chaos. The flashers not only represented a broken-down car, but a broken-down man as well. A man without hope. A man who would do *anything*.

"Anything," Jim said to the fog. "Just tell me what I have to do. Just tell me." He sobbed again, regained himself, and then screamed, "*Anything! I'll do anything!*"

He heard something in the distance. A low rumbling in the direction he'd come from. Dim side-by-side lights. A vehicle. It was moving slowly, the driver obviously being cautious in the low visibility. Jim realized at the moment he'd heard the vehicle's low rumbling engine, he had held his breath. If it was a police officer, he was screwed. Though his little tantrum had seemed to sober him up by route of increased adrenaline, he was still buzzed.

Anticipation stole the moment from despair. Jim wanted to turn his emergency flashers off, but it was too late. The approaching driver had likely already seen them, and if they halted, that would be more cause for suspicion. It would imply somebody didn't want to be seen, and blatant hiding drew attention over casualness.

The vehicle continued to approach, taking shape in the fog. It was obviously a truck. The cab took form, and Jim realized the driver wasn't just moving slowly, but with extreme caution. Not from the fog, but also from noticing the emergency beacons of Jim's car. Either the driver was planning to pass, rubbernecking along the way, or the driver was going to pull over and offer help. Jim hoped for the latter and focused on the nearing truck, as if he might have some kind of a psychic superpower that would sway destiny in his favor.

But in the weeks leading up to this moment, destiny had treated Jim and his loved ones as if they were of no more use to the universe.

The truck finally emerged fully from the fog, and Jim saw a crane protruding from the back and above the cab. It was a tow truck. It slowed even more; its emergency flashers came on, and it pulled off to the side of the road and came to a stop. Jim could see the driver faintly through a dirty windshield and assumed it was a man.

Jim was relieved. Surely someone driving a tow truck would have a lug wrench with them. He could change the tire and be on his way if the man wanted to help. If the driver smelled the stench of alcohol on Jim's breath, however, this chance meeting could still go way wrong. Hopefully, the stranger now opening his driver's side door was only partly a good Samaritan. If anything, maybe he was just looking for a late-night dollar, and he would charge Jim for assistance. That was fine, too. Jim would pay him, change the damn tire, and get home. At this point, the top goal was avoiding a DUI, and the second was getting to bed. His buzz was wearing off, and his body and mind felt exhausted.

The man stepped onto the pavement of the road, the tow truck parked in the grass behind the shoulder Jim's car sat broken down on. A chill suddenly ran down Jim's spine. His entire body trembled for just a moment at the peculiarity of what he was now seeing. He didn't believe his eyes at first, blinked them several times as if to clear up the foggy scenery, and then stared in awe.

The man was the same one from the bar. The one who had toasted Jim from across the room. The perfectly neat black suit and the red tie. A tow truck driver wearing formal attire threw Jim's assumptions so far off he thought he might tilt and fall over. The man wore dress shoes, which clicked against the road's pavement as he walked. Click, clack; click, clack.

The stranger's face was stoic as he approached, and when he stopped just a few feet from Jim and looked down at the tire, his expression changed to one of concern. He looked away from the flat tire, around as if he took in the view for pleasure, at Jim again, and said, "Well, this isn't good."

Jim hesitated, then forced a reply through his shocked demeanor. "I... Yeah... A damn flat on the way home from work. Turns out I don't have a tire iron. I have the spare, but—"

"Yes, I see the spare. You're in luck, Jim. I have a wrench you can use."

Instantly on guard, his jaw dropped. "How... How do you know my name?"

The man smiled almost devilishly and answered, "I know a lot of names, Jim. I'm in the business of knowing names."

"You were at the bar."

"Yes, I was. It's a nice little late-night place. Good music. I loved the '80s."

That statement surprised Jim because the man looked no older than his mid-thirties. The '80s ended over thirty years ago. He didn't seem old enough to remember such a distant decade.

"What business are you in?" Jim asked. "I mean...knowing a lot of names?"

The stranger looked curiously at Jim, then smiled and gestured toward the tow truck.

"Oh, shit, yeah," Jim said nervously. "Right, right."

The man's face became serious again, and he sighed. After a pause, he said, "You have more problems than just this flat tire."

It wasn't a question, and Jim was thrown off his mental balance yet again. "Other problems?"

"I'm sorry for your losses, Jim. It's an emotionally exhausting thing you're going through. I offer my condolences."

"What?"

"Your son and his family. So tragic. They were so young. Such good people. It's a damned shame God allows such things to happen. Free will and all that shit."

"Who *are* you? How do you know about that?"

"A tragic fire. Faulty wiring. The carelessness of humans often causes the demise of others. We are such a narcistic breed."

Jim wasn't sure whether he should be appreciative, angry, or in awe. His bottom lip trembled, and he wanted to say something, anything, but no words came. He stood there, staring at the man, trying to recognize him from somewhere other than the bar. But the man was unfamiliar. He didn't look like any family members or coworkers Jim knew. He wasn't a neighbor. At least he wasn't any of the neighbors Jim was familiar with. Who the hell was he?

"Are you okay, Jim?" The man looked closely at Jim, as if examining his psychological state.

"Who are you?" Jim finally asked.

The man smiled as if victorious, as if he'd been waiting for Jim to ask that very question, and replied, "I like to go by Mr. Brimstone. Seems to be quite fitting. My full name is too long. A tongue twister of sorts, if you will. My friends call me by so many different ones, but I like Mr. Brimstone, so I go by that one when asked."

"That's an odd name."

"Well, *Jim,* not everyone is named so commonly." The man grinned again, this time as if he was trying to settle Jim's nerves with friendliness.

"A tow truck driver in a suit and tie? Dress shoes?" As Jim spoke, he looked down at Mr. Brimstone's feet, then glanced back up to meet the stranger's gaze.

"I like to appear professional. I *am* a professional."

"Can you help me?" Jim sharply asked. He was beyond uncomfortable now and wanted this meeting to conclude.

"Of course I can help you. That's why I stopped."

"So, do you have a lug wrench?"

"You need more help than just a lug wrench."

Quickly, Jim snapped, "Well, a lug wrench is all I'm asking for right now. Can you help me or not?"

"You have time. No police officer will ride through here for another two hours and twelve minutes. You don't have to worry about a drunk driver charge or jail tonight. Besides, you've already sobered up. You would pass any sobriety test given to you."

Becoming irritated and impatient, Jim retorted, "You're obviously some kind of scam artist. A tow truck driver with a suit and tie. You followed me to a bar. I've heard about people like you. You find people who are desperate and use their own shortfalls to line your pockets. If you're not going to help me change my tire, then go on. I'll walk."

Mr. Brimstone's eyes widened as if he were shocked by Jim's sudden rudeness, but it was obvious to Jim the man was pretending to be taken aback. When Mr. Brimstone spoke, Jim detected mockery.

"Oh, now, Jim. Why be so snappy toward someone trying to help you? That's not polite at all. Especially considering the things I can do for you."

"I just need my tire changed, man. That's it. I need my tire changed, and I want to be home in bed, sleeping off this fucked-up night. That's all I need."

"No, it's not," Mr. Brimstone replied calmly and confidently. "You need more than just a tire, and I can help you."

"Help me with *what?*" Jim snapped again.

"Your son." Mr. Brimstone smiled.

It wasn't a comforting smile, but the smirk of someone about to pull a sinister scam on an unsuspecting victim.

Yet when those words came from the mysterious stranger's mouth, Jim shuddered. "Look, mister, I don't know who you are, but if you don't have a lug wrench, you can get back in that truck and drive away. I'm not up for tricks tonight or any night."

"This isn't a trick. It's a deal I'm offering you. A straightforward deal. Your son for your soul."

Jim's eyes widened, and he backed up, intentionally creating more distance between himself and this strange character. "Just leave, man. People like you are why the world sucks. Looking to make a dollar on someone else's pain. Just please go."

"You don't believe me." It wasn't a question.

"Yeah, I see where you're going with this. Mr. Brimstone, eh? That's your name or the name you've chosen. Whatever, man. I have to get home." Jim turned toward the fog ahead and swiveled back to face Mr. Brimstone. "I guess I'm going to lock up and walk it."

"Why would you walk?" Mr. Brimstone nodded toward the back tire.

When Jim followed the gesture, he gasped, stumbled backward, and narrowly avoided falling on his ass. The tire was repaired. It wasn't the spare tire, but the one which was blown nearly to bits only moments ago. It was in one piece, attached to the rim, fully inflated and looking nearly brand-new. Jim couldn't believe his eyes and blinked them several times. Then he went to the tire, bent down beside it, touched it, and ran a hand along the tread. He put a hand on each side of the tire and tried to shake it forward and backward. It was solid on the rim, as if it had never blown out to begin with. Still crouched down, Jim looked up at Mr. Brimstone in amazement, as if he'd just watched a miracle performed.

"How?" Jim asked as he stood up, face-to-face and only inches from Mr. Brimstone.

"I can do things, Jim. Spectacular things. Fantastic things. Unbelievable...things."

"I don't believe it." Jim glanced from Mr. Brimstone to the tire and back to Mr. Brimstone again. "It must not have been flat."

"Oh, it was flat. It's just not anymore. No lug wrench or spare tire needed. Like I said, I can do things."

"What the fuck are you?"

"Let's not get into that right now." Mr. Brimstone was still grinning.

Jim couldn't tell whether the man was entertained by the trickery he was playing on Jim, or whether the man was simply proud of the feats he could accomplish in, evidently, the blink of an eye.

"You're some kind of magician. One of those street guys who can play tricks with distraction and well-setup stunts. But I never really took my eyes off you. Just for a few moments." Jim was in deep thought as he spoke, thumbing through memories of the last several minutes. A flat tire. The fog. An odd person arrives. The tire *had* been flat. Jim remembered hearing it blow. It had sounded like a shotgun blast. There was no mistaking what had occurred, yet there was the tire on the rim, undamaged.

Mr. Brimstone reached inside his suit and produced a folded-up piece of paper and a crimson-red item with a blade protruding from the end. It looked like something someone might use to poke their finger just before testing their blood on a diabetic strip. He stepped to Jim's car, unfolded the paper, and put it on the hood. He then laid the poker beside it. The man turned to Jim. "This is the contract. You poke your finger and press the blood drops on the signature line at the bottom. That is how you sign a contract with me. Your soul for your son. You will be allowed to save him, but when your life ends, you will come with me forever. Once you sign, there is no turning back. So I suggest you think it over."

"What the hell?" Jim whispered.

"It's quite simple, Jim. Your son will live again. Your soul will be mine. There's no trick to it. Those are the only terms. You save your son, and I get your soul. Do you understand?"

Jim looked at the paper on the hood of his car in amazement. He was awe-struck. He thought of Billy Wagner and his prophetic warnings. Had crazy Billy been right? Had he dreamt this scenario weeks ago? They had all thought Billy was a drug-addicted nutjob, but now it seemed as if he wasn't off his rocker at all. Now it seemed Billy knew exactly what he was talking about.

"You save your son, and I get your soul," Mr. Brimstone repeated.

Suddenly, awe transformed into anger. Jim's demeanor changed as quickly as a beautiful spring day could become a dark and stormy one. This asshole standing in front of him, pretending to be the devil, it seemed, had just rubbed Jim the wrong way. Aside from what seemed like something out of a novel with the repaired tire, this jerk was using Jim's grief against him for pure entertainment. He wasn't asking for money, but Jim's soul instead. Jim knew now he was dealing with a higher level of senselessness than just Billy Wagner.

Jim pulled the piece of paper off the car, and without reading it, wadded it up into a ball and tossed it into the fog. He then picked up the poker and threw it in the same direction. To Jim's surprise, Mr. Brimstone stood with the same calm and cool expression as he had this entire encounter. The weirdo seemed unaffected by Jim's sudden aggression.

"I'm going home now. I don't know how you did the tire thing, and I don't care anymore. I'm going home to get some sleep. In the meantime, you can fuck off with your tricks, your games, your preying on someone in their most distraught moments. You can fuck right off."

Jim moved to enter his car, but Mr. Brimstone stopped him with words. "You might want this too."

Jim turned to look at Mr. Brimstone and saw he was pulling something else from a pocket inside his suit jacket. Something that looked like a smartphone. He extended it toward Jim. Jim didn't move but stared curiously.

"Take it. It's yours," Mr. Brimstone said.

"A phone?"

"*Your* phone."

Jim looked past Mr. Brimstone toward the fog behind them, where he had angrily thrown his smartphone in a fit of frustration. There was no way it survived that throw. It had traveled into the fog beyond Jim's sight. Too long a travel, and most definitely too powerful an impact on the street, for the device to be in one piece. The only way it could have been saved by Mr. Brimstone was if he'd actually stuck his hand out of the truck cab, while driving through the fog, and caught it. To Jim, that seemed beyond impossible.

Jim stepped away from the car and took the phone from Mr. Brimstone. He examined it for a moment, flipping it over and faceup again. He touched the screen to unlock it. The screen shined brightly, with no visible cracks from an impact, and in the top right corner the charge indicator said the phone's battery was at one hundred percent. The background picture was of Jim and Alice taking a selfie with the ocean and sunset behind them. In the electronic portrait, Jim was obviously holding the phone. This had been his background picture for years. He looked at it with sadness, because he hadn't seen Alice smile like that in what seemed like ages.

Another feeling suddenly overcame him: fear. His mind filled with the sensation of warning and an abrupt need for self-preservation. He felt something malicious, as if the surrounding air had suddenly become infected with evil. He sensed a profound badness. Jim looked at Mr. Brimstone, who still stood there without emotion, waiting for something. Waiting for Jim to offer him a soul for a saved life. Jim wanted to believe this man before him was just another lunatic in a world full of them, but there was something more, something deep and sinister.

Without saying another word, he turned once more to climb into his car. As Jim sat in the driver's seat and laid the smartphone on the passenger's side, Mr. Brimstone was suddenly standing next to the open door as if he'd teleported those few feet from his original position instead of walking them. Jim's fear grew. It was no longer a simple warning his instincts issued to him. He was becoming terrified. He started the car and reached out to pull the door shut, but Mr. Brimstone was already holding the handle from the outside.

"When you change your mind, Jim, simply shout out to me."

Jim tugged on the door, but it didn't budge from Mr. Brimstone's firm grasp.

"I'll be around. Just say my name. You can say it calmly or scream it; it doesn't matter."

Jim yanked the door with all his strength, but Mr. Brimstone had loosened his grip, and the door slammed shut with a force that made Jim flinch.

"Go home to your wife, Jim. She needs you," Mr. Brimstone said calmly through the open window.

Jim threw the car in drive and stomped the gas pedal to the floor. Tires spun and the engine grunted with effort as he sped off, leaving black tread marks from the shoulder into the street. As he drove away, he looked in his rearview mirror to see whether Mr. Brimstone was going to pursue, and lost his breath to astonishment.

There was no tow truck. There was no Mr. Brimstone. They had both vanished.

Jim nervously looked ahead and realized he was easing into the on-coming lane, pulled the car back to the right with a jerk, and checked his rearview mirror again. Fog. Nothing but blinding, mysterious fog.

Chapter Sixteen

Jim sat in his running car in front of the charred skeleton of a place that had once been the home of a growing family. After leaving the mysterious tow truck driver on the side of the road, the man in the black suit and the red tie who seemed to have vanished into nonexistence, he'd headed toward home. But that route took him past the neighborhood where his son and *his* family once lived and ultimately perished in.

Jim couldn't resist pulling in, driving to the fire-destroyed house, and parking on the edge of the property. A cleanup crew had obviously been here, because when the natural gas exploded during the fire, it had sent pieces of the home flying in all directions. Construction of the two homes on each side had to stop because of the damage from the blast. The debris from the disaster was gone, but the shell of the home remained. The building had several blast openings in it, where it looked almost like an ancient brick structure uncovered by an archaeological expedition. All glass was gone, and the windows were just openings now. The front door was no longer a neatly designed entrance, but a sloppy opening through which any person or venturing stray animals might wander. The roof was nearly completely gone, except for the right side, where it was obvious something powerful had blown most of it away.

Jim wondered whether they were in there. Obviously not physically, but maybe in spirit form. That idea was beyond his usual beliefs, but now he wanted so badly to open his mind to the possibility of an afterlife. Maybe, in a parallel dimension, they were in that house. Todd, Beth, and their newborn daughter, living their lives as if nothing happened. From the point of the explosion, maybe they passed on to somewhere they could continue forward, continue to grow and prosper in love and happiness.

To Jim, it was unlikely, but maybe he didn't know as much as he thought he did. Nobody had ever returned from death to tell the story of the other side. Well, there were no stories that could be proved. Sure, there had been probably millions of near-death experiences documented throughout history, yet those had been without proof. Nobody had left this life for days, ventured entirely into the realm of the dead, and come back to talk about it. Jim wanted so badly to believe it was possible, but when his mind leveled out and rationality returned, he realized his son was still dead, still buried in a plot with his wife and unborn child.

Jim got out of the car and left it running. He walked away without pushing shut the driver's side door. He walked through the front yard toward the home and stopped halfway there. Staring at the house, he observed the damage for a few moments, and continued forward. The front porch was no longer. Instead, there was a bare spot against the house and on the ground where it had been. The distance from the ground into the entrance was at shoulder height for Jim. He stepped closer and peered inside with his hands on the doorway threshold.

It was dark, quiet, but still somehow smelled like something burning, as if the fire were still active, or at least smoldering. That obviously couldn't be because it had been weeks since the disaster. He took a deep breath, as if he tried to clear his sense of smell. He slowly exhaled, waited, then breathed in again. The air wasn't fresh, but it didn't smell like something burning anymore. There was a staleness in the air that he took in. The odor of something sitting and rotting for ages. Although it wasn't fresh air, it was better than the smell of continuing, flaming destruction. This was a more settled fragrance, and Jim welcomed it as if it were clean spring air.

And then, as he stood there looking into the darkness, came a voice from inside the house. The voice of a man. The tow truck driver said from within the shadows, "You're wasting your time here. They are gone. Your wife needs you now."

Jim stepped back. He waited a few moments for the voice to speak again, and it did.

"Go home to your wife, Jim."

Jim stepped forward, put his hands back on the threshold, and looked into the darkness. He expected to see a male figure's shadow, but there was nothing. It was as if the voice was that of the air instead of a physical person.

"We can make the deal here if you'd like," said the voice.

It seemed to come from the center of the living room, only a few feet from where Jim stood. He squinted, tried to adjust his sight to the darkness so he could at least see a form, but there was nothing.

"I still have the papers," came the voice.

"What are you?" Jim whispered.

"I'm a dealmaker. You need only sign with your blood, and you can save him. But right now, you are wasting valuable time. Go home if you're not here to sign."

Jim glanced around. To the left, to the right, behind him. He was looking for the tow truck. Obviously, the strange character had beaten Jim to the house, but where was his truck? It wasn't on the street or visible on any of the surrounding properties. *Where was the damn truck?*

"He's not in this house, Jim. You know where your son is. There is no point in this self-torture."

Jim trembled. His hands were sweating and his knees felt as if they were about to buckle. He felt weak, as if suddenly struck with absolute exhaustion. He looked back through the doorway and searched desperately for any human form again. Still, there was none. Yet he felt another presence. It wasn't just the man's voice Jim heard, but he felt something, some kind of other consciousness, was there with him. And the more Jim felt that presence, the more afraid he became.

This thing talking to him from thin air was not of this world. It was not human, and it did not play by the same rules as humans did. It was an entity of badness, wrongness, wickedness. Something playing on Jim's desperation and despair. Whatever it was, it didn't hold Jim's best interest at heart. Hell, the thing likely didn't have a heart. It didn't need one. Its life was sustained by a power beyond Jim's understanding. That's how it arrived here before Jim did. It didn't have to drive a vehicle. Predicting Jim's likely moves wasn't necessary. It simply knew everything, and it somehow came to this place because it wanted to. No physical transport was needed because this was a thing beyond the physical body.

Then, just as suddenly as the deity had arrived, the feeling of its presence disappeared. Like tension in a room relieving, it was as instantly gone as it had manifested. Jim knew he was alone again, yet he still shook with terror. The thing was no longer in the area, but it had left behind an impression on Jim's psyche.

Jim backed away from the house without realizing he was doing so. He stumbled, caught his balance, and turned toward the car. He walked quickly, making a getaway without running, as if he were trying to trick the strange man into believing he wasn't hurrying. Once to the car, Jim looked back at the house, and standing in the doorway was the man in the black suit and red tie. A vibration of terror shot through Jim's body. The man stood in the doorway, impassive. Jim looked away, and that took effort. It was as if he was being hypnotized for several long and agonizing moments. He hurried into the car, slammed the door shut, had to fight himself to not look toward the man again, threw the car in drive, and got the hell out of there.

Chapter Seventeen

J im drove home with urgency, ignoring speed limits and only pausing at stop signs. He ran the only remaining red light, gunning straight through an intersection. He pulled into his neighborhood as if he were a bank robber driving the getaway car: tires screeched, the engine revved. His hands were slippery on the steering wheel, but he drove recklessly anyhow. He worried that if he took his time, somehow the strange, evil man would beat him home. Jim had the terrifying suspicion the man was going to hurt Alice. Maybe not physically hurt her, but get into her head and deceive her into doing something awful to herself. Jim realized he believed that man might actually be the devil himself. The most wicked of all wicked. The evil who ruled all evil eternally. The one who offered favors for souls.

As Jim neared his house, he could see the garage door was open. It was never open. And when he pulled into the driveway and his headlights illuminated the inside of the garage, Jim could see it was empty. Alice's car was gone. As he threw the car in park and yanked the key from the ignition, he glanced toward the front door. The inside door was wide open. It was usually closed and locked when he came home from work. Alice never forgot to lock that door. Even since the tragedy that had made her into a grieving, irrational alcoholic, she still secured that door out of habit. Dread built within him. Not only was something off, it was way wrong. Something horrible had happened or was happening. The devil had beaten him home.

Jim dropped the car keys in the driveway and ran toward the house, up the front porch's stairs, yanked the screen door open, and rushed inside. The living room was dark as it usually was when he came home from work, but there was a feeling about the house. Something was off. His inner warning alarm was blaring so powerfully, he almost heard it.

He yelled for his wife. "Alice!"

Of course she wouldn't answer. She wasn't there. How could her car be gone while she was still at home? He merely hoped she would be present and that there would be an explanation for the absence of her vehicle. Maybe she'd broken down on the side of the road, called for a tow, had the car delivered to an auto shop, and then took a taxi home. Maybe she'd loaned it out to someone. No, that was absurd. There was nobody in her life who would need to borrow a car. Especially this late at night. She wasn't in the house.

Her pattern of drinking had been to get smashed on one day and then recover the next. It was a two-day cycle for her. Sometimes, she got so drunk she needed two days to bounce back, but there was never a third day of sobriety. If the pattern held, today was supposed to be a hangover day. She wouldn't feel well enough to leave the bed, much less the house. When he'd left for work, she was unconscious to her world of pain and suffering, so deep in slumber, she never stirred when he kissed her on the cheek before leaving.

Yet when she didn't reply, he yelled again, panic in his tone. "Alice!"

The kitchen light was on. Its glare offered enough illumination into the living room to create shadows and for him to see the room was empty of her presence. He went into the kitchen, sweating, breathing heavily, afraid. Alice didn't leave lights on. If she was in there and not answering him, she was likely passed out on the floor. He hoped that was the case. He begged fate to not let her be hurt. But fate had been unkind to him so far. It had been a merciless dictator, taking everything of value from Jim, and sending his life in a direction he'd never even dreaded because it seemed so impossible.

The kitchen was in order. The dining table was set with summer-themed placemats and a candle in the middle. The chairs were pushed neatly in. He looked from the table to the floor, expecting to find his wife passed out on it, snoring off another alcohol-induced unconsciousness. But she wasn't. The floor was clear. He rounded the counter, which extended outward from the wall, and the floor on the other side was empty. No wife. No Alice. He realized he was disappointed, because if he'd found her sleeping, it meant she was safe at home. Not seeing her made him fear the worst.

A toppled prescription pill bottle on the counter beside the sink. The lid was nowhere in sight. He glanced next to it, into the sink, and saw the empty bottle of bourbon and the pill bottle's lid beside it. His heart felt like a train moving so quickly, it was doomed to derail. He lifted the prescription bottle, and one pill rattled inside it. As he read the medicine's description, dread took over his soul. His eyes watered immediately as he thought the worst. These were her take-as-needed Valiums. On the side of the bottle below the description and recommended doses, warnings not to drive or operate a vehicle, as this medication may cause drowsiness. Below that, instructions to call 911 immediately in case of accidental overdose.

God, no.

"Please, no," he whispered as he tossed the pill bottle into the sink.

If she'd drank that full bottle of bourbon, gone into a fit of irrational depression, and taken the entire contents of the medication, she was in danger. Not just of sleeping too long or having an awful hangover when she woke up, but *her life* was in danger.

Then he saw it. The note hanging by means of a flower-shaped magnet on the refrigerator. It was a brief note, but it said enough.

Jim, I love you. I will always love you and I'm sorry. I can't do it anymore. I can't live like this. I will always love you.

He choked on tears and ripped the letter away from the magnet, which fell to the floor with a clang and a rattle. He wadded the note and stuffed it in his pocket. Jim left the kitchen in a full panic and ran to their bedroom. He flicked the light switch on and saw the bed was still unmade. The rest of the room was in order. He had hoped to find her on the bed so he could call for help and EMS could get here to save her. She was not in the bed or on the floor. He raced out of the bedroom, saying, "No, no, no," and checked the other bedrooms. Each one he ducked inside, flicked light switches on, and glanced around quickly. No Alice.

She'd gone somewhere. She'd gotten drunk, taken the pills, and left in her car.

Where?

She had two places she visited the most: Todd's burned-down shell of a house and the cemetery where he was buried. She hadn't been at the house, and Jim couldn't remember seeing any cars on the road as he came home from there. They would have passed each other. She had to be at the cemetery.

He hurried out of the house, leapt off the porch, picked his keys up from the driveway, and jumped into his car, the driver's door still open. His smartphone had been on the driver's side seat. He picked it up and called Alice's phone. It went straight to voicemail. Jim's hands trembled so frantically, he could barely hold the phone still as he hung up and hit the Call button on her contact again. Once more, Alice's voicemail greeting answered on the other end. He waited for it to play through; then after the beep, he said, "Alice. Alice, please answer the damn phone. Please, Alice. Fucking please!"

He called the contact again, and again the voicemail greeting played. Her phone was either dead or intentionally shut off. Every time he dialed the number, he was wasting urgently needed moments. She could be somewhere dying right now. Dying or already dead.

"Not this, Alice," he whispered, and dialed 911. He couldn't wait until he arrived at the cemetery to call for emergency services. For Alice, every second counted. It was only a five-minute drive from the house. Probably less while disobeying traffic laws.

"911. What's your emergency?" the male operator answered after half a ring.

"Resthaven Cemetery on Blackhill Road. Please hurry. My wife is there, and she's overdosed on medication. I'm on my way now. Just go to where you see the car headlights. Please hurry!!"

He set the phone down without hanging up and backed out of the driveway, hitting his mailbox and knocking it over, running it over, and hauled ass down the road in the race of his lifetime.

***

As he drove the back roads toward the cemetery, memories played through Jim's mind. Their wedding. Alice in her beautiful dress. They were so young. So many years ago, that moment would stand the grueling tests of time. Their marriage had been good. Great, even. Nothing was perfect, but in the realm of romantic relationships, theirs had been as close to perfection as possible. They had rarely fought, rarely even disagreed. Two people who not only got along, but flowed through passing time, hand in hand, as harmonic and in sync as the planets in their revolutions around the sun.

And just like the solar system, and all things in nature that live and work so perfectly, as if their symbiont existence was written by something or someone of high intelligence who wanted perfect, universal coexistence, Jim and Alice intertwined as one. He loved her genuinely, with his heart, mind, and soul. Everything within him was for her, and until their son's death, there was never any doubt Alice felt the same.

It couldn't end like this. This couldn't be how things were meant to be. Tears rolled down Jim's face as he drove, holding the gas pedal once again to the floor, accelerating past the posted speed limits as if there were none. An oncoming car flashed its brights at Jim and a horn blew, its driver showing disapproval of Jim's current driving method. The brights illuminated his face, which showed a tortured expression. He wanted to scream and finally did. He screamed in anguish and sorrow. A long, excruciating shriek of frustration, grief, and even anger.

***

He pulled into the cemetery, through an entrance of memorial walls, and turned right. Now he was in the maze of curving paved arteries through the property. If he hadn't been to Todd's gravesite so many times, he would have surely gotten lost. But he knew exactly where it was. The double plot was on the edge of the back of the property to the south. Just ten feet from the headstone, a tall, thick pin oak tree stood, a crown of branches and twigs, alive with leaves, always begging Mother Nature for more sunlight. Jim remembered seeing that tree on the day of the funeral and had involuntarily forever marked pin oaks in his mind as a reminder of his son.

A left turn. Another left turn. Jim drove slower than he wanted now, as he could not take the chance of passing the gravesite where Alice might be. If her car was there, he should see it, but there were no streetlights or any other artificial illumination on the cemetery grounds. He could drive right past her car without even noticing it.

But he did see it. Up ahead. It was parked on the side of the pavement. The doors were closed, and it was shut off. That meant that when she arrived here, she was still aware enough to think somewhat clearly. She had turned the car off and shut the doors. If she was in a drunken stupor while also fighting the effects of an overdose, she would have left the car running with the doors open. Maybe even crawled out of it and to her son's grave.

Jim didn't bother to park properly behind her. He stopped the car in the middle of the roadway and jumped out. Leaving the car running and the driver's door open, he rushed toward the tree, toward his guide in the night, its tall, looming shadow beckoning him to the spot where he was urgently needed.

In the distance, Jim heard sirens. Likely the ambulance he'd called for. Several sirens approached, but too far off for relief. They weren't moving quick enough. Although he was glad there had obviously been no hesitation in response to his 911 call, he wished they had arrived right behind him. They would have to pull into the cemetery and find his spot. Hopefully, his car lights would guide them. The headlights and taillights had to be a bright and obvious beacon in this dark and dreaded place.

He saw the double tombstone, and a still shadow on the ground before it. Jim stumbled as he ran, stopped himself from falling, and raced forward. As he neared the shadow, it took a more defined form. A person laying on their front side, arms outstretched on the ground, legs together. The shape of a human sleeping on top of the burial site.

Jim stopped over Alice, who lay on the ground in the same night-gown she wore for days at a time, and fell to his knees beside her.

"Alice!"

She didn't respond to his voice.

He rolled her over. Her body was limp; her head bobbled and her arms flailed with the motion. Her eyes were closed, but not tightly. It was as if they had fallen shut and laid there, in something much deeper and more peaceful than just sleep.

"Alice, please," he begged as he gently slapped her face.

She still didn't respond.

The sirens grew louder. The emergency vehicles sounded as if they were just pulling into the cemetery, passing through the same entrance, in between memorial walls, as Jim had only moments ago.

Jim held his hand above Alice's nose. Her mouth was closed, so if she was breathing, it had to be through her nostrils. He begged the universe to let him feel the exhaling air from her, but the universe didn't reply in favor. There was no feeling of warm breath.

Stillness.

He leaned down, listened to her, and heard nothing.

"Alice!"

He gently slapped her face again.

"Please!"

She didn't move. No sign of life.

"Alice!"

He shook her.

The sirens moved closer. Jim turned to look back and saw flashing red, orange, yellow, blue lights. Several emergency vehicles approached. In the lead was an ambulance, behind it a fire truck, and behind that at least three police cars. They were a football field's length away. Too far. They needed to be here now.

Jim turned back to his wife, who he now scooped up into his arms, and pulled the upper half of her body to him. Her head was as loose as a newborn baby's. He moved his arm under it, lifted her face up toward him. He whimpered. He knew she wasn't breathing. In this moment, his wife was dead. Jim sobbed, pulled her closer, hugged her tightly. He was suddenly crying uncontrollably. Tears streamed from his face into her hair, her face against his neck. He squeezed her, as if he were saying goodbye but didn't want to. As if she were leaving on a trip they both knew she wouldn't return from.

The emergency sirens stopped. The ambulance and its entourage were now parked behind Jim's car. Doors were opening. People were yelling.

Jim held Alice close as he cried. "My wife," he whined. "Oh, God no. Alice, no."

He held her close, rocking back and forth, moaning.

A woman from somewhere behind him yelled, "Over here!"

Beams of light from flashlights on Jim, Alice, the double tombstone, the tree, the ground. More voices. Help had arrived on the scene, but they might be too late.

Chapter Eighteen

J im paced the full length of the hospital waiting room, while also trying to calm himself. Alice would be okay. She had to be. The hospital staff would likely pump her stomach, keep her on intravenous fluids for a couple of days, and then send her home with the recommendation of intense psychological therapy, or transport her straight from the hospital to a mental facility. If Jim was asked to sign papers forcing her into a mental hospital, then he would do so without hesitation. She might be irate with him initially, but she would thank him later for making such a tough decision. Considering she was now being rescued from a suicide attempt, she was obviously not currently in the right state of mind. Her depression had taken her to a depth of mental murkiness she could not simply surface from at will. She needed the most profound help available to her.

When they had brought her back to animation at the cemetery, she had not regained full consciousness, but by the time she was loaded into the ambulance, and one of the EMTs were instructing Jim that he could not ride with them but had to follow in his own vehicle, Alice was breathing. Her heart was pumping again. She had been rescued from death.

After arriving at the hospital, Jim was told to wait here, in this empty room with early-morning news playing, without volume, on two small flat-screen televisions in the upper corners on the opposite side of the room. He paced between them, and every time he walked to one corner, he'd look up at the TV for a few seconds, turn, and walk to the other one. He'd not called family yet. There was no need to wake everyone if Alice was going to be okay. Nobody else need be involved in knowing how low she'd actually sunk unless absolutely necessary. In a hurry, he'd left his smartphone and his keys in the car after parking in the attached parking garage anyhow. He couldn't call, and he wasn't leaving this place until he was sure of Alice's condition.

He'd paced for at least twenty minutes since arriving in a frantic mess and being told by a young, female staff member that Alice was being taken care of by the best, he should trust in God, and as soon as they had her stable, he would be informed. He forced positive thoughts through his mind, jammed them through the process of thought formation. But with each ticking minute—second—he found it more difficult to keep hope alive. She was breathing when they left the cemetery, so surely she was still doing so when they made it to the hospital. She had been under constant and close care by people who were trained and spent their lives saving lives, so she had to be okay.

Every time the hospital intercom sounded—someone paging someone else to call this extension, to please report to this floor, announcements on when the cafeteria was opening, Doctor so-and-so please call this or that station—Jim paused his pacing to listen, as if maybe someone might actually announce a direct message to him, letting him know his wife was alive and well and that he could now be at ease. Not a single announcement had anything to do with him or Alice, though, and he realized he was allowing himself to think in ridiculousness. There would be no announcement; the doctor would come out of one of these intensive care rooms, pull off his medical mask while removing his sterilized gloves, stethoscope hanging from his neck, and he would tell Jim Alice was stable and then give instructions on her next step of care.

Jim thought of his encounters with the character he now knew as Mr. Brimstone and wondered whether he should have just taken the deal. It sounded crazy then, but now, in a dire moment of desperation, maybe it was crazy ideas that might pull him and Alice through these dark times. Just like the night of Todd's death, when Jim had nearly taken the route by his son's house on the way home from work but didn't, and devastating consequences resulted, maybe by not taking the deal with Mr. Brimstone, Jim had allowed fate to once more take a piece from his life, which weeks ago, had been in content order.

Two different times, two decisions to go this way instead of that, to not do this or that, to not second-guess his own intuition, may have led to tragedies which didn't have to occur. Somehow, it all unraveled to his fault. Things he did, or didn't do, which brought him to this moment here and now. A dead son and a nearly successful suicide attempt by his wife. If Alice survived this moment, if she lived through it and they had at least a fighting chance toward a happy life again, then Jim would promise that from now on, when a thought entered his mind, he would act on it. He realized he must have been ignoring some sort of instinct. He would never do that again. Jim swore that, now to himself, to the powers that be, to his wife.

He paced across the room, and when he turned around after once again looking up at a flat-screen television, he saw what looked to be a male doctor walking down a corridor toward the waiting room. It was an older male with thick gray hair in operating scrubs, his mask hanging around his neck. His expression was one of sorrow. Jim froze, and his heart sank into his stomach. He had been looking forward to seeing a doctor walking toward him, but now he wanted to close his eyes, squeeze them shut, and will the doctor away.

The doctor walked toward Jim, looking Jim straight in his eyes. There was no mistaking the doctor's gaze. It was one of regret. The face of a man who was about to inform another man that his wife had just passed away in a hospital bed or on an operating table.

Jim stood like a concrete statue, his demeanor one of dread, and the doctor stopped just a couple of feet away from him. Jim could tell the doctor was forcing himself to maintain eye contact. Must've been part of the training. Don't look away from the family member's eyes when informing him or her of a loved one's passing.

The doctor spoke. His tone was somber, his hands to his side hanging in defeat. "I'm sorry, Mr. Radcliffe. We did everything we could. The alcohol mixed with the overdose of medication... There was no fight in her. If you need—"

"No," Jim interrupted. "No, don't tell me this. Please don't tell me this."

"There are no proper words of comfort right now. All I can say—"

"No." Jim's voice shook.

Then, in his mind, he could hear Mr. Brimstone's words.

I still have the papers.

I'm a dealmaker.

Mr. Brimstone's voice, in Jim's mind, replaced the doctor's. Repeatedly, everything the deity had said to Jim bounced around inside his head. As if several Mr. Brimstones occupied the space in which memories replayed themselves, overpowering any other voice or experience Jim had heard or traveled through during his life. Circling voices. Surrounding words. The doctor spoke, but Jim had faded out, was in some place like this waiting room, but the only sounds were the voice of the demon who had offered him a way to fix everything.

Your son will live again.

It's quite simple.

Your soul for your son.

Your wife needs you.

You'll be allowed to save him.

When you change your mind, Jim, simply shout out to me.

I'll be around.

You save your son, and I get your soul.

Your son will live again.

"Mr. Radcliffe."

The doctor's voice interrupted Jim's mental breakdown for a second, but no longer.

Mr. Brimstone was around. Jim could feel him. The devil himself was here, nearby, maybe standing right beside him, or behind him, or between him and the doctor. Mr. Brimstone was present and waiting.

"Mr. Radcliffe, I'm so sorry—"

Jim turned away from the doctor and hurried toward the emergency room corridor, which led to the parking garage. He broke into a jog, panicking, then a full-speed run. He was sweating, huffing, as his legs moved as quickly as he could make them. A sign pointed to the parking garage. Around another corner. He had to hurry. No time to stop. His lungs burned and his muscles ached. Physical pain and mental exhaustion meant nothing right now. He had to ignore it all. A long hallway. At the end, double doors with two signs above them. One said Exit and the other said Parking Garage.

With an urgency he had never known in his life, he pushed toward those doors, reached them, shoved them open quicker than the automatic door-motor could. He came through the doorway into the parking garage. He was on the ground level and there were only a few cars parked at this time of night. They were the hospital's graveyard shift staff. When Jim had pulled in and parked, he had ignored the

Reserved signs. He ran out into the middle of the building, where he stopped.

Jim shouted, "Mister Brimstone!"

There was not an instant response, as he expected. He wondered whether he was losing his mind, had lost it already. It didn't matter whether this was irrational or not; it was the only way to save the ones he loved the most. *He had to try.*

Louder: "Mister Brimstone!"

He pivoted to his right. Again to his right. Again and again until he'd come full circle. Despair filled his shaky voice. A last-second Hail Mary.

"Mister Brimstone!"

He waited. Turned to his left. Back to his right. To the right again.

"Mister Brimstone! God damnit! Mister Brimstone!"

He wanted to drop to his knees and weep. He wanted to give up. Jim wanted to be dead with his wife, his son, his granddaughter. If he couldn't have them back, then he wanted to be where they were. He wanted to be with them more than anything he'd ever needed. It was always all he ever desired. It was what he had weeks ago, but it seemed like it had been years. Suffering made time pass differently. Slower. Crawling from one moment to the next through a miserable existence.

"Please!"   he   screamed.   *"MISTER   BRIM-STOOOOOOOOOOOOOOONE!"*

Click, clack. Click, clack.

Someone walked in the parking garage, their dress shoes clicking against the concrete floor. From which direction, Jim wasn't sure. The sound seemed to echo all around him. It came from his left side and his right. It reverberated above and below him. He spun around to face his backside.

Click, clack. Click, clack.

There was nobody. He even looked up at the ceiling, which was the floor of the parking level above him. Could the person be up there, and their footfalls sounded throughout the entire parking garage on all levels?

Click, clack. Click, clack.

Jim recognized the sound all too well. He had heard it on the side of the road, coming from the fog, only a few hours ago. The sound of who he would come to know as Mr. Brimstone approaching to offer him the deal of an eternity. Jim froze for a few moments to listen, to focus on the direction of the sound.

Click, clack. Click, clack.

He pinned the origin of the sound as coming from his left. Whoever was approaching, they halted. Jim spun, and only a few feet away stood Mr. Brimstone, still in his black suit and red tie. His face held a steady glare of seriousness and focus as he scrutinized Jim.

"I'll make the deal," Jim said immediately. "I'll make the deal. Give me the paper. I'll do it."

Still holding a poker face, Mr. Brimstone said, "The deal is forever, Jim. Once you sign with your blood, there's no going back."

"I don't care. Please. I don't care. I need them back." He fought back tears. "I need my wife back. I need my son back. God, please."

"The deal is for your son only, Jim."

"If I save my son, I save my wife. I'll make the deal. Give it to me. Give me the paper."

"Come." Mr. Brimstone turned and walked toward a single car parked just behind him.

Jim followed.

Mr. Brimstone pulled out a folded sheet of paper, opened it, and laid it on the trunk of the car. He then withdrew a pen-like object with a blade on the end from the inside of his suit. He turned to face Jim, offered him the lancet.

Jim snatched it from Mr. Brimstone's hand. "How do I do this?"

"You poke your finger. When the blood comes, press your finger on the bottom line."

Jim stepped past Mr. Brimstone, looked down at the paper—the contract.

"How do I know you're not tricking me in some way? If you are who I think you are, you're known for lying."

Mr. Brimstone grinned devilishly. "Jim, I'm not allowed to lie about this. The contract is clear. In exchange for your soul, you will be given the opportunity to save your son. There are no tricks. I'm not allowed to trick you. It's against the rules. And if I don't adhere to them, I don't get your soul."

"My soul to save my son. Right?"

"That's right, Jim."

Without any more hesitation, Jim poked the bottom of the tip of his left index finger. Immediately, blood seeped through the tiny wound. Jim brought the finger toward a line at the bottom of the contract under which read the word "signature," and then paused. He looked at Mr. Brimstone with doubt. "No tricks?"

"No tricks."

Jim pressed his finger just above the signature line on the paper, held it there for a moment, and pulled it back, leaving a bloody fingerprint behind.

Jim looked at Mr. Brimstone. "Now what?"

Part Three

The Rescue

Chapter Nineteen

J im swiped his badge at the outside turnstile. A confirmation beep sounded, and he stood there, staring at the badge swiper, the turnstile, the parking lot on the other side of it. Absolute confusion overcame him. A moment ago, he was in a hospital parking garage, his wife in an intensive care unit bed having passed away from a suicide attempt, and a man who claimed his name was Mr. Brimstone offering Jim a chance to save his son in exchange for Jim's soul. He had, in desperation, taken the deal, pricked his finger, and signed in blood what was allegedly a supernatural contract that would give him his life back.

Now, suddenly, he was at work after finishing a shift. His work bag was in one hand, keys and smartphone in his pocket, and gate badge in the other hand. The turnstile beeped again, in a deeper tone, indicating to whoever just swiped their badge that their allotted time for passing through the gate had now expired.

"You just going to stand there?" came a coworker's voice from behind him.

Without turning around to see who it was, Jim swiped his card again. The gate beeped, and he went through it. On the other side, he stood still, staring once more at the parking lot. Cars were starting and pulling out of parking spaces. Some backed out, some simply pulled forward through the empty parking spot in front of them, and some were exiting the lot onto the main road. There was chitter-chatter from the parking lot. Coworkers fraternized before heading home to their families or their single lives.

Jim pulled his smartphone from his pocket and unlocked it. He looked at the time: 2:11 a.m. Below the time was the date: July 8. He gasped and dropped the phone. It hit the concrete of the parking lot facedown with a flat *whack*. Instinctively, he reached down, picked it up, and saw the screen was now cracked. Lightning-like veins of fracture spread from the middle of the screen outward in all directions. But the screen remained lit, and behind the fissures, he could still see the time and date. He thought they would change when he looked again, but they hadn't. The only thing that had changed was the time by one minute. It was now 2:12 a.m.

He took a deep breath, closed his eyes tightly, willed the time and date to change, and when he looked once more, they hadn't. It was still July 8, according to his phone. A profound rush of anxiety made its way through his mind, out into his body, and his legs suddenly felt weak. His hands shook. He put the phone back in his pocket and stopped a coworker who had just come through the gate behind him. A younger dude in his early twenties who Jim didn't recognize.

"Hey, man, do you know today's date?"

The man looked confused for a moment, but had his smartphone in his hand. He looked at it and then said, "July eighth, man."

The man walked away from Jim and into the parking lot.

July 8.

The night Todd died. The night of the fire.

This couldn't be a dream. He suspected it might be, but it was all too vivid to be sleeping, concocted visions. He could feel the air he breathed. Everything around him was clear, colored, real. There were no breaks in the forward progress of time and everything around him. One moment led to the next and to the next. It was all perfectly assembled. His workplace was behind him. The parking lot. His coworkers leaving. The night sky, with few stars he could see because of the parking lot lighting. It was all too real.

Dreams always had errors, like glitches in a computer program. Time skipped, scenes changed on a dime, and almost nothing made sense in dreams. He had gone from one place and time to another, but there was continuity leading up to that. Scenarios, which played out in one's mind during slumbering hours, had staggered and stuttering continuity. Often, when people wake from dreams, one of the oddest feelings was realizing that in the dream we believed it was real, and now once wide awake, it was ridiculous to have believed the dream to be concrete. Dogs don't fly. Humans don't have superpowers. We can't wake up in one house and suddenly be on an ocean beach, especially when we live in a landlocked state. But those things happen in dreams, and we believe them while we're seeing them.

This, here and now, was none of that nonsense. Jim took notice of the summer night breeze against his face. You can't feel that in a dream. At least he never had. In a dream, you somehow know there's a breeze, but it's not tangible. This was not a made-up series of events. He was here, on July 8, in the parking lot, after having clocked out just a few minutes ago, and his son's house was likely already on fire. This was his chance to rescue Todd and Beth. It was an opportunity to save his wife. And he was just standing there, trying to figure out whether it was real or not.

He rushed toward his car in the middle of the parking lot. His feet and legs couldn't carry him fast enough. Though the car was only about forty feet away, it seemed like it was hundreds of yards in the distance. The need for haste was overwhelming, and suddenly, even as he hurried, he felt as if he were in slow motion. As he approached his car, he pulled his keys from his pocket, pointed the remote key at the door, and pushed the button. The headlights flashed, and he heard an unlocking click from within the door. He pulled the driver's side door open, threw in his work bag, keys, and badge to the passenger seat, and climbed in. He reached out to pull the door shut, and something stopped it.

Jim looked up to see Adam Crane standing beside the car, with his hands gripping the top of the door.

"Somebody is in a hurry," Adam said with a friendly smile.

"Big hurry." Jim gently tugged at the door, hoping that was enough to ward Adam off.

But Adam held on tightly, and the door only budged. "Whoa, just wait a second, man. You should go have a beer with us. Long days end well with—"

Jim had no time or patience for this. Being nice would not cut it.

"Get the fuck off my car, Adam. I have to go now."

Adam looked shocked, but didn't let go.

"Adam, if you don't let go, I'm going to slam your fingers in the door. Now let the fuck go." Jim yanked the door from Adam's grip, pulling it shut with a loud slam.

He could hear Adam outside the car, his voice muffled, as he grabbed the keys from the passenger seat, jammed one in the ignition, and turned the car on. The engine fired up, and the radio blared with sports news. Jim pushed a knob inward, muting the noise, and threw the car in reverse. Jim saw Adam still standing beside the car in bewilderment as he glanced at the side-view mirror, then the rearview mirror, and backed out of the parking spot as if he were on a lifesaving mission. Tires screeched sharply as he braked, threw the car in drive, and pulled off.

He pushed a button on the door, and the driver's side window mechanically slid downward as he pulled onto the main road without first looking for oncoming traffic. He needed air because he felt like he was suffocating. The breeze from his sudden speed hit his face, and it nearly calmed him. He pushed the gas pedal all the way to the floor as the car sped off down the street. It wasn't far from Todd's house, but it was still *too far*. Ahead, there was a red traffic light and a three-way intersection. He ignored the light, slowed just enough to make the right-hand turn without flipping the car over, and halfway through the turn stomped the gas pedal all the way down again. The sound of the tires squealing as Jim gunned the engine while completing the turn was piercing. But what was more piercing was the imagined sound of his son's agony as he burned to death.

Chapter Twenty

J im stopped the car, parking it half in the street and half in the front yard, the length of it parallel to the burning home. As he jumped out, he left the keys in the ignition, motor running, and didn't close the driver's side door behind him. He rounded the back end of the vehicle in a full run toward the inflamed structure. The fire had now made its way to the roof, and the flames lunged high into the night, as if they were several glowing demons reaching frantically and repeatedly toward the sky. The entire upstairs must have been devoured in flames already.

He saw, as he looked up, every single window, four of them, had exploded outward from the heat. As he made his way up the porch, he actually ran through shattered glass on the porch stairs. A feeling of hopelessness and defeat poked at his brain. If he could see the fire and feel the heat from it outside the home, then inside there might be no corner untouched. He might be too late. He wondered how many precious moments he had wasted, earlier in his job's parking lot, when he was dumbfounded by his sudden and supernatural transition from a hospital parking garage to swiping his employee ID through a card reader on a turnstile. Every second he had wasted, the fire was growing.

Now, standing on the porch, and beneath the sound of the roaring beast within the house, he could hear sirens in the distance. Help was on the way, but the first time around they had arrived just in time to pull Todd from the fire, yet too late to save his or his wife's life. According to what Jim had learned in the aftermath of that disaster, firefighters had found Todd, at the foot of the stairs, unconscious and burned. It was determined he fell asleep on the couch in the first-floor living room, woke to the fire, and made his way toward the stairway to rescue his wife. But the fire was already full force when Todd awoke and realized what was happening, and his lungs were already suffering from smoke inhalation, making his mind malfunction due to lack of oxygen. He had made it to the foot of the stairs before collapsing into an unconsciousness he would only wake from, for a few more minutes of life, later in the hospital. They pulled him from the fire but didn't get Beth out in time. The house had exploded thanks to a gas rupture from within, caused by the fire, as the firefighters went back in for her. Not only did the exploding home take Beth and the baby she carried from life, but two firefighters as well.

Jim was at the front door. He pulled at the screen door handle, and it was only warm. He'd expected it to be hot enough to burn his hand's skin off, but was relieved that it wasn't. The screen door flew open as he was taking no chances that it might be locked. He had used full strength to pull at it. Any underestimations would waste seconds. If Todd was at the bottom of the stairs, unconscious, Jim could get him out and go back after Beth. He was still ahead of the timetable. If the fire rescue team was already here, then Jim would be doomed to not only fail, but to also die in the impending explosion, and there would be no hope of saving both or maybe even one.

Jim reached for the inner door, grabbed the knob, and pulled his hand back instinctively. The handle was hot, but not too hot to grab with protection. He stuck his hand under his shirt and used it as a glove to grab the knob again. Minimal burn, but not so bad that he couldn't grip. He tried to turn it. Locked. He tried again, but the lock was firm. Besides the doorknob lock, there was likely an engaged dead bolt on the inside.

For a moment, he considered other options. Climbing through a window was a no-go. He'd never get inside as flames had been reaching out of every window on the front of the house. Run around to the back door? No. Not enough time. If he ran all the way around this enormous house, in this vast yard, and the back door was just as secure as the front, he would have wasted what few valuable seconds he had left. He had to bust this front door in.

He stepped back and kicked the door with his right foot with as much strength and force as was available to him. The door budged; something cracked, but it didn't swing open. He had weakened the dead bolt track on the other side. Jim kicked again, and the door budged a little more than the first time, but still didn't open. A third kick, with everything he had in him; he screamed as his foot went forward, hit the door, and the door swung open into the house. With a supernatural roar, an immediate wave of barely tolerable heat slammed into Jim and warmed his face and his arms. His hair even blew in the super-heated breeze that sprang from within the house as if it had just exploded from a burst balloon. Jim almost lost his balance and stumbled backward off the porch, but he willed himself to hold strong, took a deep breath, and lunged into the burning house.

The heat against his skin was intense, but not overwhelming. Jim pulled his shirt up over his face instinctively after his first breath of smoke-filled air. He hacked through the shirt and immediately looked around the living room. Everywhere there was fuel for it, there was fire. The living room furniture, all lit: the sofa, completely engulfed, and flames from that extending to the wall behind it and the ceiling above. The smoke was thick and burned Jim's eyes, almost as if they, too, were aflame.

He closed them for a moment, then opened them again and glanced around once more. They had found Todd on the staircase, either a few steps up or at the base. Jim knew the house because he and Alice had visited several times. The smoke was too much for his eyes, and he couldn't open them completely, but he didn't have to rely on sight alone. He could use memory as a guide, so with his eyes squinted for maximum protection, he looked across the living room toward the staircase. It was an immense house, and every room in it would seem to be vast. The staircase was a good twenty or thirty feet away. He didn't see his son, though. It was a curving staircase, so Jim could see the base and the first few steps, but the rest was behind a wall that was also covered with dancing flames. The fire was quickly consuming everything in sight.

Jim started toward the staircase, but there was a loud crashing sound, and he realized, just off to his left, the ceiling had collapsed. Everything in the room above had fallen, seething in flames, through to the living room. A sadness overtook him when he realized which room upstairs had fallen through its weakened and compromised floor. A baby's bed, fire jumping about it, now lay on its side in a pile of collapsed debris just a few feet from Jim. If he'd been a little farther to his left, he would have been buried, and possibly injured, beyond recovery, amid the rubble. He looked up and saw an exposed gap between this room and the one above. There was nothing but fire up there. Soon, the entire house would explode, and almost all evidence that a family had lived here would be charred or destroyed.

The surrounding heat, as if he were in hell itself, grew in strength. His skin almost sizzled. It wasn't at that point yet, but likely, in just a minute or so, it would be. Haste was his only choice. He had one shot to get to the stairwell, retrieve his son, and drag him to safety outside.

The fire roared all around. Jim heard the searing of all matter available for the greedy flames to consume. The growling of the fire itself sounded like an orchestra of beasts celebrating the taking of property and life. He coughed through his shirt again, felt light-headed, fought it off, and continued forward.

He arrived at the staircase, stepped onto it, and went up a few steps. Lying halfway in between the first floor and the second was Todd, facedown, both hands outreached, as if he'd fallen unconscious while trying to crawl upward in desperation to save his wife and daughter. Jim saw no sign of life within his son, but he noticed Todd's skin wasn't burned too badly. The side of his face was blackened from the onslaught of heat and smoke, but not physically and permanently damaged.

Jim knelt beside his unconscious son, reached out to scoop him up, and Jim's shirt fell from his face. He had lost his only defense against the smoke, and realized if he breathed, he'd be out within seconds of smoke inhalation. Nobody would be saved if this happened. He wasn't worried about his own life, because it was no longer worth living if he didn't pull off this rescue. If he couldn't save his son, then he would also not save his wife, and with both of them gone, he had no reason to live. If he didn't make it out of here alive with Todd, then Jim didn't care whether he made it out at all. This was all or nothing.

He held his breath, and with a sudden burst of effort, pulled Todd upward. Either Todd was heavier than he expected, or Jim was weaker than he thought. Jim struggled for a few moments, but finally had Todd's arms over his shoulders. He dragged his son into a limp standing position and started down the stairs. Ahead, a wall of fire now blocked the stairway threshold into the living room. Hope seemed to drain from Jim as he hesitated, watching the fire, his legs weakening from the weight of his son and the exhaustion from his unwavering efforts.

They had to go through that wall of fire. There was no other way. They couldn't go upward. Even if that were an option, Jim didn't have the strength to pull his son's weight *up* the stairs. It was down and forward, or nothing. There was no telling how thick that wall of flames was. If it extended even a few feet from the stairwell, there would be no emerging from it safely on the other side.

Jim went for it. Doing his best to hold his breath in, he hurried forward, dragging Todd behind him. As he approached the wall of flame, the intense heat warned him to stop, but he ignored the pain, moving with determination. The flames licked his face and everywhere he had skin exposed: his neck, his arms, his hands. The sting from the fire was the most intense pain he'd ever felt in his life, but he continued on, holding a screech of agony inside himself in an effort to withhold his own breathing. If he screamed, he'd breathe; if he breathed, both he and Todd would perish.

As he entered the wall of flame, he felt as if he moved in slow motion, though he was, indeed, hurrying through it with a speed he wasn't sure he was capable of while carrying such a heavy load. A split second later, he was through the flames and in the living room again. Though the heat still burned everywhere on his body, he knew the pain was from this giant oven he was in, and not because he was actually still being touched directly by fire.

Now was not the time to stop. The smoke in the living room was thicker than even a few moments ago. He still couldn't allow himself to breathe or even rest for a few seconds. The front door seemed so far away. His legs wanted to buckle. The muscles in his arms ached from the heavy carrying they hadn't been used to for at least ten years now, since work became not so physical anymore, thanks to his rising seniority and access to easier gigs within his workplace.

He pushed forward, dragging Todd across the living room: Past burning furniture. Beneath a ceiling that wanted to fall on them and stop their progress. Past the baby crib that was now completely burned away, the mattress in it still aflame. Toward the doorway, which was still wide open.

Beyond the smoke and the flames inside the home, through that rectangular portal to freedom, Jim could see the night.

Forward. Forward. Dragging his son. Holding his breath, but about to release it. They were almost at the doorway. Jim wanted so badly to breathe, but he couldn't yet. He had to get outside first.

Fifteen feet. Dizziness came to him. Lack of oxygen was about to lay him out flat. *Forward. Push. Keep going.*

Ten feet. Hurry! Oh God, he needed to breathe. The heat against his face. Sweat dripped into his squinted eyes. He felt like he was melting alive.

Five feet. Move, move, move. Don't breathe. Not yet. No, not yet. The dizziness intensified. He was losing his balance. Now, instead of bolting straight forward, he wobbled, stumbled on something, felt fire at his feet through his shoes. He staggered to the left, taking Todd with him. The doorway was now to the right and no longer a straight shot. *No.* He regained his balance. He needed air and he needed it now.

Through the doorway, onto the porch, down the steps. He fell in the front yard, frantically inhaling a sudden gasp of air, taking Todd down with him. They both hit the ground hard. Jim rolled over on his back.

Fire engines on the street. The scream of their sirens still in the distance, but loud enough to obviously be nearby. They were approaching at top speed.

Jim laid on his back, breathing, then rolled over to Todd, who was still unconscious. The air outside wasn't fresh, but it was better to breathe than the smoke inside the house. Jim couldn't tell whether Todd, who lay on his back, his mouth agape and eyes closed, was breathing or not. It seemed like he wasn't.

Jim almost started CPR, but then remembered something: the gas explosion. This spot wasn't safe. If he didn't drag them farther from the house, the explosion would kill them. They weren't out of danger yet.

Summoning up the last of his strength, Jim grabbed Todd's hands, stood up, and moved backward toward the car, dragging his son in the grass behind him. The fire squad was now pulling in—sirens silencing, people yelling, shouting orders, preparing to fight the immense blaze and rescue anyone inside. Jim pulled Todd behind the still running car. He let go of his son, fell backward, scrambled back toward Todd.

Voices approached. Todd coughed once, twice, several times, rolled over on his side, choked and vomited. But alive.

Two male firefighters now stood over Jim and Todd, as Jim sat up, his arms arching backward to hold him steady. Todd mumbled incoherently.

One firefighter spoke. "Is there anyone else in the house?"

Jim opened his mouth to reply but coughed uncontrollably instead.

Todd mumbled more, agony and distress in his voice.

"Is there anyone else in the house?" the firefighter asked again, louder, with more urgency.

Time was wasting. In the original happening, there was nobody outside the house for them to ask anything to; they had gone straight in. Now, they were using precious moments to question Jim, who was having a hard time answering. Finally, he nodded vigorously while waving his hand toward the house, and finally he squeezed words out between coughs: "A woman. Upstairs. Hurry."

Todd finally formed words. With a raspy voice, he coughed and yelled, "My wife."

There was no time now. Too much had been wasted. As the firefighters left Jim and Todd's side and headed toward their partners, who already had their fire hoses connected to the hydrant and were shooting water at the entrance and upstairs, Jim realized they weren't going to rescue Beth. It was too late. Instead, they were going to run into the house just before it exploded.

Jim crawled to the front of the car, used it to pull himself up, and had sight of the completely inflamed house again. Two firefighters running toward the still open front door. He opened his mouth to yell at them. Nothing came out but a cough and vomit, which poured from him onto the hood of his car. The firefighters were on the porch, charging forward. Jim tried to scream again.

The house exploded. One enormous boom. Debris flew in all directions. The shock wave knocked Jim on his ass. The car shook but held its place, protecting Jim and Todd from the full force of the instant annihilation that had just occurred. Before darkness took Jim, he heard his son screaming in anguish.

Chapter Twenty-One

A cloudless blue sky, a gentle current from the west, and low humidity reigned on this July, summer day. Jim, in a suit and tie, stood beside Alice, who wore a formal dress. Beside them, Todd stood, his head hung low, in a suit, tie, and a cast running the length of his left arm, held up appropriately in a medical shoulder sling. The fire had left him with second-degree burns on one arm and showed mercy to the rest of his body.

It had not spared him emotional loss, though. A week ago, he had everything he ever asked for in life, and now he was attending his wife and unborn daughter's funeral. His face was streaked with tears that seemed to flow from a never-ending source of fluid. His body trembled off and on with the words of the speaking minister. Memories of a life that once was haunted him and gave intermittent surrender to the terror of what was now, and what was to be. If he could somehow crawl into his memory and live there forever with his wife and child, he would choose to do so.

Although he understood his father had risked his own life to save him, Todd couldn't help but wish Jim had moved past him in that burning home, gone up the stairs, and saved his pregnant wife. It wasn't ungratefulness, because Todd understood there had been only minimal moments in which to decide on a course of action, while the house was falling apart, during his father's rescue attempt. Jim's first instinct was to save his son, and there wasn't enough time to rationalize or reason with himself. He went into the burning house, found Todd, and pulled him to safety. Todd felt that maybe he would have done the same thing in his father's shoes, but he still wished it was Beth standing here, and him about to be lowered into the ground, inside of a coffin, where his remains would reside, likely until the planet no longer existed.

There were about sixty people attending the funeral of Beth and Stormy Radcliffe. Family, friends, coworkers—all there to mourn the loss of two souls taken early and unfairly from this realm into the one nobody knew anything about. As the minister spoke, the people sniffed, sobbed, prayed. Alice, standing to the right of Todd, reached out and took his hand in hers. She moved closer to her son, who was choking up, trying not to burst into uncontrollable grief. Jim scooted closer to his wife on her other side and took her hand. Together, a family united, but suffering through loss and despair.

Although this time around was emotionally devastating for Jim, it wasn't the same as before. He felt guilty that his strongest emotion was one of relief while watching the funeral of his daughter-in-law and grandchild. With the reassurance that he had done the right thing, he tried to wash away his guilt. He'd not just saved Todd, but Alice, too. Jim knew the unavoidable consequence of Todd perishing in that fire with his wife. He had lived it.

And Jim also couldn't help but feel even more guilt, knowing that he'd seen the other side of this. An eerie feeling tingled along his spine, caused by the knowing of an alternate future to this one. The future that was meant to be, but he had changed. If it cost him his soul, he would worry about that element when the time to pay the piper arrived. At his age, he hopefully had another thirty years to live. It would be quite the bummer if he was to die in a traffic accident or struck by lightning and sent to his grave any earlier than that. But it would still be worth it.

Jim looked at Alice, who was different in her grieving this time around. She was genuinely sad for the loss of daughter-in-law and grandchild, but she was more sympathetic for her son. Her grieving was an extension of Todd's this time, and she was sorry her son hurt so badly. Yet, it still wasn't the same. She would help Todd get through this, and it was a lot easier for her this way in which she had a purpose, than the other way in which all purposes, for continuing on with life, had been ultimately lost. Now, Alice would be on a mission to aid in healing, rather than one of self-destruction. She would be happy again because her happiness wasn't completely submerged in the depths of despair. This time, she wouldn't turn to the bottle. She would continue to be the Alice Jim knew and loved for so long.

Lost in thought, Jim missed almost everything the minister said. When he emerged from within his own mind and imagination, last words had been spoken, and now everyone had their heads bowed in prayer as requested by the minister. All he heard was "amen" and then the crowd dispersed. Jim noticed people walking over to Beth's parents, offering condolences and hugs. They were trying to keep it together as guest after guest approached.

Jim looked over at Alice and Todd. Alice held Todd, as he leaned in to her, bawling uncontrollably. Jim felt it was only right to approach Beth's parents and offer his sincere, yet somehow insincere, condolences.

Jim waited for the line of mostly strangers to dwindle down and then went to the grieving parents. He stepped to the father and extended a hand.

"I'm sorry. If you need us for anything, please let us know. I mean anything."

"That's kind of you." Beth's father had tears rolling down his cheeks as he shook Jim's hand. "Thank you."

Jim faced Beth's mother. A frail-looking woman. Short, black hair. Bags from never-ending stress puffed outward below her eyes. She had been crying for days. Jim didn't just assume so; he knew it. He had been beside a woman grieving the loss of her child for weeks, and he knew the magnitude of this mother's despair.

"Ma'am." Jim extended his hand.

Instead of taking it, she stood there, looking at his hand for a few moments, as if Jim had offered her something mysterious and other-worldly. Then she finally met his look, stared for a few moments more, sniffed, and wiped her eyes. "I don't hate you."

Shocked, Jim said, "I don't—"

"I don't hate you because maybe I would have done the same thing."

Jim just watched her. He wanted to speak but didn't know what to say. And aside from having no words, he didn't want to interrupt her. It was apparent she had more.

She sniffed again and choked back a sob. "I would have probably saved my kid too. Let the other die. If it was me running into that house, I would have run right past your son for my daughter. So, I don't hate you."

Jim was still speechless. He watched her eyes as she spoke. Her gaze was full of hatred and loss. Her words of not hating Jim were obviously untrue and an attempt to be civil.

She continued, "But I don't want to be your friend. And I feel like I am angry at you."

Jim said nothing.

"I'm angry at you because you decided your son's life was more important than a mother's and her child's life. That you chose one over two. I think I would have saved my daughter if it had been me instead of you, not just because she was my daughter, but because she had another life inside her. One who will never be born because you decided your son was more important."

Jim remained silent.

Beth's mother breathed in, held it, and slowly exhaled. "I'll always be angry at you for that. I won't hate you. I refuse to hate you. You thought you were doing the right thing in a moment where there was no time to think. But I don't have to like you... And I don't have to be your friend. I won't be your friend. After I walk away, I never want to see you again. I never want to see your son again."

"Sherry, that's not—" her husband started.

"No." She stopped him. "I feel the way I feel. I don't care if it's justified. A constant reminder of what happened in that house is not something I want. Mr. Radcliffe, I don't want to see you and your family again. I don't want to feel what I'm feeling right now...ever again." She turned and walked away from him.

Jim was still frozen, and the husband stepped up to him and said, "I'm sorry. She's not herself. I'm so sorry."

"No," Jim said. "She has every right. I wish you two the best. I understand her grief."

"I'm so sorry," Beth's father said again and then turned to follow his wife across the lawn.

Jim wasn't angry. He had, of course, not expected what he just heard, but he wasn't mad about it. He understood the mother's whirl of emotions. If anger helped her, then he was not one to deny her that, nor would he hold any ill will toward her. She had lost her daughter, and if blaming someone else helped her, then Jim was fine to be her target.

Jim turned to face his wife and son, standing several feet away from him, crying in each other's embrace. He wondered whether this was a dream. Because not too long ago, Jim and Alice were holding each other, him consoling her, having nobody to console him, over the death of their only child. If this wasn't a dream, then perhaps the loss of Todd had been. What didn't seem real was the one thing Jim had actually lived. But yet, it had to all be real. Every moment leading up to this very day, these circumstances. His son had died in a house fire, and Jim had relived the moment, gone into the house, and changed the past. Just as crazy Billy Wagner had predicted.

A chill passed through Jim's body. There was something else Billy had predicted. He had warned that there would be dire consequences for changing the past. The man had been right about his prophetic ramblings so far. If what Billy warned of continued to come true, then what would the price be? What would the price of changing the past be? And who would pay it?

Chapter Twenty-Two

Three months later

Billy Wagner stood in court, his female lawyer beside him. He was cleaned up for his appearance with the judge and jury: wearing a suit and tie, his hair brushed and parted neatly down the middle, his face clean and his demeanor distinguished. Although he hated dressing formally, it was essential he looked pristine for court. After all, for the first time since his life completely fell apart, he had faced a felony trial. He had argued with his attorney about what to wear, but in the end gave in to her insistence.

He was tired. Last night, his dreams had been plagued with more visions of things to come. There were elements related to those visions which certified they were of the future. One of those was the fatigue he awoke with. Evidently, seeing the future was exhausting. Another marker was that while in the dream, it felt completely real. It wasn't like most dreams, which were foggy, without color, and lacked the use of all senses. When Billy was peeking into things to come, every sense was available to him. In the one he had last night, he could see the yellow, orange, and red of the fire consuming the Radcliffes' house. He could hear the burning beast's boasting roar. The smell of smoke was not just detected, but was also so strong it was nearly overwhelming. It was like he was actually there instead of looking in through a magic crystal ball of slumbering visions.

In his most recent vision, something had been off. He only saw the house burning as it had in the other ones—firefighters, their trucks, and other emergency vehicles parked at the border of the front lawn and the street. Then the explosion came. What Billy hadn't seen was Jim Radcliffe running heroically into the burning danger. He hadn't seen the man emerging, dragging his unconscious son behind him. There had been a slight blur to the dream, too. Most of Billy's visions were clear as a crisp blue-sky day. Not last night's, though. When he'd awakened, he'd felt confused. If it wasn't for the availability of all senses, he would have dismissed it as an actual dream this time. But that wasn't the case.

The judge was an older Black woman, probably in her mid-fifties, who seemed to show a sympathetic attitude toward Billy, and especially so after hearing his back story about his mental issues, his fall from family and grace, and their ultimate impact on his life from there on. She not only looked at him with empathetic gazes, but also spoke softly whenever addressing him directly. Still, he realized that no longer being a productive member of society would work against him in the eyes of everyone here who had his fate in their hands.

The judge addressed the jury, looking over her glasses, which were obviously prescribed for close-up seeing. "Does the jury have a verdict?"

The jury foreperson, a young man with dark hair in his forties, replied, "We, the jury, have reached a verdict, Your Honor."

Billy realized he was trembling. Anticipation and anxiety overwhelmed him. He had never really been a *bad guy* until now. And although he didn't commit any acts of actual violence that day in Todd Radcliffe's backyard, he had threatened to. Billy realized what that represented in the eyes of people who truly had no idea what was going on. They did not know, and could never really possibly believe, the truth of the events which were soon to take place.

Just before being arraigned months ago, he had seen on television the report of a fire which had taken the life of a pregnant woman and two firefighters. The wheels were now in motion. The timeline had been altered. According to his dreams, that fire was supposed to kill a man, his wife and unborn child, and two firefighters. When Billy burst into that backyard on that perfect summer day, the future had intended for something else to happen to that family. Although news stories had said that Todd survived, Billy knew his own prophecies had come true. Somehow, Todd's father had gone back in time and saved his son.

The news had spoken of the funeral during which Todd's pregnant wife was buried. Billy had almost become sick with terror when he realized what was to come. A past altered was a future derailed. Destiny was supposed to run things in this universe, yet somehow Jim Radcliffe, through supernatural means, had denied destiny its bidding. By doing so, he had created a future which was never meant to be. By Billy's assumptions, that could only yield catastrophic results. Not just for those involved in the changing of the timeline, but for every single living soul in existence, not just here on this planet, but scattered throughout the vastness of all creation. It wasn't just billions of lives affected; it was likely trillions upon trillions of souls, intelligent or otherwise.

The only way to set it right was to reverse the reversal that Jim Radcliffe had initiated. The only route to redemption was for Todd Radcliffe to die. Although he may have survived that fire when he wasn't destined to, if he was to die before too much more damage to the timeline could occur, then perhaps the equilibrium of the universe would be restored. Billy would hire a hitman if he knew any or if he had the funds to do so. That was beyond the realm of his ready resources, so the only way to accomplish such a feat was for him to pull the trigger himself. Billy was no killer, and would likely perform such a task in an unprofessional and sloppy manner, which would land him in prison for the rest of his life or even on death row. That was his sacrifice to make, though. One soul for trillions. It was a fair trade.

Billy wasn't sure it would actually be a sacrifice, however, because he honestly had no desire to live any longer. His life, at one time, had been a dream come true. The house, the family, the good job: it had been as pleasing a life as possible on simple terms. Because all of that was now gone, and because there would be no reconciliation of his life, he could not look forward to a future. He didn't care to. If he dropped dead right now in this courtroom, he wouldn't complain. He would hope to not be saved, to be allowed to move on to whatever was beyond this physical life, into a realm of absolute peace.

At least, that's what he'd hope for. There would be no one for him in heaven. He sure didn't want hell either, for that place would provide even more suffering. He preferred darkness, or even something more profoundly restful than that: absolutely nothing. Ceasing to exist would be his option if he was given one.

"Could you please read the verdict to the court, Mister Foreperson?" the judge asked.

"We, the jury, find the defendant, Billy Wagner, guilty on four counts of terroristic threatening. On the single count of criminal trespassing, we, the jury, find the defendant, Billy Wagner, guilty. On the count of carrying a stolen firearm, we, the jury, find the defendant guilty."

Billy looked down at his shoes. Dress shoes. He hated them. They squished his toes together and were uncomfortable. He'd never worn such foot attire in his life, even when everything was good. Then, when having to dress up for date nights with his wife, he had a favorite pair of sneakers. Sneakers and flip-flops were all he ever wore: to work, around the house, outside in his yard, out with the wife. Dress shoes were the most uncomfortable attire on the planet, and he couldn't understand how people actually chose to wear them. A new, clean pair of sneakers actually looked better anyhow.

He realized he was distracting himself from the read verdicts. Billy knew the outcome in advance. Not from dreams this time, but simply because that's just how his luck rolled. He looked up when the judge addressed him.

"Mister Billy Wagner. It is my elected duty in this case to impose sentencing on you. Would you like to address the court first?"

Billy looked at the judge. "No, ma'am."

The judge sighed, looked down at notes she'd taken during the trial, flipped through them, and then back at Billy. "Mister Wagner, as you stand before me here today, I can't help but think of some of the unlucky circumstances of your life. I recognize that at one time, you were a different man with a different path. You were struck by mental illnesses, and I can't help but feel sympathy and empathy toward you. You are not one of the bad guys. I know you've committed a lot of petty crimes, and in the past several years you've been nothing more than a minor menace to society. My heart hurts for you because I have gone through your records many times.

"I cannot, however, after such an act as you committed to lead to this trial, simply release you on probation and expect you to search for appropriate mental treatment. With everything in consideration, I hereby sentence you to impatient treatment at a mental health facility, where you are to remain until the educated professionals there deem you fit to re-enter the realms of freedom and society."

The judge took her glasses off and stared directly into Billy's eyes. "Sir, I recommend you make the most of this opportunity. If I see you in this courtroom again, I will be given no choice but to impose maximum sentences for whatever crimes you might be convicted of. Do you understand you're being given a second chance?"

Billy couldn't believe his ears. Something somewhere in the universe had looked upon him with forgiving eyes. He had expected to be sentenced to prison, and for a long time. A mental health facility—a psych ward—was much preferable to a living habitat with gang members and true hardened criminals. Although he had no sincere hope of becoming well again inside his mind, he welcomed the chance to try.

"Yes, ma'am," Billy replied.

"Mister Wagner, do not waste this opportunity. Get yourself better. Recover your life."

"Yes, ma'am."

Chapter Twenty-Three

This place was, at one time, Todd's favorite restaurant, which was why Jim and Alice had chosen it as the place to meet for dinner. It had been three months since Beth and Stormy's funeral, and even though emotions still ran high, everyone had attempted to return to some kind of normal life. They all three returned to work, and Todd lived with Jim and Alice, even after quickly receiving life and homeowner's insurance payouts, which were exponentially high enough for him to live a decent life even without working.

However, Todd wanted to keep his job. He figured when he finally learned how to live with the loss of his wife and daughter, he would hopefully still want the career he had skyrocketed into at such a young age. Besides keeping ambitions of success alive in his heart and mind, he couldn't just sit around playing with his thumbs. For now, his job did nothing to take his mind off the memories that played repeatedly through his thoughts, but he hoped eventually it would.

Jim and Alice arrived at the Mexican restaurant before Todd, and sipped on margaritas while waiting for him to show up after work. He told them six p.m., but it was now going on seven, and they wondered if their son was standing them up. Both were on their second drink, and munching on free chips and salsa, when he finally came through the entrance, glanced around, saw them, and came to the table.

Jim noticed immediately something was off when Todd pulled his chair out and slightly staggered as he sat in it. He looked inebriated, as if he'd been drinking long before Jim and Alice took their first sip. And then Todd spoke, and his words seemed to stumble.

"Sorry...sorry I'm late. Had to stay over a little to deal with a late inbound."

"Oh, that's fine," Alice said, well buzzed from her two margaritas. "We were just going to keep drinking these until we needed a cab home." She lifted her bowl-shaped margarita glass, shook it around playfully, and then took a long drink of it. She set it down on the table a little too hard and then giggled.

The waitress, a redhead in her early twenties, was at the table. She had noticed the extra guest and immediately came to them.

"Hey, I'm Tammy, your waitress for the evening. Would you like something to drink?"

"I'll have one of those," Todd replied as he nodded toward his mother's nearly empty glass.

"Okay, a margarita." The waitress looked at Alice. "Would you like another one, ma'am?"

Alice picked up her drink and finished it in one long gulp. "Yeah. Hit me again."

"And you, sir?" Tammy asked Jim.

Jim looked at his drink, which was half full, and shook his head. "I'm good. But I'll take water. Looks like I'm the designated driver for the night."

"Oh, don't be ridiculous." Alice's voice rose to nearly obnoxious levels. "We can just get a cab."

"I'm not leaving the car here," Jim said plainly.

"Okay then," Alice said to Tammy. "No more for him. He's cut off."

"Two margaritas and a water coming up." And Tammy left the family to themselves.

"So how was work?" Alice asked her son.

"Work is work," Todd answered as he stared at the tortilla chips and salsa bowl in the middle of the table. He reached out, grabbed a chip, and ate it without dipping it into the salsa.

"I guess it's still hard to stay focused." Alice twirled the ice in her glass with her finger.

"It's hard to do anything, Mom," Todd replied without taking his sight away from the middle of the table. "I lost my family."

Jim detected light hostility in his son's voice, but said nothing. He was worried Alice might be too drunk to tread carefully with her words. Jim became nervous. He couldn't exactly caution her in front of Todd, because then there was the possibility of being too sensitive. People, even in pain, rarely appreciated being tiptoed around.

"I know, son. But you have to fight through it." Alice leaned on the table, staring straight at her son with all seriousness. "They wouldn't want you to waste away. Beth wouldn't want—"

"I know what they would want, Mom."

"I'm sorry. I just—"

"Maybe this isn't such a good idea," Todd said bluntly. "All these people around. Look at them. Look at you."

"Son," Jim broke in. "Your mom meant nothing like that. We know it's hard."

And Jim thought back to the first time around in this nightmare chain of events...when Todd had been lost to the fire along with his family, and how Alice had spiraled out of control, instantly became a grieving alcoholic and eventually took her own life. When perspective changes, so does the way we handle things. Although Alice was heartbroken over the tragedy, she wasn't as devastated as she had been. And

Jim understood that because he shared the same feelings. And once again, he felt guilty that he was merely glad his son was sitting here with them, and to a point, relieved the victims of the fire had been limited to just Beth and Stormy.

Their table became silent, with each individual in their own thoughts. The murmuring crowd around them was unheard to their ears, under the volume of their minds. Finally, the waitress returned with drinks.

After setting the margaritas in front of Todd and Alice, Tammy asked, "Are you guys ready to order or would you like more time?"

"I'd like more time with my family," Todd said, staring blankly at his drink.

Not comprehending Todd's true meaning, Tammy detected some sarcasm and forced a smile. "Okay, I'll be back to check on you guys."

Jim smiled pleasantly toward her. "Thank you."

"No problem. See you in a few." Tammy was off and away again.

Todd picked up his margarita, and to his parents' surprise, turned the glass up until he'd drunk it empty. He set it back down, smacked his lips, and belched loudly.

"Son!" Alice said with astonishment.

"What, Mom? What? Was that a little too quick?" His voice was confrontational.

Impatience rose within Jim, but he held back from interfering. He knew he should understand. He'd been there. They didn't know it. The world didn't know it, but Jim had been there. He'd lost his only child. However, he'd been allowed to change that. He'd been given the chance to go back to reverse things, and he had jumped on that opportunity. Because he could empathize with Todd in the most genuine of ways, Jim kept his mouth shut. He took a quiet, deep breath, and exhaled it slowly.

"Well, you don't want to get drunk," Alice said. "You can't drink and drive."

"You wouldn't give me a ride home, Mom? You going to make me walk?"

"Well, no." Alice paused, her intoxicated mind trying to keep up. "But you don't want to leave your car here. Someone could bust out a window. Isn't that right, honey?" She looked at Jim.

"I'm just hungry," Jim said. "Are we ready to order yet?"

"Why would I care about leaving my car here, Mom?" Todd said, continuing his irritated tone. "Why do I care about my windows being busted out? Why would that even bother me?"

"Son." Jim finally stepped in. "This isn't the place or time."

"The place or time for what, Dad? For me to be upset? For me to get smashed drunk? I don't want to be sober. The place and time are everywhere, and always, from now on. You don't know, Dad. You have no idea."

"I know more than you think," Jim snapped back.

"What do you know, Dad? Do you know what it's like to lose your wife? Your only child? Do you know how that feels? How can you even pretend to empathize? You have no—"

"That's enough." Alice's voice rose above Todd's.

"No, it's not enough," Todd contested. "How can you two go on like nothing happened? How can you just sit here at this damn table, drinking to your jolly selves?"

"Nobody is jolly!" Alice yelled.

The restaurant chatter seemed to go silent, as if suddenly everyone was watching the stewing Radcliffe family discontentment. Jim looked around, and saw nobody was looking their way, but also realized there were tables where it seemed the customers were intentionally trying to portray themselves as not being nosey.

"You think I'm just going to bounce back? You don't know. You *can't* know." Anger rose in Todd's voice.

Jim knew, though. And in an alternate flow of time somewhere, Alice knew all too well. Yet, Jim obviously couldn't reveal the things he'd been through and knew. He couldn't just tell them, because not only would it be unhelpful to anyone in this current timeline, it could be dangerous. Even to himself, because Todd and Alice would likely think Jim was as baffling as the guy who intruded on their family get-together the same day of the fire. There were so many negative outcomes to Jim filling them in on the facts. Also, even though he lived through the experience of it all, Jim still wasn't sure himself that it had all been real. He didn't trust his own eyes, thoughts, experiences, memories. It seemed absolutely impossible that his son and wife were dead, and he traveled back in time to change an event, therefore saving them both.

Alice looked on the verge of tears, and Jim interrupted Todd, using a stern and demanding tone. "I said that's enough, son."

The restaurant patrons were definitely listening in now. Suddenly, Jim heard music playing all around them. Elevator-style, Spanish-themed music. He realized it had been playing all along.

Jim noticed his son's eyes were beyond bloodshot when Todd looked into his father's gaze. Todd looked as if he'd been drinking and not sleeping for days.

Todd said, "That's enough, huh? That's enough? No, that's not enough. It's not enough for me to sit here and see you both relieved that I survived that fire, even though my family didn't. It's not enough for me to see Mom over there, drunk and giddy, as if nothing has happened." His voice rose as he spoke. "It's not enough for you to tell me to shut up, for you to think I can just turn off emotion for this little happy family get-together at my favorite restaurant." Todd stood up, swayed, and continued while looking down at his father.

Jim wanted to stand, but he was trying to keep his cool. He was trying to understand his son's behavior because he *did* understand it. Jim sat still, even though everything in him wanted to stand up to Todd.

Now the restaurant patrons weren't hiding their curiosity. They all watched the Radcliffe table's drama with intrigue.

"You're already drunk," Alice accused. "Were you drinking at your job?"

"What does it matter?" Todd asked. "Who gives a shit? It's *my* job."

"You're going to lose everything." Alice scoffed.

Todd's face changed to fake astonishment. "I'm going to lose everything? I haven't already lost everything, Mom? What the fuck do I have left to lose?"

Jim stood up with authority and faced his son.

"What, Dad?" He forced a laugh. "Am I in trouble? Am I in trouble because you people can't understand what I'm going through? Because you want to have some kind of fake happy dinner? All one big happy family, aren't we? Just a dinner, some salsa, some drinks. Just one big happy get-together because life is so great. Life is so happy. We're all just so happy here, aren't we?"

"You're out of line," Jim said.

"I'm out of line." Another scoff from Todd. "I should be cheerful, right, Dad? I should just be happy to be alive."

"You should be," Alice said. "Your father risked his life to save you."

"What if I had died in that fire, Mom?" Todd looked sternly at his mother. "Would you be happy to be alive?"

Alice couldn't answer. She sat there, watching Todd in shock.

"Fuck this. Fuck this life," Todd mumbled. He reached down and swung at his margarita glass. It fell over, ice sliding out onto the table.

"Son!" Alice yelled.

The restaurant watched on.

"Fuck my life." Todd turned to his father. "What did you think it was going to be like when you saved me from that fire and left my wife to burn alive? What the fuck were you thinking?"

Alice stood up, holding back tears of anger and frustration. "You don't say shit like that to your father. He risked—"

"He risked his life to save me. Thanks, Dad. Thanks a lot."

Todd turned to walk away. He made it a few steps before stopping at Jim's voice.

"Son, don't you walk away like this. You're too drunk to drive. Let us take you home."

"Home..." Todd paused and turned around to face his parents. "My home burned down, Dad. You were there. Remember? You saved me, but you didn't really save me." And Todd walked away, cut through a maze of sitting onlookers, bumped into one table, mumbled a quick apology, and left the restaurant.

Jim stood there for several moments, watching the exit as if he expected Todd to come back through those double glass doors to apologize. Behind Jim, Alice stood, whimpering, tears running down her face. Jim finally turned around and faced his wife. He wanted to offer comforting words, but he didn't know what to say.

"We're losing him anyway," Alice said. "You saved him, but we're still losing our son."

"He's just drunk. He'll sober up and be sorry," Jim insisted.

"No." Alice looked past Jim, past all the onlookers, and through the glass doors to the outside. "He's lost."

Chapter Twenty-Four

T odd eased the gas pedal down and the car sped up. Steering wheel in one hand, bottle of bourbon in the other, the feeling of acceleration seemed to offer consolation. As he passed one car on the interstate, traffic streetlights above blurring by, he took a swig from the bottle. He'd blown a pretty penny of insurance money on the new sports car, and the shiny red vehicle wasn't disappointing him. The bottle of alcohol, however, was. He'd put three-fourths of it in his body over a period of three hours, and he felt barely buzzed. He wasn't sure whether he was misinterpreting his level of inebriation, or whether his emotions were so high, he was almost immune to the effects of straight liquor.

All the windows were down, and the feeling of the wind blowing in through his hair, the cool October air against his face, gave him something he needed. It wasn't relaxation; it was the actual feeling of moving fast, as if he were flying away from this place, this city where he'd lost everything he loved the most. The faster the car moved, the more released he felt. An emotional prison of grief and turmoil would hold him and eventually ruin him if he didn't get away.

He realized the roar of the engine and the howl of the wind weren't enough sound, so he set the bottle between his legs and turned on the radio. The perfect song was playing: "Kickstart My Heart" by Mötley Crüe. The beating of the drums, the wild, carefree sound of the lead guitar, the intensity of Vince Neil's voice was all somehow as calming to him as a lullaby might be to a three-year-old at bedtime. Todd tapped the steering wheel to the beat of the song as he gunned the car around a semi-truck. Someone on the expressway, somewhere nearby, blared their horn. He looked in his rearview mirror and saw another car's headlights almost on his ass. He had cut them off with his bold and rambunctious maneuver. Todd flipped the trailing driver his middle finger through the rearview mirror, pushed the gas pedal harder, and sped off.

Now he was nearing ninety miles per hour. The streetlights went from intermittent blurs to one foggy, long line. He imagined he was in a ship, flying through outer space. The streetlights were stars shooting by, and vehicles were other ships. Perhaps he would be lucky enough to lose control and crash head-on into the guardrail, ejecting himself from the car through the windshield, and ending this miserable second chance at life.

He wished his father hadn't saved him. It would all be over right now. He would be at absolute peace, and perhaps he would be with his wife and child in another realm or dimension, in a place where they could be together for eternity, free from the fear of separation by untimely death. A place where death held no power over them; a place where they could complete what they started in this awful world.

As he raced the car forward, several motorists blew their horns angrily at him. Pissed off that not only was he blatantly and fully ignoring speed limits, but also that he might just hurt someone else with his reckless driving.

"Don't worry, folks," he mumbled, realizing his speech was slurred. "I got this. Nobody's going to get hurt but me."

The lines on the roadway had become one long one because of his speed, and Vince Neil sang in a tone that pumped Todd up mentally

while simultaneously helping him to not give a shit. He could wait
for a clearing in traffic, spin the car to his left, and probably hit the
guardrail so hard he'd fly through the windshield. The car might flip
up into the air and hopefully land on him. Surely there would only
be a few moments of pain before he checked out forever. But if he
made such a move, suicide attempt by vehicle, and he didn't die, but
instead became wheelchair-bound for the rest of his life, his loved ones
having to feed him and wipe his ass because of near full paralyzation,
he would still also be living with the profound grief he felt now. To
be so handicapped that he wouldn't be capable of a second attempt to
depart this universe was his only deterrent.

His parents seemed as if they expected him to just move on, like
everything that had happened was simply a part of life. He held no
genuine anger toward them, realizing they were only trying to be
there for him, but also couldn't understand their ignorance of the
profoundness of the circumstances. His defiant outburst had shocked
them both, and their reaction had unpleasantly surprised him. What
did they expect him to do? Did they really believe he could just continue life blissfully? They thought he could be good ole Todd, and things
could instantly return to normal?

He sped forward and took another drink from the bottle. The
bourbon no longer burned his throat, and, because of that, he realized
he was finally intoxicated. It wasn't the cars, lights, and street lines
that had changed, but his perspective of them. And it wasn't only
speed that blurred them all together; it was inebriation. He was wasted
drunk. If his mind wasn't full of memories from a past with a family he
would never know again, he might overcome intoxication's influence
on his actions and slow down, head home, go to bed, and sleep it off.

But the cocktail of disaster in his mind and body forbade rational
decision-making, and he didn't care. He'd done the right things all

his life, and life had dumped on him in return. It had thrown one single knockout punch directly into Todd's soul, and everything he was had not just been knocked into dormancy, but had been ejected completely from him.

This was the new Todd. Fuck the rules, because the rules never gave a damn about him. The rules never cared for Beth and Stormy. In fact, his straight and narrow lifestyle had only rewarded him with tragedy. He couldn't handle it anymore. It had only been a few months, but the murk was so thick, all hope of escaping it was lost. He could not simply pull out of this and carry on with his life.

His head felt heavy. He took another long gulp from the bottle, finishing its contents, and tossed it out the window. With the music blaring, the wind, and the sound of passing traffic roaring through the open windows, he didn't hear the glass bottle crash and explode on the pavement. He would have loved to hear it—the sound of destruction, the audible confirmation of something else, other than his life, annihilated.

The crazy man had entered his backyard on that summer day, waving a gun and declaring impending doom for Todd and his family. Throwing about accusations at Dad about saving Todd and somehow altering a future that destiny had predetermined. That man, Billy Wagner, had told Beth she and her daughter wouldn't survive. And everything he had rambled on about eventually came true.

Todd still wondered, even in his current drunken state, how his father saving his life was an alteration of a future already written. In the natural flow of events, Dad had arrived on the scene and risked his own life to save Todd. How was that a violation of destiny's plans? Was his father supposed to show up and just watch the house burn? From Dad's description of the events, help was already coming when he arrived. The fire had well progressed, and Dad had decided the sound of sirens was too far away. There wasn't enough time to wait for them to show up and do their hero stuff.

Almost immediately after Dad had pulled Todd from the fire, as rescue personnel showed up and were running into the house after Beth, a gas leak caused by the fire had ignited and destroyed the house in one enormous explosion. Two firefighters lost their lives. It *was* a *natural* flow of events. What kind of father *wouldn't* have charged, without caution, into a burning home to save his son's life? What exactly did destiny have in mind?

Lights flashed. Not directly in his face, but somewhere nearby, creating a distant strobe effect in his vision. He blinked several times, assuming it was the streetlights as he saw them through drunken sight. But that wasn't it. Something else was flashing either beside him or from behind. He suddenly realized the flashing light was multicolored. Red, blue, red, blue, red, blue.

He looked in his rearview. That's where the light was coming from, reflecting from the mirrored glass into his eyes. It was from a vehicle hot on his tail. Red, blue, red, blue, red, blue. Then he heard the siren, loud and demanding.

Todd glanced at the speedometer. It claimed he was traveling at ninety-two miles per hour. And finally, he realized he was being pulled over. This might be his chance. He could flee, cause a huge police chase, get the pursuing officers riled up and frustrated; then, at the end, he could jump out of the car and pose as if he pointed a weapon at them. They would all instantly open fire. His body would be riddled with bullets before he hit the ground, dead as his family, his soul on its way to be with them.

Ahead, there was no traffic. He had passed the city limits minutes ago. There wouldn't be congestion on the interstate at this time of night, this far from the city. He was in the next county over, which

wasn't heavily populated. Todd might come upon a tractor-trailer occasionally if he continued on, but there would be no real obstructions.
He could lead the police on a high-speed chase for miles. Maybe even
until he ran out of gas.

He checked his rearview mirror again. Red, blue, red, blue, red,
blue. The siren screamed. The police car behind him weaved from left
to right to left to right, as if its driver was considering pulling up beside
Todd, or was using the police car's motion to grab his attention, as if
the siren and the lights weren't enough.

Todd looked at the speedometer. Ninety-three. With his right foot,
he nuzzled the gas pedal down a little further.

Chapter Twenty-Five

E arly morning, the sun was just below the eastern horizon, its glow spreading out and across a clear sky. A comfortable breeze. All of nature's elements worked together in preparation for a mild autumn day. Jim was asleep on his back, his arms at his sides, snoring heavily. Alice lay on her side, back facing her husband, sleeping silently. Dawn's early light entered the bedroom window and passed through nearly transparent curtains.

Jim's smartphone, laying faceup on his nightstand, vibrated. The entire table rumbled along with the incoming call. The vibrating stopped after around two minutes, paused, and then started again.

Jim stirred in his sleep and turned toward his wife. Still slumbering, he put an arm around her. She was undisturbed in her deep and peaceful rest. Jim's phone stopped vibrating again, and then Alice's phone on her nightstand followed suit.

She started, her eyes opening slowly, and looked toward her phone. It went silent, and she closed her eyes and fell back to sleep.

But then she was awakened again, to the sound of Jim's phone vibrating. She realized someone was trying desperately to get hold of either of them. She rolled over, pushing Jim's arm away, and said with a half-awakened voice, "Jim."

He mumbled and rotated onto his back, still not awakening.

"Jim," she said louder, tapping his shoulder.

His phone went silent and then started again.

He opened his eyes, staring straight up.

"Honey." She nudged his shoulder. "Someone is calling."

"What?" he said sleepily.

"Your phone. My phone. They're going crazy."

"Shit," he said. "What time is it?"

"I don't know. Answer your phone. When I got up to pee last night, Todd wasn't in his room."

As if jolted to life by his wife's words, Jim pivoted toward his phone. He looked at the screen and saw an incoming call from a phone number instead of an actual programmed contact, felt panicked, and picked it up. He hit the Answer button and held the phone to his ear.

"Hello?"

"Jim Radcliffe?" came the voice on the other end.

A voice Jim instantly knew he recognized but couldn't match it to a face in his mind.

"Yes. This is Jim."

"This is Officer Mitchell with LMPD. You may not remember me, but I was one of the arresting officers in your son's backyard the day that Billy Wagner threatened your family. I've got Todd here at the station."

"What?" Jim sat straight up, blanket falling away from his bare torso.

Immediately, Alice's expression became one of alarm in response to her husband's sudden change in demeanor.

"He's okay," Officer Mitchell said. "But I need you to come to the district station. He was pulled over for reckless driving. Failed a sobriety test and a breathalyzer pretty badly."

"He's not in jail?"

"No, sir. The arresting officer recognized your son from the news. He cut him a break, considering the tragedy he's been through. You're going to have to pick up your son. He's still not sobered up from the amount of alcohol he drank last night. His car is on the side of the interstate. We didn't tow it because if we had, we would've had to charge him. He's passed out drunk in a holding cell."

Even though Jim was concerned for his son, he couldn't help but realize that Officer Mitchell didn't remember the last conversation between him and Jim. It was because that conversation never happened. When Jim had charged into the police station demanding justice served on Billy Wagner, accusing that the man must have had something to do with the fire, it was before the reset which allowed him to save Todd. Because Todd was rescued this time around, Jim was complacent with the new set of circumstances. He hadn't gone to the police station to accuse Billy. This really was happening. All of it. He had actually been granted a do-over and executed it. The timeline had been changed, just as Billy Wagner foresaw.

Jim felt a touch of shame. He hadn't *cared enough* to go on a rampage over Beth's death as he had his son's. Content Todd was with them again, Jim had a guilty questioning of himself. Had he given a damn at all about Beth? And if he didn't, then how much did he let his own wants overrule what was important to his son? When you love someone, you want them to be happy. Jim had considered none of this. He'd simply acted on wanting his wife and son back, and when he accomplished that through some kind of strange supernatural means, he was done.

Alice now sat up in bed, frowning at Jim as she listened to his phone conversation.

"I'll be right there," Jim said.

"Thank you, sir," Officer Mitchell said and then the call ended.

Jim looked at Alice. "Todd was pulled over. He was drunk. Driving recklessly. They didn't arrest him. He's only being held until someone picks him up."

"Jesus," Alice muttered.

"We have to go get him."

"Let's go."

Jim dropped his legs off the bed and just sat there for several moments, staring at the floor. Todd showed up drunk and enraged for dinner. Now he was driving intoxicated so erratically, he was pulled over by the police. Jim's son seemed to slip into more than just grief. Fading away into something more dangerous than moving on from losing loved ones. This was going into a dark abyss of irrationality and self-destruction.

Jim wanted to think he was just overreacting. After all, the first time around, losing Todd had driven Alice to instant alcoholism. It seemed of the three, Jim was the only one who handled the tragedy with a level head. Was it because he didn't care as much about his loved ones as others did? He remembered wanting to lose it, wanting to explode into grieving fits, when Todd had perished in that fire, but couldn't. Of course he had cried, but just crying and that's it? Over his own son? He had finally given in to the need to explode on the side of a road, but that was after his car had broken down. Why did it take a flat tire to bring forth a flow of emotion from him? He knew he loved his son and his wife. Jim knew he cared deeply for Beth. And the granddaughter on the way—Jim had felt excitement for that, had fantasized about what he would do as a grandfather.

But had he cared as deeply as he was supposed to? He hadn't accepted Mr. Brimstone's offer until *after* Alice had killed herself. Why did it take that for him to drop to a level of desperation so deep that he was willing to ask for help from someone he thought was scamming or taunting him?

From behind him, Jim heard Alice's voice. "What are you doing? We have to go."

He realized he'd gone into a trance while sitting on the bed and hadn't moved for minutes. Alice was already up and getting dressed behind him. He snapped out of it and stood up.

"I don't know. This is all...confusing."

"Confusing? What do you mean by that?"

"I can't explain it."

"There's nothing confusing. Are you concerned with Todd's behavior? How would you behave if you lost your wife and kid? Our son is grieving. We need to be there for him."

Jim knew all too well how he would behave, but he definitely couldn't tell Alice that. He stood up. "Let's go get our son."

***

The same female officer stood behind the counter when Jim and Alice entered the police station. Jim realized that because of the reboot of the timeline, she wouldn't remember having met him, because now it hadn't happened. This was their first meeting. Jim looked around the lobby and saw all the wall hangings from the first time hadn't changed and were in the same places.

After they informed her of who they were, the officer disappeared through the doorway behind the counter. A few minutes later, she emerged with Officer Mitchell behind her. He came around the counter and immediately extended a hand to Jim, who shook it, and then to Alice, who followed her husband's lead.

"I'm sorry to have to meet again under shitty circumstances. I'm also very sorry for your losses. I can't imagine."

Alice immediately got down to business. "Where's our son? Where's Todd?"

"He's in the holding cell, ma'am. He's sleeping it off. He woke up about an hour ago, puked his guts out, then passed out again on the cot in there. When my officer picked him up, your son was extremely drunk. He was wasted, speeding close to one hundred miles per hour. Swerving in and out of traffic."

"Jesus," Alice said.

"He could have killed himself, or somebody else. I can't tell you how severe this could have turned out. He's lucky. Everyone around him was lucky. My officer immediately recognized your son from the news about the fire and took pity on him. That's actually against strict policies. The law isn't supposed to bow to anyone. Nobody is above the law. You two understand the enormous favor my officer did for your son and your family?"

"We do," Jim answered. "We'll take care of him. Get him some help."

"I know your family has been through a lot. Billy Wagner was sentenced to inpatient mental therapy over his little fiasco in your son's backyard. Thanks to your affidavits, he won't be getting out anytime soon. The man is messed up and needed the help. Not a bad guy, just a messed-up guy. I know of your tragedy, and I'm sorry about that. Nobody should have to endure such a loss."

Jim sensed a "but" coming. He was right.

"But we can't just let your son zoom around town, tanked on liquor, putting innocent citizens at risk. This is a one-time thing. He gets pulled over again like that, the usual consequences will apply to him."

"We understand," Alice said.

Officer Mitchell scrutinized them for a few moments. "His car is still on the side of the interstate. If I catch him driving today, he'll be locked up. He's so drunk it's going to take a couple of days to sleep it off. The entire basement down there smells of booze, and he's the only one in the holding cell section. That's how much he drank. He had to be only moments away from passing out at the wheel."

Jim was getting irritated. Although thankful the police had cut his son a break, he felt scolded. And Officer Mitchell's constant pounding of Todd's errors, damn near implying he was a shitty person, was causing Jim feelings of spite. He understood. He got it. Todd got drunk and put people's lives in danger. It was a terrible thing. An awful thing. Both he and Alice knew it was wrong. They weren't teenagers who needed intense verbal reprimanding. They would do something about it. Put Todd in some kind of treatment or psychological therapy. They were going to take action and not just let it slide.

Todd had been fading since the funeral. It was time to force him to get his head on straight. He could grieve all he needed, but he also needed help with his now full-powered depression. Otherwise, he would end up in the ground with his wife and child. And Alice would eventually end up in a plot of her own.

"Understood," Jim said, faking patience.

"I'll go get him." Officer Mitchell disappeared through the doorway.

An awkward few minutes followed. The female officer stood behind the counter, tapping away on her smartphone as if she were texting someone. Jim and Alice stared at each other, glanced around the lounge, looked at their feet, played with their own fingers. Jim wanted to express his discontent with Officer Mitchell attempting to chisel the impression of Todd being a horrible person into their minds, but cautioned himself against saying anything in this station where other ears could hear. He didn't want to stir up feelings of resentment that might lead to Mitchell changing his mind about pressing charges. Jim thought it might be too late for that, but he wasn't sure. He was no legal expert—or even a novice.

When Officer Mitchell led Todd into the lobby, through the doors behind the desk, Alice gasped.

Jim's attention had been wandering around the room, but now turned toward his son. Todd looked awful. Though they had seen him less than twenty-four hours ago, he looked as if he'd been gone for years and aged badly. His appearance was one of exhaustion and surrender: deep bags of darkness below his eyes, his face long and tired, his clothes wrinkled as if he hadn't changed them in weeks.

He looked at his parents but didn't acknowledge them. Instead, he walked right past everyone, turned back, and asked, "Am I free to go now?"

"Yeah, you're good to go," Officer Mitchell replied.

And with that confirmation, Todd exited the police station.

"He looks awful," Alice said to Mitchell.

"He's putting himself through some shit," Jim said.

"I understand he's going through something horrible, but your son needs to clean his act up real quick," Officer Mitchell said. "A lot of people deal with what he's dealing with. They don't all turn to self-destructive behavior. We're talking on a scale of endangering others. Your son should be in jail awaiting arraignment right now. My officer gave him a break. That's not going to happen again. Next time, he'll be charged."

"We understand," Jim said.

Alice was still staring toward the exit. Her expression was as if she'd just watched a zombie walk out those doors.

"Get that man some help. He can't do it on his own."

"Thank you," Jim said, and he grabbed Alice by the hand. "Let's go."

She looked up at him, shock still on her face, and surrendered to his lead.

Chapter Twenty-Six

U pon his arrival at the inpatient mental facility, Billy immediately began plotting his escape. There were two levels to this government-run agency, and he learned the floor he was to be housed on was lighter security than the one below ground. Downstairs, as everyone called it, was where they put the more severe cases of mental illness. People who were likely to hurt themselves or others spent most of their days in a maximum-security lounging area, with nearly one guard for every patient present.

On the first floor, where Billy was, there were only three security guards on two shifts of twelve hours each. The patients on this level were believed to only have minor mental issues, sent here by the courts to actually get better and eventually be allowed back into society. There were even a few who had arrived after Billy did and were already released. The lounging area on the first floor was a more laid-back atmosphere, where fraternizing was as loosely watched as a high school lunchroom. These were the patients who were trusted, and Billy was one of them.

As his plan went into motion from day one, he befriended several of the other patients he had chosen and assumed he could most likely win over. And by the end of his second week, he had created a loyal posse. Four other patients.

There was Ralph, the older guy in his mid-fifties, his head full of gray hair and his ongoing act of coolness. Ralph was always in character, trying to appear calmer than he really was on the inside.

Then there was Edward. The younger guy, in his mid-twenties, who was here because he became so obsessed over ridiculous conspiracy theories, people in his life thought he was a walking red flag for an eventual attempt to overthrow the government on his own. He had hurt no one or even threatened to, but somehow the courts thought he could use inpatient therapy to clear his head of conspiracy fog and return to being a normal and productive member of society.

There was Thomas. A gigantic man in his thirties. At least six and a half feet tall and nearly three hundred pounds of pure muscle and strength. He was here because he was considered to be on the edge of a mental breakdown after his wife left him for his brother. Thomas was an angry man, and definitely not one to piss off. But even given his size, and what seemed to be impending physical aggression toward a particular member of his family, he was deemed harmless enough for the minimum-security floor.

The fourth man was in his early thirties. Joe was a quiet person who had also suffered a mental breakdown over a job he'd lost. By his own words, he didn't go to work for a week in protest of having only received a fifteen-cent raise for the year. Upon returning, he was discharged over no-call no-shows. Unable to handle the fact that his peaceful little rebellion had cost him his employment instead of earning him a higher rate of pay, he turned to drinking and fits of rage around his own home. His wife had taken a mental inquest warrant out on him, hoping to get him right again, and here he was, now a member of Billy's little, quickly assembled gang.

The five of them sat at the same table every day, telling stories, sharing laughs, endeavoring into deep discussions of religion and science, government and anarchy, family and friends, pleasant experiences and bad. A regular lunchtime group, just like in high school or middle school. They spent most of their days together and were only separated during their individual counseling sessions, during which they all also received their daily doses of medication.

Sitting at the table, Ralph had been verbally reminiscing when he'd lost his virginity at age seventeen. They were all laughing and carrying on as if there wasn't a care in the world, when Billy took the conversation to a more serious path.

"Okay, guys, you know we're not supposed to be in here. None of us."

"It's the government," Edward said. "It's always the government. This is the place where those of us who resist end up. I guess it's better than prison, but it's still wrong."

"You think everything is because of the government," Thomas said.

"I concur with Thomas," Ralph said.

"Everything is because of the government," Edward said. "They have their hands in *everything*. If you don't see it, then you're part of the problem."

"Well, I'm definitely sure the government put me here because of everything I know," Billy said.

"What do you know?" Joe asked, genuinely interested.

"Well, I know time travel exists. I was about to save the world, the universe, and they locked me in here because they thought I was crazy. But I'm not. My dreams have proved it."

"Your dreams about the horse races?" Joe asked.

"Yeah. Dreams *like* those," Billy said.

"The fire. The house fire. That lady and her baby," Ralph said.

"That's the one," Billy answered.

Ralph raised an eyebrow. "If that man changed the timeline, there will be serious consequences for all of us."

"Paradox," Joe said.

"Exactly," Edward said.

"They put me in here to stop me from fixing it," Billy said. "They don't want me to save the world because it's all a part of their plan. The man who was saved is probably someone they need for their idea of the future. He's going to play a part in their huge plot."

"What's the plot?" Edward asked.

"I don't know," Billy answered. "The dreams are unclear on that. But they are clear that Jim Radcliffe went back in time and changed the outcome of that fire. He saved his son. He saved his son and altered destiny."

"If this is true," Thomas said, "then what are you supposed to do about it? How can you do anything? You're stuck in here like the rest of us."

Billy couldn't help but smile. He immediately withdrew his smirk, though. He had been working on them since he'd arrived in this place, and it had taken such minimal effort to find and manipulate the handful of people he would need to execute his plan of escape. He realized that by escaping, he would eventually be captured again, and his consequences the next time around would be harsher. He would end up in prison for several years. Yet, being in jail for years of his life was not a deterrent to fixing what had been broken.

More was at stake than just his life; the lives of billions hung in the altered equilibrium of the universe. To those who put him here, he was merely another crazy person, lost to insanity because his wife had left him. But he knew he was more than that. The dreams had come true way too often for him to ignore the one that warned him of profound consequences. The one stirred up by Jim Radcliffe's venture into the past to change certain outcomes.

Billy had to get out of here, had to find Todd Radcliffe, and kill him. It was the only way to set things right. Todd wasn't supposed to be alive. He should have perished in that fire. He *did* perish in that fire. It was the bidding of destiny, and Todd's father had denied destiny of its plan. Billy didn't know what Todd's future was. He only knew that Todd wasn't supposed to *have* a future.

"You need to escape," Edward said. "You have to get out of here."

Ralph said, "If it has something to do with the future, then this man must be stopped before he causes whatever paradox his further existence will create. The universe does not like paradoxes."

"We're on the low-security floor," Edward said. "I've scoped it all out since I've been here. They trust the patients on this floor more than they should. Government arrogance. They underestimate every person who's brought here."

"I've done the same," Billy said to Edward.

"Well, do you have a plan?" Joe asked.

"I do. I need your help. All of you."

"Count me in," Edward said. "Any chance to put the government in its place."

"I'll help," Ralph said. "We are talking about something which is beyond ourselves. In this universe, on this plane of existence, we are so tiny we barely even exist. When given the chance to make a difference, one cannot pass it up."

Thomas said, "I'm down to fuck some shit up. Just tell me where and when."

Joe said, "I don't know, man. I miss my wife."

"Isn't she the one who put you in here?" Billy asked.

"Yeah," Joe answered. "And I want to get out as quickly as possible."

Billy thought for a moment and then said, "I have a role for you in my plan that won't get you into much trouble. Actually, all of you can help without extending your stay here by too much. You'll get a bad conduct reprimand, but that's it. I'm the one who's escaping. I'm the one who will be in deep shit. But I don't care. I have to fix things. I'm the only one who knows exactly what's going on besides Jim Radcliffe. The only motherfucker who can set things right is me."

"You in, Joe?" Edward asked.

Joe hesitated, a faraway look in his eyes, and then said, "I'll help. This better not land me in prison."

"It won't." Billy smiled. "It's a simple plan, and you guys might at most be stuck in your rooms for a few days. That's it."

"Well, what are we doing and when?" Edward asked.

"Friday. Two days from now."

"Why Friday?" Ralph asked.

"Because it's supposed to rain and storm all day Friday," Billy said. "Perfect cover for an escape. It's hard to see a person running away in a thunderstorm with torrential rainfall."

"And what's the plan?" Joe asked.

Billy leaned back in his chair with deep thought on his face. There was a plan. He'd been working on it for three weeks now. He looked around at his soon-to-be coconspirators and studied each of their expressions. They all appeared confident and unbothered, except for Joe. He would spend the next full day working on Joe, boosting his morale toward the mission at hand. Billy couldn't have any of them backing out on him at the last minute.

If that happened, he wouldn't escape, and further attempts would likely be thwarted by him being thrown into the maximum-security basement of this hellhole for a long time. He might even end up back in front of a judge and eventually sentenced to prison, while the universe fell apart, because of the paradox Jim Radcliffe had created. All of existence relied on Billy's escape. There could be no mistakes or second thoughts.

Billy leaned forward. "Okay, here it is. I need you guys to pay attention. If you have any questions, ask. This has to go off without the slightest mistake. Joe…"

Chapter Twenty-Seven

A lice walked through her backyard garden. There were only a few plants still alive in the middle of this fall season. She stepped past each withering vine, pulled at branches, knelt and felt the hard ground from which they were growing, stood up, and continued on to the next.

Jim stood on the edge of the garden, watching his wife, but his mind was in a far-off place. He wondered what things would be like now if he'd saved Beth, instead of his son, from that fire. Would Alice still be here, possibly a renewed energy from having a grandchild in her life after having lost her only offspring? Would she have gone as far into depression as she had the first time around, when there was nothing to distract her from profound, completely enveloping grief?

Every time these thoughts ran through his mind, Jim hated himself. He traveled through self-loathing via the road of the feeling of selfishness. These sentiments were triggered by his understanding that things weren't going like he assumed. He had saved his son, but nobody was living happily ever after.

Jim told himself he needed patience, and repeatedly fought off the pondering over what-ifs. This current turmoil his family was enduring had to only be temporary. They would come through this dark cloud of Todd's overwhelming and consuming psychological misery together. Eventually, they would all find the light at the end of the tunnel, and move toward it into a normal life again.

But were those thoughts also selfish? Was Jim showing an inability to feel empathy? Was he more concerned about overall peace than his own son's mental state?

"We had quite the harvest this year." Alice ran her hands along a jaded and slumped-over tomato plant, her back facing Jim.

"Plenty of fried green tomatoes."

"You and those fried green tomatoes. Your son used to eat the hell out of them with you. Now I wonder if he's even eating at all."

"He eats," Jim said. "Just not like before everything."

"We're going to have to talk him into getting help, Jim." She turned around and faced her husband. "He can't just keep sleeping it off. The drinking and driving...he could have killed someone. He could have killed himself."

"I agree. I don't know how to handle something like that. What do we even say to him?"

"There are other routes besides just convincing him he needs help."

"Other routes?"

Alice looked up at the sky. An autumn overcast blocked out sunlight. The gray ash clouds made the day match the bleak mood. A gloomy blanket of misery and uncertainty.

Alice said, "Legal ways. We can have him committed."

"And have him hate us?"

Alice forced a smile. "He would never truly hate us. Sure, he'd be mad, but once he was okay again, he would be thankful."

"A little soon to be throwing him in a padded room, don't you think?"

Alice knelt again, ran one finger along the dirt, drawing a faint line. "Too soon would be better than too late."

"How do we know the difference? How do we know what to do?"

Alice stood up again, looking at Jim with pending tears glossing over her eyes. "We have to follow our instinct on this. It's not like there's a guidebook for this kind of thing. We have to act on love."

Jim released a sigh of frustration. Not frustration that Alice was pushing immediate action, but because of a feeling of despair of the overall circumstances. Everyone's mental state was in danger. They were all on the brink of psychological collapse.

"Acting with our heart and not our minds might be the worst thing to do," Jim said. "We're older than that. We're smarter than that."

"What else can we possibly act on?" Alice's voice hinted at irritation. "He's our son, not a job or a project. What else should we allow to drive us besides our love for him?"

"I wasn't saying we don't love him," Jim said. "I'm saying that if we act on emotion, then we make the wrong moves. He needs our help, and we will give it to him. It's a delicate time for him, Alice. We don't think things through, we could fuck him up even more."

Alice's voice rose with anger. "How much more could he be fucked up, Jim? How worse does he have to get? We don't do something now, we'll end up losing him. You can't always just sit around, waiting for things to get better. Goddammit, Jim. Goddammit."

"You act like I had something to do with all of this," Jim fired back. "You don't think I see him hurting? You don't think it gets to me?"

"Then show it."

"Show what, Alice? Somebody has to keep a level head around here. What do you want me to show? You want me to fall apart too? We can all just fall apart and nothing good comes from that."

"Blah, blah, blah. You're full of nothing but words. You won't *do* anything."

"I don't do anything? You have no idea what I've done. What are you now? Some kind of psychiatrist? You think you know the answers to everything just because you love a son? You know how many people love their kids and make poor decisions? You know why, Alice? Because they don't think. You want to run on emotion. Emotion won't fix things."

"What will?!" she screamed. "What will fix things, Mister Expert? He could have died! You just want to wait until he does! I can't lose my son. *I can't lose him!*"

"You haven't lost him! He's in that house right there, sleeping it off! He's safe!"

"He's not safe from himself, Jim! You don't care. You don't even fucking care!" She stomped past him and toward the house.

He swiveled as she walked by, not pursuing her. "Where are you going?"

She stopped, and without turning to face him, Alice said, "I'm going to check on my son, Jim. Something you don't seem to care enough to do."

"You have no clue," he mumbled at her.

She turned to face him; her expression was full of rage and frustration. "No, Jim. *You* have no clue." She stormed into the house, slamming the inner door shut behind her.

Jim stood there, dumbfounded, for several moments before following her in. As soon as he stepped into the house and shut the back door behind him, he heard the doorbell ring. It must not have been the first ring, because just a moment later he heard the front door open, his wife's muffled voice, and then a man speaking. Jim went into the living room.

Standing in the foyer, a middle-aged man in a suit and tie. He carried a briefcase and had a somber expression pasted to his face. Alice and the man were already engaged in conversation.

"He's asleep right now," Alice was saying. "He had a rough night."

"There's no need to wake him," the man said. "I'm Archie Baskins. I'm the regional manager for distribution."

From behind Alice, Jim said, "Come on in. Have a seat. I have a feeling this isn't good."

"Sure thing." Archie followed Jim and Alice into the living room.

"Coffee?" Jim asked.

"No thanks." Archie waved one hand in a declining gesture. "I can't stay long."

"You want to have a seat?" Alice asked, her voice full of worry.

"I'm good. I appreciate it, though," Archie answered.

"We are Todd's parents," Jim said. Neither he nor Alice sat down. "This is Alice and I'm Jim."

"Pleased to meet you," Archie said. His voice was nervous. "Although I do regret the circumstances under which we are meeting."

"Well," Jim said, "let's get down to it. I assume Todd is fired."

Archie sighed, as if about to deliver a serious blow. "Let's not say he's fired. Because he's not. It's not termination. Hopefully, this is temporary."

"Suspended?" Alice asked.

"Something like that." Archie took another deep breath and let it out slowly. "We have to replace Todd. He's not coming to work. When he does, he's showing up drunk. He's behind in every aspect of his job, and it's affecting the entire operation here in Louisville." Another sigh as Jim and Alice listened. "We understand what happened. It's an awful tragedy. We know this. We don't expect anyone to go through what

Todd has and still be on top of their game. Especially this soon after. Three months, six months...hell, even a year may not be enough."

"It's tough on him. He lost everything," Alice said.

"Yes, ma'am. It is surely tough on him. And we know that. I'm having such a hard time with the right words here. I want you to know we're not heartless or cold. It's a business, and it can't stop because someone is having personal problems." He paused.

Alice and Jim remained silent.

Archie continued, "Personal problems aren't meant to downplay what's happened to him. I just don't know the right words. This is so sensitive."

"The company has to go on." Jim helped Archie out. "I understand what you're getting at. You can't let the ship sink because one sailor is sick."

"That's exactly it. I don't want it to sound inconsiderate or apathetic. It's not that at all."

"I'm following you," Jim assured Archie.

"Thank you," Archie said with a soft sigh of relief. "We're replacing Todd as of immediately. He needs to take this time to get better. We're not leaving him hanging. His health insurance benefits will remain in place for a year. We're giving him six months' severance pay. We will—"

"That's fired," Alice said. She looked from Archie to Jim. "Severance pay is fired."

"Ma'am, fired would be complete and immediate separation from the company, including pay and benefits. This is not what we're doing. When Todd gets better, he can come back. If we don't return him to his position, we'll find something for him. We know this is a mess created by tragedy. We know he's mourning. I can't imagine what he's going through, and I'm not going to pretend to. But like your husband said, we can't let the ship sink."

"Seems like low-key abandonment to me," Alice said.

"Alice." Jim gave her a look that told her not to get excited.

"I'm just saying," she replied. "This sounds like he's being fired."

"Let the man talk," Jim said.

"Look," Archie said. "Todd is our top performer. The numbers his leadership produces are tops in the company. I don't just mean in this city. I mean, in all the cities we're located. Not just regional, but nationwide. We value Todd's capabilities as if they are gold. But for now, he's got too much going on, and those numbers have plummeted. We have to move on. At least temporarily, we have to put someone else in the driver's seat."

"We understand," Jim said.

Alice said, "No, we don't. You're abandoning him in a time of need."

"I'm sorry, Mrs. Radcliffe. I wish there was another way. We had several meetings over this. This is what has to be done for now. I have some paperwork." Archie laid his briefcase on the sofa behind him and popped it open, pulled out a stack of papers, and offered them to Jim.

Jim took them.

"This is a briefing of what benefits will continue. His pay for the next six months is outlined. Nothing needs to be signed. We just printed out some information for him. Like I said, we aren't heartless. There is even a list of top-notch mental care providers in there. The company will pick up any co-pay required if he sees someone on that list. When he has a clear bill of health, he can contact me, and we'll talk."

"This is just going to sink him further," Alice snapped. "This doesn't help. Those papers don't help. First, he lost his family, then his sanity, and now his job."

"Alice," Jim said.

"This is rock bottom for him," Alice declared. "This can't help at all."

"Alice." Jim interrupted again. "Not now."

"What do you mean by not now? When? They're dropping him like a bad habit."

"I have to go." Archie closed his briefcase and picked it up. "I'm truly sorry. I don't know what else to say."

"You could take those papers back and let my son keep his job. Just give him a few weeks off."

"He's been declining for months, ma'am. I'm sorry, but this is a decision come to by more than one person. It wasn't simple."

"Of course it wasn't," Jim said.

Alice turned around, her face showing anger, and looked up at her husband in defiance. "You agree with this shit?"

"Again, now is not the time," Jim said.

"It seems to be the time to abandon our son." She faced Archie with ire. "You can leave now."

"I'm sorry, ma'am." Archie stepped past them toward the front door. "I wish this wasn't the circumstances."

"Of course you do," Alice said sarcastically. "Business is business. Right? People don't matter. Only money."

Archie wanted to reply, thought for a moment, but then exited the house without a word, leaving Jim and Alice to themselves, not in agreement once more.

"You just take it easy on everything, don't you?" she asked Jim. "Just let everything go without a fight."

"You think I can step in and change their minds? Who do you think I am? Some kind of magician?"

"You can speak up."

"And say what?"

"I don't know. But you don't even try. It's like you don't care. You just let everything flow past as if it's all okay. It's not okay, Jim. Nothing is okay."

"We need to make sure our son gets better. This isn't the end. You heard the guy. They are not just firing him. They want him to get better."

"It's a wonder you even ran into that house to save anyone," Alice snapped. "It's a wonder you didn't just stand there and watch and say, 'Welp, there's nothing I can do.'"

"What the fuck is wrong with you?" Jim asked, distress rising in his tone. "Why would you say something like that to me? I ran into that fire and pulled him out. Did you think that would be the end of it all? That his wife and kid would die in that fire, but because he lived, we could just all suddenly go back to a normal family life?"

"With a little support from his parents, yes. Eventually. Of course not instantly. But he's not got the support of his parents, does he? Just his mother. His father wants to stand back and just let everything happen."

Her words were more than stinging. They packed a punch, even though Jim knew Alice didn't know what had actually happened. She didn't know about the first time, when nobody survived the fire, and Jim had watched her slow demise, until she finally lost her grip on caring about anything and ended her own life. She didn't know what he'd given up to save her and Todd.

Jim had sold his soul to the devil to save them.

Chapter Twenty-Eight

Darkness in all directions. A forever void. There's a sound. Millions of tiny fingers tapping erratically on glass. The pace of the tapping speeds up, then slows. It's coming in waves. Steady. Faster. Slower. Steady. The nothingness all around, intertwining with the ongoing pitter-patter, should be relaxing, but it's not. It is a sign of something to come. Something bad is on the horizon. It's approaching in the company of dread, danger, suffering, death.

A male voice originates from somewhere nearby, yet also far away. It reverberates through the pattering and the blackness. It says, "Madame President—"

Another male voice, this one filled with panic: "Three made it—"

The rapping grows louder, softens, quicker, slower, steady.

The bad thing is approaching.

A heavy feeling in the chest. Anticipation of a disaster that will affect millions of lives. Billions. All the lives. Every single living soul is about to be snuffed out. The feeling of apprehension is giving way to complete horror. Shaking legs. Trembling hands. Brain feels as if it's being squeezed in a vise.

"Madame President—"

"Three made it—"

"My God, what have—"

A female voice says, "They would have—"

"My God—"

"Madame President—"

More voices. A few have become a crowd. Distinct words have become incoherent chatter. The tone of them all is the same: panic. They are still growing in number. So many people. They're all afraid. Something out of a nightmare has occurred. Something more than bad or horrific. The tension is squeezing. Crushing all souls into a compressed, united terror. Regret. Tentativeness.

Suddenly, the voices soften. Something is coming. My God, it's horrific. Something is coming.

From overhead, the sound of a low-flying jet plane. It's as if it is cruising only a hundred feet from the ground. It's passing by directly above. Look up. Just darkness. Darkness still reigns everywhere. It's not a jet plane. It's not a plane at all. This is something worse. Something much, much worse. Terror. Shock. Panic. Something so awful. God, no.

"My God—"

"Madame President—"

"My God—"

An explosion. It's so loud the ears hurt. It's so powerful it must be something as big as the moon crashing into Earth. So forceful. So disturbing. So thunderous. The fear is overwhelming.

Rumbling approaches quickly. There's no chance to run. There's nowhere in the darkness to hide. It sounds like a stampede of a billion animals is coming this way. It is not a stampede. In the distance, a glow crossing the entire plane of sight and rising from the horizon. The glow is growing stronger, the stampede louder. The glow and the stampede arrive simultaneously. A flash of light, thunder so loud, as if it originates within the ears.

Blinding light.

Deafening thunder.

"My God—"

Billy awoke. His eyes opened mechanically, like a human-replicated robot powering up for the day. He didn't move at all, staring straight at the ceiling with his arms at his sides and his feet protruding from a thin white blanket. There was a gray gloom cast across the ceiling, as if daytime had attempted to arrive, but a vast, strong overcast had limited it. Rain drummed against the barred window glass like millions of insects crashing into it as they tried to enter the room.

It was Friday morning, but it was early. Usually, at seven a.m. sharp, members of the facility staff entered the rooms, waking the patients for morning fraternizing in the lounge. They were allowed caffeinated coffee, but no sugar added to it. Caffeine was okay, but any other form of unnatural stimulants wasn't. Then, one at a time, the patients had their one-on-one with Doctor Jameson in his office. Accompanied by a security guard, they were given their daily medication, and then a bullshit counseling session. The guard waited outside the room for the psychological element of the meeting.

Today was the day. Billy had gathered his posse of five, counting him, over the past few days, and they had planned out today's escape with profound detail. Although they all seemed to have their doubts and some reservations, Billy was confident they would stick to the plan, and he would make it out of this place today. He knew what consequences awaited him after an attempted escape, and how much worse they would be if he were successful. But this was his last chance to save the universe. He could not waver in his resolve. The show must go on so that the bigger show *could* go on.

Today was the day Billy Wagner would become a hero. Though it would be an unknown deed to the world, it was for the good of all things that existed. There could be no doubt. There could be no hesitation. Only resolve and steadfastness must prevail. Otherwise, everything now and in the future would be lost and destroyed.

It was all up to him.

Chapter Twenty-Nine

The morning lounge was full of patients and chatter. Some were having coffee, some were drinking water, and a few sat at the windows, staring into a rainy outside world they had been forcefully removed from. Billy and his clan sat together at a table in the center of the room. This had become their usual spot. Just like a lunchroom in high school, everyone had tables they habitually sat at. There was no official assignment or designated seats, but naturally, over time, people were creatures of habit, and once comfortable, returned to the same spot daily.

The only person missing from the table was Joe, who was in session with the psychiatrist. The other four, including Billy, who was the only one with coffee, were quietly going over the escape plan.

"We don't have to hurt anyone, right?" Edward said. "We can pull this off without hurting anyone."

"You have to make it look real, though," Billy said. "It might help to land a few punches on each other. But no, don't actually hurt anyone. The idea is for this to go off with only me being in any serious trouble."

Ralph leaned forward, his gray hair a mess from a night of tossing and turning. "What are you going to do when you're out there?"

"Out there?" Billy nodded toward the windows, which were covered on the outside with drops of rain. The grayness of the day was evident even through the rain-spangled glass.

"You don't have a car," Thomas said. "You can't get away fast. They'll have you back in here in less than an hour. It's not going to work."

"I'm going to run like hell," Billy said. "I know this city well. I've spent years homeless and getting everywhere I need by foot. The rain will camouflage me well enough. Sure, eventually I'll be caught, but not before I do what I have to do."

"You're really going to kill that guy? The one who shouldn't be here?" Ralph asked. "Seems there'd be another way."

Billy didn't immediately answer. Instead, he seemed to stare off into another time and dimension for a few moments. His expression was one of deep, ominous thought. Finally, he said, "I don't know. I'm not a killer. But one life for billions? He's not supposed to be here anyhow. The way I'd do it would be a lot better than the way he was supposed to die months ago."

"In a fire," Joe said from behind them.

They all looked at him as he took his empty seat.

He said, "The man was supposed to die in a fire. But he didn't. How do we know this isn't the way it was supposed to happen? How do we know his destiny wasn't to die and be brought back somehow? What if this *is* the way things were meant to be? Wouldn't we then be conspiring against destiny?"

"No," Billy said sharply. "My dreams. I can't see clearly, but bad things will occur because he was brought back. He's going to do something bad, or one of his future children will, or maybe someone he affects negatively will. Something terrifying is going to happen because of the altered timeline. I know this. I trust my dreams. They've never let me down before."

From behind them, a male voice, one of the security guards, said, "Ralph, you're next."

They all turned around to see the guard across the room. Billy breathed a sigh of relief that the guard wasn't close enough to hear their conversation. They had become so engrossed, their voices were no longer in a whisper.

"Be back in a few, fellas," Ralph said as he got up and left the table.

In a dreadful tone, Joe said, "You're next, Billy. They always call you after Ralph."

"We're really going to do this," Edward said.

"You okay?" Billy asked Edward. Then he addressed everyone at the table. "You guys good?"

"They will know we're involved with your escape attempt," Joe said. "They won't dismiss it as coincidence. They'll know."

Billy maintained a cool and calm demeanor. "They will probably think it at first."

"We may end up in prison right alongside you," Joe said.

Billy said, "I will vouch for you guys. I'll say I saw an opportunity and took it."

Edward said, "They'll investigate. They'll go back to the cameras they have all around this place. They'll see us sitting at the same table, day after day, conversing. There's no telling how many times one of us has looked around to check if someone might hear us. The video footage of us sitting here will be suspicious."

"Look around," Billy said as he did so. "There are regular groups sitting at tables every day. Certain people naturally flock together in places like this. It's just like being in school."

"I'm not so sure," Thomas said. "I feel like we look suspicious, and they all don't."

"That's paranoia," Billy said. "That's all it is. They won't know. They won't know as long as we all stick to the story. If one of us breaks from the story, then the whole aftermath will derail." Billy leaned in.

"*We have to stick to the story.* No matter what. They'll try to trick everyone into snitching. One of us cracked, they will say. They'll say Joe said this and Ralph said that. Don't believe them. Just stick to the story and it will all be fine. That's the most important thing. I can't stress it enough. *Stick to the story.*"

"I won't crack," Thomas said.

"I'm good," Edward said.

"Stick to the story," Joe said. "Most important thing. Got it."

"No matter what they say," Billy said.

"Right," Joe said.

Billy leaned back again and glanced around the table. He studied his coconspirators' faces. Their expressions. Their demeanor. Every one of them had the look of worry. He suddenly wasn't sure he'd vetted them well enough before choosing to befriend them for the sake of his escape plan. None of them looked confident, and any of them might falter when in an interrogation room. But after watching everyone in the unit closely, they were the only ones he felt were strong-minded enough to help him. Sure, they had been easy enough to manipulate, with nothing more sophisticated than the truth, but, their sagacity was an obstacle. Who with a level head would try to pull off an assisted escape with the threat of prison looming as a result?

Edward said, "I'm not sure it really matters. We're talking about the government here. If they want to pin us with crimes, they will. If you succeed, and the story goes public, they will need scapegoats. That will surely be us. We will be guilty, too. I don't think the worry is whether we'll be charged with some kind of escape accusation, but how stiff the punishment will be for it."

"I'm not prison material," Joe said.

"Not sure what prison material is," Thomas said. "I know I can handle myself physically in the slammer, but mentally, not so sure. I'm a big guy, but I don't think I'd handle confinement so well."

Billy looked at Thomas. "What do you think this is here?"

"Yeah," Thomas replied. "But there are no bars here. We're not incarcerated with hardened criminals. We were all sent here by what is considered a light sentence. Prison would be different."

Joe slapped his hands on the table and sighed. "I don't know, man. I don't know."

Billy felt his chance of escape slipping away. If any of them balked, he was screwed. The world would be screwed. "Guys, we are doing this for a greater cause. They'll come full force at *me*. I will be the one who escaped. They will forget all about you guys."

"I'm not backing out," Thomas said. "I'm just preparing myself for the worst."

"The worst won't be as bad as you're expecting," Billy said.

"It's always the worst for me," Joe said.

"Yeah, same here," Thomas said.

Edward said, "Every damn time. If I have any luck, it's bad luck."

"You guys in or out? I have to know before I go in that room with Doctor Jameson. We good?"

Silence gripped all of them. Thomas and Edward stared at the table while Joe played with his thumbs. They all had somber expressions on their faces. Looks of hopelessness and doubt in themselves. Worries of consequences that might extend their captivity by years.

"I don't know, man." Joe finally broke the silence, and Billy's heart sank into his gut.

Billy leaned toward Joe. "We can do this. It'll work."

Edward said, "You promise to take all the shit when it hits the fan?"

"Full responsibility?" Thomas asked.

"Yes," Billy answered enthusiastically. "I swear to you guys, the focus will be on me. I'm going to kill a man. They won't even think about you all. All eyes will be on the murderer, which will be me."

Thomas plainly said, "I'm in."

A sigh from Edward. Then, "I'm in."

Joe still stared at the table as if his mind were in some far-off place. Billy looked at him; he looked back at Billy, and said, "I'm in, man. I hope you're right."

From behind them, Ralph said, "I'm in. Let's save some lives."

None of them sitting at the table had realized Ralph was back. They all looked up at him, and Billy turned to face him with a smile.

Billy said, "Thank you, man."

"Let's do this thing." Ralph took his place at the table in the only remaining empty seat. "Let's fucking do this thing."

They all looked at Ralph in shock. Not only were they not used to seeing him pumped up in any type of enthusiasm, but they had never heard him cuss.

Billy was concerned mostly with Joe's hesitation.

"Joe," Billy said. "Are you sure? If you are going to back out, now is the time."

Joe stared at the table for a moment, a visceral expression on his face, and finally said, "Yeah, man. I'm in. I won't let you down."

From behind them, a guard across the room yelled Billy's name.

"It's time to roll, boys," Edward said.

"This may be the last time I ever see you guys." Billy stood up.

"Until we're all in prison," Joe said sarcastically.

Billy looked at Joe. "The only one going to prison will be me."

The guard across the room called for Billy again.

Billy said to his partners, "Good luck to you all. In life. Get your heads right after this. Go back out into the world and live a happy and normal life. Got it?"

Ralph said, "Sure thing, man."

Edward said, "You bet. Good luck out there."

Thomas said, "Good luck, man."

Joe remained silent.

With that, Billy turned and crossed the room, his face expressionless, his motions fluid, yet somehow dreading. He wasn't a true criminal, and he definitely was no Harry Houdini, but the show must go on. It was time to get out of this place and set the universe back on its proper path.

Chapter Thirty

The guard, who was the biggest of the small crew watching over this psychiatric unit, waiting for Billy outside the door of the counseling room, was known as Frank. He was a man in his thirties—big muscles, tall, black hair in a perfect crewcut. Although Frank was huge and intimidating upon first sight, when the patients got to know him, they learned he was mostly a giant teddy bear. Although he seemed like the softer and easier-going version of the Incredible Hulk, the patients dared not test him. Nobody wanted to find out the hard way if Frank had a mean, enforcing side.

Like all the guards, he had a utility belt, and on it the only really fierce weapon was a yellow and black taser. Billy always supposed the bright yellow was to make sure nobody, who might decide to take on one of the guards, missed seeing the weapon first.

"Good morning, Billy," Frank said. For such a large and bulky man, he had a soft voice.

"Frank," Billy replied.

"All good today?"

"Yeah. A little trouble sleeping last night. But other than that, all good."

"The weather outside is perfect for a nap." Frank looked past Billy and toward the room's windows. "Supposed to rain all day. It definitely has me feeling tired."

"Well, it's Friday. Right?"

"Yeah. For most people. It's hard to pass up the overtime, though. I volunteered to work Saturday and Sunday."

"Supposed to rain all weekend, isn't it?"

"Yep."

"Maybe we'll both sleep good tonight," Billy said.

"Sure hope so. There's no better rest than when you can hear the rain tapping away on the roof and windows. So relaxing. Deep sleep and all that stuff."

"Sure thing," Billy agreed.

"Well, the doctor is ready to see you. Shall we?"

"Let's do this," Billy replied.

They stepped into the room, and Frank shut the door behind them.

Doctor Jameson, an older man dressed in casual clothes underneath a white hospital jacket, gray hair combed neatly to the left, sat at his desk. In front of him, an open laptop. There was a badge, with the doctor's name and picture on it, clipped to his jacket breast pocket. That ID card was the focus of Billy's impending plot. Billy eyed the badge discreetly and then glanced away from it.

To the right of the laptop, a small plastic cup of water, and another one with two pills in it. Doctor Jameson sat straight up, shoulders even, in perfect posture. He looked like the kind of person who did everything by the book, including how he conveyed himself to others. He seemed like a man who was probably never out of character, even when he was off the clock and out in his personal life.

"Good morning, Billy."

"Good morning, Doc."

"Have a seat."

There were two chairs in front of the desk. Billy chose the one on the right and sat up straight as if to follow Doctor Jameson's lead.

Frank stood behind them. He would remain in the room while Billy took his medication, but would leave when the counseling session began.

When Billy was seated, Doctor Jameson said, "How has your day been so far?"

"Uneventful."

"Well, I suppose that's good in a place like this. Did you have any dreams last night?"

"No," Billy lied. "It's been awhile since I've had any. Maybe this place is what I needed."

"Do you think the medication is helping any?"

"I'm really not sure. To be honest, the dreams were never really frequent."

Billy shifted nervously in his chair. He was waiting for the signal that the plan had gone into motion. It would be a loud event, and so far, the silence from outside the door disturbed him. Was his crew backing out? It was supposed to happen thirty seconds after the door to this room shut. So far, nothing. Surely more than thirty seconds had passed.

The doctor noticed Billy's worried demeanor. "Are you okay, Billy?"

"I'm fine. You need more comfortable chairs. These things are awful."

"I'll see what I can do. In the meantime, less focus on the chairs and more on why you're here."

"Of course," Billy agreed with a smirk.

Two, three minutes now? Were they all backing out, or was it just one of them holding up the plan? Billy wondered who was the most in doubt and was most likely to throw a wrench into things. It had to be Joe. Joe seemed less enthusiastic about the whole idea of saving the universe, and more afraid of personal consequences. Had he talked the others into changing their minds? Billy couldn't proceed without his accomplices. If they pivoted, he was stuck here, and all hope of restoring the timeline would perish.

"Let's take your medicine. We have two pills here. One is a mood balancer, and the other is a light medication for anxiety. They will make you a little tired, as usual, but you won't be sedated or feel like a zombie."

"Not a fan of zombies." Billy leaned forward and took the cup with the two pills in it. He dumped them into his mouth, picked up the water, and washed the pills down his throat. He placed both cups back, precisely where he'd picked them up from.

"Is that intentional?" the doctor asked.

"Is what intentional?"

Maybe Ralph. Maybe Ralph, in all his calm intelligence, had reasoned with the others and convinced them jail time was not worth the risk they were being asked to take. Billy could see Ralph smooth-talking the others into backing out. Now maybe they all sat at that table, discussing how to deal with the disappointment they were going to cause in Billy.

"You placed the cups back exactly where you picked them up from."

"I don't like disarray. I like to put things back where I found them, or where they are meant to be kept. Is that bad?"

"No, it's not bad. Just another observation. While we're here, I will make several character observations. You already know that."

"Yes, I do." Billy threw a cheesy grin Jameson's way.

Then it finally happened. From outside the door, a muffled ruckus arose. Doctor Jameson looked past Billy toward Frank. Billy swiveled around and looked at the bulky guard, who was spun around and looking at the office door as if he had see-through vision and was trying to observe where the sudden disturbance came from. There was shouting, and then the loud sound of a crash, and more yelling.

Frank turned around and said to Jameson, "You good in here?"

The disturbance continued beyond the closed door and seemed to become louder and more frantic.

Doctor Jameson, with a slightly distraught look on his face, said, "I'm good. Billy is no threat. Go see what that's all about."

"Got it." Frank opened the door.

Instantly, the yelling and shouting were no longer muffled. It was so loud, it seemed as if it was just outside the room. But it was several feet away in the lounging area. So many escalated voices. Tempers were exploding, and it sounded like a full-blown bar fight. Another crash of something solid against something, as if a chair had been thrown, or a table flipped, or both.

When Frank emerged from the office, he immediately saw a chair fly across the lounging area and crash into a table. Two dudes at the table instantly stood up, their tempers triggered, and hollered in the direction the chair had flown from. A table in the middle of the room had been flipped. Chairs lay on their sides. To the right of that, Edward had just slammed Joe onto another table, instantly breaking its legs, and both the table and Joe fell to the floor.

Just a few feet from that action, Thomas had Ralph in a headlock, and they had stumbled into a table where another man had sat before, barely hurrying to his feet and dodging the two fighting patients. The near victim tried to separate Ralph and Thomas, to which Thomas responded by releasing Ralph, and shoving the once bystander, now turned white knight, backward, causing him to stumble over a chair and nearly lose his balance.

Across the room, the other two guards, Jacob and Dave, were already trying to pull Edward and Joe apart. Dave, seeing the commotion across the room between Thomas and another patient, looked at Edward and Joe for a moment, found himself amid indecision, and then ran across the room toward them. Neither guard had pulled their tasers just yet.

The two angry men whose table had been the target of a flying chair now engaged with Edward and Joe, trying to break them up. Jacob was in the middle of them, and Edward threw a punch that landed against one of the angry men's jaw, who in turn, took a swing at Edward in instinctive retaliation, but accidentally decked Jacob on the side of the head. Jacob responded by turning while swinging a punch of his own, which missed the angry man completely but landed hard against Joe's jaw, who stumbled backward, regained his balance, and charged at Jacob. It was now an all-out brawl.

Another chair flew across the room. Frank broke free from his frozen trance of astonishment and ran toward the center of it all.

In the office, Billy and Doctor Jameson sat listening in awe. Billy eyed the doctor's security badge, realizing he needed to act now. But something stopped him. He was not an aggressive man, and an assault on any one person would be difficult for him to initiate outside of self-defense. But the longer he waited, the less likely he was to pull off his planned escape.

"What the hell has gotten into them?" Doctor Jameson asked.

"I don't know," Billy said, his voice shaky. His nervousness was unhidden.

Doctor Jameson picked up on Billy's unsure tone and hesitated. "Billy, what the hell is going on out there?"

A loud growl of anger sounded from outside the door. Another object crashed. Someone yelled, "Comply, goddammit!"

Billy didn't answer the doctor. Instead, he sat frozen, trying to force himself into action. His arms and legs didn't want to move. His body refused to do what his mind commanded of it. He was going to blow the whole thing if he didn't act right now.

Another voice outside the room shouted, "I will fuck you up!"

"Let go!!"

"Comply! Comply now!"

Billy stared at the badge. It was his only way out, and there was only one way to get it.

"Billy?" Doctor Jameson said.

The commotion in the lounge wasn't letting up. It seemed to intensify with every passing moment. Billy had to make his move now, because at any second, the guards would subdue the hectic situation. He stood up and looked down at Doctor Jameson. "I'm sorry, but I need that badge."

Shock on his face, the doctor scooted his chair back from the desk, but didn't stand up. "This is all a ploy, isn't it? All that out there is an escape plan."

"No," Billy said. "Call it a moment of opportunity. I need that badge."

Billy followed Jameson's sudden change in sight toward a button on the wall to the right. It was a panic alarm, which would likely lock everyone in, regardless of security badges or authorizations, until any irregular situation was confirmed to be under control. If pushed, an alarm would probably sound, notifying even the downstairs heavy security to an urgent event in the building. There was a small army in the maximum-security branch of this institution. Once alerted, escape would be impossible.

"If you try to escape, you'll go to prison for a long time, Billy. You need to sit down and wait this out. Don't be stupid."

"There is more at hand than you realize, Doctor. I need that badge."

The doctor looked at the panic alarm, back to Billy, and back to the alarm.

Billy said, "Don't do it. Just give me the badge."

"You realize as soon as you leave with this badge, I'm going to push the button, right? You can't escape from here without doing something violent. Are you really a violent person, Billy?"

Billy realized the doctor was right. There was no way to do this without rendering Jameson helpless, at least for a few minutes. Billy looked at the desk for something to tie the psychiatrist up with and saw nothing. There was a landline phone, but it was wireless. Of course, there would be nothing he could use as a weapon in a mental facility. The chair and the desk were the only objects that could be weaponized, and Billy didn't want to permanently or even accidentally injure the doctor.

The doctor looked as if he were positioning himself to make a dive for the panic button. He leaned just a tad toward it. He was measuring the distance between him and Billy, and himself and that damn button. Billy realized if he allowed Jameson to make the first move, there wouldn't be time for him to react.

Billy leapt forward and slid across the desk head-first, knocking the laptop, phone, and other items to the floor. As he crashed forward, he reached out and grabbed the doctor by the shoulders. They both hit the floor, Jameson's chair toppling over with them.

The doctor let out a shriek and screamed, "Help!"

They rolled together on the floor, both grunting, and Billy tried to position himself behind the doctor. But Jameson squeezed away. His only focus was getting to that alarm. Billy realized when they fell, they had fallen toward the button, and he had only aided the doctor in getting closer to it. The doctor heaved forward, and Billy grabbed him by the leg, tried to pull him back. Jameson kicked, landed a heel against

Billy's nose. A sharp pain shot through Billy's face, and he nearly let go of the doctor's leg, who was now only a few inches from reaching his target. Billy didn't let go, though; instead, he reached out with his free hand, grabbed the doctor's other foot, and pulled them together.

"You'll be in prison," Jameson mumbled. Then he screamed, "Somebody help! Helllllp!"

Even though they were both the same size in build, Billy was stronger. He let go of the doctor's leg and foot, and threw himself upward and on top of Jameson. He then rolled them both over, placing himself behind the doctor as they struggled. That last effort had moved them farther from the alarm.

The doctor tried to yell again, but now Billy reached around Jameson's head with one hand and placed it over his mouth. The yell was muffled and barely even audible over the struggle in the lounge.

"I'm sorry, Doctor, but there are things more important than either of us," Billy said as he brought his other arm forward and around Jameson's neck. When he squeezed that arm toward himself, he blocked the doctor's airflow, and Jameson's eyes widened as he assumed his assailant was about to choke him to death.

He flung his arms outward, trying to loosen Billy's grip, but Billy held on as if he were fighting for his own life. The doctor tried to reach back with both hands. One of them grabbed a handful of Billy's hair; the other slapped at his face.

Billy squeezed harder. He wasn't trying to strangle his combative opponent to death, but wanted to render him unconscious. The doctor kicked his legs out, pulled at Billy's hair, slapped backward at his face, but Billy didn't budge. He could feel the doctor's efforts weakening. Another kick from both legs, but this one was much less energetic. The doctor's arms stopped flailing about. One more kick. Weaker. Jameson felt tense in Billy's grasp, but that tension was loosening. Finally, Jameson's arms went limp, his legs fell still, and his body became flaccid. He was unconscious.

Billy let go and laid there for a few moments with the doctor on top of him, waiting to see whether his surrender was a trick. The doctor didn't move.

Billy rolled an unconscious Doctor Jameson off him. The doctor fell still on his front side. Billy pushed himself into a kneeling position and pulled Jameson toward him and onto his back. His mouth was agape, and slobber leaked out through one side of his lips. Billy brought his face within inches of the doctor's and listened intently for a few moments. The commotion of the lounge brawl made it hard to hear anything in the room. Billy inched closer and turned an ear toward Jameson's mouth. He could not just hear a soft breathing, but could also feel gently warm breath against the side of his head. The doctor was fine and off somewhere in la-la land.

Billy noticed the doctor's shoes. White, casual sneakers with shoe-strings. He could use those strings to tie the doctor up, making it harder for him to awaken and go straight to the emergency alert button before Billy could make it out of the building. He glanced around the room and realized the only thing to bind the doctor to was a desk and a few chairs. The time it would take to tie him up wasn't worth it, because Jameson could wake up and easily drag any of those would-be binding posts across the floor.

Billy just had to hurry his ass out of there and pray he made it outside before the alarm was sounded. Once outside, it wouldn't matter. The rain was pouring; the day was dim from cloud cover, and he would vanish from anyone's sight when he made it a hundred yards or so from the building. This area was almost surrounded by woodland, with a main road leading west and east. On the other side of the woods to the south were commercial businesses: fast-food restaurants, gas stations, various other merchants, and a highway. To the north of the woods, a middle-class neighborhood.

The woods and the storm were perfect cover until Billy reached his current intended destination. That happened to be about five miles away to the south, but five miles was nothing for him. He'd spent the last several years walking everywhere anyhow. Five miles was a breeze. From there, he would take a public transit bus to his next destination where, if his dreams proved accurate, Todd Radcliffe would be waiting for him. Oh, Todd didn't know he was waiting for Billy to arrive, but nevertheless, he would be there, and Billy would do what had to be done.

He pulled Jameson's security badge away from its clip on the doctor's jacket breast pocket, looked at it, and then back to the doctor. As if showing it to Jameson, Billy held the badge out. "I'm sorry, Doctor, but I really needed this."

Billy stood up, looked toward the doorway, and back to Jameson. "Sleep well."

By the sound of it, the bar-room brawl in the lounge was still going strong. Billy headed to the door but stopped just before the threshold. He took a deep breath, told himself not to hesitate when he left this room. The floor had a simple layout. All he had to do was step out, turn right, and head down the hallway. At the end of that corridor, there were automatic double glass doors that would open when he held the security badge near a reader on the wall. Through those doors, another short corridor, and two more double glass doors, also activated by a badge scan, which led to the outside. He needed to just walk out the door, turn right, and go without looking back, no matter how much the noise from the free-for-all in the lounge tempted him. He realized he might still be spotted by one of the guards and hesitated a little longer. He turned around and looked at the doctor.

The white medical jacket.

Billy walked back to Jameson, kneeled beside him, and carefully slid the jacket off him. He then stood up, put the jacket on himself, and paused. It was a tight fit, as the doctor was actually a smaller man than even Billy, but from across the room and in the middle of battle, the guards might be too preoccupied to notice details. Especially if they only saw Billy from the back side.

He paused again before leaving the room, took a deep breath, and stepped into the hallway. As soon as he did so, he heard a voice only a few feet away. Someone talking in his direction. It was Frank's voice. Frank had already been on his way to the room, panic in his tone.

"Doctor. You need to push the—"

Billy automatically looked toward Frank, and Frank recognized him through his generic disguise.

"Billy, what the fuck are—" Mid-sentence, Frank realized exactly what was going on. Not just that Billy was in Jameson's jacket, identification badge in hand, and was trying to escape, but that this entire mess had been part of a premeditated getaway plot.

"Shit," Billy said, and he hightailed it down the hallway. The double doors were a good thirty feet away, which seemed like a hundred yards now that he was on the front end of a foot race. He made it about halfway before he felt Frank's forceful grip on one of his shoulders.

"Where do you think you're going?" Frank said through a grunt as he yanked Billy back.

Billy was helpless against Frank's seemingly preternatural strength, lost his balance, and stumbled in reverse.

"I never really liked you," Frank said as he wrapped an arm around Billy's neck and dragged him backward. "Just another crazy like the rest of them."

Billy tried to drop through Frank's choke hold, but that took him nowhere. Instead, the attempt weakened his foothold on the ground, and now he was really being dragged. He tried to twist, kicked a foot forward. No good. He grabbed Frank's arm with both hands and realized he'd dropped Doctor Jameson's identification badge. It was lying on the floor, faceup, about ten feet away.

Backward. Backward. Frank dragged and Billy struggled.

"You might as well settle down, you nutty fuck," Frank said.

Billy was a bit surprised that Frank was so hateful. The entire time he'd been locked up here, he really believed Frank liked him. Evidently, the muscle man security guard was an excellent actor.

"You little wimp. Stop squirming before I break your neck. This is an escape. I can do whatever I want to you and get away with it. Do you hear me?"

Billy threw a wild punch, hoping it might land just in the right spot on Frank's face to cause him to loosen his grip just a tad. The punch landed against Frank's forehead, which must have been made of steel, because Billy felt like he might have fractured a few knuckles. Extreme pain in his fist, Billy grunted.

"Ha!" Frank exclaimed as they neared the office, Billy losing hope and almost ready to surrender. "You stupid shit."

Frank was going to take them to the office and push the panic button. Either that, or he was going to take Billy into the room and beat the shit out of him. Either option meant the escape was a failure. If the escape failed, the world lost. Everyone lost if Billy didn't get away. He had no strategy, though, for fighting a man whose strength was a hundred times more than his own. He was a rag doll in Frank's clutches.

"Did you really think you were going somewhere?" Frank asked as he pulled Billy along.

Billy still struggled, though his energy level had been sucked from him, along with any hope. This was it. Game over. Frank was now pulling them both through the doorway into the office, where Jameson still lay on the floor, unconscious.

Just when Billy gave up completely, when he realized there would be no escape today, something odd happened. At first, he was frozen in shock, thought maybe Frank was having a seizure of some kind. Frank began to shake and moan. His grip around Billy tightened for a moment, and Billy felt Frank's intense and sudden vibrations passing through his own body. It was as if Frank had stepped on a fallen live wire, and electricity was shooting through him.

Frank moaned, and it sounded like he was doing so through the spinning blades of a desk fan. Then, Frank fell to the floor, right beside Jameson, dragging Billy down with him. As soon as they hit the floor, Frank's grip let go of Billy.

Billy rolled away from the seizing security guard and looked back at him in awe. There was a wire leading from Frank's body outward. Billy followed the wire and, in the doorway, saw Joe with a yellow taser gun in his hand, wire extending from it to Frank. Joe held the trigger, a look of determination on his face.

"Go!" Joe ordered Billy.

Billy scrambled to his feet just as Joe let go of the trigger, ceasing the voltage from the gun to Frank. As Billy stumbled past Frank, Frank moaned and reached out. He grabbed Billy's foot and pulled back. Billy hit the floor again, falling forward on his front side, but caught himself with both hands. With his free foot, he kicked back at Frank and made contact against the huge guard's face, who grunted, but didn't let go.

"Again!" Billy looked at Joe and yelled. "Zap the motherfucker again!"

"Gladly," Joe replied, added a grin, and pulled the trigger.

Electricity shot into Frank's body once more, causing him to let go of Billy's foot, who quickly crawled forward a couple of feet and stood up. Joe wasn't letting off the trigger, and Frank was frozen in paralysis, staring at both Joe and Billy with rage.

"Get out of here," Joe said. "I got him." He nodded toward Frank.

Not just stunned that today's hero was the most timid of their small team, but also grateful for what Joe had done despite dooming himself to a prison sentence, Billy said, "Joe. Thank you. I—"

"Go, man! Go save the world!"

Billy ran out into the hallway, leaving Joe to take care of business and suffer his own eventual consequences. As he hurried toward Jameson's ID badge on the floor, he heard the commotion in the lounge area continuing on. He didn't look back, though. He scooped the card up and ran toward the double doors.

In the office, Jameson came to and saw Joe standing over Frank, continuing to administer quick jolts to keep the guard on the floor. Jameson immediately sprang into full consciousness and awareness, rolled over, and crawled toward the panic button.

"No, you don't," Joe yelled as he dropped the taser and threw himself toward the doctor. Joe's shot was perfect, and he landed on top of Jameson, wrapped his arms around the doctor, and rolled them both away from the panic button.

Even with all the voltage that had passed through Frank's body, he was still conscious, and as soon as Joe collided with the doctor, Frank quickly pulled himself to a crawling position. He fought the aftereffects of the taser and crawled toward the panic button.

In the hallway, Billy was at the double doors. He held the badge to the reader on the wall. There was a beep, but the double doors didn't click, signaling they could now be opened. Did the card not work? He wiped it against the white jacket he was wearing and held it up to the reader again. Another beep, but the doors didn't open.

"What the hell?" he mumbled as he wiped the card again on his jacket. Then he noticed there was a black stripe on the back of the card. He looked at the reader again. There was a card-sliding slot.

In the room, Frank was at the button. He reached out to push it. Suddenly, his arm was in the grasp of someone's hand. It was Joe. He had pulled himself away from the doctor and grabbed Frank's arm just before Frank could push the button. With his free hand, Frank punched Joe right in the nose. Joe let out a yelp and hit the floor, unconscious. Frank grinned at the fact he'd just knocked out a man in one punch, and turned toward the panic button again.

Billy swiped the card through the reader. There was a beep and then a click from the double doors. He breathed a sigh of relief and pushed them open.

Frank smashed the button.

An alarm sounded just as Billy passed through the doors. He ran into a small lobby and saw that there was a red and blue light above the exit doors spinning like lights on top of a police car. He hurried to the exit and swiped the card, expecting that it wouldn't work now that the building was going into lockdown. He was wrong.

The doors clicked; he pushed them open and ran through. As soon as he cleared the doors, they slammed shut automatically, and he heard them lock behind him. He hesitated for a second, turned around and looked back, saw there was nobody pursuing him from the other side. Billy then hauled ass through the parking lot in the dark and rainy day.

Water pellets shot against his face. The air was crisp and chilly. He crossed the main road, stood on the edge of the woods, then looked back again. The downpour was so thick, he could barely see the building he'd just escaped from. He turned and ran into the brush. As he pushed his way ahead, bushes and thorns scraping at his skin, his face, he could hear the alarm dimming through widening distance. He was nearly out of breath but kept moving forward. He tripped over some protruding roots in the ground, stumbled, stayed on his feet, and ran. Billy ran like he was running for his life, and then pushed even harder, as if he were the only man who could save humanity.

Chapter Thirty-One

J im stood inside the garage, staring out at the pouring rain, his hands on his hips and his mind traveling through the past. It was a dark, cool, and tenebrous day, but it seemed every day was like that, even when the sun shined, free of any cloud-covered obstruction. He wondered, if he could again go back to the night of the fire, knowing what he knew now, would he do it all differently? It seemed no matter the scenario, the only correct path would have been not to toy with the past. The consequences of doing so were severe. Even though in the original scenario, he had somewhat blamed himself for what happened to his son, his son's family, and his own wife, at least Jim knew deep down it really wasn't his fault. He had almost traveled the back way home that night and decided against it.

But had he done so, and arrived at the fire at the same time in the first go-round that he had in the reboot, he would have pulled Todd from the house and Beth and Stormy would have perished anyhow. Jim had realized while standing there in the garage that the supernatural entity, who had granted him a chance to go back, had timed everything as to the minute Jim would have arrived that night anyhow. Mister Brimstone had given Jim the opportunity to reverse the decision to take his normal route home from work. That's where the timeline remake's starting point was. There was no coincidence. It was all by design.

Brimstone hadn't wanted the rescue attempt to be easy. He had wanted the thrill of the game and probably watched the entire scene from nearby, tossing whatever form of popcorn a supernatural being might favor while watching a suspense movie unfold.

Jim had thought Mister Brimstone was a neutral force somewhere in the middle of good and evil. Even though the man with the black suit and the red tie had demanded Jim's soul in return for the deal to finalize, Mister Brimstone had given Jim an option to reverse a tragedy that had affected him and his family like no other event could. That was the good in Mister Brimstone.

Now, though, Jim questioned whether his mysterious benefactor wasn't a benefactor at all. Now he wondered whether this was some cruel game, initiated by an evil, bored demon who got off on human suffering. The torment was going to occur no matter which direction the timeline went, but the added element of it being by Jim's own decision-making was an additional layer of entertainment for the demon. This time around was worse than the first time. There was no arguing against that.

"If I could go back and do it again, if there was a next time, would I save him?" Jim whispered to himself. "Would I save my son, save my wife, or would I let them go, knowing that it was me who decided their fate?"

He sighed. He'd come to the garage to perform an oil change on his car, but when he'd opened the garage door and looked outside, he'd suddenly not wanted to do anything but stand there, staring at Mother Nature's depressing display. It was a little after ten in the morning, and he didn't have the energy for car maintenance. He didn't have the energy for anything but staring and pondering. He looked at Todd's car, parked in the driveway, and wondered what Todd was up to.

Just as that thought hit Jim, Todd stepped in front of the garage. Rain soaking him and a bottle of booze in his hand, his expression was one of obvious intoxication. He just stood there, staring at his father for a few moments.

A nervousness ran through Jim's body. The way his son glared at him in silence, drunk, but something else too. Accusingly. Jim wanted to say something. He wanted to tell his son to come in out of the rain, but his mouth didn't move. He remained still and silent, waiting.

Todd lifted the bottle to his mouth, took a swig, and stepped in from the rain. He stood only a few feet from his father, and their gazes connected.

"How did you know, Dad?" Todd's voice was shaky. The bottle he held was half empty.

Sincerely confused, Jim asked, "Know what?"

"You knew about the fire. How did you know?"

Jim felt exposed without a ready excuse. Caught in the act of something he'd not expected to get caught for. He didn't know what to say. He knew exactly what Todd was talking about. His son need not explain. But how could Todd know? What had he pieced together?

"Was it the man? The weird guy in the backyard? Did you see him again? Was he right?"

"That man was a nutjob," Jim said.

"But he knew something. Something was going to happen, and he knew it. You were going to save me, that's what he said. He said Beth and Stormy were going to die. He never said how, though. How did you know, Dad?"

"What are you accusing me of?"

Todd scoffed. "I know you didn't start the fire. There's something else, though. You said so yourself that day. Before the guy showed up. You said you never take the back way home. You take the back way *to* work, but the highway home. How is it on that night, you showed up to save me? How did you know?"

Obviously, Jim couldn't tell Todd everything. He couldn't tell his son that some man in the fog showed up and gave Jim a special pass to travel back in time and change things. "I didn't know anything. I just went that way. I can't explain why. I don't know why."

"No." Todd shook his head, forcing a fake grin. "That's not going to cut it, Dad. You fucking knew. Make it make sense. How could you possibly know? What else did that weirdo say to you? Did he tell you it was going to be a fire? Did he set it? Did that man kill my wife and baby? If he told you he was going to do it, why didn't you stop him?"

"No, son. You're wrong. They said it wasn't arson. The man was in jail. He couldn't have set it."

Todd swigged from the bottle. "How the fuck could he know? How the fuck could *you* know?"

"I told you—"

"I know what you fucking told me." Todd's words slurred. He was beyond drunk. A cocktail of intoxication and growing rage. He was becoming aggressive in his stance. Like he was bucking up to his father. His lips quivered with an irate energy. He held the bottle so tightly in his hand, Jim wondered whether the glass would shatter.

"It was luck. Luck for you," Jim snapped. "If I hadn't showed up, you'd be buried right beside your wife. You were saved. You're *alive*." Jim hesitated and then stepped forward. "By the grace of pure luck, you survived. You get to live your life. Yeah, it's hard going forward right now, and you will never completely get over your losses, but *you get to live*. You get to chase dreams and be something. Beautiful days and peaceful nights are what you get. You ungrateful asshole. I risked my life to save you. You think that's nothing? You walk around with your bottle, drinking yourself as close to the grave as you can. Out there drinking and driving. Putting others at risk because you feel sorry for yourself."

Jim's voice rose. He stepped forward again and pointed at his son in accusation. "You have the nerve to stand there and complain about being alive? People die young every day. You had a loss. It's rough. It's tragic. A nightmare is what it is. But you're alive, son. How dare you scoff at that? You were given another chance that so many people aren't allowed to even sniff. You stand there and complain."

"You call this another chance?" Todd scowled. "You were selfish. You didn't want to lose your son. You never once thought about the consequences of saving me and not them. Had you saved my wife and my child, at least Beth would have our daughter. Some kind of motivation to go on with life. Someone to love. She would have had our child, and they would have moved past the tragedy of losing me. You left me with nothing. All because you wanted to save *your* kid. Peaceful nights? I don't know what peace is. You selfish son of a—"

"It wasn't just you I lost!" Jim yelled. "Your mom was suicidal! I had to save *her* too! Your mom was suicidal, you ungrateful, overgrown asshole. She was drinking herself to *death!* Do you understand that?" Jim choked backed tears. "I hadn't just lost *you!* My wife!"

Suddenly, Todd showed confusion. He looked at Jim as if his father had spoken in a foreign language. Todd stood there, trying to process what Jim had just said.

And Jim realized exactly what he'd done. He'd spoken of the first time around, before his deal with Mr. Brimstone. A chain of events that hadn't actually happened now because Jim had gone back in time and stopped them from occurring. Jim's mind panicked as he scrambled to find the words to save himself.

"What do you mean, Mom was suicidal? When was Mom suicidal?" Todd asked, puzzlement in his voice.

Jim opened his mouth to speak, but words didn't come out. There were no words. He couldn't make the save. He stood there looking as bewildered as his son.

"When was Mom suicidal?" Todd repeated. "When was she drinking? Mom doesn't drink. When did she ever have an actual drinking problem?"

"I don't know what I'm saying," Jim said.

Todd cocked his head and looked at his father, who was trying like hell not to make eye contact with his son.

"What's going on here?" Todd asked. "What are you not telling me?"

"Nothing. This is going nowhere, son. Go lay down. Go sleep it off."

With sudden rage, Todd threw the bourbon bottle across the garage. It crashed against a wall and glass showered to the concrete floor.

Jim flinched and looked at his son through anger. "You're going to clean that up," Jim demanded.

"No. I'm not. But let me tell you something." His words were so slurred, he barely got them out. He swayed where he stood, so drunk that standing still had become a complicated task. "Let's go ask Mom about her out-of-control drinking. Let's go ask her about her suicidal condition."

"No," Jim said. "I told you, I'm tired and babbling."

Todd scoffed. "You mean you're lying? Lying to save your own ass once again. Ha! There's not an unselfish bone in your body, is there? Maybe you need to lose something close to you to understand how I feel."

"I know how you feel."

"Don't you fucking dare. You have no clue. Your wife is in that house right now. Alive! Your only kid is standing right in front of you. Alive! You don't goddamn know. You couldn't know. But maybe there's a way you can find out."

"Son—"

"Don't call me that. If I was your son and you actually gave a fuck about me, I wouldn't be here right now. But there's a way you can know. There's a way I can share this feeling with you. You want to feel it, Dad? You want to *really feel it?* The only true empathy is one of experience. You want to feel this, Dad?"

"Don't do anything stupid. You can't undo some things. Hurting yourself will prove nothing."

Todd faked a laugh, as if what Jim had just said was of the highest level of absurdity. "Hurt myself? Nah. That's not what I'm talking about."

Jim watched his son with profound scrutiny.

"Maybe you need to know what it feels like to lose your wife." Todd had lowered his voice. A deep tone of contempt. "Maybe then you'd understand."

"Are you threatening your own mother?"

"Maybe it's not a threat, Dad. Maybe I need to go in that house right now and take your wife away from you."

Jim stepped to his son, sprang to him in a quick motion, as if he were going to attack. He stopped just as they were nearly nose-to-nose. At the top of his lungs, Jim screamed directly into Todd's face so powerfully, Todd felt his father's breath. "Don't you threaten your mom! I'll drop you right here! I will beat your ass right here!"

Todd didn't back down. Instead, he held his spot in front of his father, and said in a low, almost evil voice, "Go ahead, Dad. Take a swing. You want to hurt me? Take a swing, Dad."

Jim lost control. With a roar of frustration and both hands, he reached out and shoved Todd with all his might.

Even though they had been in each other's faces, Todd was stunned by the sudden burst of physical aggression and had no time to react. He flew backward, instantly leaving his feet, and landed on his back. He scrambled and sat up in the rain-soaked driveway, now with heavy precipitation pelting his face. Todd sat there staring at his father through rage, and Jim was certain his son would get up and come at him.

"That's okay, Dad!" Todd yelled as he clumsily got to his feet, staggered, and finally held himself still. "You can't always be around! You can't always be here to protect her!"

"You son of a bitch!"

Todd faked a laugh in spite. "Maybe. Maybe, Dad." Todd pulled his car keys out of his pocket. "I'll see you soon, Dad. You're going to feel what I feel. I'll see you soon."

Todd turned his back on his father and went to his car parked at the bottom of the driveway. He opened the driver's door and looked at his father. "You're going to know, Dad! I'm going to go say goodbye to my life, and then you're going to do the same."

He got in the car, started it, backed out of the driveway without putting his seat belt on, and stomped on the gas pedal. Tires squealed like a demon screaming through eternal suffering as he sped off, leaving his father standing in the garage.

Chapter Thirty-Two

Billy stood on the front porch of the shotgun house, drenched by tenacious falling rain. He knocked again. He had made it to this neighborhood in just over an hour, hurrying through backyards, crossing streets, passing through several wooded areas. The neighborhood was an old one, all the houses the same and only separated by about ten feet each. There were back alleys and side roads, wire fences around the front yards and back. Most were poorly maintained, as this was a low-income area of the city. Beside the door Billy had knocked on was a window covered only with plastic, which seemed to vibrate in the wind from the storm.

Billy waited several seconds before knocking a second time. Finally, the door opened, and standing on the other side of the threshold was Logan Mason, in shorts and a T-shirt, his thin brown hair unkempt.

Logan's facial expression was a stoic one. "Billy Wagner. What are you doing around here? I thought you were in jail."

"Can I come in? It's kind of wet out here."

Logan stood to the side, gesturing Billy to enter the house.

Billy obliged.

"Let me get you a towel. Dripping water all over my spotless home." Logan disappeared down the hallway.

Billy stood still on the inside of the doorway and waited patiently while looking around the living room, where there was a lingering, powerful stench of marijuana. The room was nearly as dark as the storm-plagued outside, with dim lighting from ceiling fan lights, covered in dust, and only two of the four bulbs working. A yellow and orange sofa, ripped and worn, sat against a wall which at one time was painted tan, but now was soiled with nicotine stains from years of cigarette smoke. A generic, rectangular coffee table sat a few feet from the couch, covered with overflowing ashtrays, old newspapers, paper plates with food stains, empty packs of cigarettes, and a pipe with its bowl darkened from marijuana resin.

Logan reappeared with a stained white towel in his hands and tossed it toward Billy. "Here, dry your rat ass off," Logan instructed.

"Thanks." Billy caught the towel and dried his head, his face, his hands. He patted the towel up and down his shirt and pants, rubbed the top of his shoes, then the bottoms of them dry. He held the towel out toward Logan.

"The table," Logan said.

Billy walked across the living room and gently placed the towel on top of the newspapers on the table.

"What are you doing here?" Logan skipped the small talk. That was always his way of doing things anyhow. "I thought you were in the slammer."

"I got probation from trial," Billy lied. "I'm a free man as long as I don't fuck up."

"So then, let me ask you again, Billy. What are you doing here?"

"I need a piece."

"I just sold you one not too long ago."

"Well, obviously, they took it away from me. I can't really ask for it back."

"They didn't charge you with carrying a stolen firearm? There were no serial numbers on it. I always scratch them off."

"No," Billy said. "Well, yeah. But those charges were dropped, believe it or not."

"Talk about luck."

"I know. So, can you help me out?"

Logan watched Billy curiously for a few moments. "Help you out? That doesn't sound good. I guess you don't have any money."

"I'll pay you later. I'm fresh out of jail. I haven't had time to get any money."

"You still having those dreams?"

"Yeah."

Logan smirked. "Any of them profitable lately?"

"No. Just gloom and doom shit. Probably just normal dreams."

"No horse races, eh?"

"Not for a while."

"How you gonna come up with the money, then?"

Billy sighed. "You know I have my ways. I won't stiff you."

"What do you need a gun for?" Logan asked.

Billy waited a few moments, then answered. "I need it for—"

"No." Logan held up a hand, gesturing for Billy to stop. "I don't want to know. The less I know, the better. You know I'm just going to give you a light pistol, right? I can't give you anything good without money up front. There are a few pieces I can front you."

"I only need one," Billy said, holding up a one gesture.

"Yeah, I'm only going to give you one. I'm just saying I have a few to choose from. You have ammo?"

"Fresh out of jail, man," Billy reminded Logan.

"Right. So you need the gun and some bullets on front. You're a needy sonofabitch. You know that?"

"There's nobody else to turn to, man."

"You're not gonna kill anybody, are you?" Logan asked with a stern look.

Billy held up his hands. "No, man. I ain't no killer. You know that."

"Well, considering what you were locked up for, who knows?"

"I didn't hurt anybody."

"Maybe you were going to."

"No," Billy said flatly.

"You get caught with a piece I gave you, you better keep your trap shut."

"Didn't say anything last time."

Logan hesitated, watching Billy closely. "You know what happens if you talk. You know—"

"Come on, man. Am I known for running my mouth?" Billy sounded frustrated. "Have I ever snitched on anybody for anything?"

"Well, with you being on probation, and wanting a damn gun, you get caught, you're fucked. Being fucked will make a person consider ratting his people out. You get yourself fucked, *you're* fucked. You get it?"

"Yeah, man, I fucking get it."

"Don't get testy with me, motherfucker. I'll march your ass right out the door, back into the rain, empty-handed. I gotta be sure is all. Don't get smart-ass on me."

"I'm not."

"I'm looking out for *me*. What happens to you is something I don't give a shit about. I'm not doing this as a friend. We're not friends, Billy Wagner. You understand that?"

"I do," Billy answered with a quick nod.

"I don't need friends. I need me and me only. Friends will just stab you in the back. I ain't up for getting a knife in my back. You feel me?"

"Yes."

"When you gonna pay me?"

"A couple of weeks is all I need."

Logan looked Billy over for a few moments. "A couple of weeks, eh? I can depend on that?"

"Yes."

"Okay then. A couple of weeks. A couple is two. Two weeks. Two weeks from today. Right?"

"Two weeks from today, man. Maybe before that."

"That's fourteen days, motherfucker. *Fourteen days.*"

"Fourteen days," Billy agreed.

Logan examined Billy again. "If I don't have my money in fourteen days, I'm going to break your fucking arm. You're gonna have a hard time surviving in your homeless world with a broken arm."

"Yeah, man, it'd be rough."

"You know I'm older and tired," Logan said. "By 'kick your ass,' I mean I'll have my people fuck you up. It won't just be me, man. And it'll hurt. It'll hurt bad. You like pain?"

"I hate pain, man. Two weeks, you'll have your money."

Logan folded his arms. "That's fine, then. I'll give you a piece and some ammo. Two weeks."

"Two weeks," Billy said.

Chapter Thirty-Three

Jim rushed into the house, soaked and dripping from the persistent deluge outside, in a frantic panic. He needed his car keys but, because his mind was in a disarray of emotions, could not think of where he'd left them.

Alice came down the hallway in a nightgown, her hair a tangled mess from having just awakened, with a look of concern on her face.

Jim moved from side table to side table, looked at the coffee table. Nothing. He went to the keyholder on the wall in the kitchen doorway. No keys hanging.

"Jim?" Alice asked.

"Keys. Where are the keys?"

"What's wrong?"

Jim stopped his search and went to his wife. He looked down at her, and the expression of panic and other mixed emotions on his face disturbed her. Immediately, her expression suddenly matched his. He said, "He's drunk again. Rambling on about revenge."

"Revenge?" Alice gasped. "Revenge for what? On who?"

"On *me*." Jim ran his hands through his hair. Looked around the room nervously and then back to Alice. "For saving him. For not saving Beth. For not saving Stormy. Alice, he's lost it. He threatened to hurt you."

"He's not going to hurt anyone. He's just drunk. Jim—"

"You didn't see what I saw, Alice. You didn't see the hatred in his eyes, the spite in his voice. I've got to catch him. I've got to find him before he does something stupid."

"Do you know where he went?"

"I have a clue. He said he was going to go say goodbye to his life. He's going to the cemetery. I can't think of anywhere else. Alice, he said he was going to make me feel what he feels. I believe him. I believe him, Alice. He meant every word. When I leave, you need to lock up everything. If he comes back here, call the police."

She flinched in shock. "I'll do no such thing! I'm not calling the cops on my son. He's been drinking. They'll lock him up."

Jim put his hands on his wife's shoulders and forced a gentle tone. "He's probably safer there than anywhere right now. The man is not himself. He's snapped, and he's drunk. You can't trust someone like that, no matter *who* they are."

"Jim, he wouldn't hurt me. He wouldn't hurt *us.*"

Jim let go of Alice and walked into the kitchen, leaving her standing there in bewilderment.

"My keys," he said.

"The bedroom," Alice said. "On your table. I saw them there last night."

He hurried past her, down the hallway, and returned almost instantly with a key ring jingling in his hand. He stopped and looked at her. "I'm going to find our son. We can't just keep doing nothing. He's getting worse and needs help."

"Okay. Go find him. I'll stay here in case he shows up."

"Alice," Jim's tone was dead serious, "do not let him in this house. He's dangerous right now. You understand?"

"I'm not turning my son away. I can talk to him."

"No, Alice. Don't let him in. Call me if he shows up. I'll take care of it. Do not trust him right now."

"You're overreacting. Go get our son."

"I love you." He touched her face with both hands and kissed her on the forehead.

She met his gaze with love and admiration, respect and gratefulness. "I love you, Jim. Go get him. Bring him home safe, please. Please, Jim. Bring him home safe."

"I will," he said and then hurried out of the house.

Alice went to the front door and watched as her husband backed out of the driveway, heard the engine gun as he pulled off. Tears in her eyes, she sniffled. Could Jim save Todd again? This time around would be a lot harder than saving him from a house fire. This was mental illness brought on by depression. Could Jim save Todd just one more damn time?

Tears rolling down her cheeks, Alice said, "God, please let him save our son. Just one more time. Just this next time. Please, God, protect my son."

Chapter Thirty-Four

Todd drove into the front yard of the lot that was once occupied by his home, his family, his life. He steered directly from the street onto the front lawn, leaving heavy tire tracks in the muddying soil. When he slammed the brakes, the car slid and came to a stop just a few feet before crashing into the home's foundation, which was the only remaining element of the burned-down dwelling.

Cleanup crews had finally demolished the skeleton of the house, but had yet to clear the foundation, which wasn't whole anymore. It was chipped and cracked, broken and crumbled in some places. The property looked like it had been hit by a focused, powerful earthquake. The incomplete houses on either side were also condemned and likely scheduled for demolition, as they had suffered irreparable damage from the explosion—windows broken out, visible structural damage on the sides closest to Todd's property.

The rain hadn't slowed at all. Mother Nature seemed determined to drench the entire city, as if she were trying to cleanse it of its sins. Todd left the car running, opened the driver's door, and tried to climb out. The softness of the muddy ground, alongside his inebriation, caused him to lose his balance. He stumbled forward and fell. Lying on his front side in the mud, he turned his head, and, for several moments, didn't move. He didn't want to get up; had no desire to stand ever again. He didn't care to even breathe anymore, and no longer wanted anything to do with this life.

It was all a scam. Life. Love. Family. Love only led to loss, and that loss cut so deep he wondered whether, even in death, his soul would suffer.

Water splashed, and mud covered his face as he smashed a fist into the ground. He fought back tears. He didn't want to cry anymore, but he couldn't stop it. He laid there, choking on his own cries, pounding fists, and shrieked so powerfully as if trying to expel the pain through voice.

On cue, the downpour intensified. It went from a steady deluge to nearly torrential rainfall. Todd pushed himself to his knees and looked at the house's foundation. He looked up further, as if maybe he could at least see the ghost of the home that was once there. He went back in time in his mind, saw his family inside. His pregnant wife making a glass of unsweet iced tea. Him coming up behind her, putting his hands on her waist, kissing her gently on her neck.

"Good morning, beautiful," he said to her.

Enjoying his loving touch, Beth smiled. She looked straight ahead and gave herself to the warmth of the moment. Then she closed her eyes so softly, and tilted toward her husband as he kissed her on the back of the neck again.

"Good morning, my handsome man," she whispered.

"How's the wife this morning?" he said in between neck kisses.

Beth turned to face Todd, her face glowing with happiness, and kissed him on the mouth. He returned her affection and then kissed her cheek.

"The wife is fine," she said.

He put his hands on her pregnant belly, now six months along, and massaged it. "And how's our daughter this morning?"

"Feisty," she said. "Don't move. Wait a second."

He obeyed, and a moment later, he felt a sudden thump. His eyes widened with excitement, and he smiled as Beth said, "You felt her. She's strong, isn't she?"

"Yes," Todd said, still not pulling his hands away. "There! Another one. She's lively."

"Always."

"You can sleep through that?"

She released a quick laugh. "When I'm exhausted. You think you could sleep with a child tossing and turning and kicking and punching inside you?"

"Well, I'm a man. I can sleep through anything."

"That you can," Beth teased.

A little girl, blonde, maybe five years old. She was riding a tricycle with a balloon tied to the handlebars via a long string. Her face had patches of dirt on it from where she had been playing in the yard. Her hair was unkempt and wild. She was smiling, laughing, riding that bike down the street. Pedaling as fast as possible with her little legs. The first time she'd been set free to ride on the road. Todd and Beth stood in the driveway, cheering their daughter on. Their unborn daughter.

Unborn. Unborn forever. Little Stormy Dawn would never live, and this wasn't a memory; it was a fantasy of something never to come. Suddenly Beth disappeared. Vanished into thin air as if she just abruptly ceased to exist. That's exactly what had happened the night of the fire. One moment she was alive, a life growing inside her, and then the next she was dead.

Panicking, Todd looked out into the street at his exuberant daughter. *She's going to disappear, too.* Terror and dread gripped his soul. He had to save her. At least he could save Stormy. She deserved to live. She had a right to her first breath of air and a chance to make her place in this world. He couldn't let her die again. *No, not again. Please, not again.*

He bolted out into the street, running as fast as he could toward his daughter. She was too busy enjoying the ride to see him coming after her. Down the street. She was moving damn fast for a kid new to riding bikes. She was too submerged in loving life to know it was about to all end for her.

Suddenly, the bike wheels sparked. Then they caught fire. Stormy continued onward, still beaming, still the joyous, free-spirited child. She was oblivious to the life-threatening danger. The blaze made its way up the body of the bike. The pedals caught fire. Stormy looked down and saw her feet engulfed in flames. Behind her, Todd was running with all his strength, yet he seemed to fall farther behind with each moment. Her legs were on fire, but she continued to pedal. Faster, as if she could ride away from the burning beast crawling up her legs.

Stormy screamed just before her torso and upper body were swallowed in searing terror. Her face, as she shrieked in horror, began to melt. Lit strands of hair flew in the wind behind her, floating like feathers from a phoenix as it soared across the sky. Now she was a racing fireball, moving down the street so fast. So damn fast.

Todd's legs wanted to quit. He was exhausted but couldn't let himself slow down. He refused to give up. His baby girl. He could still rescue her.

Her screaming was like that of something escaping hell, immersed in flames as it climbed out of the dark, suffering pits onto the earth. Todd cried. He yelled her name. He pushed harder. His legs moved quicker than he could physically keep up with. He stumbled, moaned, and fell forward face-first onto the street.

Laying in the yard. Rain bombarding his body. Mud covering his face. Todd was crying. He wept so hard he could barely breathe.

His anguish was overwhelming. He rolled onto his back, and the sky dropped rain onto his face, in his eyes. He blinked the water away. Something stood in front of him. His vision was so blurry, but it looked like a man standing on the other side of rain-spangled glass.

Todd blinked again and his sight partially cleared. The man seemed to hold something as he stared down at Todd. Todd rubbed his eyes, and his sight was now unobstructed. A man stood there with a gun, and Todd recognized him. It was the crazy guy from his backyard. The one who had burst into their family get-together, waving a gun and shouting psychotic accusations. Todd sat up with effort as the mud was so soft it could have been quicksand.

The man stepped closer and pointed the pistol at Todd.

"I really didn't expect to find you here." The man spoke. "My dreams said you would be, but I don't know. I didn't think it would be this easy."

Todd said nothing, still sitting in the mud, afraid to stand up.

"Guess I got lucky, didn't I? Maybe it's just my lucky day. Not so lucky for you, though."

"What do you want?" Todd asked with contempt in his voice.

"To fix the timeline, Mr. Radcliffe. I gotta set things right, and there's only one way to do that." He gestured toward the gun with a head nod.

Chapter Thirty-Five

J im stepped out of the car, wipers fighting vigorously to keep the windshield clear of the falling rain, and left it running. He left the door open and walked across the cemetery grounds. He passed tombstones, ignoring their faces, and approached the plot with the wide concrete headstone. On it, both Beth and Stormy's names, with their dates of birth and demise, chiseled in fancy lettering. His shoes sloshed in the saturated ground as he approached. He noticed immediately some grass had grown over the burial plot, but it was still mostly bare, having only been filled in a few months ago.

Jim had expected to find his son here, grieving through bourbon intoxication, drenched with rain, and in a state of hopelessness only the ones who loved him genuinely could rescue him from. But Todd wasn't here, and Jim visited the site anyhow. He couldn't be here and simply leave without stopping to offer his respects, his sympathy, his love. If by some chance there was an afterlife, and Beth and her daughter could see into the universe of the living, how would they feel if Grandpa drove by their gravesite without acknowledging it?

He stood in front of the plot, looking down at the names on the stone. Beth had been so young, and, having not even been born yet, her child even more so. Jim knew some day this would be his destiny. His wife's destiny. It was the future of all those born into this beautiful world, into a life full of opportunity and hope. But every life ends, just like every day gives way to night. Eventually, it was always the darkness that won. Tomorrow didn't always come, not for organic life or for even the life of the entire universe. As galaxies spread apart throughout all of creation, as stars put more distance between themselves, as civilizations on Goldilocks planets rose and fell, they were all headed toward one final and shared ending: darkness. Even the universe was meant to die, eventually.

So it seemed a cheated act to take lives so young, to forbid anyone from living into old age and wisdom. If everything ends, then the only point of life was to *live*. So where was the fairness in extinguishing any flame earlier than its expected span? Yet, Jim thought, in a universe where the only true reason was to live and then end, there could be no actual point. And without a cause, the only realistic goal could be just to extend it as long as possible, enjoy all that happens in between, and when the end comes, be grateful the opportunity of life was even granted. Even if one only gets a taste of it, like making a dish and testing it, enjoying the flavor, and then tossing it into the trash. Just a taste. Nothing else.

Pointlessness could only suggest that reason didn't exist, either. Come, enjoy, leave. No more and no less. Fairness had nothing to do with any of it. Without fairness, there could also be no God. Because a true God would have treated Beth and Stormy more fairly.

Jim realized he was silently crying. He wanted to drop to his knees and pound the ground. He wished he could scream, face-to-face, at whoever, or whatever, was responsible for all the pain his loved ones were suffering. If only there was a subject at which he could point an accusing finger. He wondered whether that finger should be aimed directly at himself. Had he let things be, as Billy Wagner had warned him to do, his son would rest peacefully where he truly wanted to be: beside his wife in the grave Jim stood before.

Right now, Alice was at home suffering emotionally yet again. This time, the last time, next time: there would be suffering no matter what. The key event, the house fire, was meant to change lives by whatever forces of nature deemed it to be so. Jim had interfered and, therefore, caused even more misery.

Mr. Brimstone. Was he at fault with all of this? Was he the one who started the fire, thus kicking off a series of events that would replay, reboot, and play themselves out repeatedly for all eternity? Save Todd. Save Beth and Stormy. Save Alice. Save himself. Who was Jim rescuing in the end? Did it even matter now? What was set in motion was rolling downhill with the velocity and determination of the most dense boulder tumbling down a steep mountainside. Jim couldn't stop it again. If he could, should he? If there *was* to be a next time, what would he do? Stand there and watch the house burn, knowing that people he loved were inside dying? Had this all been some kind of test by a higher power, and he had failed it miserably? Should he have let it be? What person, who knew love, could allow others to die when there was an option to save them? Should Jim have chosen the natural selection of life-and-death over heroism?

This inner turmoil didn't matter. Jim tried to shake it off, but it stuck to him just like the rain. It soaked his soul and saturated it with conflicted misery. What was done was done. Yet it wasn't so simple. It should have been. He must move forward. Hanging onto mistakes, without taking action, would only bury him and his family further in anguish. He knew this. We learn the most from our failures. But how could he learn from this? If ever given the chance again, simply don't change the past? There would be no other opportunities, because the one he had tried to take advantage of was a supernatural serendipity. But it wasn't serendipitous. Not at all. It was an error.

Jim stared at the headstone. The names. The dates. There should have been a third carved into that grave marker. Jim had stopped that, and it was the mistake of a lifetime.

***

Alice was on her knees, beside the open cedar chest, in her bedroom. On the floor, and scattered about, were several pictures. She and Todd together when he was a baby. Some of just Todd. Some of her and Jim, Jim and Todd, all of them together. Every single photograph was a frozen moment of forever happiness. A family of love and laughter. The dearest moments held still for anyone to look back on. She held one picture in her hand. A family portrait, professionally taken, in which Todd was only three years old, a huge smile on his face, and plastic sunglasses covering his eyes. There were several poses photographed that day, but this one was the most accurate representation of the family. A life that was mostly happy. Almost complete and absolute bliss. And even the hard times weren't so hard. They had done a good job—her, Jim, and Todd. They had done the family thing right.

She laid the picture in the scattered mess on the floor and reached in for another one. A photograph of Todd, outside in the backyard, in the middle of the spot where her garden would eventually be. There was a hole in the ground that had been dug by Todd with a small garden shovel, which was lying on the ground. Todd was five or six years old in this picture. A big cheesy grin on his face as he held up a small tin box with the lid closed. Alice remembered there was something in the box. Something they meant to bury and dig up years later. When she eventually started her garden, during Todd's late teens, he had asked about the box. Should they dig it up now? They didn't, though, because Alice told her son it hadn't been long enough. They would do so when Alice and Jim were old people, and they would then, alongside grandchildren, dig up the box, and enjoy revealing the time capsule idea to a new generation of the family.

Alice examined the picture for a few moments, tears strolling down her cheeks, with deep consideration. It was still there now. The box. Beneath the garden. She wanted that container. She wanted to see what was inside it. Nothing came to her when she searched her memory for its contents. How could she forget? Wasn't that the idea, though? Bury it, forget about it, then dig it up decades later.

She dropped the picture in the cedar chest and left her bedroom. In the kitchen, she fumbled through the utility closet until she found a small hand-sized gardening shovel. Alice headed to the back door, opened it, and stood there. It was a cold and rainy day. The ground was likely saturated and muddy. The air was probably brisk with a powerful bite. That didn't matter. She wanted that buried treasure. She *needed* it.

She opened the door and headed out into the wet, chilly, autumn day. Raindrops hitting her face were so cold they nearly stung. There was a steady breeze, almost as if Mother Nature herself tried to force Alice back inside. She would not surrender to the harsh elements. She would not back away. As soon as she stepped off the porch, crossed the narrow sidewalk, and her bare feet sank into the mud, she paused for an instant.

No, this didn't matter. For her son, for her family, Alice had to push forward. This weather and its bitter offerings were only a minor challenge compared to what her son was going through. She would feel guilty if she gave up now. Just some mud, cold water, and chilled air. Nothing at all compared to the fate Beth and Stormy suffered.

Alice looked up at the gray sky. Icy raindrops hit her face, fell into her eyes. She looked ahead, toward the center of her dead garden. Right in the middle was where she needed to dig. The treasure awaited. She wasn't sure what good it would do to dig it up, but she was going to do it. Alice moved forward, crossed the yard, stepped into the garden. She slopped through the quicksand-like ground and fell to her knees, the impact emitting a splash of mud and water. Already soaked from head to toe, Alice drove the tip of the shovel into the ground with a grunt of determination.

Chapter Thirty-Six

Todd and Billy stood, soaked in relentless rainfall, only a few feet apart, staring at each other. Todd's expression was one of anger and confusion. Billy's was one of false confidence, even though he was the one holding the gun, which he had pointed at Todd's chest.

His finger was behind the trigger, as if he had no intention of pulling it. He knew what he was here for and what he *had* to do, but wondered why his finger wasn't on the trigger. Was he subconsciously reconsidering his intentions? He glanced down, quickly, at his trigger finger, and then back at Todd. Billy was wavering in the moment he was meant to shine. This was where he changed everything back to the way it was supposed to be, yet his finger wasn't ready, and perhaps not willing, to carry out the plan.

"You started that fire," Todd accused.

"No," Billy answered. "I was in jail when your house burned down."

Todd made a quick move, as if to test the waters of leaping at Billy, and Billy raised the gun up a few inches, now aiming it at Todd's face.

Billy warned, "Nuh uh, man. Don't do it."

"How did you know?" Todd asked.

"I've always known things. Dreams. I have dreams. Usually they're clear. Most of the time, I can see everything as it's going to happen. With you, the dreams were clear at first. Yet in later ones, there were details left out. I think it's because it wasn't set in stone. The vision was telling me I can still change things. I can save humanity. That it doesn't *have* to be this way."

"You're insane," Todd said. "I'm going to fucking kill you. You killed my wife. My daughter was never born because of you."

"I may be insane, Mister Radcliffe, but I didn't kill your family. I'm not a violent man."

Todd scoffed and looked at the gun.

"This is out of necessity." Billy nodded at the pistol. "I don't want to do this."

"You're a fucking nut," Todd said. "If you didn't set that fire, then you had someone do it for you. You're just another crazy."

Todd took one step forward, and Billy tensed up, but he did not back off and still held the gun on his target. He moved his finger from behind the trigger to on it, ready to fire when the moment came.

"Don't hesitate, you psycho," Todd said. "If you're going to do it, then do it."

Todd stepped forward again. Now only a couple of feet separated them.

Billy opened his mouth to say something but was stopped silent when Todd took yet another step forward, closing the gap between them. The gun was now only inches from his neck. Billy's hand trembled. His entire body did, and it wasn't from the cold of the air or the rain. He was afraid. In his mind, he tried to hype himself up. He offered himself a quick reminder of why he had to do this and what was at stake. Something so much larger than himself and his conscience. But he was no killer, even when he *had* to be one. Just this one time. And would it really count as murder, considering what its purpose was? The inner turmoil was a sudden hurricane washing up on the shores of his conscience.

The breeze blew the potent smell of alcohol from Todd's breath to Billy's nose. Todd wasn't afraid. He was drunk and angry. He was a living, lost soul after everything he'd been through. This man had nothing to lose and would probably welcome death. It seemed he was begging for it, how he stood there, not only unwavering, but challenging. Rage, depression, and alcohol stimulated him.

Billy's mind commanded his finger to pull the trigger, but the finger disobeyed. The two stood there, toe-to-toe: one with a mission and one who didn't give a damn about anything anymore. He tried to remind himself once again of the importance of this moment, and that perhaps it had something to do with that dream on the morning of his conviction, which had been a vision, but an unclear one. Was that about this moment?

In that vision, the house was on fire, but nobody entered or left it. Couldn't be. Because that moment was in the past from this current one. Whatever happened *then* couldn't be affected by what he did *now*. But *now* he was faltering. And if he let *now* move forward without the proper action, then from *now on* was doomed.

"You fucking chicken-shit," Todd snarled. "You don't have the guts. Do I have to do it for you?"

And to Billy's dismay, Todd leaned forward and pressed his forehead against the gun's muzzle. Billy almost yanked the gun back, and then internally scowled at his own lack of commitment. He forced himself to hold it steady, but still didn't shoot.

"Does this help?" Todd pressed his forehead so hard against the gun now, Billy had to use strength to hold the line. "All you have to do is pull that fucking trigger."

"No," Billy mumbled. Epiphany gripped him and translated what he already knew into audible words. "I'm not a murderer. I... I can't do it."

He started to pull the gun away, but Todd grabbed it by the barrel and held it still to his own head. Billy tried to yank it, but his opponent used more force.

"There's another way," Billy whispered. "Wait for more dreams."

"There's no other way, you worthless piece of shit," Todd insisted through his hatred.

Billy tried one more time to pull the gun back but couldn't win this tug-of-war battle. He was now terrified, and that fear had taken his adrenaline and drained his strength. Suddenly worried he might accidentally fire, Billy let go of the gun and stumbled backward. His feet slipped in the mud, and he fell to his back with a soft thud on the wet ground. He kept his focus on Todd, who now stood before him with a gun in his hand. The weapon was now aimed at Billy, and Todd had a menacing smirk of victory on his face.

"What now, coward?" Todd almost roared above the consistent sound of falling rain.

Billy scrambled, slipped, and struggled backward. His arms and legs were a flurry of desperation on the softened ground. He finally made it to his feet, still facing the enemy, and backed away, so carefully, as to not fall again.

Todd advanced on him with confidence. "I know you killed my family."

"No."

"I know somehow my dad must've been a part of it."

"You're drunk, man. You're drunk and hurt."

"How did he know? How did my dad know to show up just in time to save me?"

Billy backed up. Todd continued forward.

"I don't know your dad. The fire was an accident. I don't know how he knew."

"I'm going to put a bullet in your head if you don't tell me how he knew."

"I don't know."

Todd raised the gun to aim it at Billy's head. "Tell me. Tell me now!"

"It was my dreams! I'm telling you, he didn't know! I had nothing to do with it! He had nothing to do with it!"

"You're nothing but a coward in all this! Tell me how he knew! Tell me now! Tell me now, motherfucker! God damn it, you tell me!"

Billy turned to run, almost fell, but quickly recovered. The ground was too slick, and a run was only clumsy jogging. He ran toward the street, and just before he reached the unscarred blacktop of a new neighborhood, he heard the gun fire. A blunt force to the back. He flew forward into the street, landed on his side, and rolled into a crawling position.

The pain was beyond any he'd ever felt. A fire had emerged from inside him, and his legs felt so weak. The pain was so intense, he struggled to maintain consciousness. Tunnel vision in and out. Stars forming in his sight. His arms almost like pudding, he crawled forward, tried to pull himself up, but only collapsed back down again. He could feel a warmth against his back while blood from the wound soaked it, as if the rain fell from the sun itself.

Billy stood clumsily. He wavered from left to right like a drunk struggling with inebriation. A boxer who was trying not to give in to the powerful knockout blow he'd just taken. He swiveled, staggered, and faced his enemy.

Todd was walking toward him, the gun still held up and aimed.

"You can't get away with killing someone's family, man," Todd said. "My daughter. My damn daughter. She wasn't even allowed to be born."

"I didn't kill anybody. I'm not a killer," Billy struggled in between gasps.

"You won't hurt anyone else!" And Todd shot Billy Wagner again.

A blast to the gut. Billy held both arms against his now gushing, bleeding belly, like a child acting dramatically over a tummy ache. He wobbled forward, the momentum of unbalance taking him back into the yard and toward Todd. Tripping over his own feet, balance was no longer a factor in his fading life. He tried to hold himself steady, but the pain and loss of blood were now stronger than his own will. Breathing was nearly a useless labor. Billy's sloughing was only stopped when he ran into Todd, who caught him with one arm and held him steady. Billy's head laid on Todd's shoulder, his legs only holding him up because of his attacker's assistance.

Todd spoke softly into Billy's ear. "Whatever you and my father had together, it ends today."

"You're wrong." Billy spoke through agonizing pain.

"It's too obvious. Do me a favor, will you?"

Billy tried to talk, but he was fading away quickly. Only a gasp escaped.

"Can you do me a favor?" Todd asked again.

"Fuck you," Billy snarled.

"Tell my wife and kid I love them, and I'll see them soon."

Even though he already knew Todd was going to kill him, those words caused Billy a chilling pause. He held his breath, closed his eyes, and braced for the final shot. He wanted to fight for his life and see another day, but just didn't have the strength to reach for it anymore. He was spent, bleeding out, confused by a cloud of physical torment.

Todd had the gun held in between them, and knew it was aimed right at Billy's chest. Their embrace was like that of one brother holding up his injured sibling. But this moment had nothing to do with love. Todd pulled the trigger. The report was muffled in between the two clinching enemies and the falling rain.

Billy grunted and went limp.

The sudden weight of his now lifeless body was too much for Todd's one arm and his intoxication, and he dropped Billy to the ground, face-first in the mud.

Chapter Thirty-Seven

The sky seemed as if it would never empty, but Alice dug frantically anyhow. Driving the shovel into mud and scooping it out, throwing it to the side. Stabbing at the soft ground, sometimes placing the tool beside the hole she'd made and using her hands in place of it. She grunted with effort and urgency. It was as if she needed that treasure now, and the longer it took for her to find it, the more chance of it somehow disappearing was likely. As if there were some supernatural nemesis beneath the ground, also digging upward in search of the same item she was.

Alice felt wholly panicked. She threw glops of mud to the left and to the right. Grabbed the shovel and brought it down into the hole with full force, tossed it to the side, reached her hands in again. The borehole she'd made was at least three feet deep and just as wide in diameter. She had to be close. She searched her memory, and the retrieved visions worried her. They hadn't dug this deep on that day. As a child, Todd had been enthusiastic about the project, and eager to put the box in the hole. He'd tried several times, but she had stopped him, explaining that if the cavern was too shallow, dirt would eventually wash away, and the treasure would be exposed for potential thieves to come along and snag it up.

"Isn't that deep enough?" he had asked, the box in his hand.

Alice could see these memories clearly, but when she searched deeper for the container's contents, she couldn't, for the life of her, remember what was in it.

"Come on, Mom. That's deep enough."

What was in that damn box?

"Let me put it in. Let's bury it now."

Alice wanted her past self in this memory to ask what was in the box. She could remember everything but that, so maybe if she could just tweak the memory a tad, she'd know what was driving her so furiously, other than physically possessing something her lost son had once held. Like it would bridge the past to the present, and she could again feel those moments stronger than the ones she endured now. Maybe the specific contents weren't really important, but that physical connection to the past was. Somehow she might forget, just for a damn moment, all the current turmoil, and linger in a time that was more simple.

"Maybe we should put more stuff in it," Todd said.

After a quick chuckle, Alice said, "It's full enough already. You don't want it to bust open, do you?"

"Yeah, but there's more room. All we have in it now is—"

That was it. The memory *did* contain the secret of the box's contents. But right there in that moment, right as Todd was about to inform her all the way from the past, the memory stopped. It didn't disappear, but it became silent. What force of nature, or space and time, didn't want her to know?

She dug in the mud, still going at it as if her life depended on it. As if the life of everyone she loved teetered on the edge of an emotional cliff, the answer to which she needed to know stopped in the memory, teasing her sanity. Alice dug like she was clawing her way not just a few feet to where a magic container of nostalgia lay in rest, but all the way to the core of the planet. With mud on her face and her arms, patches and smears on her wrinkled and soaked nightgown, she looked like a woman plagued with insanity and a mission with no real end-game scenario in reach. A madwoman who had fallen completely off the rocker, she grunted and moaned with frustrated determination. With each lump of mud tossed to the side, hope diminished within her.

Right now, all she'd had was hope. If she lost that, then she lost everything: her son, her husband, her reasons for living. Hope was an element of life and emotion that kept humans going, even in their most dire moments. Without the companion of hope, only despair could exist. When despair ruled all, then direction and meaning lost touch with reality. If reality was nothing but gloom and doom, where was the motivation to keep going?

Though Alice wasn't a drinker, she wanted a shot of bourbon or tequila. Something to numb or even banish the rush of dreary emotion rising within her. Something to take the despair and flood it out. She could stop right now, go inside, down a few drinks, and then return with a numbness that might help her with her current chore. Now her thoughts were getting the best of her, and everything in the world was through a pessimist's eyes.

Holding the handle in both hands, she raised the shovel over her head and brought its cutting edge down into the deep orifice with all her strength, accompanied by a shriek of fury. She had hoped it would hit something solid, stop with a loud clank or bang, but the tip only penetrated more mud. She did it again, harder; her scream louder. Only mud. Again. Again. Fully enraged bursts and thrusts. Again. She screamed and threw the shovel across the yard. She grabbed mud with her fingers, throwing it in all directions. Her actions became more frenzied. Peaking insanity. More mud. More. More.

"It's gone, Mom," came Todd's voice from behind her.

At first, she thought it was his voice from a memory, from his childhood. She stopped cold in her actions, looked into the deep emptiness of the void she'd dug as if she'd see his face in there. But the voice hadn't been that of a child. It was as deep as a full-grown man's tone. She realized the words had come from here and now, from her grown son standing behind her. The rain suddenly intensified as if her realization had made bigger the leaking hole in the sky.

"I dug it up years ago. Almost right after we buried it," Todd said, his words slightly slurring.

As soon as Alice realized he was struggling to talk, she thought she smelled the powerful aroma of alcohol.

Without turning around to face him, Alice asked, "Where did you put it?"

"I threw it away. I was afraid you'd find out. I threw it away. All of it."

Something about his voice made her uneasy. He spoke with an arrogant confidence, not someone who was ashamed of something he'd done. A matter-of-fact kind of tone. Along with his slur and his overconfident cadence, Alice knew there was something more out of place here than her sanity. A chill ran through her body. She realized the sound of his demeanor frightened her. The hairs on the back of her neck seemed to warn her of danger from her own son. Something was way off here. Way the hell off.

She wanted to turn around, but she was afraid to. If she faced him, and actually saw what she was already sensing in his voice, then she would be justified in being scared of her own child. She didn't *want* to fear him. Not Todd. Not her kid. But if she continued to kneel with her back to him, was she leaving herself open to some kind of impending attack? She tried to believe Todd surely wouldn't hurt her, but was that legitimate confidence or foolish naivety?

"What was in it?" she asked, still trying to chase the sensation of warning out of her own mind.

"Nothing important. Nothing that matters now. Maybe it mattered then and could have mattered now, but it doesn't anymore. Who gives a fuck what was in it?"

His hostile words nearly took her breath away. Now she wasn't just afraid to turn around, but she was scared, frozen. Whatever he was planning to do, he was likely waiting for her to face him. If he wanted to hurt her from behind, he would have already done so.

Alice was saddened suddenly. Saddened at the fact that she was on her knees before her own son, wondering how he planned to harm her. Though she'd not seen him or looked into his eyes, she could feel it. He meant to do more than confront her over something; he meant to do something to her she might never forgive him for. She'd thought the despair she felt minutes ago was at its peak, but now it was even stronger.

"I care," she said. "What was in it, son?"

He scoffed. "Some pictures. An ultrasound. Baby pictures. A pacifier. A baby bottle nipple. A lock of hair from my first haircut. A baby footprint on laminated paper." His voice rose as he spoke, as if his own words enraged him. "Things I'll never have again. Stormy's ultrasound pictures were lost in the fire. She never got her first haircut or sucked on a pacifier. No footprints. Nothing left, Mom. She didn't get to live."

He paused for a moment, and Alice's fear intensified.

"Because of Dad. Because of your husband. He killed them!"

As if she were spring-operated, Alice finally turned to face him, anger instantly taking over her fear, words already coming from her mouth as she swiveled on her knees. "Your dad saved your—" She stopped. Todd held a gun. And it was aimed right at her face.

"What are you doing?" she gasped, and stood up with some struggle, her feet wanting to slip on the mud.

Todd closed his eyes tightly for a second, opened them again. There was pain in his glare, but it wasn't alone alongside rage, hatred, bitterness. Alice had been accurate in her detection of the smell of alcohol. Todd's eyes were bloodshot, as if he'd been drinking for days. The devil was in his scowl.

When he didn't answer, she repeated herself, adding one word to the previous question, hoping it would remind him of who she was to him, and him to her. "Son, what are you doing?"

"I'm going to show Dad what it feels like, Alice."

"Mom. I'm Mom. You call me Mom."

"Alice," he insisted. "For these last few minutes of your life, you are Alice to me."

Chapter Thirty-Eight

J im stood before the gravestone, memories flashing through his
mind like a teacher showing math cards to a first-grade student.
Instead of seeing numbers and calculating solutions, though, Jim was
identifying the moments, the places, the faces, and activities. His inner
turmoil was an interrogation of his own decisions, pounding away at
him as if he'd committed a crime, cruelly urging him toward confes-
sion. He had already confessed to himself, but maybe he needed to
do so to his son. Face Todd and admit he'd made the wrong decision.
Though the circumstances were beyond any heartfelt apologies, perhaps if Jim acknowledged his selfishness to his emotionally tortured
son, healing could at least begin.

His smartphone vibrated in his pocket. Jim ignored it and continued on in thought, looking for epiphanies that might start the path
toward happily ever after. Maybe happily ever after wasn't attainable
anymore, but at least a contentness that offered some kind of permanent closure, and his relationship with his son not healed, but at
least mended. A Band-Aid that would cover the wound for life, not
washing off in the downpour of any future strife.

The phone went still for just a few moments, but then started to
buzz again. It was as if the caller was nagging at him, like an anxious
child tugging at his shirt. Something important. When it stopped
and then began once more, suddenly Jim felt importance upgrade

to urgent. He pulled the phone out of his pocket and looked at the screen. It was Alice.

His voice was shaky when he answered, and Jim realized for the first time since standing here in the rain that he was drenched and freezing.

"Hello, wife," he said.

She didn't reply with words at first. Instead, he heard sniffling, as if she had a sudden cold. But then her voice came, and her words were outlined in whimpering. "Oh Jim," she wailed.

"Alice, what's wrong?"

"Jim, I don't know what we did wrong. I don't know."

Jim heard a voice in the background. A male voice, but it was so muffled the words were inscrutable.

"What's wrong, honey? Are you okay?"

"No," she cried. "No, I'm not. I don't know what to do." She spoke like a child blubbering after just being injured in a bike wreck, trying to explain through agonizing tears what had just happened. "He's lost his mind. He's gone. We've lost our son." Her voice trailed into a struggling squeak. "He's lost, Jim. I don't know what to do."

Then the male voice in the background again.

Next came Alice's voice once more, but this time it sounded as if she held the phone away from her face. She said, "No. No, you don't—" Distant mumbling.

"Jim," came Todd's voice. He held the phone now. His tone, in just one word, was full of demand.

The fact he'd called Jim by his name instead of Dad triggered an inner alarm.

"Son, what's going on? What's wrong with your mom? What's she talking about?"

"Where are you?" Todd asked.

Todd's tone was so off, Jim felt a chill run through him that wasn't from the icy rain pelting against his face.

"I went for a drive. Just to think."

"Doesn't sound like you're in the car." Interrogative. Demanding. Cold.

"I had to stop for gas," Jim lied. "Now, what's wrong with your mom? Is she okay?"

"No, Jim, she's not okay. She's not going to be okay."

"What? What's going on? Son—"

"Don't call me that. Neither of you will ever call me that again."

"What the hell is going on? I'm coming home." Jim turned away from the gravesite and started toward the running car.

"Yeah, come home, Jim. There's something I want you to witness. Come home quick, man. You don't want to miss this."

"Stay on the phone with me. I'm coming. I'm on my way. Put your mom back on the phone. Son, please. Don't do anything stupid. Put your mom back on the phone."

Silence.

"Son, goddammit, put your mom on the phone."

No reply.

"Are you drinking? Don't do anything stupid. Todd—"

"Come home, Jim. I have a surprise for you."

"Todd, don't you hurt your mother. Son—"

The call ended.

The car door was still open and the wipers running. In a sudden, hastened state, Jim climbed in, pulled the door shut, and sped off without bothering to fasten his seat belt, wheels peeling out on the puddling blacktop.

Chapter Thirty-Nine

J im saw Todd's car parked in the front yard as if he'd lost control of it while pulling into the driveway, and then slid on into the grass, leaving deep, ponding tire tracks in the soaked ground. Jim put the car in park and looked at the glove box. Inside it was a small handgun Jim kept for self-defense purposes. In a city where carjacking was becoming a near epidemic, he'd bought one for him, and one for Alice, a few years ago. It had remained in that glove compartment ever since. Loaded, the safety on, and never used or even touched, the need for a firearm had thankfully never become necessary.

But now, Jim stared, wondering whether he should take it inside with him. Todd had sounded profoundly inebriated over the phone, and with his depression sinking him lower and lower into a state of unpredictability, he might actually now be so far gone he could, or would, actually hurt someone. Rain tapped on the car's roof, drops covering the windshield intermittently between wiper blade swipes.

He was nearly angry at himself for even considering that he might need a lethal weapon in a confrontation with his own son, but that feeling quickly gave way to a once more nagging unsureness. He wasn't being illogical. Jim might actually need the gun, at least for the sake of bluffing. The safety would never be disengaged if he pulled it on Todd, and he would keep his hand behind the trigger instead of over it. He wondered whether he should empty the ammunition from it before even leaving the car, but realized now he was already taking too long, sitting there debating himself, while something awful might be going on inside that house.

He reached across the passenger seat, opened the glove compartment, and pulled out the pistol. He double-checked the safety. It was engaged. He shoved the gun in one pocket, and his smartphone in the other. Keys in hand, he got out of the car and hurried toward the front porch, tackled four stairs in two steps, and rushed into the house.

As soon as he stepped from the foyer into the living room, glancing around, hectically searching for Alice, he heard her yell for him from the kitchen, obviously alerted to his arrival by the screen door slamming shut.

"Jim!"

He reached into his pocket for the gun, decided against pulling it out, and hurried into the kitchen. When he crossed the threshold, he immediately looked to his right toward the dinette set, and his heart felt as if it nearly paused for a long moment and then accelerated into overdrive. Alice sat at the far end of the table, her hands folded on its surface, and a look of pure horror mixed with despondency on her face. Her sad eyes were red from crying immoderately. Standing behind her, with a bloodshot glare and a slumping stance, was Todd. He held a gun and had it pointed right at his mother's head.

Again, Jim wanted to reach into his pocket and pull the piece he'd brought with him, but he convinced himself that mental keenness was more needed now than brute or lethal force. If he pulled the pistol, Todd might instinctively pull the trigger on his. Jim was no quick-draw ace, and it was impossible for him to beat his son to the punch. At least for now.

Jim felt suddenly saddened at the thought that he was now in a standoff with his own kid, and that his initial instinct had been to shoot Todd. Never would he have imagined these circumstances on himself, or any of this family. But he also would have never conjured up, even in his wildest dreams, the events of the past few months. It was as if it was all one everlasting hallucination.

"Alice, are you okay? Has he hurt you?" Jim asked while he stared Todd down, who had a foul smirk on his face. Jim suddenly noticed the potent smell of alcohol. Todd had consumed so much, the stink from it was unavoidable even from across the room.

"No. Not yet. Jim, he's drunk. He's not thinking clearly at all. He really believes you killed his family or had something to do with it."

"Hey guys," Todd waved the gun back and forth, "I'm right here in the room. I'm still here."

"Where did *you* get a gun?" Jim asked.

"From our friend. From *your* friend."

"Who?"

"The crazy guy from our backyard." Todd pointed the gun at his father. "Don't pretend you don't know him. I'll put a bullet in Mom right now. Don't even pretend, Jim."

Perplexed, Jim said, "I don't understand. When and why did he give you a gun?"

"He was going to shoot me. I guess finish the job you two started out to do. But he couldn't do it." Todd's tone was that of a bad guy in a movie, boasting about his plan before tying the good guys to the railroad tracks, with an approaching train whistle blaring in the distance. "He just couldn't pull the trigger. So, I took it from him. I'll tell you, I had no problem pulling the trigger myself. It felt natural, right, *good,* to put down the motherfucker who took my family from me. Watching him turn to run. Shooting him in the back. He tried to play ignorant, but it didn't get past me. Never again. Nothing is getting past me anymore. I saw through him. I shot him more than once, too. Each time felt better than the one before. I held him in my arms, Jim. I held him in my arms as I fired the fatal shot. You should have seen him. Oh, how the mighty fall."

"Jesus, son. Where is he?" Jim asked in obvious distress.

"He's lying dead in front of my house. What used to be my house before you two schemed to take it away from me. My family..." He choked back tears, paused to regain what weak steadiness he could in his demeanor. "That murdering piece of shit. He's lying dead in the yard...in a puddle of his own blood. Like roadkill, Jim. He's reduced to a useless carcass in the mud. Gone, gone, gone."

Pleading, Jim said, "You killed an innocent man, son. He was in jail. He had nothing to do with the fire. Just a lonely, crazy man having bad dreams. You killed an innocent man, son. Oh, God, son. An *innocent man.*"

"So innocent that he came to that house with a gun, pointing it at me, about to kill me. He was there to do to me what I did to him!"

"Give me the gun, son," Jim demanded as he reached out a hand and started around the table.

"Stop right there!" Todd demanded as he aimed the muzzle at his mother's head again.

Jim froze, backed up, with both hands up in a submissive gesture. "What are you doing, son? I hope that safety is on."

"Nope." Todd turned the side of the firearm toward his dad.

Even from the ten-foot distance, Jim saw the safety was not engaged.

"You can lay it on the table. I won't touch it. Just lay it on the table."

"I don't think so, Jim."

Alice sniffled. Elbows on the table, she hid her face in her hands.

"What if it goes off? You want to accidentally kill your own mother? Will that bring back Beth and Stormy? Is that what you think?"

Suddenly enraged, Todd pointed the gun at Jim and yelled, "Don't you say their names! Never again!" He jabbed the gun back and forward as he spoke. "You don't get to say their names. You let them die. You planned it. You and that crazy guy!"

"Oh, son," Alice said in between sobs, not uncovering her face.

"What the fuck is wrong with you?" Jim asked, hands still out.

"Tell Alice, Jim," Todd said through clenched teeth and restrained rage. "Tell her how you knew."

"I didn't know. I told you it was coincidence...from earlier that day. I just decided to ride by and check up on you. The house was on fire. I went in."

"No. It's too perfect. The timing is too perfect. You knew. You fucking knew." Todd prodded the gun through the air again. "You. Fucking. Knew. Tell us how. Tell your wife how you knew. There's only one way, Jim. The crazy guy told you. He had to tell you in advance."

Alice raised her face away from her hands, impatient courage in her voice. "You really believe your own father would try to hurt you or your family? What has your father done over the years of loving and raising you that makes you think he'd do something so awful?" Her voice rose. "Were you abused, son? Were you beaten or neglected? Was your childhood made so bad by your father that you believe he'd ever hurt anyone?"

"You shut the fuck up with your pitiful attempt at logic," Todd snapped at his mother. "He knew that fire was going to happen. Who gives a shit how I was raised? Something went wrong somewhere with that motherfucker." Todd continued to aim the muzzle at his father. "Tell us how you knew!"

"No," Jim said firmly. "I didn't know. If you want to shoot somebody, shoot me. Your mother had nothing to do with it. I saved you and let Beth and Stormy die. That was *my* decision. I had no time to rationalize. I had no time to think. The house was ablaze. I ran in. I saved my son. On instinct, I saved my son. On love."

Todd had tears running down his face now. Tears of rage and other emotions. Mourning. Regret. The ongoing realization he'd lost his wife and daughter forever dripped from his face onto his shirt. He swayed slightly from left to right and back again as if he fought his drunkenness to stay conscious. His bloodshot eyes were barely slits as they tried so hard to close, to bring unconsciousness to him. He fought it off, lazily aiming his weapon at his father.

"I don't get to do it again," Jim said. "If there was a next time, a re-do, knowing what I know now, I would do it differently. Because I love you, I would save them first. I would put my selfishness aside. I would sacrifice you for what I know you would want. I'm sorry, son. I failed."

Todd seemed to fade away, but with a burst of determination he fought off the inebriation and jammed the muzzle against his mother's head.

Alice gasped and froze.

Jim's body wanted to leap forward, across the table, at his son, hands out, to grab the gun. He knew he wouldn't make it, though. If he moved in any way that made Todd flinch, Alice would take a bullet to the head. Jim held completely still, frozen in terror. He knew if he extended this confrontation as long as possible without incident, Todd's body would give in to his overindulgence in alcohol, and he would hopefully pass the hell out. More time. Surely not too much more. Just a few more minutes. Todd was fighting it, but the fight in him couldn't last much longer.

"I never thought my life would end up like this," Todd whispered. "I did nothing wrong. I went through school, doing what I was supposed to. Beth and I met. I loved her. We were perfect for each other. I got the job. Worked so hard. Moved up. I waited. We waited until we could do it right. I got promoted."

"Son," Jim's words were gentle and cautious, "you did everything right. It wasn't your fault. It was a fucked-up accident."

Alice had a gun to her head, wide-eyed and silent. She was afraid to even breathe and did so as carefully as possible. Slow, steady breaths. Her hands were flat on the table, her gaze forward and fixed on her husband.

Todd swayed to the right and back again. Seeing this, and focused on the gun at his wife's head, Jim almost gasped aloud. Todd was fading quickly. He struggled to keep his eyes open while his finger was still on the trigger. Jim worried his son might reflexively pull it if he passed out, reporting one fatal shot before crumpling to the floor.

"What did I do that was so bad?" Todd sounded like a child trying to speak through miserable wails. "What did Beth do? What did Stormy do? What...what did we do? Why us? Why them?" Todd flinched as if he were slapped in the face, fighting the coming darkness with every ounce of determination he had left in him. He met his father's gaze. "Why, Jim? Why?"

"You didn't. Nobody did. It was a tragedy. It was bad luck. You weren't chosen by anything or anyone because of something you've done wrong. Bad things happen to good people all the time, son. It's part of life. We have to go on. If Beth were here right now, what would she say to you? What would your daughter think if she were here right now, watching you hold a gun to her grandmother's head? See, this is all wrong. What you're doing here isn't rational. You're going to hurt someone. And then what will you do? If you shoot me or your mother right now, what will you do after that? What's next if you kill one or both of us right here? What will you do next, son?"

Todd stumbled to his right and inadvertently pulled the gun away from his mother's head. He was near the darkness of an unconscious state. His eyes fluttered. He waved the gun around recklessly. A loud bang like a powerful firecracker popped inside the kitchen. Drywall pieces exploded from the ceiling and rained down onto the table. Todd had pulled the trigger as he staggered.

A quick moment of opportunity. Jim sprang into action, coming around the table in the direction Todd stumbled, with more speed than he knew his body was capable of. In an instant, he was close enough, and grabbed Todd's gun hand by the wrist. Jim had reached for the gun itself, but his aim was off. With Todd's wrist in his hand, Jim brought his other hand up for the pistol. Todd put all his weight into a backward motion and slipped out of his father's grasp just before Jim would have grabbed the firearm. Jim stayed with his son, lunged forward as Todd stumbled backward, waving the weapon wildly. Another shot. Shreds of cabinet wood above the kitchen sink splashed in all directions.

Alice screamed. Arms over her head as if in a tornado drill, she came out of the kitchen chair like a spring that had been triggered by the latest gunshot. She scrambled around, hunched over, away from where father and son were battling it out. She stopped just at the doorway of the kitchen to the living room and turned back to look. Mid-flee, she considered running back in there to help Jim, but was unsure whether she would just be in the way and might obstruct his efforts to subdue their drunk and enraged son.

Jim had grabbed the gun's barrel, but Todd's strength was enhanced by alcohol, and he yanked it back away from his father. Jim charged and tackled Todd, hoping the impact of them falling to the floor would cause Todd's grip on the weapon to come unglued. They hit the tile, Jim on top. Todd tried to roll away, and Jim realized he had no choice but to weaken his son. There was only one way he could do that. He made a fist and decked Todd right in the face.

Blood splattered from Todd's instantly broken nose, and he let out a rage-filled shriek. With all his strength, he swung the gun at his father's face, who was instantly knocked back, with stars in his vision. Todd tried to crawl away, but Jim was on top of him again in an instant.

"This isn't who you are!" Jim squeezed the words out with a grunt of effort.

Todd tried to squirm away, but Jim had him held to the floor like a father holding down a tantrum-throwing child. Todd slipped his free hand from his father's grasp, who immediately had hold of it again.

"Son!" Alice yelled from the other side of the table. "Todd, please stop! Just stop!"

An enraged glare from Todd, who continued to struggle with his father. Todd said nothing but grumbled with each tug or pull. He was dragging them both along the smooth kitchen tile. Finally, he stopped with a huff and went completely still.

"Please, son," Jim said. "We can get you help. Let go of the gun, and let's get you some help. You don't have to deal with this alone. Me and your mother will be beside you the whole way."

"We're here, son," Alice said through a whimper. "I swear, we're both here for you. We love you. We love you so much." She came around the table and was almost at their feet, looking down woefully.

Jim thought the hard part was over and loosened his grip on both of Todd's wrists.

For a few moments, Todd laid still, catching his breath.

Jim lessened his hold a little more. "I'm going to let go of you. I want you to let go of the gun first. Let me take the gun, and we can sit here as a family and talk this out. Together, we can figure out what we need to do to help you. To help us all. A family, son. As a family."

With no hint or warning, Todd screamed with hatred as he lunged upward, head-butting his father in full force.

The blow was powerful, and Jim became helplessly dazed, falling off his son and onto his back. He tried to roll toward Todd, but his son was quick and pulled away. When Jim missed his target, all his strength gone, he rolled just far enough to stop on his back, looking up at a ceiling that was spinning. His stomach felt nauseous, and consciousness was a fleeting state.

"No, son!" Alice screamed and backed up a few steps, stopped only by the outreaching counter behind her.

Todd was inspired by the sudden shift in advantage, and quickly straddled his father.

Jim tried to roll away but was too significantly weakened by the blow his son had delivered to his face. The entire room was a quick-turning carousel. He couldn't focus on one point, not even his son who now sat on him, looking down at him with blurred spite.

"We'll do this together," Todd slurred in mockery. "We're a family, son. We'll get help together." Todd punched Jim in the face, who was so close to darkness he didn't even mumble or cry out.

His face just jerked involuntarily from the power of the strike.

"Todd, stop it, for heaven's sake. Stop this shit right now!" Alice screamed.

"We're just one big happy family, aren't we?" Todd said. "You're all one big happy family. You have your wife. Your kid isn't dead. *You* are one big...happy...family." Todd swayed just a little, caught himself. He blinked his eyes several times as if he, too, fought off dizziness. He shook his head quickly, trying to jerk clear vision back into his sight.

Jim lazily reached for Todd's gun, missed, and his hand fell back to the floor.

"Oh, you want this?" Todd waved the pistol just inches from his father's face. "Don't pass out yet. I want you to witness something. I want you to watch like I watched my house blow up with my family inside. I want you to see this, *Dad*."

Jim watched Todd through foggy vision. Son rambled on while father said nothing.

"Oh, son. What are you doing?" Alice asked.

Jim, still silent, still watching.

"We love you so much," Alice said. "So much." She was crying.

"We love you so much," Todd mocked his mother. "We love you so much. We...love...you...so...much."

Todd turned away from Jim, faced his mom, and aimed the gun at her.

She gasped.

"We love you so much." He repeated her words again. His cadence was so full of hatred and spite. "Will you love me after this?" He raised the gun more, steadied his aim on his mother—

From below Todd, Jim screamed. Loud, long, and piercing, he shrieked with all that was in him, raised up with a gun that he'd slyly retrieved from his pocket. Yelling, roaring with agony, Jim pulled the trigger. Again. Again. Three quick shots echoed around them.

As each round impacted and pierced Todd's body, he jerked, yanked, dropped his gun, and with a stunned expression, turned to face his father.

Jim brought his gun hand down, crying as if he wanted the entire world to know and feel his torment.

Alice screamed at the top of her lungs with her face in her hands, her entire body trembling.

Todd fell off his father and landed on his back, staring at the ceiling, wheezing, gasping. Blood was already pooling around him. The side of his shirt—one hole, liquid red pouring from a wound. Warmness against his back from two other gushing punctures.

"Call an ambulance," Jim ordered Alice as he pulled himself into a kneeling position beside his son.

Alice acted as if she couldn't hear her husband above her own verbal horror.

"Do it now, Alice! Call an ambulance."

With all her willpower, Alice moved toward the kitchen table, grabbed her smartphone, and frantically dialed 911. She fell to her knees just above her son's head.

"Todd, stay with us. Stay with us, son," Jim said gently, his voice trembling.

Todd tried to talk but coughed instead. Blood leaked from his mouth, off to the side of his face, dripping on the floor. He moaned, tried to roll away, but Jim grabbed and held him steady.

Alice was hysterically giving the 911 operator an address, screaming that her son had been shot and they needed to hurry.

"Dad." Todd squeezed the word out as he choked and turned onto one side.

Jim hovered over Todd, gently rolled him onto his back again. The stream of blood from Todd's mouth intensified like water boiling over onto a hot stove.

"Son, please just keep breathing. Fight for it, son. I'm with you. Your mother is here."

Alice was off the phone now and still kneeling just above Todd's head. She leaned forward and looked down into his face. She was trying to control her crying, speaking in between sobs. "Son, I'm here. We're here. We love you. We love you so much."

"We love you so much," Jim repeated.

"Todd, please stay awake," Alice begged.

"Keep breathing," Jim said again. "Just keep breathing. Please, son."

"Mo...Mom. Dad... Dad," Todd struggled through fierce pain. "Dad."

"I'm here." Jim held his son steady. He touched Todd's face. Gently brushed his hair back from his forehead. "I'm here, and I love you."

"Oh, God, Jim. God, no. Please, please, please," Alice whispered.

"I'm sorry," Todd said through a sudden cough, which pushed more blood from his mouth. "I'm so sorry."

"It's okay, son. We love you. Stay with us," Jim replied gently.

"Stay with us," Alice mumbled. "Just stay with us."

Todd tried to move, but his father held him still and said, "Don't move, son. You need to stay like this. Just trust me, son. Trust me, please."

"Son," Alice said.

"Dad..." Todd's voice was raspy, choppy, and so weak.

"Son," Jim replied.

"Please... Next...next..."

Jim said, "I love you, son. I love you so much. My only child. My boy."

Alice tried to speak, but couldn't through her sniffling, held speechless by terror.

"Dad, listen...to me."

"I'm here."

"Save my wife. My kid." He coughed out more blood. His voice weakened even more.

Jim didn't know what to say. He held his silence and listened.

"Next time, Dad. Save them. Promise—" He choked for a second, coughed. "Promise me, Dad. Do it now. Save them."

Knowing his son needed to focus on breathing and staying awake, Jim replied, "I will, son. I promise. Next time, I'll save them. I swear it. You need to breathe. Stay awake."

"Next time, Dad."

Jim started to reply but realized Todd had just exhaled his last breath in this life. His son's eyes, wide open, went blank, and his body limp. Suddenly, Jim knew what had happened, and so did Alice, who shrieked in agony.

Jim swiped his badge at the outside turnstile, and a beep emitted from the card reader. On the other side was his work parking lot. He held the badge up and looked at it. In his other hand, his work bag. In his pockets, his car keys and his smartphone. He held the bag up too, regarding it with bafflement.

The card. The bag. This night. The kitchen scene during which, in defense of Alice, Jim had shot his own son, had instantly transformed into this. Work. It was after the shift. Joyful chatter in the parking lot distance, people happy to be headed home or to wherever their post-shift endeavors led them. He realized his face was dry from tears and free from the pain inflicted upon it by Todd during the scuffle, which was only moments ago. There was an urging in his soul. Something pushing at him to hurry the hell up. The fire.

A deep warning tone emitted from the turnstile, informing whoever had just swiped their card that they would now have to do so again in order to pass through. Jim looked through the still gate, into the parking lot, his face frozen in confusion.

"You just going to stand there?" came an impatient male voice from behind him.

Jim was holding up the exit line. Suddenly, he got it; he understood what was happening to him yet again. He dropped the bag, swiped his card once more. Beep. A green arrow lit up in an electronic display at the top of the turnstile. He rushed through, ran across the parking lot, also dropping his work badge to the pavement while reaching into his pocket for his keys. He was here at the night of the fire again.

Part Four

Next Time

Chapter Forty

As Jim ran across the parking lot toward his car, he reached a hand into a pants pocket and retrieved his keys. He frantically hit the unlock button several times as he approached his vehicle. Headlights flashed, indicating the car doors were unlocked. He almost reached into the other pocket to pull his phone out and check the time, but decided against that because it might slow him down a fraction of a second. He didn't have that to lose, and he already knew the time. It was 2:11 a.m., as it had been the first time he'd played through this scenario.

He pulled open the driver's door, slipped into the seat, and reached out to pull the door shut with one hand while starting the car with the other one. Sports talk was booming on the radio. No time to turn it off. That would take at least a second. By letting it play and focusing on getting the hell out of there, Jim might gain another precious moment to use toward his impending rescue attempt.

The door stopped. Just like last time, Adam Crane stood beside the car, holding the door open.

"Somebody's in a hurry," Adam said with an affable grin.

Jim didn't reply. Adam had held him up by at least a full minute, maybe more, the first time around. Now, Jim had a chance to get those urgent moments back, and there was no nice way to do it. With all his strength, he yanked the door out of Adam's grip, slamming it shut and leaving his coworker with a look of shock on his face, and shaking his hand from the pain of having a door handle ripped suddenly from his clutches.

The engine was running. Without putting his seat belt on, Jim threw the car in reverse. He didn't even check the rear or side-view mirrors when he stepped on the gas. If he hit someone's car as they were passing behind him, he didn't care. He would have just taken off anyhow and dealt with the hit-and-run consequences later. The car backed out of the parking spot at high speed, tires protesting.

Adam instinctively moved back from the vehicle with such force he stumbled and almost fell on his ass. He stood there, eyes wide, as he watched Jim speed out of the parking lot, not stopping to check both ways at the main road, engine gunning; then he disappeared into the night.

Jim flew through the three-way intersection at the end of the street, ignoring traffic lights or any potential oncoming traffic. When he successfully made the turn without incident, and zoomed forward, he breathed a sigh of relief. He wanted to roll his window down and feel the night air against his face, because he knew it might at least be somewhat calming, but didn't want to take the time or lose focus on driving. He needed this car to go as fast as it could. Rolling the window down might lose him about one second. A second not lost was a second gained.

On the main road, he saw the speedometer hit ninety-five. *Faster.* He needed more speed, but the pedal was already to the metal. His entire body was soaked in sweat. It dripped from his forehead into his eyes, and he blinked it away. Maybe he should have opened the window, if at least for cooling his head. If sweat blurred his vision at the speed he was traveling, he might run off the road, crash the car, and save nobody while also killing himself. He blinked several times again, kept blinking. The constant movement of his eyelids might deflect anymore dripping perspiration, but he also couldn't focus if he was struggling to see through the flickering of a 1920s film. He had to wipe his brow, which meant taking one hand off the steering wheel for a split second.

He was on a straight stretch of roadway, so he took the risk. He reached up, wiped with a brisk movement, and when he pulled that arm away and grabbed the steering wheel again, he saw the deer. He knew it would come up quick, and reminded himself that the first time the animal had not run out in front of his car, yet Jim had still swerved just a tad into oncoming traffic as an involuntary reaction. That might have cost him a few miles per hour in speed and, once again, precious seconds.

This time, he willed himself to hold the car straight and bolted past the deer, which turned and ran away from the road as the wind from Jim's speeding car hit it. Jim, however, did not see it flee from the roadside, because he didn't give a damn about anything behind him, and wouldn't check the rearview this entire race. If a speeder-hunting cop, running radar, clocked Jim at this reckless pace and pulled out behind him, that officer would just have to follow Jim to the house. As a matter of fact, that wouldn't be a bad thing. There would be two rescuers instead of one—a better chance to save everyone in that house.

Up ahead, there was a sharp curve to the left, and it was approaching quickly. Jim didn't want to slow the car, and cringed, knowing he had to brake. More time lost, but if he flipped the car, he would never arrive at the fire's scene. He wouldn't save Todd. Beth and Stormy would perish once again. Jim took the curve with extreme caution, feeling the car slide as he tried to maintain as much speed as possible.

The railroad tracks. He crushed the gas pedal again, and the car felt like it went a few inches airborne as it cleared the tracks. Like he was on some kind of amusement park ride that simulated motion, the car bounced on its shocks and Jim's head hit the ceiling several times. He held the steering wheel steady, though, remained focused on the road, and continued forward.

Now he was on the main road through a neighborhood. The speed limit was thirty-five, and he exceeded that by forty-five miles per hour. He would never travel through a residential area with such recklessness on any other occasion, for fear of strolling citizens or children on bikes. There were sidewalks, but people didn't always use them. And there was nothing guaranteeing that a child on a bicycle wouldn't lose control and accidentally stray into the street. It was past two in the morning now, and if there were kids out playing on the road, then there were deeper issues with parenting involved. Jim risked it and continued at an absurdly high speed on a street with no artificial lighting besides a porch light here and there.

"Please hurry. Please fucking hurry." He mumbled to himself as he drove, as if he could encourage himself in this moment of urgent hope.

The four-way stop was ahead now. Last time, he had slowed enough to avoid any vehicles which might have already stopped and were about to advance through. There were bushes just on a residential border at the street, which obstructed his view to the left. The last time through, Jim had slowed significantly to avoid any possible oncoming vehicles. This time, however, he had the advantage of knowing there were no cars coming. He slowed enough to avoid momentum sliding him off the street and through a yard, but he didn't ease up on speed as much as he had before. A loud screeching from his spinning wheels against the blacktop as he swung the car right, a sound loud enough to wake up every household in the immediate area, and he launched forward again.

His mind wandered toward Mr. Brimstone, the sinister character who Jim thought was offering a lifesaving favor, but was only truly using tragedy for entertainment. That's why he sent Jim back to a point where he could save Todd, but with no time to spare. It was like the mysterious man in the black suit and red tie was watching from somewhere nearby with a bunch of his buddies, and they had all placed their bets on whether Jim could make it or not. Maybe there were several gambles, with odds set: Jim not saving anyone two-to-one odds. At twenty-to-one odds, Jim was saving just Todd. Jim saving everyone at one-thousand-to-one odds. Perhaps there was even a betting line on whether Jim would die too, and nobody survived.

Once more, he wondered exactly what Mr. Brimstone *was*. He obviously couldn't be human, having supernatural powers to manipulate actual space and time. To offer any living being a do-over, and being capable of delivering on that, was a preternatural ability. Was he a demon, a god, or maybe even an alien from some distant galaxy? Whatever he was and wherever he was from, he wasn't benign. He was evil, because no good conscious being would play games like this. These were malicious practices beyond even simple murder. Like holding hope in front of someone's face, just out of reach, and waving it back and forth like a pendulum.

By the time Jim had the car up to sixty miles per hour, he was upon the turn that put him on Todd's street. In the distance, he could see the glow of the fire. It was an eerie scene, flickering orange and yellow melding into the darkness of night around it. Jim felt as if his heart had stopped the moment he saw the radiance from the developing disaster. If his windows had been down, he would have smelled smoke, and might even choke on it, as he neared the house.

When he pulled into the yard, stopping the car parallel to the engulfed home lengthwise, Jim's eyes became wide with awe. The fire was a cruel, destructive force already consuming the roof, blasting out windows. It seemed to warn Jim with a psychic message to stay away, to run away, to not dare enter. As flames reached upward and outward, black smoke bellowing and disappearing into the darkness of night, it seemed to have a malicious, living soul. An evil, ancient warlock taking an elemental form in the present, and its only intention was to kill as painfully as possible.

Jim's body tingled with fear—not for himself, but for the victims inside. He'd wasted no time, but felt he was once again too late to save everyone.

The driver's side faced away from the house, and Jim knew when he carried out Beth and Todd, he would have to place them on this side, using the car as a shield from the gas explosion that would happen within just the next few minutes.

He swung the car door open and hurried out, stumbled over his own feet, clumsily avoided falling, and ran around the back of the car. As he approached the house, the ferocious beast disintegrating it piece by piece, he paused. The last time he'd heard sirens in the distance, but this time he didn't. He glanced down the road, listened, and heard only the fire's roaring voice. He was earlier this time. Maybe, just maybe, he *could* save them both.

But now thoughts ran through his mind from the months after having saved Todd. The misery caused the alternate timeline to not offer any more solace than the original. How many times had he doubted his own actions of saving his son from that fire in the past few months? How often had Jim wondered whether he was right in interfering, and whether Billy Wagner's warnings had been accurate? What if he goes into this house, saves Beth and Todd, and an even worse future occurs? Could there be any bad in saving them *both*?

All these doubts, these reflections, happened in a flood of his mind over just a few quick moments of time. He looked to his right and listened for sirens, but still heard none. He was still ahead. Way ahead. There was plenty of time to make things right, to bring everyone safely out of the burning house, get them behind the car to protect them from the impending explosion. Standing here in contemplation only diminished his odds. The last intact upstairs window of the house blew out, and a fist of flames reached into the night. Jim ran forward and leapt up onto the porch.

Chapter Forty-One

He already felt the heat from the fire. It was in there waiting for him, but sent warning messengers as waves of warmth. The first time, Jim had taken the time to grab the doorknob. This time, he knew better, and threw one solid kick, with all his strength, into the center of the door. It kicked in with a loud crash, ripping the dead bolt through the inner doorframe. Jim instantly looked away from the doorway, knowing from before that a wave of heat would attack him like angry and enthusiastic guard dogs suddenly freed from their chains. The heat wave brushed all around him and proceeded on. Jim turned, faced the door, took a deep breath, and charged into the inferno.

The fire's sweltering breath was instantly intense, and its surrounding voice was even louder. The smoke suddenly in Jim's lungs threatened to overcome him before he could make it even to the stairwell, so he pulled the top of his shirt over his mouth and nose like a mask. Immediately, the air he breathed felt better. Although his lungs burned less, they still burned. Just as before, he knew he had to act without hesitation.

Every second. Every damn second.

He made it to the stairwell, and laying there as before, on his front side with his arms reaching upward on the stairs, was Todd, unconscious from smoke inhalation. Jim let out a gasp of desperation. His eyes watered not just from the smoke and the heat, but from the thought of stepping past Todd to go save Beth. Jim reached down and nudged his son. Todd didn't move.

"Todd!"

No reaction. Jim could see Todd was still breathing, but for how long could he continue to do so? Before, Jim had pulled him from the house just in time. Now, if Jim went up, retrieved Beth, hauled her down the stairs and outside, and then ran back in for his son, would Todd already be dead? Jim reminded himself that he was ahead of schedule for this rescue operation, and by the time he made it back into the house after saving Beth, maybe he would be right at the same pace as before. There was too much thinking; too much calculating. No time for that. He had to move.

"Son!" he yelled as he slapped Todd on the side of his face. Jim's shirt facemask fell down off his chin, and he quickly put it back in place. Todd seemed to react to the smack, but only unconsciously. He didn't spring to life or even open his eyes. The smoke was too much, and Jim wasn't going to successfully get his son up and going. There was no more time to waste, and he forced himself to move past Todd and up the stairway.

When Jim reached the top of the stairs, he immediately saw Beth lying on her back, unconscious, with her arms out. His eyes moved to her belly, a pitcher's mound with a baby inside it. Seven months pregnant. Precious life. It looked as if Beth had crawled from the bedroom, trying to stay below the smoke, but had succumbed to it anyhow, and rolled onto her back, knowing she was passing out, to avoid crushing unborn Stormy Dawn, and hoping someone might rescue her before she and her child perished. Jim tried not to break down as he remembered the funeral...Beth's mom admonishing him. But now Beth was alive, and Jim could change everything. He could give that woman her child and her granddaughter back. Hope was still around, and it was reminding him to hurry the hell up.

He went to and knelt beside her, holding his shirt over his mouth and nose with one hand, and jabbed at one of her flustered cheeks with the other. She didn't move, but Jim could see she was breathing slowly, as her chest and belly rose and fell with each struggled, unconscious pant.

"Beth!" he yelled. "Beth, wake up! Wake up!" He was louder than the voice of the fire, but barely. She didn't respond. He couldn't stay here all night trying to bring her back to the conscious world. There was a growing beast consuming the house. Jim was going to have to carry her, baby and all.

Beth was a smaller woman, probably weighing no more than one hundred and thirty pounds with a baby in tow. He carefully slid both hands underneath her and his shirt fell off his face again. There was no way to keep the makeshift mask in place. He was going to just have to pace his breathing until he got her outside. He knew he was going to suck smoke into his lungs, but if he could keep that at the bare minimum, he could make it out. As he stood while lifting her, he realized he wasn't as strong as he thought he was. His arms immediately felt weak, and his legs wobbled. She laid limp across his arms, and he adjusted her closer to his body, which relieved some of the strain on his nearly incompetent strength.

When he finally felt as if he had as comfortable of a hold on her as possible, he carried her toward the stairs. He willed his legs to hurry, while focusing primarily on balance. His knees wanted to fold, but he demanded they hold steady. At the top of the stairwell, he hesitated. This wouldn't be easy. If her weight shifted forward, they might tumble down the stairs together, right over the top of Todd, and end up in a disastrous pile at the bottom. Jim steadied himself, paused, encouraged himself, and down the stairs he went.

Taking each step as if he were just now learning to walk, he made it most of the way down without fault. When he reached where Todd still lay unconscious, he over-adjusted the side-step, lost his balance, and almost fell. He was quick to his wits, though, and threw his entire weight to the left against the stairwell wall. The wall caught him; he leaned on it, exhaled slowly, and pushed himself forward.

When he did this before, as he carried Todd to the foot of the stairs, a wall of fire had formed and blocked them. He had to run through it then, suffering only minor burns from the charge. This time, there was no wall of fire, and Jim knew he was still early. Still ahead of last time's event clock. He felt a rush of enthusiasm and hurried forward. The front door was still wide open. Not far now. He would have Beth to safety and could come back for his son.

Halfway across the living room, his legs wobbled, and his arms felt the strain of a weight they wouldn't dare handle under normal circumstances. Beth slipped forward, and he knew he was about to drop her. Everything in his body wanted to surrender, but Jim refused. He picked up the pace, almost running, and made it to the open front door and onto the porch. When he cleared the doorway, he gasped for clean air. It was too close to the house to be completely free of smoke, but it was enough for him to catch his breath. Panting like a dog after a game of catch, he knew he wasn't done yet. As weak as he felt, as tired as his muscles were, he couldn't put her down. She wasn't safe until she was on the other side of the car because the house was eventually going to explode.

After rounding the back of the car with Beth, he fell to his knees. He let her gently roll out of his arms and onto the ground on her back. Her arms flopped outward, and her head fell to the side. As soon as her face touched the ground, she mumbled something, stirring. Her eyes fluttered.

Sirens in the distance.

Jim looked over his shoulders and saw flashing strobe effects of emergency vehicles approaching. They were about to turn onto this street. He was almost out of time.

"Jim... Jim..." Beth mumbled from the ground.

He looked down and saw her eyes were barely open.

Sirens closed in.

"Beth, I need you to listen. Can you hear me?"

She continued to look at him through a confused glare. Her lips moved, but no voice came out.

Sirens. Louder.

"When the firefighters get here, tell them not to go into the house. The house is going to explode. Tell them to get away from it. Tell them it's going to blow up."

Louder. Closer. He was losing time. *Todd* was losing time. Jim anxiously looked over his shoulder. The emergency light beacons were brighter. Just down the street.

Tick, tock; tick, tock.

Beth looked at him without replying.

"Nod your head if you hear and understand. The firefighters will see you and come to you first. Tell them the house is going to blow up."

She nodded softly, and said, "Todd."

"I'm going in for him." Jim stood up, looked at the house, and back down at Beth. "I'm going to get him out. Tell them, Beth. Tell them to stay away from the house. It's going to blow. They'll die if you don't tell them."

Jim left her lying there and hurried around the car toward the inferno. The sirens were so loud now. The lights from the emergency vehicles, approaching from just down the street, were so vibrant, they danced with the flickering glow of the fire. He'd lost so much time. For most of the duration of the rescue attempt, he'd been way ahead. Somewhere along the way, he'd faltered in pace, and now was trailing the game clock.

Up the porch stairs, through the doorway. A blast of heat barraged his body. He immediately squinted to protect his eyes from the searing air. When he stepped in, the sudden swelter against his face caused him to lose balance. He staggered to the left, reached his hand out for something, anything, to hold his balance, and met nothing but air. He wobbled farther to the left, his momentum carrying him away from the targeted destination. Jim willed his legs, his body, to even out, and they reluctantly obliged. When he finally steadied, he looked toward the stairway. There was a wall of fire in front of it—growing, widening, lengthening. The last time through this, he was on the other side of that wall of flames when it incarnated. He was falling even further behind.

He coughed uncontrollably, still standing there, his thoughts now clouded with the poison of the smoke. A dizzy spell came and went. He needed to lunge forward to the wall of fire and the steps behind it, where his son lay unconscious, about to burn to death. From Jim's perspective, the barrier of flames between him and Todd was growing in all directions. That meant it was also likely making its way up the stairs, too. He needed to go now.

There was suddenly an extra crackling to the voice of the fire, yet it wasn't from the fire itself. It came from overhead. Structural failure was occurring in the ceiling, and he remembered exactly what it was just an instant before it happened. The ceiling caved in with a loud rumble. Heavy debris, burned pieces of ceiling and the upstairs floor, items that had been in the aloft room. It all fell on him, immediately knocking him to the floor, pushing him down, forcefully holding him. A sharp, agonizing pain in his back, his hips, his neck, his head—a sudden force against his right leg as if it'd been struck with a hammer. He was on the floor, facedown, beneath everything that had just collapsed from above. It was all on fire, too. Profound heat burned along his backside.

He tried to push forward, crawl out from under it, but a harrowing pain in his leg, as if it had been bit into by a monster with razor-sharp, knife-length teeth, hampered his efforts. He knew the leg was broken. There was no time to baby the wound, though. He had to act as if it didn't hurt at all. Jim closed his eyes, pulled and kicked, screamed in agony and tenacity.

Push. Pull. He moved forward.

He'd never felt so much pain in his life. A one-two punch from the fire and his leg. His face was drenched in sweat and his eyes burned from it. *Forward.* Jim felt himself sliding out from under the debris, but it was taking too long. He didn't have too long to take, though. He commanded all his strength to the front lines of this battle, and pulled and pushed with one last thrust. The pain was so much, he couldn't stop screaming.

He was past the debris, felt its weight had gone, and looked back. The burning baby bed. Stormy was secure, outside in her mother's womb. She would someday sleep in a different baby bed, alive and well, thriving, growing up in this world, safe and sound.

He looked forward and to his right. He could only see the ceiling above the stairwell now. Fire stood guard over his path to Todd in full force.

Jim tried to stand up, yelped in pain from a sudden sharp jab in his broken right leg, and fell back down flat. Again, he tried to push himself up. His face squinched in physical torment, and once more he failed to stand. Continuing to cough, now ash-spangled saliva dripping from his mouth and hands flat on the floor, he once again called all his strength to arms. Screaming, he pulled himself up to his feet, his leg powerfully protesting, and took aim with his body. God damn, the pain was so unbearable, but he bore it.

Forward quickly, he limped—fast, fast, forward, stumbling, howling with resolve, forward, struggling, so fast, to the wall of fire. *God, don't stop now. Forward.* He submerged himself into the flames, his suffering screeches something from another planet. His face, hands—*oh God, his leg, his leg*—through the wall of tormenting heat, forward, staggering. The stairs had to be close. Jim dove ahead, emerged out of the other side of the fire wall. His left toe hit the first step, and he fell toward the stairs, willed himself mid-flight to fall upward, succeeded, and landed right on top of Todd.

Jim could no longer control his breathing. It was fast and sucking in smoke-tainted air as he rolled off Todd and onto his own back. His broken leg's pain wasn't subsiding. He gritted his teeth and clenched his fists. Every inch of his exposed skin felt like it was covered in flames. Jim looked up at the ceiling, wondering how much time he had, and then realized he had none left. In his condition, even under the circumstances of a clear and sunny day, he would struggle to carry, or drag, Todd the distance from here to the front yard.

From his right peripheral, he saw movement. Jim slowly turned his head toward it and saw Todd stir again. Jim rolled to his side and lifted himself up to where he was looking down at his son's face. Todd coughed; his eyes opened partially, closed again. More coughing. Todd was coming to, but it was too late. The house was going to explode any second now. It was too damn late.

Suddenly, more motion to the left, from the foot of the stairs. Jim quickly turned and saw the silhouette of a figure in the dancing fire's center. His heart suddenly felt alive with hope, but he fell onto his back again, weakness infecting every muscle. It could only be a firefighter coming to rescue them. Probably several of them, covered in protective gear, walking through the flames as if they had a supernatural immunity to them.

Closer, the figure took on more of a solid shape. Jim noticed the character's head did not appear to have a helmet on. Its outline was too well defined to be wearing bulky fire-protective gear.

Closer. A red tie. The man walked out of the fire and onto the steps, towering over father and son. It was Mr. Brimstone—an ominous expression on his face and a rolled-up piece of paper in one hand.

More movement. Todd. Jim looked at his son and saw Todd was also staring, through partly opened eyes, at the man.

Mr. Brimstone stepped up the stairs and kneeled in between father and son. Todd was in and out of consciousness. One moment he stared at Mr. Brimstone in struggling awe, the next he was out again, coughing in his sleep. Jim glared in bewilderment.

Mr. Brimstone held the rolled paper out. He shook his head in disappointment. "Mister Radcliffe, you have violated the terms of the contract."

Jim hacked, caught his breath. He tried to speak, but as soon as he opened his mouth, he coughed. His lungs burned. His throat stung. He again tried to talk, but the only sounds he could produce were rattles and wheezes.

"No need to speak, Mister Radcliffe. You killed your own son, thus resetting the deal. But you hadn't broken it just yet. You voided the bargain when you saved the woman and the child. That's not what we agreed on."

Mr. Brimstone unrolled the paper, and showed its face, a dried, bloody fingerprint at the bottom, to Jim. "These are clearly written stipulations, sir. There's no misinterpretation possible. You've nullified the contract." He stood up. "We no longer have a deal." And he threw the paper upward. It floated in the air, downward, behind Mr. Brimstone, like a leaf from a tree, and into the fire. The breath of the surrounding heat knocked and pushed the paper around, catching it on fire, and then blew it deeper into the flames and out of sight.

Todd wheezed and opened his eyes again. Moaning, he tried to sit up, but he had no strength and only barely moved. He gasped, waved an arm upward and dropped it, limp, back onto the stairs.

Jim reached over and took his son's hand.

Todd stared at Mr. Brimstone again, tried to speak, hacked up soot and slobber, choked, and returned his father's grasp. Todd was too weak, his lungs already polluted with thick toxin, consciousness and unconsciousness dancing in his mind.

"I'm here, son," Jim assured him. "I'm with you. I love you, son. I love you so much."

"Oh, how heartwarming," Mr. Brimstone snarled. "I can send you back, Jim. A new deal and you can still save him."

Jim shook his head slowly, darkness and tunnel vision swirling around. "No," he hissed.

Mr. Brimstone said, "You can still have your son back. He can live. As a father, isn't your most precious priority in protecting your children? What kind of father are you if you don't even try?"

"Dad," Todd whispered.

Jim squeezed Todd's hand even tighter with reassurance.

Mr. Brimstone said, "You can still save him."

"No," Jim mumbled again. He fought off the dizziness, the oncoming unconsciousness, shaking his head. "No. No, no, *no!*"

With a look of disappointment on his face and contempt in his voice, Mr. Brimstone said, "Humans. Your capacity for compassion and sacrifice will always be your most self-destructive traits. What a shame."

Mr. Brimstone backed up a step. "Good day, Mister Radcliffe."

He turned around and walked into the fire, fading as he departed, the same as he'd arrived. His figure became an outline, attacked by lapping, flaming tongues, and then he completely disappeared like a ghost crossing a dimensional border between life and death.

There were only a few seconds left before the house would explode. The clock was ticking, with the chance to escape long gone. Jim rolled over to his side and pulled his son close to him.

Todd's eyes opened so slightly. He looked at his father and said, "Beth."

"She's safe. Beth and Stormy are safe." Jim coughed after pushing the words out. The sudden hack burned from within his lungs, up his throat. He moaned in agony.

"Dad."

"I love you, son. I've always loved you. I will *always* love you."

Todd tried to speak, but only a raspy breath escaped his mouth. He squeezed his father's hand, closed his eyes. The fire's heat sucked the life out of both their sweat-soaked bodies.

Jim squeezed back. With his other arm, he pulled himself even closer. Any moment now. Any split second now, it would be over. The explosion would kill them both instantly. Jim doubted either of them would feel a thing. He thought of the day Alice told him she was pregnant, and then the confirmation doctor's appointment. The fetus heartbeat, so fast. The echoing sound of it through the ultrasound speakers. He had held Alice's hand just as he now held his son's. Alice lying on the sheet-covered medical bed, her head cocked back, and watching Jim's reaction while he viewed the screen. Them looking at each other. Love in their expressions. Alice smiling. The heartbeat. Jim grinning. The touch of their hands. So tight. Forever love. They were going to have a baby. A family. Happily ever after.

Just before the smoke overcame him, and just before the house exploded, Jim smiled.

***

The fire truck pulled up first and stopped on the street. The sirens went silent but still flashed their rotating lights out into the surrounding night. Firefighters unloaded out of the truck, voices barking orders and others confirming them. A rush of sound. The fire's roar, on the other side of the car, seemed too near Beth as she lay there, her eyes opening just as an ambulance pulled up and its wailing screams hushed.

She could remember seeing Todd's father, Jim, kneeling beside her. In her memory, his lips were moving, but she couldn't hear his words. She looked up. Thick clouds of smoke were moving overhead, but in between them, the clearest of night skies, stars showing themselves intermittently through the haze. Doors opening and slamming. What was happening? Why was she out here? Where was the smoke coming from? Who were the voices? Why the sirens and why did they all shush?

She remembered being in the house. Waking up, coughing, in bed. Her room filled with smoke. Trying to get up and run, realizing the home was ablaze, and dropping to her knees to avoid the poisonous product of consuming flames. She was overcome and became too weak. Lying on her back in the hallway, she tried to call out for Todd, but only a squeak had escaped her mouth. Darkness.

She could again remember Jim kneeling above her. He had dragged her out of the fire—saved her and the baby—and then gone back in for Todd. Where were they now, though? She was coming to consciousness quicker. Where were her husband and his father? Still in the house? Jim had said something to her. He'd told her to warn the rescue workers of something? *What, though? What had he said?* She struggled to open the memory like a corrupt computer file. *What was the damn warning?*

"Ma'am, was there anyone else in the house?" came a male's voice.

Beth cocked her head backward. A man in full firefighting gear towered above her, looking down. As soon as they made eye contact, he knelt beside her and repeated, "Were you the only one in the house? Is there anyone trapped inside?"

Jim's words finally came through in her memory.

The house is going to explode.

Tell them the house is going to blow up.

I'm going in for him.

It's going to blow.

They'll die if you don't tell them.

"The house." Her words felt as if they were made of barbed wire, scratching her throat and the inside of her mouth, as she forced them out. "Don't go in."

"Ma'am, is the house empty?"

They'll die if you don't tell them.

The house is going to explode.

They'll die—

They'll die—

"It's going to—"

"We need to know. Is there anyone in there? Please try to remember."

"The house is going to explode." She finally pushed the words out clearly, repeating her father-in-law. "They'll die if you don't tell them. It's going to blow."

She noticed a firefighter running by with a hose, and two others behind him, toward the house. The one kneeling beside her, his eyes lit up with alarm, and he stood up, screaming at the others, reaching down, taking Beth by her armpits, as gently as he could, in this moment of urgency.

"Gas leak, gas leak, gas leak!" he yelled.

The one with the hose dropped it and turned away from the house. They all altered their courses instantly while repeating, "Gas leak, gas leak!"

"Behind the truck!" someone yelled.

"Help me out with her! Get over here!"

Suddenly, someone had Beth by her ankles. She was off the ground, moving in suspension away from Jim's car. She, and the firefighters who had her, moved so quickly. The sky above. Clouds of smoke. Stars. Flashing blue, red, yellow lights. Fire flickering and growling in the distance. She glanced to her left, to her right, toward her feet—saw the man in fire gear, his face covered with sweat, his expression one of struggle. Gliding coarsely above the ground. Where were Todd and Jim? *Her husband.* Where was he? Still in the house? *Please don't be in the house.* Where was he?

"Todd," she tried to yell, but only mumbled.

"Behind the truck, everyone. Hurry."

"Behind the truck!"

"It's going to blow!"

"Go go go! Behind the truck!"

"Go go go go go!"

"My hus—" She saw the fire truck in her peripheral. Around it. Into the street. Firefighters, EMS workers...all ducking behind the huge red truck with shiny metallic ladders on the side. Suddenly, the loudest burst of thunder she'd ever heard in her life. A deafening explosion that seemed to last for several seconds. A wave of pressure against her body; she rocked in the firefighters' grips.

The sky suddenly lit up completely yellow and orange, as if the apocalypse was occurring. The giant fire truck moaned and creaked against the pressure of the explosion. Debris of all sizes fell around, some of it showering down on them. Ashes fell like gray snow, landing softly against their faces, nestling on helmets and in Beth's hair. She looked up, and the stars were gone. The night sky was blanketed with the cloudy remnant of disaster.

"Todd," she sobbed. She was hyperventilating. "Todd. My hus—My husband. My husband."

A firefighter yelled, "Is everyone okay?"

Chaos sounded all around her. The rescue workers' voices seemed to come from within a nearly soundproof bubble. She struggled to hold on to consciousness, hoping that in the complex mixture of people shouting, checking in and up on each other, engines from emergency vehicles running, lights still flashing, she might hear Todd's voice, or see him emerge from the smoke that dominated the air.

"Ma'am, are you okay?" came an anxious male voice from above.

Beth looked up, saw his blurry face, and realized he was not Todd. Her husband would not have called her ma'am, yet she still allowed her hopes to flow when she heard the voice.

"My husband," she mumbled. "He was inside."

"Stay right here. We don't know if you're injured. Don't move."

"My husband. Where is…where is he?"

But the man was gone. He'd disappeared into the distance, through the smoke, among the sources of many more panicked voices. Ashes fell softly onto Beth's face as she looked upward, tears streaming down her smoke-charred cheeks. Upward, hoping Todd's face would appear at any moment. It didn't. No more faces showed themselves as she passed out, struggling to breathe, her back hurting, cramps in her abdomen. The stress of the events—the fire, the smoke, her husband missing—took a toll on her. So much pain. The baby. Stormy was coming. She was coming now. Darkness and silence.

Chapter Forty-Two

The gate slid shut behind Billy Wagner, and he spun around to look back. A tied-up sheet containing clothes and belongings over his shoulder, he watched the guards and the prison warden, on the other side, walking away from him. He looked up and saw his breath against the backdrop of a clear blue sky. The sun was just passing the border between morning and high noon.

He turned around and looked down the road. A public transit bus was approaching. It had been ten years since he stood on the outside of prison grounds. He had a bus ticket in his pocket but felt like he wanted to walk. Ten years. Ten years gone. All because Alice and Beth Radcliffe had given victim testimony at the trial.

On that day, they were emotional, with good reason. Not too long before, both had lost their husbands in a merciless fire. Alice had lost not just her spouse, but her son as well. Their testimony, toned with mourning and anger, had convinced the judge, and she'd sentenced Billy to a full decade in the slammer with no chance of parole. He wasn't young when that happened, and the time lost in his mid-life years was a harsh punishment for simply waving a gun around and issuing a few threats.

"Habitual offender," is what the judge had said in defense of the prison term handed down. But it had been more than that. Two grieving, crying women had sealed the deal.

The bus stopped beside Billy, and the door opened. He hesitated. His legs were tired already, but there was work to do. If he walked to his intended destination, where he was to hopefully acquire a firearm, he would waste time. Enough of that had already been thrown away. Ten years had passed, and things were in motion. The dreams had plagued him during his stay in prison. The same dreams repeatedly, night after night, month after month, and so on. He could hear the explosions right now. The voices. *Madame President. Millions dead.* Rockets firing overhead. A once beautiful sky now littered with smoke from lethal missiles, soaring to and from, crashing into their targets. *Armageddon.* He could still stop it.

The bus door was open and waiting. The driver, sitting there, stared at Billy with impatience. The diesel engine idled. Destiny was not only calling, but rushing him. He could still save the world, maybe the universe.

Billy stepped onto the bus, dug his ticket out of a front pocket, and handed it to the driver, who scanned it in and dropped it through a slit in a metal box attached to the floor. The door shut behind him. He walked down the aisle, the only soul on the bus, as it began to move forward. He sat down on a bench seat, scooted to the window, and looked through its dirty glass. The blue sky again.

He could keep it clear and beautiful, but he would have to issue a sentence of his own. Judge, jury, and executioner. It was all so clear now. More clear than when he went into prison. Before, his attention had been on the grown son of Jim Radcliffe—Todd. But Billy realized that, for the first time ever, his dreams had been more cryptic. Todd hadn't survived the fire as Billy thought he would. Maybe Todd escaped and lived on in another timeline, or in an alternate universe, but it was the unborn child who should have been Billy's focus. He should have killed Beth Radcliffe the day he barged into that backyard, but the dreams of that future had been foggy. He realized they were vague because the future was still forming, settling in, being written.

The last few weeks of his time behind bars, the dreams had cleared for him. Now it was more than evident what the future planned, a future that would not exist if that baby girl hadn't survived the fire. She wasn't supposed to live, but had, and now posed a threat to the entire world. Eight billion lives were at stake. Billy could still save them all.

He had to find Stormy Radcliffe, who would be ten years old now, and end her life. He had to make her future disappear.

Billy laid his head on the backrest, closed his eyes, and fell asleep. There were no dreams this time; just deep, replenishing rest.

Chapter Forty-Three

A woman and a child, hand in hand, walked through the cemetery. Dry leaves crunched beneath their feet, still falling intermittently around them. The little girl, ten years old, with her wild brownish-blonde hair, wore blue jeans and a cute blouse, comfortable attire for this perfect, sunny, and seventy-five-degree autumn day. The woman, in sweats and a short-sleeve shirt, led the way as they passed grave markers...some basic, some tombstones of marble with fancy lettering. They stopped at the center foot of two plots. One headstone read "Jim Radcliffe. Loving father, husband, and grandfather." The other one read "Todd Radcliffe. Loving father, son, and husband." Woman and child, mother and daughter, Beth and Stormy, stood there, staring down at the markers.

Stormy let go of her mom's hand and stepped forward, but Beth quickly reached down, put an arm around her child, and held her back.

"No," Beth said. "This is good enough. You don't want to step on their graves. It's bad luck."

Stormy said nothing, but stood still, looking down at her father's plot.

"You're ten now. I guess you're old enough to understand what happened."

Looking up at her mom curiously, Stormy said, "I already know. They died in a fire."

Beth looked at Jim's headstone. *Loving father, son, and husband.* She said, "There's a little more to it than that."

"They didn't die in a fire?"

Beth looked down, and their gazes met. "They did. But there's more you should know. You should know the courage of your grandfather. He died a hero."

"How so?"

Beth kneeled and took Stormy's hands in hers. "You're here. I'm here. We're both alive because of your grandfather. We were in that fire. You were in my belly." She hesitated, seeing that night again in her memory. Lying on the ground, looking at a smoke-polluted sky, waiting for Todd to appear. He never would. She could see the hospital. The labor and delivery room. Just a couple hours after her father-in-law had sacrificed his life to save her and child, after her husband had perished in a fiery explosion, Beth had given birth to Stormy. Life had ended tragically, yet also began miraculously, on the same day.

"How did you get out? How did we get out?"

"Your grandfather came in and saved us. Your grandma says he was driving home from work, and for some reason, took a different way. He rode by the house, saw it was on fire, and came in after us."

"Why didn't he save Dad?"

Beth choked on emotion, and a tear streamed down her cheek. "He tried. After he pulled us from the fire, he went back in." She held it back. *Don't cry. Finish the story.* "He went back in for your dad. There wasn't enough time, though. There was a gas leak, and the house blew up."

"They died together," Stormy said. "An explosion. They died at the same moment."

"Your grandpa saved more than just us. The house was going to explode, and he knew it. He warned me. He told me to tell the firefighters, and I did. They were going to charge into the house without caution. They would have died, but they didn't. Your grandfather gave his life so others could live."

"A hero," Stormy said.

"Yes." Beth choked again. "A hero."

Silence.

Beth stood up. She held Stormy's hand and faced the gravesites once more.

Beth said, "You could be a hero someday. Maybe you'll grow up to be a firefighter or a doctor. You know? They do hero things every day. Every night. All the time. I'm sure your dad is watching every second of your life." She paused, sniffled, and continued. "Doctor actually sounds better. You don't have to die in a fire to be a hero. There are so many ways."

"I want to save the whole world someday," Stormy said. "I want to be president. There are more good things I can do as president."

"President Stormy Dawn Radcliffe." Beth smiled. "That rolls off the tongue pretty good. You can do it, you know? The first woman president. You can change the world if you want to. You just have to want it bad enough."

"The world needs saving, for sure," Stormy said.

Beth felt a little sadness at that statement. A ten-year-old with a cynical view of the world, of humanity. So young to feel so dreary.

"Well, if anyone can do it, you can," Beth assured her. "I know you can. You're so smart. You're a damn smart kid. If you want to be president, then be president."

"No," came a male voice from behind them.

Both Stormy and Beth swiveled to face Billy Wagner, who stood maybe ten feet away, a tombstone behind him, with a gun in his hand. He aimed the weapon straight at Stormy. Beth gasped and pulled her daughter close to her. Stormy looked at Billy in confusion.

"You're supposed to be in prison," Beth snapped. She stooped down, wrapped Stormy in her arms.

"You didn't get the word?" Billy asked. "I got out two weeks ago. I thought victims were supposed to be notified."

"What do you want?" Beth asked angrily. "Why are you pointing a fucking gun at my daughter? Put it away. Put it away now, god-dammit."

"No," Billy said firmly. "There's no putting anything away. Your daughter is going to grow up to do bad things, Mrs. Radcliffe. Such horrible things." He shook his head as if he were trying to eject wicked visions from his mind. "I can't let it happen. I'm sorry."

"You're sick. You know you're sick. Why don't you put that gun away and go get help? Go get help so you can be a decent human instead of some asshole running around with a gun, threatening people. She's a kid. She's not hurt anyone. She's never going to. She's a good kid."

"She's not going to be a good adult," Billy replied, sadness in his tone. "I don't want to do this. I'm not just some psychopathic piece of shit. I know what's going to happen. That day in your yard...I thought your husband was the one. The dreams pointed at your husband. But they were only the beginning of a chain of events. It was always about her. Stormy Dawn Radcliffe. She's the one I should have been worried about. She is going to do a lot in the years to come. A lot of bad. I have to stop it."

"You're gonna have to kill me first," Beth said, rage building.

"I understand that. Two lives to save billions. Yes, I understand that."

He had allowed the gun to lower as they spoke, but now it was time to end the conversation.

"I'm sorry, Mrs. Radcliffe. I wish there was another way."

He raised the gun, put his index finger around the trigger, took a deep breath—

A shot fired. Birds scattered from nearby trees. Another loud bang resonated throughout the cemetery.

Billy's body jerked with each report. A third one. He dropped the gun, stumbled backward, his expression enveloped in shock. His legs hit the tombstone behind him, and he flipped back-first over it. He crawled toward the gun, which had fallen just a few feet from him. Blood soaked his shirt and spilled out onto the ground. He was inches from the firearm.

Stormy screamed. Beth covered her daughter's face, pulling both of them backward. They trampled Jim Radcliffe's burial plot, stopped only when they were halted by its headstone.

Billy was close to the gun, struggling to breathe, gasping, coughing up blood, which poured out over his chin. Another shot struck his body, his chest, and he rolled onto his back, staring straight up in a gaze of forever.

Alice was at least twenty feet away to the left, a gun in her hand. She lowered it and ran toward Beth and Stormy. The child was hyperventilating, rocked with terror, trying to pull away from her mother, who fought with everything in herself to hold her child tight and safe.

Earlier, as Alice drove, Beth in the passenger seat and Stormy in the back, Beth had asked her mother-in-law, "Do you mind if we do this alone this time?"

"Alone?" Alice asked with a soft look of surprise on her face.

"I think she's old enough to know now. I want to be the one to tell her."

After a quick few moments of thought, Alice replied, "Yes. I understand that. There's a bookstore just across from the cemetery. I'll stop in there and see if they have anything new of interest."

Alice had become an avid reader of fiction over the years. Until Jim's untimely death, she read a few novels per year, but since then, she consumed herself with reading and gardening. He'd left behind a life insurance policy that paid everything off and left Alice comfortable, without the need to work.

However, over a few months' time, she'd grown deeply depressed and paranoid. She'd bought a gun and begun carrying it with her everywhere. The experience in the backyard, that summer day so long ago, had changed her. Then, when Billy Wagner's crazy predictions kind of came true, she worried he might return to finish the job. Todd and Jim had died, not Beth and Stormy. So while Billy's prophecies missed the bull's-eye, they still hit the board. He'd been handed a lengthy prison sentence at the conclusion of his trial, thanks to her and Beth, but he was also in jail the night of the fire.

Alice could never shake the suspicion that Billy Wagner still had something to do with the disaster and death of that horrible night, regardless of what investigators determined after supposedly thoroughly examining the scene's aftermath.

At Jim and Todd's funeral, Alice was pleased to see so many of Jim's coworkers showed up to offer emotional support. Evidently, her husband was a well-liked guy at work. There was always the odd conversation she had with one particular associate of Jim's, though.

"It was strange," Adam had said. "When he was leaving work, I tried to get him to have a few drinks with me and the guys. He hadn't gone out with us in a while. So, I figured I'd try to talk him into it. Back in the day, Jim was actually the life of the party. Nothing bad. We just had a few beers every now and then, and when Jim caught a buzz, he could crack jokes and get everyone laughing like nobody I know. But he was in such a hurry that night. Rude like I've never seen him. Like he had somewhere urgent to be. An emergency. I thought maybe something was going on at home. Such a hurry. Sped out of the parking lot."

That was the night Jim died, and it sounded as if he left work knowing the fire was happening, or was going to. According to arson investigators, the disaster was sparked by faulty wiring. When further investigation occurred, it was not only determined it was an accident, but an act of God, basically. So how could he have known?

Eventually, Alice settled it in her mind that Jim must have obsessed his entire shift over Billy Wagner's macabre predictions, and by the time he clocked out, felt like he knew something awful was likely to happen. So he raced out of work, paranoid that the psycho in his son's backyard had planned some sort of attack, or home invasion, against Todd and Beth. It was pure luck that Billy was right about *something* happening. Jim had arrived on the scene just in time to save Beth and Stormy, and then perished when he went back in for his son.

The gun went everywhere Alice went. She knew if Jim was still alive, he would have cautioned against it. Although he carried a pistol in his car, he never took it out of that glove compartment. She had it tucked in an armpit holster no matter what store signs forbade bringing firearms inside. One could never know, especially in today's society, when a firearm might be needed for self-defense in a parking lot, inside the store, or even at a bookstore.

Above all else, she always expected Billy Wagner would show up, just like he had out of nowhere before, waving his own gun around and making threats. After being thrown in prison over that incident, which no doubt was influenced by her and Beth's testimony, next time he might actually pull the trigger. Alice was ready for him. For the last ten years, she had prepared to face him. She knew how to use her firearm, thanks to several training classes at the gun store and countless target practice sessions. She knew there was a broad chance she might never need it, but if she did, she was ready. More ready for Billy Wagner than she'd ever been for anything in her life.

Alice stopped at Billy and looked down at him, the gun still in her hand. If he moved, she would shoot him again. She even aimed it at him, while looking at the wounds she'd inflicted from a suitable distance, as they hemorrhaged blood onto the ground, his clothes and body soaking in it. He looked straight up, eyes wide open and empty of life. Whatever he was staring at, it was nothing in the world of the living. Satisfied he was not now, and would never again be, a threat to her or her loved ones, she holstered the gun underneath her jacket and went to Beth and Stormy.

The ten-year-old child was terrified, but was no longer screaming. Her mother was holding her tight.

"It's okay, baby girl." Alice tried to comfort her trembling granddaughter. "It's okay. You're safe. I'm here. You're safe. It's okay."

Now, the only piercing sounds of the day were approaching emergency vehicles. Someone must have heard the shots and called 911. Alice kneeled beside Beth and Stormy, and put her arms around both of them.

In the huddle, Beth, with tears of horror in her eyes, looked at Alice. "Is he dead?"

"He won't ever hurt us again," Alice said. "Never again."

"Who was he?" Stormy shakily asked.

"A very bad man," Alice replied. "A terrible man who will hurt no one ever again."

Epilogue

President Stormy Dawn Radcliffe stood in the center of the bunker room, surrounded by her top appointed generals, the Secretary of State, the Chairman of the Joint Chiefs of Staff, the Secretary of Defense, and, of course, Vice President Norman Wheeler. The walls were covered with several giant strategic monitors with military commanders sitting in front of them, hectically punching away at keyboards, changing the screens on the monitors from one view to the next, to the next, from live views to strategy maps, to statistical readouts, to live views, back to military maps.

Madame President had never questioned her decision for these preemptive strikes. Russia was increasingly becoming a rogue nation over the years. She'd realized it since she was thirteen years old. Even at such a young age, when she should have been thinking about boys and hanging out with friends, playing sports maybe and picking up bad habits, she knew what she wanted to do with her life, and never swayed from her goals. A senator representing Kentucky by age thirty-five, and after twelve years of serving on the country's Congress, she had run for president as an independent. Stormy was the first independent to win the presidency since Millard Fillmore, a member of the Whig party, in 1850. She had beat out the Democrat and Republican by a landslide, her on-the-fence policies capturing the votes of 70 percent of the country, on Election Day. She was the overwhelming choice.

Though she didn't run on her foreign or military policies, her focus had always been to hit Russia before Russia came after the United States. She knew the Russkies were coming for her country. Since the Cold War began over a hundred years ago, both the USA and the Soviet Union had stockpiled nuclear weapons. When the Soviet Union fell, there was a sigh of relief from the USA. But in 2022, when Russia invaded Ukraine, the rise of a new Soviet Union had begun. After the liberation of Ukraine, several nations surrounding Russia had dropped from NATO, and joined the new Soviet Republic of Europe. Some of those countries knocked on the SRE's doors, requesting admittance out of fear, while others, with Soviet-infiltrated governments, claimed to join this new union for economic objectives.

Stormy had worried about the SRE all her life. And she wasn't alone in her paranoia. Most of the United States felt the Soviets were up to no good, building uranium enrichment and nuclear power plants in every state it had captured or acquired.

Leaders of the great USA—Congress, presidents—had done nothing to ensure the continuing longevity of the country, and as the SRE grew, so did the uneasiness of citizens all across the world. Other members of a shrinking NATO looked to the USA for leadership, yet the USA only stalled in actually taking some kind of action against the SRE.

Stormy was elected president, the first female one in the history of America, and immediately started to plot this preemptive attack. The Soviets were a danger to the entire planet, and Stormy felt she was Earth's savior. On this day, she had gathered military leaders in this bunker, and at noon, the war had begun. Several nuclear missiles launched and flew toward the Soviet motherland of Russia and its controlled states. Millions would die, but it would be to save billions from the inevitable. She knew they would return fire, and nukes would be in the air and headed for the USA, but she had confidence in the missile defense system she had pumped billions of dollars into during her first two years in office. All had come together as she planned, and now she stood in this bunker, leading an attack that would ultimately save the world.

The mood of the room was panicked. She knew not a single soul agreed with what she was doing. They had all tried to talk her out of it, and she feared a mutiny which, thankfully, never came. The officials she was surrounded with all upheld their subordination to her, and the strike launched as planned.

A garbled mess of radio transmissions, from other military installations running missile silo sites, came through loudspeakers underneath the giant monitors. Reports came in of confirmed nuclear weapons launches. Successful interceptions as the Soviets retaliated. Transmissions from other world leaders demanded to know why the USA had done this without collaborating, or even informing them of, such dire actions. One after the other, calls came through. President Stormy and Vice President Wheeler took them, explaining that all would be okay. This was for peace. Sometimes violence was the only way to achieve a longer-lasting harmony. There had been no choice. The Soviets were a threat to the world, and the USA had to eliminate that.

"Emergency transmission from Los Angeles, Madame President," one of the operators sitting before the monitors said. He pulled his headset off and spun his chair around, a look of terror on his face. "Madame President..." He hesitated, tears in his eyes. "One got through. LA has been hit."

Another operator, who continued staring up at one monitor, said aloud, "Live footage on monitor C coming through courtesy of a weather station just outside LA city limits. This is on a twelve-second delay."

On the monitor directly above, a distant view of Los Angeles, clear blue skies above what appeared a peaceful city, the sun at high noon. From this perspective, the city looked empty of human life despite a light blanket of smog that was barely detectible through the video feed. Then, something headed toward the city out of the sky. The reflection of the sun made tracking the missile with the naked eye easy. It flew in between a patch of tall buildings. Nothing for a split second. Then, the silent explosion as this feed was video only. The blast of light from the center of the city was blinding; it covered the entire monitor, then white noise. The room went silent as everyone present instantly realized what had just happened.

A general from the back of the room said gloomily, "Over five million people live in LA."

Madame President broke the stunned and horrified silence of the room. "They would have hit us first. They were planning it. We know they were planning it." She looked around. Some still stared in awe at the white noise on the LA-focused monitor, and others looked at her with the same glare. "There was reliable intelligence. We *know* they were planning something. We need to stay the course now and mourn later. The world is counting on us."

"Madame President," came a disappointed voice from behind her.

She spun around and saw her vice president looking at her in disbelief.

"This is the only way, Norman. You know it is."

Another voice rang out. It came from another operator at the monitors. "Three made it through. We are confirming two more hits. One in St. Louis and another in Louisville, Kentucky."

Louisville. Stormy went to the operator, standing directly behind him, and put a hand on his shoulder.

"My God," came a voice from behind her.

Another one to her left was sobbing.

Behind her, Norman Wheeler said, "My God, what have we done?"

Stormy said to the operator, "These are confirmed hits?"

"Missile defenses are shooting down incoming left and right, but some are making it through."

"Do we have a live view of Louisville?"

"We did." The operator punched keys on a keyboard and looked up at a monitor. "That's our view of Louisville."

The monitor was static, flipping up and up and up, like the vertical hold on a television needing manual adjustment.

Stormy looked at the screen. Her jaw dropped, eyes filled with horror.

A voice from behind her said, "Madame President."

More incoming reports from other operators. One of them said, "God damn, they hit Tallahassee. I didn't think their capabilities were that far-reaching."

"New York just shot down two incoming."

"California hit again. LA."

"They're getting through. Reports of missile defense systems malfunctioning from the East Coast."

"They're coming in from everywhere!"

"LA."

"Seattle."

"Lansing."

"Chicago. Oh God! Chicago is gone!"

Stormy still stared at the same monitor. Flickering static. *Louisville, Kentucky.*

"Mom," she whispered. "Grandma." Her lips trembled. "I'm sorry. I'm so sorry."

***

With Beth behind her, Alice moved the walker forward, toward her garden, which was thriving this summer: tomatoes, strawberries, collard greens, green bell peppers, and jalapeños. Alice, at age eighty, had never remarried or even dated since the death of her husband so long ago. Beth had remarried and lived a happy life with her second husband, but never went a day without missing Todd. Eventually, her second husband passed away from a heart attack during her daughter's first Senate campaign.

Coincidentally, that was when sciatic nerve issues struck her forever mother-in-law. Beth's home had been a rental, while Alice's had been paid off with life insurance money when Jim passed away. So, Beth moved in with Alice to help her out, and they lived through their years more like sisters than in-laws.

A few years ago, Alice's sciatica intensified and, because of her age, doctors refused to operate. Instead, they chose physical therapy, massage machines, and medications. Some days were okay for Alice, and some were awful. As far as the lingering pain, it would never completely subside or vanish. It eventually affected her ability to walk, thus landing her in a wheelchair for ventures away from home, and a walker in and around the house.

What seemed to console Alice more than anything was her plants. During the spring, summer, and the beginning half of autumn, she completely submerged herself into gardening, and that worked better than any physical therapy or medication.

"What was really all that stuff on the TV?" Alice asked as she held herself steady with the walker, preparing for another step forward to the garden.

"It was too scary to watch," Beth replied. "Something going on with LA. News reports were confusing. Seemed hectic. I turned it off because I hate bad news. Whatever it was, it definitely wasn't good."

Alice took a cautious step, paused, moved the walker forward, paused again.

Stormy had offered to let them move to the White House with her when she won the presidency, but both had declined. Beth was actually afraid of what Stormy had become, and had dreaded the final product of her daughter for many years. Stormy's paranoia started when she was just a teenager, but, simultaneously, was also the backbone of the young woman's drive and ambitions. A star student in middle school, high school, and all the way through college, Beth knew Stormy would achieve her goals.

But she felt dread more than she felt proud of her determined daughter. Stormy's theories, and paranoid fears, were actually scary, and Beth had never once voted for her daughter. She felt ashamed that she thought of her own kid as an upcoming female Hitler, but all the signs were loud and bold that Stormy Dawn Radcliffe should never be in charge of the United States in any manner.

Yet somehow, Stormy had built a large base of constituents. They didn't just choose her; they loved her. She could do no wrong in their eyes. If she was to walk out into the middle of the street, on live national television, and mow down a crowd of babies with an Uzi, while laughing devilishly, her followers would support her with excuses of validation for her actions, or claim those things didn't happen.

Stormy was dangerous for this country, and for the world.

Although Beth and Alice declined the invitation to live in the nation's capital, Stormy still kept in contact with them at the beginning. The calls were daily, but some were just a few minutes because the president of the United States did not have time to hang on the phone like a chatty teenager. There was a country to run. Eventually, those calls became less frequent, and their durations sometimes just a minute or two.

Then, during the past few months, the calls rarely came at all. Beth knew something was stirring. The dying communication from her daughter wasn't the only tangible evidence, but something in her intuition told her more was wrong. Maybe even something god-awful was coming. Stormy's own rhetoric during those phone calls was eerie, chilling, and something to fear.

Just a few minutes ago, as Alice was in the kitchen making coffee, Beth had been sitting on the sofa in the living room, scrolling social media websites on her smartphone, with the television playing in the background. There was breaking news, and the emergency broadcast system's all too familiar tone coming from the TV. She heard it as background noise at first, but then the alert went off, and was interrupted by a national affiliate with breaking news. A report of something happening in Los Angeles. Something happening *to* the city. Panicked reporters. Anchors leaving professionalism behind and talking hysterically from behind the news counters. Something horrifying.

Nukes. LA hit. Millions dead.

Alice came from the kitchen, trying to use her walker while holding a cup of coffee. She'd heard the commotion on the television.

"What's going on?" Alice had asked from the kitchen doorway.

Beth immediately grabbed the remote control, turned the television off, went to Alice, and took the coffee cup from her.

"Let me get that for you," Beth said. "Let's go to the garden."

Her voice was shaky, and Alice detected Beth's trepidation.

"What's happening?" Alice asked. "You look like you just saw a ghost."

"Nothing. Some kind of celebration in LA became a little too wild is all. They flipped some cars, burned some couches. Barely newsworthy. Let's go outside."

Alice scrutinized Beth for a moment and then dubiously said, "Oh, okay. Well, that's fine. We can just leave the coffee in here. Let's go check the garden."

"Yes. The garden," Beth agreed.

Now they were outside, Alice inching toward the garden with the help of her walker, Beth staying close as possible just in case her elderly and ailment-inflicted mother-in-law seemed about to take a fall.

It didn't feel right out here. There were no birds, no breeze, and no summer insects. No lawnmowers rumbling as their owners pushed them down one strip of lawn and back on another. The usual sound of kids playing somewhere in the distance was as absent as the occasional car engine humming by was. So much silence, as if the entire world was holding its breath and bracing for something awful.

Alice moved forward another step, her walker supporting her.

The silence was finally broken. Something overhead. A plane. A jet plane, maybe. It was in the distance at first, but quickly moving closer. It sounded like it was coming right at them. Whatever it was, it was definitely nearing and losing altitude. At first, Beth could tell the roaring noise was coming from the west, but within just a few moments, it sounded as if it was all around them. So close.

Beth and Alice looked up. Directly above them in the sky, an object leaving a trail of thrust behind it. It was moving nearly lightning fast;

not just flying across the sky, but shooting, zipping across it and at a downward slant. Whatever it was, it was definitely going to crash.

It rocketed past, and the sound of its roaring engine faded, faded, faded.

Beth trembled.

Alice stared, in awe, east in the bogey's direction of travel.

A deafening boom.

Rumbling in the distance, like an approaching stampede of giants.

Blinding light.